Regency

LORDS & LADIES
COLLECTION

*Two Glittering Regency
Love Affairs*

Perdita
by Sylvia Andrew
&
Raven's Honour
by Claire Thornton

The *Regency*

LORDS & LADIES
COLLECTION

The Regency

LORDS & LADIES
COLLECTION

Sylvia Andrew &
Claire Thornton

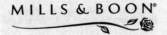

MILLS & BOON®

MILLS & BOON and MILLS & BOON with the Rose Device are registered trademarks of the publisher.

First published in Great Britain 2006 by
Harlequin Mills & Boon Limited,
Eton House, 18-24 Paradise Road, Richmond, Surrey TW9 1SR

THE REGENCY LORDS & LADIES COLLECTION
© Harlequin Books S.A. 2006

The publisher acknowledges the copyright holders of the individual works as follows:

Perdita © Sylvia Andrew 1991
Raven's Honour © Claire Thornton 2002

ISBN 0 263 84425 0

138-0306

Printed and bound in Spain
by Litografía Rosés S.A., Barcelona

Perdita

by
Sylvia Andrew

Sylvia Andrew taught modern languages in Cheshire for many years, ending up as vice-principle of a sixth form college. She now lives in Somerset with two cats, a dog, and a husband who has a very necessary sense of humour, and a stern approach to punctuation. She has one daughter who lives in London and with whom she shares a lively interest in the theatre. Sylvia divides her time between Somerset, London, and a small cottage in Normandy. In spite of a career in teaching, she describes herself as an 'unrepentant romantic'!

To Simon

CHAPTER ONE

THE GIRL STOOD shackled to the post in the corner of the huge courtyard. Someone with a belated sense of decency had covered the shreds and tatters of her clothing with a cotton cloak, and a trick of the moonlight silvered the folds and gave grace to the emaciated body. Her head was slightly raised, and a sudden breath of wind lifted her matted hair away from her face. The moonlight flooded over her, revealing the pure profile, the proud lift of her chin and the slender lines of her throat. The man standing in the shadows caught his breath. His instinct had not played him false this afternoon. She was perfect—Artemis the huntress in person. Indeed, she resembled nothing more than one of the statues he had so recently seen on the Acropolis, an impression which was increased by her immobility, the apparent indifference with which she faced her fate, and the cool silver light in which she was bathed.

"Sir! Sir—there's the guard now."

The whispered warning drew his attention to the figure making its way along the battlements towards the courtyard.

"It'll be some minutes yet, Tom. Are you ready? You remember what you have to do?"

"Yes, your lordship. I can't answer for them two heathen, though."

The Earl smiled. Tom would never admit that the two Berbers standing behind him might prove necessary or useful. But on tonight's adventure they were essential. Danger was in the air. The Pasha had accepted his bribe, it was true, but that did not necessarily mean he would keep his word and see that the guards were blind. His mind turned to the scene in the Dey's palace that morning.

"I'm obliged to you for the provisions and water, Mehmet Pasha."

"It is nothing, Lord Ambourne. A trifling gesture of hospitality to a storm-tossed traveller; nothing more. If I can serve you in any other way, of greater significance, then I am honoured to do so."

The Earl hesitated, then spoke. "There is one other thing you could grant me..."

Mehmet Hussein Pasha, Dey of Algiers, grinned his shark's grin and said gently, "All I have is yours to command, my lord. My poor people have already experienced your princely generosity in return for the water... You have only to tell me, and it is yours."

"You have some prisoners in your courtyard—not, I think, of your race?"

There was a little silence. The Pasha's thoughts were racing, in spite of his appearance of judicial calm. What was this Englishman up to? Behind the Earl's air of indifference lay a purpose which the Pasha had not yet divined. He carefully considered the man before him. Hair that was almost black, a strong face with cool grey eyes, an arrogant high-bridged nose and a hard, disciplined mouth. There might be passion there, but if so it was well under control. The Pasha was in the habit of looking for men's weaknesses and exploiting them for his own ends. It would be difficult to find any in this man. What was his interest in the wretches below? Was it that they were French and therefore should be deported or tried in their own country? Or was he anxious to make sure that they would be punished adequately here? Europe, as the Pasha knew only too well, had strong views on piracy in the Mediterranean. Only two years ago their ships had bombarded Algiers, and since then the Pasha had walked an uneasy road between his former associates and the ever-watchful Mediterranean fleets.

"They are French, my lord," he said finally. "French pirates. We captured their ship, *Le Faucon*, two days ago after they had attacked one of our own merchantmen. Unfortunately the captain and senior members of the crew were blown to pieces attempting to escape from the sinking ship in a longboat. What we have here are the pathetic remnants of the crew, not worthy of your attention, I assure you. They will all die tomorrow."

The Earl got up and walked to the window overlooking the courtyard. "They are not all men, Excellence. One of them is a girl. I might pay well for her."

The Pasha was startled out of his customary urbanity. "Pay for a pirate? A girl? What girl? Ah—my lord, you jest. The woman in the courtyard? That is nothing for you. She is a pirate's drab, a piece of scum, not worthy of your slightest breath. Her own master left her to drown or be captured." Then, as the Earl remained silent, he added, "The other members of the band shun her. They say she has the evil eye, that she is what you call a witch. That is nothing for you." He sat back, his composure restored, and smiled knowingly. "No, no, my lord, there is little enough to comfort a man in that one. But if it would please you to look through this window…" He led the Earl over to the other side of the room. A fretted window overlooked a scene to delight the eye of any wanderer. Fountains played in a sheltered courtyard full of flowers and sweet-scented shrubs. Cushions were scattered on the lawns, and on some of them lay members of the Pasha's seraglio. "The choice of them is yours, my lord."

"Tempting as these sights are, Mehmet Pasha, I regret I must forgo the pleasures they promise. The girl prisoner would not be for such a purpose, I assure you."

The Pasha frowned. The Englishman's directness annoyed him. This was not the way business was conducted in Algiers—at least not with a Pasha in the Ottoman Empire and high in favour with the Sultan himself. Still, the girl was to die tomorrow, along with the rest of the trash in the courtyard. She was worth little enough to him. How much would she be worth to the Englishman? He looked at the face above him, but the lean, tanned features revealed nothing. He sighed. "Alas, my friend, the girl is the Sultan's prisoner, a condemned associate of pirates. It would be difficult and dangerous to release her."

The Earl restrained his impatience with difficulty. Until recently this old fox in front of him had been a close associate of the pirates that had ravaged the Mediterranean for centuries. However, to remind the Pasha of that now would hardly further his cause. He said carefully, "But, Excellence, does not the Koran say that women should be protected and treated gently, as befits their weaker constitution?"

"The girl is one of a band of infidels, my lord. The Koran says nothing of such a woman."

The Earl decided not to fence any longer. He had come prepared, after all. As he spoke he drew from his finger a pearl ring of singular beauty and contemplated it. "I understand your scruples, believe me. But is there not a way this matter could be arranged to our...mutual benefit?"

The Pasha's eyes gleamed. "My lord, the Sultan's laws are absolute. On the other hand...the guards, it is true, are sometimes less vigilant than they should be. I have often spoken to their commander on this subject. A prisoner might well escape—especially when, for example, the muezzin calls the faithful to prayer…''

''One hour after sunset. I think I understand you. There remains but one detail.''

''What is that, my lord?'' asked the Pasha eagerly, his eyes on one of the largest and most lustrous pearls he had ever seen.

''I must see the girl at close quarters. I must be sure.''

In spite of his curiosity, the Pasha was too anxious to possess the pearl to make any objection. They descended to the courtyard, where the late-morning sun was blazing down mercilessly on the wretched band of prisoners. The Pasha had spoken the truth. The men had distanced themselves from the girl, who was crouched, head bowed, in the minute amount of shade afforded by the post to which she was chained. Squatting down beside her, the Earl took her chin in his fingers and pulled her head up. Startlingly dark blue eyes blazed into his, then sharp teeth bit hard into his thumb. The Algerians gasped when they saw the drops of blood on his hand, but the Earl did not release his hold.

''Take the drab away!'' screamed the Pasha. ''Take her away and beat her!''

''No!'' said the Earl. ''The injury is nothing. Leave her where she is, I pray you.'' Then, as the Pasha, resenting this usurpation of his authority, would have spoken, he added deliberately, ''Look at her. She is a pearl beyond price.'' He looked at the Pasha and smiled. The Pasha slowly smiled back, and the smile turned into a laugh and then a roar.

''Truly a pearl,'' he spluttered, pointing at the bundle of rags on the ground. The courtyard rang with the sound of his laughter.

"Then we are agreed?" said the Earl, frowning at the fury in the girl's incredible eyes. He slowly released his hold.

"Agreed," said the Pasha, still chuckling. "A pearl beyond price."

Now, EIGHT HOURS LATER, as the moonlight streamed over the girl, the Earl smiled grimly. The success of his plan was worth a dozen such pearls. This step was but the first of many. Away in the distance a ghostly wailing began, was taken up by others until the air was filled with the sound—the muezzin. It was time. He nodded to his three companions. One of the Berbers went swiftly to the stairs, where the guard might appear. It was wise to be cautious— the Pasha might have taken the pearl without actually earning it. The other Berber ran forward to the girl, wielding a murderous-looking axe. With one mighty swing he severed the chain which bound her to the post. Meanwhile the Earl, with Tom's help, had taken hold of their prize.

"Quickly, Tom, the gag in her mouth. Ouch! The devil! Yashid, take her feet! Hold up the rest of the chain, man!"

Struggling, kicking, uttering muffled little cries, the girl was carried out on to the causeway, which led to their dinghy. Halfway along it she stopped her struggles, as if she was suddenly drained of energy, and the Earl gave her over to Yashid to carry. She was no weight, except for the fragment of chain still attached to her ankle. They waded out to the dinghy and the Berber dropped the girl in the bow, where she lay motionless as they cast off, making for the ship, which lay at anchor in deeper water. No sound of pursuit came from behind them. The night was tranquil under the moon and there was just enough breeze to make sailing sure. But when the ship was almost within reach the Earl gave a sudden shout. "Tom! Catch her! Quickly!"

smell acquired during her brief sojourn in the filthy courtyard.

"So which is it to be, Tom? The bath or London?" When the man still hesitated, the Earl said impatiently, "Believe me, Tom, if I have to bathe the slut myself you will return to England as soon as I can arrange it." Tom remained silent. "Dammit, I need your help, Tom. The matter needs discretion. Who should I trust but you? I've known you all my life. You know very well we have no abigail, so what am I to do if you refuse?"

Tom nodded reluctantly and set to. The bath was filled and waiting when he looked curiously at the girl by the porthole. She had taken no interest in the discussion but was staring out at the night. "Er—madam? Will you step this way, please? Miss?"

The girl ignored him. The Earl gave a snort of laughter and said, "I fear your courtesies are wasted on the jade, Tom. Tell her simply to take her clothes off and climb into the bath. Meanwhile I need some food. I'll find the steward."

"Oh, no, sir, don't leave me. I'll do it, but don't leave me alone with her! Come on, girl, do as he says and get in the bath! I don't think she understands English, sir. You tell her in French."

When the girl continued to ignore them both the Earl grew impatient with what he saw as an assumption of modesty on the part of a woman who had been living with a gang of pirates. He strode over, picked her up and dumped her in the tub, clothes and all. "Now get on with it, Tom!"

He disappeared. Nervously Tom approached the girl, only to find her shivering uncontrollably. "Now, don't take on so. I'll do your face first, shall I? That's the ticket. That's the way; you help, then we'll both be happy. Look, I daresn't turn me back because of what you might do, but

I promise not to look, if you know what I mean. Let me take some of these rags off your back. That'll be a start. Lord love us!''

Tom's concern was not because of the girl's emaciation, bad though that was. What had caused him to exclaim was the state of her back and shoulders. They were covered with a network of bruises, weals and burns. Tom had been with his master at Waterloo, and had travelled widely with him since, but this evidence of deliberate cruelty shocked him. With gentle fingers, which no ladies' maid could have rivalled, he quickly removed the rest of the girl's rags and helped her out of the bath. He fetched salves and one of his master's fine linen nightshirts. When the Earl returned she was dry and lying in a makeshift bed on a couch in the day cabin.

''The steward is bringing some food for you and the girl, Tom. I've dined. Are you ready for it? Ah, good! You've dealt with our little friend, I see.''

''I have in a manner of speaking, sir. But I'd like you to see this. I wouldn't treat an animal like this and that's a fact.''

The girl was still shivering as Tom gently lifted her up, pulling the nightshirt from her back to reveal the dreadful scars. The Earl frowned.

''Do you think the Pasha's men did all that, sir?''

''No, some of those scars are old ones, though I very much fear she had that beating today after all. What a life she's led, poor devil! I see you've put something on them.''

''What we've got, which ain't much. What do you think we should do, sir?''

''I think she needs some food—something easy; a little gruel, perhaps. Then she probably needs sleep more than anything else. After that we'll see.'' By now Tom had lost his inhibitions about looking after a female, and he dealt with the girl with an unexpected deftness before tucking into a hearty meal himself. Meanwhile the Earl sat in his chair, frowning at his thoughts. "We must put back our plans for a month or two, Tom. The girl is little use to me the way she is. I'll leave her with Sheikh Ibrahim when we call there to deliver the two Berbers to their home. I think I can persuade him to treat her. We should be there in two days, not more."

Tom was still preoccupied with what he had seen. "I suppose she might not have felt it as much—being brought up to it, so to speak," he said to himself without much conviction. "But how's she borne it? Sir, do you realise that if we hadn't of found Miss Linette when we did she might...she might have... It doesn't bear thinking about!"

"But I have thought about it, Tom," said the Earl softly. "Ever since we brought Linette back from that doxy's house in London I've thought about it. And about the animal that put her there."

"This plan you were mentioning, sir. Is it something to do with Miss Linette? I shouldn't have thought this one'd be fit company for Miss Linette. I mean, look at her! What are you thinking of doing with her?"

"I'm using her to teach someone a lesson, Tom," said the Earl grimly. "One he won't forget. I mean the girl no harm, but I bought her for a purpose. She's a tool; no more. Let's hope she survives, for she's the key to my whole scheme."

Later that night, when Tom had gone to his bed, the Earl sat considering the slight figure on the couch. She was in a restless sleep, muttering unintelligibly and occasionally moaning. Where had she come from? She was probably French, of course. It didn't really matter—French or English, she would do for his purposes. But she'd need a name, a new one, for her own would probably be highly unsuitable. He sat in thought for a moment or two. "Perdita. Yes, that's perfect. Classical but apt. Perdita, the lost one!" Her eyes flew open, and once again he was astounded by their depth of colour. In that pale face they burned like a dark blue flame, like sapphires. There was something in them... He got up calmly, and walked to the door of his cabin. On his way out he looked back, smiling sardonically. Perhaps the Pasha had been right after all. The slut was a witch! All the better for what he had in mind.

THE VOYAGE WENT smoothly, and in two days they were close to their destination. This was a small bay to the west of Tangier, where lived a man skilled in those arts of medicine for which his ancestors had been famed throughout Europe. The Earl had made his acquaintance some years before, and had good cause to be grateful to him. Sheikh Ibrahim was now an honoured friend, and though the two men met infrequently they were able to pick up the threads of their friendship with ease. It was the Sheikh who had persuaded the Earl to take the two Berbers with him on his journeys through the eastern Mediterranean.

The Earl and Tom were much relieved at the prospect of making an early landfall. Perdita, as she was now called, had been in high fever ever since the first night. Tom had done what he could, but the resources of the ship were small. If she was to have a chance of survival the sooner she was in a doctor's hands, the better. Throughout her illness the girl had muttered and even shouted, but never so clearly that they could deduce who she was. Even her nationality remained uncertain, though they assumed that, like the rest of the pirate band, she was French. The Earl felt some pity for the girl, but he was impatient at the threat to his plans. He could, he supposed, replace her, but it would be difficult to find another so ideally suited to what he had in mind. He was intrigued by her, too. How did someone who had lived in primitive squalor come to have an air of such dignity and grace? These were attributes which could serve him well, but he wished he knew where she had acquired them!

They were received with great joy by the Sheikh and his household. He declared Perdita's condition bad but by no means hopeless, and saw her safely bestowed in his private apartments under the care of his own daughters. Then he led his guests into the salon, where he regaled them with refreshments and demanded an account of their travels. The Earl knew what the Sheikh wanted to hear. He had little interest in the antiquities of Greece, Turkey or Egypt, but was eager to hear what was happening in Athens, Istanbul and Cairo. It was not difficult to satisfy him, for the Sheikh had friends all over the Ottoman Empire and the Earl had been charged with numerous messages for him. But though he talked freely of his adventures in these great cities the Earl was singularly reticent about the girl—a fact which did not go unnoticed by the Sheikh.

When they had exhausted their supply of news—at least for the present—the Sheikh sat back and looked quizzically at his friend. "And now, my lord? Do you make for home and England? Or are you to visit your estate in France? You will note that I am far too discreet to ask you outright what you intend to do with your...protégée through there."

"What I do now depends in some measure on what you suggest. The girl, as you have seen, needs care and treatment. I was hoping you would undertake that."

"Of course, of course. It isn't necessary even to ask. I

think we can cure her—to some extent at least. You realise that some of those scars will fade, but they may never disappear entirely?"

The Earl nodded soberly.

"But what then, my friend? I hope I do not presume on our friendship too far when I point out that she is a most unlikely companion for the Earl of Ambourne—here or anywhere else." The Earl raised an eyebrow, and the Sheikh said apologetically, "I could not help noticing, even in my brief examination, that the scars on her body are not those one acquires in the salons of London or Paris, or even in the houses of joy in those cities. You are not indulging in some generous but unwise act of chivalry, I hope?"

"My days of chivalry are over, Ibrahim."

"I know, I know. You will tell me that they disappeared when you lost the use of your arm at Waterloo. But my treatment seems to have cured that. I notice you are using it quite freely. Why is it that I could not cure your soul? Or is it not the injury, but something else that eats away at your spirit? My friend, my dear friend, you are not seeking some form of vengeance, are you? Perhaps for what happened to Mademoiselle Linette?" The Earl's face darkened and he walked to the window. The Sheikh continued gently, "Now I have offended you. Forgive me. I must not judge when I know so little of the story. You will, I am sure, talk to me if you feel you can do so. Meanwhile I will use all my skills to heal the flesh of that poor wretch in there. Damage to the spirit is more difficult to repair, but we shall do what we can. Let me take you to your room."

The Earl turned again, and the Sheikh was distressed at the implacable look on his face. "You have never seen Linette, Sheikh Ibrahim," he said. "She was a lovely child. Open, generous and happy. Linette is a pet name, but indeed I think it is apt. We have a little English bird, the linnet, and Linette was just such a happy spirit—not clever, but infinitely lovable. She spent her early childhood in France, but when her father died she and my aunt came over to live with us in England. They lived with us at Ambourne for over twelve years, and they were happy years. My own father died when I was still quite young and I became the head of our house, with all the responsibilities that held. Linette was one of them.''

''Did you fall in love with her?'' asked the Sheikh.

''Not as a man loves a woman he wishes to marry. But Linette needed all the protection we could give her—she was so trusting. Even when she grew older she felt nothing in the world could do her harm; evil simply did not exist. Yes, she trusted us, and we failed her,'' he said bitterly.

''What happened?''

''My aunt had been in ill health during the autumn of 1814, and it was decided she should take the waters at Bath. She went in November, leaving Linette with my mother at Ambourne. I was in Vienna all that winter and I suppose my mother felt dull and lacking in company. She invited friends to stay, among them my mother's god-daughter, a lady who had at one time persuaded herself that she would like to become the Countess of Ambourne. I had disabused her of the notion. She brought with her a new acquaintance, a certain Piers Carston. Spurred on by her ill will towards me, Georgiana Compton persuaded Linette to believe herself in love with Carston. She encouraged secret meetings, overcame Linette's scruples and later aided the pair to elope. Carston must have had some hold over her, for she would not otherwise have abused our trust so grossly.''

The Earl had obviously reached a difficult point in his

narrative. His voice remained calm, but his hands were clenched round his glass. "Carston himself was motivated by greed. You see, he had been deceived by the apparent affluence in which Linette lived into believing her an heiress. When he discovered this was not the case..."

The Earl paused and the slender glass cracked. Drops of blood appeared on his thumb, which he absently wiped away.

The Sheikh put out his hand. "Take your time, my friend. This is very painful."

"I have nearly finished, Ibrahim," said the Earl sombrely. "Piers Carston had taken Linette to London. When he found that she was not the heiress he'd imagined, he refused to marry her and abandoned her there in one of the worst quarters of the town. It took us a week to find her, and when we did...we were horrified by her condition. She very nearly died. Our innocent, who had never had a malicious thought in her life, who knew nothing of evil or inhumanity, had been deserted by the man she loved and left to God knows what sort of life in the stews of London. She was sixteen years old. Would you say that this man should not be punished? I am not so forgiving. But I am not seeking vengeance, Sheikh Ibrahim. That is too melodramatic a word. Say rather that I am about to exact justice. I have sought this man for over three years. He is now in London and I have found the weapon with which to punish him."

"You draw a fine line between vengeance and justice," said the Sheikh gravely, "and if, as I suspect, the 'weapon' is now lying sick in my apartments, then you must take care it does not rebound on you. To use human beings thus is a dangerous exercise."

The Earl smiled. "When have I ever shunned danger, Sheikh Ibrahim? Tell me that!"

CHAPTER TWO

THE BIRDS IN THE OAK trees outside had been arguing for some time. The noise of their angry chatter coming in through the window had woken her. Her skin was hot and sore and her head was aching. Her limbs were stiff. She must be ill. Mama would come soon, she was sure, and then all would be well. Mama would send for Dr. Williams and then she would be better... She closed her eyes and slept again... Strange! She was asleep, and yet she could feel herself being lifted and turned. Gentle hands were bathing her forehead, then putting something soothing on her back. That hurt! She drank gratefully from the cup that was put to her lips. Had she fallen from her horse, perhaps? She couldn't remember. Mama would tell her... Later...

When she next woke up the pain in her head was less severe. The birds were quiet, but she could hear voices outside. She slowly turned to look at the window. What was wrong? This was not her room! The window was in the wrong place. Perhaps they had moved her bed... No, the room was completely strange to her. Where was she? Where was Mama? Then she heard a voice she recognised. It was a man's voice, crisp, decisive, talking in French. The last time she had heard it he had been speaking English... Suddenly memory came flooding back in a series of pictures—the two men on the Englishman's ship, the courtyard in Algiers, the capture of *Le Faucon* and her life with the pirates. Oh, God, no! She remembered it all now.

She was back in the nightmare that was reality. In her weakness and despair she groaned, and slow tears forced themselves down her cheeks. There was an instant flurry of silk and a breath of perfume, then cool hands were wiping her face and forehead and giving her a drink. She slipped into sleep again.

It continued like this for some days. The girl hovered between sleeping and waking, while her poor battered body regained strength. In her more lucid moments she forced herself to face what had happened to her in the years up to the sinking of *Le Faucon*, and as her body grew stronger so did her determination to return to the stoicism she had possessed before her illness. She accepted the gentle care of the Sheikh and his daughters passively, but met all overtures of friendship with silence. This act of will took its toll, and the Sheikh became seriously worried about her state of mind. On the morning of the Earl's departure the Sheikh voiced his concern. ''I am satisfied that the battle for the girl's physical well-being is almost won. All she needs now is rest and care. When you return I hope she will be fully recovered. But I am more concerned about her refusal to communicate with her fellow humans. It is not only a question of language, I am sure. She has erected a barrier, which will take time and skill to overcome. I wish I knew more of her history. What is her name, for instance?''

''I know very little, Ibrahim,'' said the Earl. ''Only that she was arrested on the pirate ship *Le Faucon* one or two days before I found her in the Pasha's courtyard. I don't even know her real name, but, as it is almost certainly unsuitable, I named her Perdita.''

The girl was shamelessly listening in the room overlooking the garden court in which the two men were sitting. She smiled ironically. Her real name was most certainly inappropriate. Perdita would do very well.

"You English and your Shakespeare," murmured the Sheikh. "Yet I suppose it is apt—the lost one. However, if I remember correctly Shakespeare's Perdita was found to be a princess."

The Earl laughed. "Oh, I very much doubt that my Perdita is anything of that nature, Ibrahim! That's the crux of my plan—the slut is so very unworthy, so absolutely low. She's part of the scum of the Mediterranean, and she's perfect!"

The Sheikh looked serious. "I do not wish to bore you again with my anxieties about your plan, my friend. But I beg you to be very careful when you are playing with the lives of others. That is Allah's prerogative—and Allah is jealous of his powers."

"You are too concerned, Ibrahim. The girl is a tool, no more and no less. I promise you that when I have finished with her she will be no worse off than she was—in fact, she will have a much better life. Why, she will have an establishment of sorts, and fine clothes and jewels."

"I cannot believe that your values have become so crassly material, Lord Ambourne!"

"No, they are not, I hope. But hers might well be. Now, how long must I wait before coming again?"

The Sheikh considered, pulling at his beard. "I would like to keep her here until she is fully restored—in mind as well as body. But I fear that would be too long for you. Shall we say three months?"

"Two at the most, Ibrahim. Concentrate on curing the girl's body. Leave her mind to me!"

They went into the house soon after, and silence fell in the garden. Upstairs in her room, Perdita was left with much food for thought. She was to be involved in a plan, that much was clear. It was also clear that the man who had brought her here did not think of her as a person at all, only as a—what had he called her?—a tool. He had called her other things, too. She wrinkled her brow in an effort to remember. It wasn't only 'slut' or 'scum'. There was something else... She had it! He had called her a 'pearl'. When she'd lain in the filth of that courtyard he had called her a pearl, and then the courtyard had filled with cruel laughter—more cruel than anyone there realised. Well, over the last two years she had taught herself to expect nothing more. She would survive this, as she had survived the catastrophe that had put her on the pirate ship in the first place and the torment and isolation that had followed. But she had only done that by learning to be strong, by refusing to be affected by the world around her, by shutting it out. She must exert herself. It would be so disastrously easy to relax her guard with the Sheikh and his daughters, for it was a long time since she had experienced such loving care. She must not let it weaken her.

TWO MONTHS PASSED, and the Earl's ship had just been sighted. He was expected within the hour. The Sheikh was sitting in the garden with Perdita. Rest and food had transformed her. She was still slender, but her face and figure had acquired the bloom of health. Her long hair was a cloud of dark brown silk held back in a jewelled cap, and the combination of her sea-green kaftan and those deep blue eyes made of her a picture to delight the most critical eye. The Sheikh regarded her with pleasure, but then he sighed. In spite of all his efforts she was as distant as ever. He had reasoned with her, tried persuasion on her, had asked his daughters to amuse her—all in vain. She suffered their ministrations patiently, was always courteous, but refused to talk to them. He had tried to trick her by speaking at length in Arabic and then suddenly switching to French or even English. He knew she understood at least one of those languages, but she was never caught out. He was astonished at the strength of purpose to be found in such a delicate frame. Over the weeks he had become increasingly certain that there was a mystery about the girl. He had the absurd impression that she could easily be the princess the Earl had so laughingly dismissed, for she had breeding in every line. He was anxious for the Earl to see her, but not at all happy at the thought of Perdita's departure.

Perdita, too, regarded the Earl's imminent arrival with mixed feelings. She, too, was apprehensive about her unknown future. But she was much more eager to go. She knew that if she stayed much longer with the Sheikh and his family she would be unable to keep the detachment she had so painfully regained. She was beginning to return their regard for her, and she dared not let that happen. She looked at him now, his eyes full of kindly concern. He took her hand and addressed her in French, "And so, Perdita, the Earl will be here very soon now. Are you ready to go? I doubt it. I wonder whether he would let me keep you a little while longer. But would that serve any purpose? You widen your eyes. You're afraid, but of what? You do not wish to stay here, is that it? Are you afraid of us? Or can it be that you are afraid of yourself? If that were so it would be progress indeed. You shake your head. Perdita, I beg of you, do not shut us out like this. I know a little of what you have suffered, and I believe you have armed yourself against any further pain by rejecting human contact—even life itself. Oh, yes, you may shake your head again, but I know of your attempt to end your life in the sea... I have surprised you?"

Perdita had never been more strongly tempted to confide

in this man, to explain to him why she had jumped into the sea at Algiers. For twenty-four hours she had believed herself to be close to death in the Pasha's prison. She had come to terms with the thought of death, even welcomed it as a way of escape from a life that had become insupportable. When the Earl had removed that way of escape she had impulsively tried to take her own life. She knew it was wrong, and knew she could never do such a thing again. Life was to be borne, stoically if necessary, but never thrown away. She looked at the Sheikh. He seemed to see through to her very soul. He said softly, "Well, Perdita, I think we understand something of each other after all. Perhaps words are not always needed. Fight your battle, my child, but if ever you should need a refuge I would be happy to offer you one. Lord Ambourne is a man of honour and feeling, but in this instance I fear his judgement is impaired by his hatred of the man who betrayed his young cousin. Ah, you understand hatred? You have felt the same emotion? For the captain of *Le Faucon* perhaps? No? I wonder who? You will not tell me? Well, then, I will say to you what I will say to Lord Ambourne: hatred is destructive. You might or might not succeed in destroying the object of your hatred. You will certainly succeed in destroying your own happiness." Then, when Perdita smiled bitterly, he added, "Happiness is still possible for you. Do not shut the door to it. And now that is enough. Remember what I have said. You have the courage and spirit to help Lord Ambourne. Use them wisely."

A bustle inside the house warned the Sheikh that his guest would arrive within minutes. He bowed to Perdita and went in. She got up and walked restlessly about the garden, her thoughts in turmoil. The Sheikh's words had made a deep impression on her. But she would not, she *could* not now surrender the fortress she had built to pro-

tect herself. So much courage she did not possess. As for
Lord Ambourne, she would wait to see what was to come.
Of one thing she was certain. His opinion of her was so
low that nothing she felt or thought would hold the
slightest interest for him. It was better it should be so, for
then she could remain indifferent to him in a way she could
never dismiss the Sheikh. All the same, she was curious
to see this man who held her immediate future in his
hands. She remembered very little—grey eyes in a tanned
face, an impression of strength, an authoritative voice, an
ability to speak French as fluently as he spoke English.
That was all.

She looked up to see the object of her thoughts standing
in the garden doorway. Her memory had not been at fault.
He had grey eyes, hair that was almost black, and a strong,
rather hard face. He was tall, and dressed well but plainly
in fawn buckskins and a dark maroon coat. For an unguarded moment his eyes widened with astonishment and
something more. She did not know what it was, but it filled
her with a peculiar excitement, almost a sense of recognition. But of what? He took a step towards her, but then
stopped abruptly, and his face, which had been alive with
feeling, became expressionless. When he finally spoke his
tone was cool. ''I would not have thought it possible that
you could be so changed. I must congratulate the Sheikh
on his work.''

She looked at him silently, still dazed by what had happened.

''Ah, yes, Sheikh Ibrahim did say you were not yet talking to us. A pity. But he is sure you understand French,
so in the absence of any other evidence I will assume you
understand me. I am returning to Europe tomorrow, and
you will accompany me. In your room you will find some
European clothing.'' He looked her up and down. ''Fetch-

ing though those garments are, as I'm sure you are aware,
they are hardly suitable for the rigours of a northern European winter. You will consult with the seamstresses here.
They have my orders and will see that you look respectably dressed. I expect to see you ready to sail with me at
nine in the morning.'' As she continued to stare at him he
said irritably, ''Go, girl, go!''

Sadly she returned to her room. Now that the moment
had come she was reluctant to leave this oasis in the desert
that was her life. She refused to admit, even to herself, that
the Sheikh and his daughters had taken a place in her heart.
But she had been reminded of her status by the Earl's tone.
To him she would always be something lower than a servant.

In this she did the Earl less than justice. He would never
normally have spoken to a dependent in such tones. The
truth was that he had been disorientated by the unexpected
feeling that had overtaken him on seeing Perdita. For years
he had prided himself on his self-control. Born into a family with large estates, he had inherited the title early and
accepted its responsibilities as fully as he enjoyed its priv-
ileges. As a young man in Regency London he had, of
course, enjoyed the favours of various ladies in that pleas-
ure-seeking world. And his birth and wealth had made him
a tempting prospect to ambitious mamas and their mar-
riageable daughters. But he had easily avoided all the traps
laid for him, had never experienced any emotion he could
not control, other than hatred for Piers Carston. Not, that
was, until he had looked into Perdita's eyes on the night
he had taken her from Algiers. Now, at the sight of Perdita
in the garden, his calm assurance had deserted him
again...! He reminded himself that he had been abroad for
too long. Such unaccountable lapses would soon be forgotten after his return to Europe.

The time for them to leave was soon upon them. Perdita
had been caught up in a whirl of fitting and stitching, with
little time left to come to terms with her departure. Before
she knew it she found herself on the shore in her new
European clothes, waiting patiently while the Earl took his
leave of his host. Then it was her turn. While the Earl
looked sardonically on, the Sheikh kissed her cheeks and
said with a mischievous look, "You would make an ideal
wife, Perdita, for you never answer back!" Then more
seriously, "Remember, my daughter, you have a refuge
here if you should ever need one. Now farewell! Go with
Allah's blessing and protection!"

The Earl was making for the ship and the girl followed
him. Suddenly she turned back, caught the Sheikh's hand
and kissed it. "*Merci*, Sheikh Ibrahim," she whispered so
softly that no one else could hear, "*merci.*" Then, without
looking at him again, she followed the Earl to the ship for
France.

PERDITA SAT IN HER CABIN, examining her new clothes.
There was nothing else to do, for a cold wind was blowing
outside and the seas were rough. Besides, Tom had
brought a message that she was to remain inside. He had
obviously been coached, for he made no comment on her
appearance, nor even gave any sign that he had seen her
before. She wondered if the Earl was suffering from sea-
sickness, and rather hoped he was. It was therefore a disappointment to hear his incisive voice on the deck a few
minutes later, giving some directions to Tom. No seasick-
ness there. She turned back to her clothes with a sigh. They
were very pretty, of course. It was a long time since she
had seen such lovely materials—pink Italian silk and pale
blue jaconet muslin for two of the dresses, midnight-blue
merino wool for a third, grey kerseymere and dark blue

velvet for the pelisses. The undergarments were all of fin-
est cambric or lawn. There were even two matching hats
and a luxurious cashmere shawl. The gloves were Limer-
ick, and the slippers of softest leather. Perdita was still
feminine enough to enjoy parading in her new wardrobe,
curtsying and bowing. She was pleased to discover that
she had not forgotten the art. It had been so long…dear
God…so long! She sat down, overcome with a sudden
vision of herself at her first party. It had only been a small
affair, but it had promised to be the door to a delightful
new world. She had worn pink silk then, and it had been
a great success. Afterwards Mama and she had planned
what she would wear for her come-out the following year.
The question of whether white lace would be too 'old',
and if it should be worn over white, pink or blue satin had
seemed overwhelmingly important. Of course as the heiress to the Taverton estates she would be assured of an
excitingly successful season… But by the following June,
when she would have been dancing at her first London
balls, her mother was dead and she…and she… She hid
her face in her hands. Whatever happened to her in the
future she would never go back to the happy world of her
girlhood. That would remain closed to her forever, for she
was now unacceptable in any decent society. She sat there
for a moment, then rallied herself angrily. What was she
doing? This was no way to survive! This was what happened when one relaxed one's guard! She had been closeted in her cabin without air or exercise for far too long.
To hell with the Earl and his stupid commands! She flung
open the door of her cabin and marched out on to the deck.

A gust of wind caught her as she came out, forcing her
to clutch her bonnet. The kerseymere pelisse was not really
thick enough for the weather, but she was determined not
to go back. She walked briskly round the deck, enjoying

the strong fresh air. However, her enjoyment was curtailed when she turned a corner and walked into the Earl. The ship gave a sudden lurch and she found herself clutching his sleeve. When they were disengaged he turned on her.

"What the devil are you doing out on deck? I gave strict orders you were to remain in your cabin!" In the face of his anger she adopted a stratagem she had learned to use with Legrand, the Captain of *Le Faucon*. Looking as stupid as possible, she behaved as if she had not heard him. He continued in tones of contempt, "I know you heard me, so don't try your tricks on me! Or were you too anxious to show yourself in your new finery? That's not meant for pleasing the sailors, my girl. The bonnet's an expensive one from Paris—it's wasted on them. Save it for London!"

Perdita's mind was racing behind her expression of stupidity. How could she punish him for his unpleasant insinuations? With a masterly look of hurt incomprehension she took her hand away from the bonnet. She regretted the necessity, for it was a fetching grey velvet lined with pink silk. The wind swept it into the air. It hovered for a moment, then went sailing down into the churning sea. Then she put her hand to her mouth.

The Earl was furious. He narrowed his eyes and said softly, "If I were sure you had done that deliberately, you little slut, you wouldn't sit down comfortably for a week." She could see him debating whether to pursue the matter, then he suddenly turned on his heel and left her. As he went he shouted to Tom to escort her back.

Perdita returned to her cabin well pleased with her short expedition. The Earl, it seemed, was not as in control as he would like to be. There was scope here for some fun. She did not deceive herself that she could win any serious battle between them, but it was pleasant to have got the better of him in that little skirmish. Detached she would remain, but she might derive some mild amusement from needling the great man! The fact that she refused to talk was already a source of annoyance to him. She must see what else she could think of. It might while away the weary hours.

Unfortunately the Earl proved very elusive for the rest of the voyage. When he saw her he treated her with apparent indifference, but since she had all her meals in her cabin they did not often meet. Until she learned what sort of establishment was to be her home it was difficult to make plans, so she spent most of her time in stultifying boredom. However, the Earl did arrange for Tom to escort her on a walk round the deck every morning. It did not disconcert Tom that she was silent. He talked enough for both of them, and Perdita learned a great deal about the Earl's home on these walks. She found it difficult to reconcile the man she knew with the picture Tom drew of him, and put it down to an old servant's partiality. Towards the end of their voyage he said in some embarrassment, "I wouldn't never have thought you could turn out so well, miss. You might not talk much, but you do have an air about you, no mistake. I take back what I said. I think you and Miss Linette would do well together. I hope you'll be very happy at Belleroi."

He scuttled away, leaving Perdita in a rueful frame of mind. After years of isolation from gentleness, concern, even goodwill, she was now meeting them wherever she went! She jumped as a voice behind her said, "What a pity Tom isn't going to be at Belleroi to act as your champion! How do you do it, Perdita? First the Sheikh, and now Tom. Well, I have a use for those arts of yours. But do not employ them too indiscriminately. The cowherds at Belleroi are very susceptible!"

Thank you, my lord, thought Perdita. It is a relief to

know that if I am ever in danger of forgetting my true position I can be sure you will remind me. Though I cannot like you, I am truly grateful to you. And she went into her cabin without looking round.

They landed at Cherbourg and were soon in a carriage, on the last stage of their journey. She had learned from Tom that, in addition to his estates in England, the Earl had inherited a small estate in a quiet corner of Normandy, and guessed that he was taking her there. It was dark as they came through a cluster of cottages and up the long straight drive that led to the house. She was so travel-weary that she noticed little of their arrival. She was taken up to her room by a stout woman in black, who gave her some soup, undressed her, and put her to bed. She was asleep before the door was shut.

CHAPTER THREE

PERDITA WOKE EARLY the next morning after a refreshing sleep. She lay there for a moment in the darkened room, and then got up to open the curtains. It was barely light. The long straight drive along which they had driven the night before stretched in front of her. It seemed to go on forever. At the far end were two massive cast-iron gates, flanked by wide stone pillars. To the left and right, about a hundred yards from the house, stood two identical little lodges, and flowerbeds and lawns were laid out in rigorous symmetry around them. She shivered. It all looked so cold, so formal. She shivered again and realised that it was, in fact, very cold! She had spent so long in the Mediterranean that she had forgotten how sharp autumn mornings here in the north could be. After all, it was already November. She splashed her face with water from the jug on her wash-stand and dressed, putting on the thickest of her three dresses—the dark blue merino. Hastily throwing the grey pelisse over her shoulders, she slipped out of her room and sought the stairs. In two minutes she was outside.

The air was intoxicating. It had a crisp freshness that no wind of the Mediterranean had ever possessed. She savoured it for a moment while she stood listening for signs of movement around the house. The servants were astir in the kitchen, which must be behind the house, and she could hear a child's voice among the other noises. But the main rooms along the front were curtained and silent. She had

time to explore. When she reached the lodges she turned
and looked back. The house was a small château. The symmetry of the gardens and lodges was echoed in its façade,
but the grey stone was softened by creepers, which had
been allowed to grow over the lower half. Two rows of
windows stretched across the front. The lower ones obviously belonged to a series of large reception rooms on the
first floor, and above them were the bedrooms. A line of
small windows in the roof probably belonged to the servants' rooms. The whole building showed signs of recent
repair—perhaps since the restoration of the monarchy in
France.

A servant, dressed in black, was walking stiffly up the
drive. He bowed when he reached her and said in a voice
that was formal but managed at the same time to convey
his disapproval, "*Mademoiselle*'s breakfast is served in her
room." Meekly she allowed herself to be conducted back
to the house. There was little point in ignoring him; she
needed to find out more about the house and its occupants
before deciding how to behave. Besides, she was ravenously hungry!

Her room was charming in the fresh morning light.
Draped muslin softened the tall windows and furniture, and
rose-printed chintz hung from the brass curtain-poles. The
same rosy chintz covered a small couch and two chairs. A
fire burned in the pretty marble fireplace opposite the bed,
and in front of it stood a tripod table with a tray. She drank
the hot chocolate and ate the crusty rolls, butter and quince
jam with relish. She was just exploring a tiny dressing-
room, which opened off her room, when a maid appeared
to escort her to the library. After hastily washing her hands
and face she followed the maid downstairs.

The library was a lovely room on the first floor. She was
gazing in admiration at the long windows and the books

lining three of the walls when a cool, well-known voice said, "Come here, Perdita."

The Earl was sitting in a wing chair by the fire, dressed plainly in a dark tobacco-brown coat and buff pantaloons. On the small table at his side was a pile of papers and books, one of which lay open on his knee. She contemplated disobeying him, then decided it would be better not to challenge him until she knew more.

"Sit down," he said, without looking up from his book. This was too much! She looked at him blankly, her stupid expression firmly in place.

"Do not, I beg of you, imagine I am deceived by that bovine look. You understand French perfectly, and I have no time for tricks. There's a great deal to say to you. Please sit down." Happy to have wrung a "please" out of him, she sat. He shut his book and looked at her thoughtfully for some minutes, while she stared into the fire, trying to shut out all consciousness of the long figure sitting in the chair on her left.

"You are about to embark on a strenuous course of study, Perdita. During the next six months you will be trained—I will not say educated—in what is necessary to give you the outer appearance of a lady. You will have a chaperon, who will also instruct you in deportment, and tutors in dancing and music. You will be given the elements of reading and writing—at least enough to write your name."

He paused, and Perdita looked at him in astonishment. Could this really be happening? Was this man telling her that he was about to make her into a lady? She did not know whether to laugh or cry at the bitter irony of the situation. She had spent two years trying to forget all she had learned of gentleness, concern for others and the courtesies of polite Society. Now she was to have six months' training to 'acquire' them. Life was surely full of strange twists!

"Perdita, I have told you I am not deceived by this idiot's stare you employ. I am convinced that you use it to hide what you do not wish the world to see—such as, God knows why, triumph at the loss of a very pretty bonnet." Caught off guard, she turned her head swiftly to look at him. "Yes, I thought as much—you did it deliberately! Was it a somewhat childish effort to annoy me? The loss of the bonnet was yours, not mine! But then, I have long given up divining the thoughts of women. To return to the tasks ahead. I will assume that before the time is out you will regain the use of your tongue, and when that happens you will be taught to speak correctly."

Perdita found herself wondering what use this high-born aristocrat had for a pseudo-lady. What was he up to? Well, she would wait and see—the situation would not be without its piquancies. She realised he was talking again. She must concentrate on what he was saying.

"When I have finished with you, which will be within a year, I will see that you have enough clothes and jewels to set yourself up in the profession I imagine will suit you best. There is no reason why you should not enjoy a very comfortable existence from then on. It will at the very least be an improvement on your mode of life with the pirates."

Perdita was torn between resentment and laughter, but finally forced her mind into its preferred mode—that of detachment. She would need a clear head if she was to succeed in the delicately balanced game in front of her. The man was no fool.

"However, I should warn you, Perdita," the cool voice went on, "that if you refuse to do as I have said you will be sent back to the Pasha in Algiers with my compliments. Do you understand me?"

She stood up quickly. There were some things to which she could not remain indifferent. It was as she had thought. She might win skirmishes, but she would never win the major battles. He had all the heavy weapons in his hands. But that wouldn't stop her from resisting his attempts to destroy her self-respect. Whatever had happened in the past she had always kept an inner core of integrity. She wasn't going to let Lord Ambourne succeed where so many others had failed.

He let her go then, merely saying that she was to present herself in the library at two o'clock that afternoon to meet the first of her tutors.

In her room she found the stout woman in black, who had helped her to bed the night before. She introduced herself as Madame Lebrun, the housekeeper. She was obviously curious about Perdita and disappointed not to be able to converse with her. Perdita ignored her as far as possible, and at length the woman finished what she was doing and went out with a sniff. Madame Lebrun was indiscreet enough to recount her experience to the other servants, and this, coupled with their uncertainty about Perdita's true position in the household, caused them to treat her with unfriendly suspicion. This well suited Perdita's passionate determination to remain totally self-contained, depending on no one for friendship or company.

"I SHALL DO what I can, milor'," said Monsieur Champollion doubtfully. They were in the library, and Perdita had just met the little music master for the first time. "The time is very short. And *mademoiselle* does not talk, you say?"

"Not yet, anyway," murmured the Earl, looking sardonically at Perdita. "However, we have every reason to believe that she will eventually."

"But how am I to teach her the theory, or test her knowledge, if she cannot answer me? She could perhaps write it down?"

"Well, not yet, Champollion. Mademoiselle Perdita has not yet mastered the art."

"Not write?" faltered Champollion. "She can't write?"

"Champollion, if you cannot manage to teach her some rudimentary little tunes—enough to tinkle out at some insipid evening party—then say so. I will find someone else," said the Earl, growing impatient.

Perdita surveyed them both in silent amusement. What fun she was going to have. Who would have thought that such an unpromising episode in her life would turn out to be so diverting! She straightened her face when she saw the Earl's eyes on her.

Monsieur Champollion was hastily protesting his complete confidence in Mademoiselle Perdita's ability. "She will soon have a repertoire of the most delightful little tunes, milord. You will see. Very soon." He left, looking doubtfully at Perdita and mopping his brow.

"What amused you just now, I wonder?" said the Earl. "Was it Champollion? The poor man is convinced he has an impossible task, but he would not dream of admitting it. Are you so unmusical? You must not underrate yourself, Perdita. You may well discover you have an unexpected talent for music. It will complement your other…talents." Perdita's eyes flashed and she jumped up. "What has angered you now?" said the Earl impatiently. "The ladies in the kind of establishment I imagine you would aspire to—in London, or Paris perhaps—are not simply stripped and bedded, Perdita. They must entertain their clients. A little ability in music will not come amiss."

Perdita walked to the window, struggling for calm. Whatever he said she must not let it affect her.

He continued scornfully, "Oh, come, now! You surely don't imagine that I am ignorant of what you have been, Perdita? I assure you, your assumed indignation is really quite unnecessary. By all means act the modest young lady when we are in the public eye, but abandon these histrionics when we are alone. I bought you, knowing you for a strumpet, and you are of value to me because of it. Sit down, and listen to what I have to say." Perdita turned round and gazed at him defiantly, staying where she was. He said softly, "I am not accustomed to being defied in my own house, Perdita. Come here and sit down!"

When she still refused to move he got up swiftly and caught her by the arm. "What is it, Perdita?" he said dangerously. "Are you trying to have me believe that no man has ever held you like this? Kissed you like this?"

He kissed her violently, even passionately, but though he was angry there was an innate tenderness in his kiss that turned Perdita's heart over. She had never experienced anything like it before, and for a moment it filled her with a surprised delight. Then she struggled to pull herself away. He released her with a laugh and stood looking at her contemptuously. "My God, I must congratulate you, Perdita. If I did not know you for what you are—a slut, a drab from the dregs of the Mediterranean—that air of artless innocence might well deceive me." Perdita walked swiftly to the door. He made as if to stop her, but then hesitated and said merely, "Consider carefully what I have said, Perdita. You will have time, for I do not wish to see you again today. Tomorrow you will meet your chaperon and other tutors. Be here at the same hour. Go now."

Perdita was glad to be alone in her room. She needed a respite. The strange and lovely emotion she had experienced was so new to her that it would take time to recover her self-possession. But recover it she must. Bitter unhap-

piness lay ahead if she allowed the Earl or anyone else
any power over her real self. To him she was a tool, no
more. It was essential she returned to her former detached
dislike of him.

When they met the next morning it was as if the afternoon before had never been. The Earl's behaviour was
intimidatingly formal. He presented her to Madame
d'Espery, the elderly aristocrat who was to chaperon her,
Signor Calvi, her dancing master, and Père Amboise, the
local *curé*, who would teach her to read and write. If she
had not been so antipathetic to the Earl she could have
admired his competence in dealing with them all. Not only
were the lessons admirably arranged throughout the week,
he had also seen to it that she had free time in the afternoons for fresh air and exercise. He soon dispersed any
gratitude she might have felt, however.

"Understand me, Perdita, you are not to stray far from
the house on your outings, nor are you to indulge in any
of your tricks with the fellows of the neighbourhood. They
are simple souls and I am quite sure you could bewitch
them out of their senses." He looked at the lovely face
before him. "Quite sure. If you are wise, however, you
will resist the temptation to do so."

PERDITA'S TIME was soon heavily engaged with her lessons, so-called practice sessions and walks. She saw very
little of the Earl, for during the hours of daylight he was
out on estate business or closeted in the library with his
agent, and in the evenings he visited his neighbours or
dined alone. But, even when he was out, the château was
dominated by his presence and Perdita resented this. Her
walks became precious to her, for then she could escape.
Madame d'Espery was content to let Perdita walk alone,
as she herself preferred to spend this time "resting" in her

room. As long as Perdita was back in good time for their early-evening meal she was left to her own devices for the whole afternoon. She quickly discovered that the gardens behind the house had none of the formality of the front, but were designed in the English style, with large trees scattered in the lawns, which sloped up to woods at the back. In the distance to the right a large lake was a haven for flocks of water birds. Though the weather was grey and cold, Perdita loved her walks. The park was extensive enough to give her the illusion of total freedom, and she was happier, discovering its wild beauty, than she had been for some time. At this season there was little by way of leaf or flower, but the undergrowth was full of small animals that scuttled away as she approached, and when it grew colder left their tracks on the frost-covered ground.

She was almost on the far side of the woods one day when she heard a soft whimpering. Some animal in pain! Turning swiftly in the direction of the sound, Perdita picked her way through dead branches and brambles until she reached her goal. A girl of about her own age lay there, holding her ankle and crying. Her huge grey eyes were wide open in terror. "No! No! Leave me! Don't touch me!"

"I'm not going to hurt you, I promise," Perdita quickly assured her, dropping on one knee beside her. "Tell me what's wrong. Is it your ankle?"

The girl stared at Perdita for a moment and seemed to be reassured by what she saw. "Yes, I fell. I was looking for Toto." Then, to Perdita's dismay, large tears gathered in her eyes and rolled down her cheeks. She gave a helpless little sob. "I've lost my dog. And my foot hurts. What am I to do?"

"Well, I should imagine the first thing is to see about your ankle. Let me feel it." Perdita was not without experience, and she soon established that the girl had not suffered any serious damage. "I think you could walk if I helped you," she said eventually.

The girl clutched her arm. "Oh, no! I couldn't. The pain!"

"Then I must leave you to get help," said Perdita, rising. "It will be dark soon. We can't stay here."

"Don't leave me. Please don't leave me!" In her agitation, the girl rose to her knees. Perdita took advantage of this to help her to her feet, and they had soon struggled to the edge of the wood. Here the girl collapsed. "I can't go any further. My foot hurts," she sobbed. "And where's Toto?"

Perdita looked at her in exasperation. There was only an hour or so of daylight left. The girl must be made to walk. "Toto might have found his own way home," she suggested. "He might be looking for you there. Can't you try again? I'll help you all I can."

"Toto's a she, not a he," said the girl, looking up at Perdita indignantly.

Perdita was amused. It was cold, it was growing dark, the girl seemed unable to help herself, but she could still get annoyed with her rescuer over her pet dog! She looked at the flushed face before her. The girl was ethereally lovely, with silver-grey eyes, delicately pink cheeks and pale gold hair. The tear-stains on her cheeks only added to her air of fragility. Perdita sighed. She had already become far more involved with this spoiled child than she'd wanted—even to the point of breaking her rule of silence. What was she to do? "Come on," she said lifting the girl to her feet. "Lean on me and hop."

They had gone a fair way along the path when they were hailed by a man's voice. A minute later a young giant came running up to them. "Eliane, what's happened? I've been looking for you everywhere."

"My foot hurts dreadfully, Philippe, and I've lost Toto! Help me!"

"Toto came back hours ago. That's what worried us so much. Here, I'll take you home." He swept the girl into his arms and started off down the path. Perdita hesitated for a moment, then shrugged her shoulders and turned back through the wood. The girl was safe, and her task was finished.

IN THE DAYS that followed Perdita found herself wondering where the girl, Eliane, lived—perhaps on the other side of the hill. She was certainly lovely, though probably spoilt. Perdita had an impression that the girl had been ill—she was very thin. How old was she? That was more difficult to judge. Eliane's face and person were those of a girl of about twenty, Perdita's own age, but her manner and speech had the simplicity of a much younger person. And who was the young man who had come so peremptorily to the rescue? From what she had been able to see in the fading light, he too was fair, though his hair was a darker colour than Eliane's. He was certainly handsome and certainly strong—striding off over rough ground like that with the girl in his arms! He'd seemed to treat her like some precious jewel to be jealously guarded and protected. But then, there was something about her which aroused a protective instinct. Look at the way she, Perdita, had rushed into speech in order to reassure her. Well, whoever they were, she hoped they were not too closely acquainted with the Earl. Explaining her sudden ability to speak might prove difficult! For a day or two she waited apprehensively for a summons to the library, but when none came she decided with relief that either the Earl was not on visiting terms with Eliane's family or that the girl herself had not thought Perdita's part in the adventure worth mentioning.

The days grew shorter as November passed into December. According to Madame d'Espery, the Earl would soon return to England to spend Christmas with his family, and she redoubled her efforts to teach Perdita the usages of polite society. She was sure the Earl would invite them to dine with him before his departure and was eager to show that Perdita had made some progress. Perdita was equally eager to demonstrate that she had not! At first she had derived no little amusement from deceiving her tutors, and what the Earl had called her 'bovine look' was much in evidence. However, for one of Perdita's lively intelligence the pleasure in fooling such easy prey soon palled—it was far more difficult to hide her familiarity with the ways of a great house and her growing appreciation of living in a civilised society once more. But, whether it was easy or difficult, she remained determined to disguise her real self from everyone in the château—especially its master. Her refusal to talk and her failure to "improve" satisfied her desire to thwart the Earl wherever she could. In a situation where he had almost absolute power over her future she cherished these small secret victories over his domination. Accordingly, when Madame d'Espery announced that they were invited to join him the following evening, Perdita felt both apprehensive and excited. However boringly simple it was to deceive her tutors, the Earl himself would be a far greater challenge. He wished to see what progress she had made. Well, so he should, thought Perdita, though if his expectations were high he was due for a sad disappointment!

She spent some time and considerable thought on her preparations the following day. She must leave some hope of improvement, for it would not do to give the Earl such a disgust of her that he would find her unsuitable after all and send her back to Africa. That must be avoided at all costs. Her resources were slender, but she made ingenious use of them. The unexceptionably simple rose silk gown acquired quite a raffish air when draped lavishly with lace from the top of her dressing-table and finished off with a purple spangled scarf given to her by one of the Sheikh's daughters. A painfully tight use of curl-papers the night before had enabled her to twist her hair into a riot of elaborate curls. She was pleased to observe that the addition of a small paper flower found in one of the bedrooms did not improve her appearance.

When this vision appeared in the salon before dinner Madame d'Espery dropped her fan and sank into a chair. It amused Perdita enormously to see the stunned look on the Earl's face, but his expression quickly returned to its normal impassivity. Madame d'Espery found her voice and suggested that she should take Perdita upstairs...

"I will not hear of it," said the Earl blandly. "Perdita has clearly spent a great deal of effort on her appearance tonight and it would be cruel to spoil her enjoyment. May I escort you into the dining-room, Madame d'Espery?"

Perdita was left feeling baffled by the Earl's reaction. She had fully expected to be ordered to remove her trailing draperies, and was somewhat disconcerted at being forced to manage them at the dining table. The Earl was at his most charming during the splendid meal that followed. Perdita knew that her chaperon had lost most of her own wealth in the Revolution and was almost one of the Earl's pensioners, but there was nothing to suggest this in his manner to her that night. Madame d'Espery positively sparkled in his company, and Perdita watched and marvelled. So fascinated was she by the exchanges between her companions, so relaxed in the convivial, candlelit atmosphere, that she almost forgot her own role. She was reminded of it by the Earl. Part of her lace trailed on to her plate, and had become caught in the cutlery. She was making a discreet effort to disentangle it when she caught the Earl's eye. His lips were twitching with amusement. Furious at herself and him, she pulled the lace free, picked up the leg of wild duck from her plate and, staring at him, defiantly bit into the flesh with gusto. The look of amusement vanished, to be replaced with a frown. At this she meekly put her duck down and then slowly licked her fingers one by one. Madame d'Espery's shocked "Mademoiselle Perdita!" made her jump, so absorbed had she been with the Earl. "*Mademoiselle*, have you forgotten yourself?"

Perdita looked apologetically at Madame d'Espery and wiped her fingers carefully on her lace. At Madame's gasp of outrage, the Earl said, "Pray, do not upset yourself, Madame d'Espery. Your charge has by no means forgotten what you have been teaching her. She is merely playing her favourite game—'Bonnets', I think she would call it. She forgets what a dangerous game it can be."

Madame d'Espery was too agitated to question the Earl's cryptic remark but said, "I really think it would be better, Mademoiselle Perdita, if you removed those... additions to your very pretty dress. I do assure you, it does not need them. And you would probably feel better if you cleaned your fingers with a little soap and water. Wait, I will ring for Jeanne to take you upstairs to attend to it."

As Perdita reached the door the Earl's voice stopped her. "Perdita!" He paused until she turned. "Remove that flower from your hair. You need no such embellishments."

As Perdita followed the maid upstairs she was in a confused frame of mind. On the one hand, she had undeniably demonstrated her lack of company manners. But, on the other, the Earl had not been convinced, and she had only succeeded in upsetting Madame d'Espery. But when she returned to the dining-room Madame d'Espery was restored to good humour, and Perdita found she had lost the desire to play any more tricks. After dinner Madame d'Espery suggested that Perdita should play something for them. "I am sure dear Monsieur Champollion has taught her a little tune."

Perdita's flagging spirits were revived at the thought of what she might do at the piano, but after a quick glance at her the Earl protested that he had had enough entertainment for one evening and took them into the library. "I set out for England tomorrow, but I think we have made all the necessary arrangements, have we not? Perdita will continue with her lessons and I expect to see much improvement when I return." This was said with a warning glance at Perdita. "Now I would like a word alone with Perdita, *madame*. Will I see you tomorrow morning? I must set out in good time."

"Then I will wish you goodnight and *bon voyage*, Edward. Pray convey my best wishes for the season to your mama. We hope to see her at Belleroi before too long." At the door she paused. "It is early days yet, Edward. Pray do not be too harsh with Mademoiselle Perdita. She has much to learn, I know, but she does try so hard. I cannot conceive where she has been, but I am sure she means well." Her voice faded as she left the room, and Perdita was left alone with the Earl.

"Madame d'Espery has a more charitable view of your intentions than I, Perdita. On the other hand, I believe I have a higher opinion of your intelligence. You begin to intrigue me. I ask myself if you are playing some deeper

game of your own. That would be foolhardy beyond belief,
I assure you.''

Perdita shifted uneasily. This was getting too close to
the truth for comfort. She would have turned away but he
pulled her back. ''Am I right? Was tonight's display part
of a larger scheme? You surely cannot aim at being sent
back to the Pasha? Or is it the Sheikh you long to return
to? Answer me, Perdita!''

He was growing impatient, and Perdita felt a sudden
surge of triumph. For a brief moment she had the upper
hand. The Earl would wait for longer than he imagined
before she would tell him anything of herself. Her lips
curled in scorn as she thought how easy it was after all to
frustrate this autocrat, for all his money and his power!
But the Earl had seen her reaction, and her insolence en-
raged him. Her ridiculous curls fell to her shoulders as he
shook her like a doll. ''Damn you, Perdita! What lies behind your silence? Tell me, you jade!''

He was white with rage, and such was the force of his
anger that Perdita's elation gave way to fear. She took an
involuntary step back, but then her pride came to her rescue and she stopped where she was, forcing herself to look
at him calmly. He seemed to sense her fear all the same,
and with an expression of self-disgust he turned away. He
said bitterly, ''The men on the ship called you a witch. I
begin to believe them. You make me behave like a savage,
like one of them.'' He stood in silence for a moment and
then turned back to her. ''There is some mystery about
you, Perdita, and I intend to fathom it. But not tonight. It
is late, and I have much to do before I leave for England.''

Perdita's hand trembled as he led her to the door. He
said abruptly, ''You have no real reason to fear me, Perdita. Not if you deal honestly with me. But are you capable
of honesty, I wonder?'' He took her chin in his hand and

held it for an ageless moment. Perdita was hypnotised by
his eyes. They seemed to be reaching towards her inner-
most thoughts, and she saw them darken with a different
emotion. Again there was the fleeting sensation of a wordless recognition. Slowly he bent his head and kissed her
lingeringly. She willed herself to be still, fighting for self-
possession, but it was hopeless. He seemed to be drawing
her soul from her body. The kiss deepened and grew more
passionate, and Perdita was lost in its spell. Gently the Earl
released her, but then, cupping her face in his hand again,
he murmured in wonder, "Such a lovely face. Such magical eyes. Such enchantment in the lips." Perdita looked
at him, words trembling on her lips, but they died, still-
born, as he said, "Though I know you to be everything I
despise, you still weave such a spell that a man could
almost forget it all and ask for nothing more than to be
your slave. How the devil do you manage it, Perdita? How
can such corruption appear so damnably innocent?"

Perdita almost cried out at the pain caused by his words.
She had to call on her considerable strength of will to hide
her distress. There was a short silence, while the Earl
stared at her broodingly. Then he shook his head as if to
clear it, gave an incredulous laugh and said, "I can't believe it! Is that your game? To be my mistress? Oh, no,
Perdita! Lovely though you are, I am more fastidious than
you think. No, no, you are everything I looked for, but not
for my own enjoyment." As she made no move, he said,
"You will not be disappointed in the role I have in mind
for you, Perdita. Remember the rewards if you play it well!
Now it is more than time for you to go to your room. I
will see you in the morning before I leave."

That night Perdita took herself severely to task. Her life
had become too comfortable. A man had only to kiss her
for her to forget the bitter lessons of the past two years.

Trust no one, depend on no one. Life is not a game, but a battle for survival. Perdita against the world. Had she not learned that over and over again? She pushed away the thought that this particular man affected her as no one had ever done before—not even in her weakest moments.

By morning she was calm again. It was as well, for overnight the Earl's attitude had hardened. His parting words to Perdita were harsh. "Do not imagine my absence will make things easier for you, Perdita. Madame d'Espery will supervise your conduct, and my servants, too, are vigilant. You may be sure I will hear of any...escapades. Remember the Pasha in Algiers, for I have not forgotten him."

After he had gone, however much she resolutely denied it to herself, Perdita felt his absence. His face was no friendlier than those of the servants, but, though there was danger in their encounters, at least there was some excitement. The house seemed dead without him.

CHAPTER FOUR

SOON AFTER THE EARL'S departure Perdita was furious to find that she was being spied upon. She could never quite catch sight of the "spy", for whoever it was was adept at disappearing from view whenever Perdita turned round. So when one day she saw that her follower had whisked into a cupboard to keep out of sight she locked the cupboard door, and pocketed the key. Then she went to her music lesson, leaving her captive to cool his or her heels in the cupboard for an hour. When she came out of the music-room the house was fizzing with agitation.

"Have you seen Colette, *mademoiselle*? No, of course you haven't. Silly of me to ask, really," said one of the maids as she scurried past.

Colette? Who was Colette? Perhaps Colette was her captive. She went to the cupboard and gingerly unlocked the door. Lying asleep on the sheets and pillows inside was a little girl. The light woke her, and with a roar of fright she rushed out of the cupboard and down the stairs, shouting for her grandmother. Perdita laughed ruefully. Her "spy" had been a curious small girl!

"I am sorry to see that *mademoiselle* regards the terrorising of a little girl as amusing," said a frosty voice. It was Madame Lebrun. She swept past Perdita and went downstairs. Perdita started after her but then stopped. What was it to her? The child would find her grandmother and would get a great deal of sympathy from all the servants, who would be sure to lay the blame on the stranger in their midst. They would avoid her even more, and everyone would be satisfied.

Colette however had not been at all put off by her experience in the cupboard. Two days later Perdita found the child following her outside in the grounds. When she stopped Colette stopped too, some distance away. "You're not a witch, are you, *mademoiselle*?" Perdita smiled and shook her head. "The others said you were but Grandmère said no, and I think she's right because you don't look like one at all because you've got such a nice smile." Somewhat breathlessly Colette came along the path, and after a moment's hesitation took Perdita's hand. "Let's go for a walk, shall we?"

That was the beginning of a strange, secret friendship. Colette was an adventurous ten-year-old and, for her, forays into the main body of the house were a source of interest and excitement. They went on many walks together, and Colette's quick intelligence and quaint remarks kept Perdita constantly amused. Colette seemed to sense that Perdita did not wish to speak inside the house, but when they were outside Perdita's silence did not last long. The child simply bombarded her with questions until they were answered. So once again Perdita found her defensive wall of silence breached. Where the Sheikh's subtleties had failed, the need for an immediate response to Eliane's terror and Colette's curiosity had succeeded. Or perhaps it was just that time and a peaceful existence in civilised society had worn Perdita's resistance down. Whether she wanted it or no, life was sending out slender tendrils to catch her and draw her back into its fold.

CHRISTMAS CAME with a deal of celebration in the servants' quarters, but not much joy in the rest of the house.

Perdita was on her own most of the time, for Madame d'Espery was confined to her room with a bad cold. She was touched when her elderly chaperon tottered downstairs on Christmas morning to escort her to church—so touched that she behaved beautifully, and was rewarded with an invitation to *madame*'s room for a glass of hot wine.

Madame warned her about Colette. "*Mademoiselle*, I hope you do not encourage the cook's grandchild to come into the house. I have caught her twice recently lurking about the corridors. She is harmless enough, but she knows very well that the servants' quarters are the proper place for her. She has no mother and, fond though she is of her, her grandmother Rosanne is too busy in the kitchen to pay much attention to the child. Colette should really be sent away to her other relations, but then her grandmother would be unhappy. Monsieur le Marquis would never agree. And it is true that Rosanne is a superb cook."

Perdita looked her puzzlement. Who was Monsieur le Marquis?

"Do you not know? The Marquis de Belleroi. The Earl." As Perdita continued to look puzzled she went on, her tongue stumbling over the English names, "Edward Robert Justin de Cazeville Rotherfield is the fifth Earl of Ambourne and fourth Marquis de Belleroi. He inherited the French title and this estate from his mother's family, the de Cazevilles. Surely I told you that, *mademoiselle*?"

They spent an amicable hour together, after which Perdita persuaded the old lady back into bed, for she could see that the outing to church had taken a great deal out of her. The rest of the day she spent alone, for even Colette had deserted her in favour of the fun and laughter in the servants' hall. As she sat in the library, pictures from the past went through her mind. The great hall at Taverton, full of holly, ivy and mounds of spiced apples. Her father tossing her up on to the pony that had miraculously appeared in the stable one Christmas morning; her mother's face when Perdita gave her a penwiper she had made. And then that last Christmas. Perdita shuddered. Mr. Carston, with his white face and heavy features. How could her mother have married him? She had been lonely after Papa had died, it was true, and at first Mr. Carston had seemed all tender concern. She had paid for it dearly, poor little Mama. That last Christmas her mother had been so ill after the stillbirth of a child she should never have had that Perdita had hardly left her bedside. And Mr. Carston... That was enough! She must stop herself there.

She got up and looked along the shelves for her next book. Having been starved for so long of literature of any kind, she was having a feast of it now. French classics predominated, of course, but she had come across some modern English novels tucked away in a corner. She settled down to *Persuasion* and soon forgot her troubles in the world of Anne Elliot. She had just finished a chapter when the housekeeper came to put out the candles. She slipped the book down the side of the chair before Madame Lebrun saw it, and followed her disapproving back upstairs to bed. Christmas was over. Perdita lay awake long into the night, wondering where she would be and what she would be doing the following Christmas.

THE WEATHER DETERIORATED after Christmas Day. High winds whistled round the château, blowing flurries of snow against its walls and building up drifts along the roads. Perdita spent most of her afternoons in the library, eagerly reading all she could, for when the Earl eventually returned it would be more difficult to find the opportunity. However, on New Year's Eve the wind dropped and the sky cleared. The view from the library windows was breathtaking. White lawns and silver trees were dazzling in the bright sunshine, and Perdita could not stay indoors. Clad in her heaviest clothes, with her cashmere shawl around her, she ventured forth.

At first she stayed close to the house. The snow was still deep in places, and she was not certain of her footing. Then the crisp, clear air and the brilliant light enticed her to be more adventurous and she found herself eventually on the shore of the lake. It was completely frozen over and the waterfowl were having difficulty in landing gracefully on the ice. She stood there, laughing at their antics, for a while, but then reluctantly turned to go back—it was very cold.

"Hello! I say, hello!" It was the young man who had collected Eliane from her. He came skating across the lake, red scarf flying and arms swinging. A lock of dark blond hair had fallen over his eyes, and his cheeks were red in the cold air. "Don't go!" he said, coming to a swirling halt at the edge of the lake. "Mademoiselle d'Harcourt would like to meet you again. She's just over on the other side."

"Mademoiselle d'Harcourt?"

"Yes. Eliane," said the young man. Perdita had to hide a smile at his reverent tone. He continued, "We all met when Eliane hurt her foot. I'm Philippe Fourget."

"Of course. Where is she? I can't see her."

"Oh, she's not skating. She can't. She really isn't strong enough."

"Then how am I to meet her?" asked Perdita. "There's a lake between us, and I haven't any skates."

"Well, I thought," said the young man hesitantly, "that is to say, if you would permit me, I would walk you across the ice. It's really not difficult. There's a layer of snow on it." As Perdita hesitated he added, his hazel eyes pleading with her, "Do come! Mademoiselle d'Harcourt wants to thank you—and she needs company. It's not far."

Though it was clear that Eliane's wishes were the young man's command, Perdita was not at all sure that she wanted to meet her again. Furthering the acquaintance would almost certainly lead to complications. On the other hand, the house seemed very dull, and it would be fun to try walking on the ice. She held out her hands and they started moving slowly off. She fell once or twice on the way over but was quickly picked up, and arrived breathless and laughing on the other side.

Eliane was there, wrapped in furs and looking like the Snow Queen herself, with her silver-grey eyes and wisps of pale blonde hair peeping out from under her fur hood. "I'm so glad Philippe persuaded you to come, *mademoiselle*. Come quickly into the house; it's so cold out here, and you need to recover after your walk. You're very brave to cross the ice like that. I could never do it."

Taking Philippe's arm, Eliane led the way to a sprawling half-timbered house, which lay some distance back from the lake. Their wet outer garments were taken by a curtsying maid, and they followed Eliane into a large, low-ceilinged room. The outstanding impression was one of old-fashioned comfort. The huge log fire easily warmed the room to its furthest corners, and bowls of dried flowers and herbs scented the air.

A grey-eyed woman got up as they entered and came towards them. "Eliane, you're not cold, child, are you? Come near the fire. Philippe, I'm glad you've come. And this is Eliane's rescuer. *Mademoiselle*, you're welcome. Come, sit down here." Then, as they settled themselves, she said, "You see, we do not stand on ceremony here at Beau Lac, *mademoiselle*. I am Marguerite d'Harcourt, Eliane's mother. Eliane has not even told me your name."

Perdita was in a quandary. What was she to say? She knew of old that nothing was secret for long in the country. But the contrast between this house and the château suggested that the d'Harcourts' acquaintance with the Earl would be slight. Perhaps an abbreviation of her real surname would suffice.

"My name is Perdita, ma'am. Perdita...Taver. Is your daughter's ankle quite recovered?" This was enough to turn the conversation, though Perdita had the impression that Eliane's mother knew more than she was admitting. Her eyes had widened when Perdita had given her name.

During the next hour Perdita had opportunity to observe the little group. Madame d'Harcourt had been a beautiful woman, but now, in middle age, her face was lined, and in repose it was sad. Eliane had obviously been very ill some time ago and was still not fully recovered. Her mother watched her constantly and, each time Perdita caused Eliane to laugh, Madame d'Harcourt gave a small nod of approval. Perdita got the impression that the family was not as rich as it had once been—they apparently lived comfortably but very quietly. This encouraged her in her hope that the family had little contact with Belleroi. Philippe sat tongue-tied most of the time, only responding to direct questions, except when Eliane spoke. He was obviously head over ears in love with the girl, and she in turn seemed to draw on him for confidence and support.

It had been a long time since Perdita had enjoyed the company of people of her own age and upbringing. Through chance she had become acquainted with Eliane in the guise of her former self, with none of the problems that dogged her present life, and she was happier than she had been for a long time. It was a glimpse of what her life might have been if her mother had never met and married Frederick Carston...

Eliane proved to have a more attractive personality than had appeared at their first meeting. She had a delightful laugh, clear and childlike, and had obviously decided that Perdita was a friend. Perdita was often reminded of Colette, except that Colette was more robust and, she thought, more intelligent. They talked in generalities at first, and then Toto came in and their conversation turned to pets. The room often rang with their laughter as each in turn, including Madame d'Harcourt, told a favourite story. Perdita could see difficulties ahead, but for the moment she enjoyed the hour.

Refreshments were brought in, and when the tea-tray was removed Perdita suddenly realised that it was getting late and got up to go. By the time her cloak had been fetched the light was fading fast. Madame d'Harcourt insisted that she should come again. "It's some time since I have heard Eliane laugh so much, Mademoiselle Taver. You have been better than any physic for my daughter. She goes out rarely in the winter, and I am dull company for her."

"Thank you, I would like to come if I may," Perdita was surprised to hear herself say. "But has she no other friends in the neighbourhood, Madame d'Harcourt?"

"Until very recently my daughter was unwilling to meet anyone other than Monsieur Fourget, *mademoiselle*. You cannot imagine how pleased I am to see her enjoying the company of someone new."

Perdita promised to come again when she could. Philippe insisted on escorting her home, and together they set off on the road to the château—the lake was judged to be too dangerous in the half-light. Perdita was amused to find that Philippe talked of Eliane all the way.

At the gates of the château Perdita paused. It was now almost dark, and if Madame d'Espery had found she was not in the library she would be looking for her. But time had to be found for a request. "Monsieur Fourget, I would like you to do me a favour and not ask any questions about it. Will you do it?"

"I think so," he replied cautiously.

"Then will you please leave me here? Let me go up to the château by myself. And...and...should anyone ask you about me would you say as little as you can? I...I...well, I don't talk when I'm in the château. Don't tell anyone I talk to you and Mademoiselle d'Harcourt. Please."

"But why ever not?"

"You did say you wouldn't ask. I'll tell you sometime, perhaps, but not now. I must go; they'll be watching. Goodbye, Monsieur Fourget. Remember, you've promised!"

She ran up the drive and into the house, reaching the safety of her room without, she thought, being observed. She quickly changed into dry clothes and was waiting for Madame d'Espery in the salon when that lady descended for dinner.

FOR THE NEXT MONTH or more Perdita lived a kind of double life. At Belleroi she was the silent, rather stupid ward of Monsieur le Marquis. She was dismally slow to acquire the requisite social graces, and failed to show much progress with her tutors. Meanwhile she secretly continued to work her way through the Earl's library, enjoyed her outings with Colette, and when she was with the d'Harcourt family at Beau Lac she behaved as normally as any other well-brought-up young lady. She had a genuine love of music, and was delighted to discover that the d'Harcourts shared this pleasure. She and Madame d'Harcourt often played together, and even Eliane was occasionally persuaded to join her in a duet. They had a common love of literature too. Madame d'Harcourt even had some novels by the same English authors as Perdita had discovered at Belleroi. They read aloud from them, and Perdita's lively rendering of the absurdities of some of Jane Austen's characters was very popular.

Only once did she try to tell Madame d'Harcourt something of her true status. This was an act of heroism, for she was growing to depend on their friendship. But before she could get very far Madame d'Harcourt interrupted her.

"Mademoiselle Perdita, I am aware that your scruples are asking you to tell us something about yourself, which you would prefer us not to know. Let me say that I am content not to know it. I have observed you carefully since you have been visiting us. I know you will understand this, for you have seen how protective I am of Eliane. However, I do not believe you would willingly do her any harm, and your company has done her a great amount of good. As long as you are pleased to visit us I am well content to receive you. Now let us talk of something else. What is your opinion of *Waverley*—or have you not yet finished it? I have just received another by the same author, but I find the historical setting somewhat remote for me."

Afterwards Perdita was to ask herself how she could have been so blind. All the evidence was there, had she been alert enough to read it. Perhaps she was simply too happy enjoying the present to question it.

The snow disappeared, leaving behind it muddy paths and wet fields. Then came blustery winds to dry up the meadows and blow some of the newly placed slates off the roof of the château.

"You should not go out, *mademoiselle*; it is dangerous in these winds," protested Madame d'Espery, who was swathed in an exotic collection of shawls and scarves. "I cannot understand the modern passion for fresh air. We managed very well without it when I was a girl, I assure you. Monsieur le Marquis will be back any day now—what will he say if he finds you have been injured, or even killed? Tell me that.''

Perdita would have said that Monsieur le Marquis would regard it as a great bore, since he would have to start all over again with another ''tool'', but she contented herself with giving an apologetic smile. She was not going to give up her visits to Beau Lac because of a slight breeze!

The winds were still high a few days later when she was returning earlier than usual from Beau Lac. Eliane had been slightly feverish, and her anxious mother had called the doctor. Perdita had been willing to stay to keep the invalid company, but Madame d'Harcourt had urged her to go home. ''If Eliane is developing a cold, Mademoiselle Perdita, I would not wish you to catch it. You should go back in any case. The winds are dangerously high. Take care!''

She took the short cut through the woods. There were signs of spring wherever she looked. A few late snowdrops were tucked in among the dead leaves, and primroses and celandines could be seen on the edges of the wood. She came out on to the lawn and stood there, looking about her. The air was full of swirling movements and clouds were scudding across a bright blue sky. On her left ruffled waves were racing over a dark blue lake, and in front of her lay the château. She suddenly felt a sense of exhilaration. It was as if a great weight had been lifted from her shoulders. She was alive! She was a whole person! Whatever the future held, she could face it—not with stoicism, but with courage, not to reject life, but to challenge it. She ran laughing down the slope towards the house. A figure came racing up to meet her. Strong arms snatched her up and threw her to one side as a huge branch came crashing down from one of the lime trees on the lawn. She fell to the ground with the Earl on top of her.

"You stupid fool!" he said, fighting for his breath. "Don't you know better than to walk under old trees in a wind like this?"

She sat on the ground, dazed and bruised. "I'm sorry," she said. "I didn't look. You saved my life, I think."

"Not for the first time, either," he said. "Come on. Get up. You can come into the house and explain how you've suddenly found your voice. Or are you going to tell me it was the shock?"

CHAPTER FIVE

THE EARL AND PERDITA faced one another in the library.

"It was the shock," said Perdita with a straight face.

"I see," said the Earl resignedly. "I suppose I have only myself to blame for handing you that excuse on a platter. We shall no doubt eventually establish whether it is true or not. Meanwhile you will want to change, Perdita. Your clothes, I mean. Our tumble in the mud has made them rather dirty."

Perdita escaped to her room in some confusion. Little though she liked to admit it, she had been considerably shaken by her narrow escape. It was ironic that she had just discovered how precious life was when it had so nearly been snatched away from her. And it was the Earl who had saved her. What had he said? "Not for the first time." That was true, he had saved her life in Algiers, but life then had had no value for her. This time it was different, and she was grateful to him. She took some time to change her clothes, for she was strangely reluctant to go down.

Meanwhile the Earl was equally glad to be left to himself. He had dismissed his valet, and was sitting in front of his bedroom fire. The vision of Perdita laughing as she ran down towards the house was hard to dismiss from his mind. He had sent for her after his arrival, only to be told she was out walking, and was in the garden looking for her when she had suddenly emerged from the wood. She had looked magnificent. Her hair was streaming back in the wind, and her clothes were blown against her body, revealing its lovely lines. No marble Artemis this, but a vital elemental force. The sight of the broken branch which was threatening her had horrified him, and he had raced to save her without stopping to think. It had not surprised him that she had spoken, and he suspected she could have done so much earlier had she wished. But the quality of her voice was pleasing—low-pitched and musical. And, though there was an elusive accent, her French was not as uneducated as he would have expected. He wanted to hear more of it. He began to be very interested in meeting her again. At last he might have some answers to his questions.

Of the three at dinner that night only Madame d'Espery was completely at ease. She was amazed that Perdita had so suddenly regained her speech, and said so often. She went into a flood of reminiscence of other miraculous cures, which she or her friends had witnessed.

Perdita was grateful to her. She was in an unusual state of indecision, which reduced her appetite and made her reluctant to engage in any conversation. What was she to do? Was she to carry on the rest of her deception of the Earl and his household? After his prompt action that afternoon it seemed unnecessarily churlish, yet to confess that she had been wasting her tutors' time, largely for her own mischievous amusement, needed a degree of courage she was not sure she possessed. Watching the handsome head bent towards Madame d'Espery, she was once again impressed by the Earl's charm tonight. She would not have credited him with the patience with which he listened to the old lady's ramblings. She sighed, crumbling the roll by the side of her plate into even smaller pieces. She started guiltily when she saw the Earl's eyes on her.

The Earl too was quiet. While responding courteously

to Madame d'Espery he had been watching his pirate girl. This afternoon she had been a vision of spring itself— Persephone come to glowing life. This evening, with her rose silk gown, bare of any ornament, her dark brown hair simply dressed on top of her head, her sapphire eyes hidden under lowered eyelids, she could have been mistaken for a modest young lady of fashion. Though she was nervous, her manners were unexceptionable. Madame d'Espery had wrought a miracle, and the girl herself was a revelation. He was amazed at the chameleon qualities she showed. But which was the real Perdita?

After dinner he suggested they should adjourn to the library, since the salon was too large a room for such a small company. He saw that they were comfortably settled, watched as Perdita arranged Madame d'Espery's shawls, and then sat down himself. One of the servants brought him a glass of cognac, and he sipped it slowly, savouring its aroma.

"I compliment you on your pupil, Madame d'Espery," he began, lazily inspecting Perdita's face and figure. "She makes a charming impression."

Perdita looked up swiftly. Had there been a slight emphasis on the word "impression"? He stared blandly back at her and said, "And you, Perdita. Do you feel you have benefited from Madame d'Espery's time and patience?"

Madame d'Espery was not yet accustomed to the idea that Perdita could speak for herself. "She is a charming girl, Edward, and is slowly acquiring a modicum of decorum. Her behaviour at dinner tonight was, in my opinion, exemplary—a vast improvement from our last dinner together. Do you not agree?"

"Certainly, certainly. A little quiet, perhaps?"

"That is no real fault in a young lady. And you forget, until this afternoon Perdita did not have the power of speech." Perdita's colour rose as the Earl looked quizzically at her. But Madame d'Espery was pursuing her own train of thought. "I must confess, I have been somewhat puzzled by your ward, Edward. She appears to have no notion of sewing or drawing, and indeed her ignorance of all the uses of polite society is astonishing. Forgive me *mademoiselle*. I do not mean to hurt you, but you know it to be true. How can this be?"

Devilment lurked in the Earl's eyes. "Ah, yes, Madame d'Espery," he said. "Perhaps Perdita could explain that herself."

Perdita rallied. She would not let the Earl put her out of countenance. "Why, ma'am, I believe it is because I spent so much of my life removed from civilisation. I have only recently come to France."

The Earl listened in amusement to this evidence of Perdita's quick wit. She could not have chosen an excuse more likely to satisfy her tutor. For Madame d'Espery civilisation began and ended within the borders of royalist France.

"Of course," that lady said, gravely nodding her head. Then she continued, "However, I do not perfectly comprehend, *mademoiselle*, why you should find it so difficult to learn. Am I so poor a teacher?"

Once more Perdita was forced to rely on her wits. Somewhat desperately she said, "You are an excellent teacher, ma'am. Madame d'Espery has told me much of the great world she lived in before the Revolution, Lord Ambourne. Does his lordship know the story of the Duchesse de Nevers and the Duke of Hastings, ma'am?"

Madame d'Espery was not sure, but was happy to repeat it. Perdita was safe for the moment from further questioning. Her evasion had not been lost on the Earl, however, and he made a note to pursue this matter on another occasion. Meanwhile he sat back to enjoy Madame d'Espery's slightly scandalous reminiscence and to observe Perdita in the flickering firelight. He was fascinated by her. He had seen her grace and dignity even in the filth of Algiers. In the Sheikh's garden he had been surprised by her loveliness. But only now did he realise what a barrier she had been putting between herself and the world. Now that barrier seemed to have vanished. It wasn't just that she now talked; as she sat quietly listening to Madame d'Espery her face was no longer closed and wary; it was alive, mobile, even vulnerable. When Madame d'Espery's story reached its ridiculous climax Perdita's eyes were alight with amusement, and a delicious gurgle of laughter escaped her.

Madame d'Espery sat back with a satisfied sigh. "And now, Edward, I think I should like to retire to my bed. We live so quietly here in the normal way that this evening's excitement has quite done me up. Ah, you may smile, Edward, but when one is my age one no longer has the resilience you younger people take for granted. Come along, *mademoiselle*. Goodnight, Edward." Then she added with a roguish smile, "I hope my story did not shock you!"

"I assure you, Madame d'Espery, till tonight I had always regarded the Duke as a pompous bore, but your tale puts him in a different light altogether! Wait—I'll have some candles fetched."

He escorted them to the foot of the stairs, watched as they slowly went up, then returned to the library. He was standing looking into the dying fire when he heard a slight sound behind him. Turning, he saw Perdita coming into the room and was filled with sudden pleasure. She, too, had felt the evening incomplete. He walked forward and took her hands. They trembled slightly as she said, "Madame d'Espery sent me for her shawls, Lord Ambourne. They're on the chair."

"And I was vain enough to think you had come back to talk to me."

"You forget, my lord. You bought me. You have only to send for me if you wish to speak to me." Her head was bent and her eyes veiled. He took her chin in his fingers and pulled her head up.

"The first time I did this you bit me, Perdita. Do you remember? Are you going to bite me again?" Once again dark blue eyes looked into his, but this time they were troubled. "What are you afraid of, Perdita?" he whispered. "That I shall kiss you again?"

He pulled her mouth to meet his and gently kissed her. At first she tried to push him away, but then as the kiss grew sweeter and deeper he drew her into his arms. She slowly put her arms round his neck and pressed more closely to him. After a while they drew back, and the Earl, holding her against his arm, looked at her searchingly. At first he was smiling slightly, but then with a muffled exclamation he snatched her back and kissed her again, more passionately than before. He kissed her as if he could not hold her closely enough, could not have enough of her. This time when they parted the Earl walked over to the fire. He was shaken. He had kissed many women, but never before had he felt so moved.

Perdita swiftly picked up the shawls and moved to the door. "May I go now?" she said, hugging the shawls to her as if for comfort.

"What is it between us, Perdita? And what am I to do about it? There's something about you... Yes, you may go. Come, I'll escort you to the stairs."

At the foot of the stairs they paused. "Goodnight, Lord Ambourne," Perdita said in a subdued voice.

He had the ridiculous impulse to take her in his arms again and comfort her, but restrained himself. ''Goodnight, Perdita.'' Then he added, smiling ruefully, ''I have a notion that Perdita, the lost one, has found herself, and it is I who am lost. I wonder what will come of it?''

Perdita went up to her room, her head spinning. Found herself? Found herself? What a laughable notion! She was lost in a maze of rioting emotion. All her life, all her experience had not prepared her for this. She got herself to bed without noticing what she did. The treasured silk gown lay in a heap on the floor, the rest of her clothes on top of it. She lay there, her thoughts churning, for half the night. Finally she reached a measure of calm. The Earl still did not know her full story. Perhaps when he did he would treat her kindly, let her go to live a modest life somewhere in England. Tonight they had both been in the grip of a strong emotion. If nothing was done to change the situation the Earl might even overcome his repugnance for her past and suggest she should become his mistress. That she could never do. Deep within her she knew that, for all her self-discipline, the Earl of Ambourne could cause her more pain than anything she had known before. She must prevent that by telling him her true history. And then leave him.

Perhaps she could go to the Sheikh? Having decided that she would tell the Earl everything tomorrow, she fell into a troubled sleep.

Unfortunately the decision was taken out of her hands. She overslept, and by the time she saw him again it was too late to attempt any harmonious solution to her problem.

The Earl, too, lay awake for part of the night, thinking of Perdita. Where had she acquired her air of quality? How had she retained it in the rough company in which he had found her? Was she a victim of circumstance—or was she

a consummate actress? He debated what he should do. He
had lived so long with the thought of exacting justice for
what had happened to Linette that he was reluctant to
abandon it now. But Perdita had somehow or other ceased
to be a tool, had become instead a real person, someone
perhaps worthy of respect. He felt he could not use her as
he had planned, though what he was to do with her he
could not think. He fell asleep, still pondering the question.

The next morning was a busy one, and the Earl rose
early. Belleroi was once again a large and thriving estate
and demanded a great deal of attention. The Revolution
had passed over this quiet spot in the heart of the Norman
countryside almost without trace. But the land and more
especially the house itself had suffered from neglect during
the period when its half-English owner had been unable to
visit it.

He spent the first part of the morning seeing his agent,
the master mason and various other members of his little
community. Monsieur Champollion grew increasingly anxious as he waited his turn. Finally he was admitted.

The Earl was sitting with his back to the window, at a
huge desk covered in papers. He was writing. The little
music master clutched his hat nervously and waited to be
noticed.

"Champollion, forgive me. I did not see you there.
Now, how have the music lessons progressed?"

This was the very question Monsieur Champollion had
been dreading. "Monsieur le Marquis...milor', I...I..."

"Speak up, Champollion; it's surely not as bad as
that?" said the Earl, smiling.

"But it is, Monsieur le Marquis. I have succeeded in
teaching your ward nothing! She seems incapable of re-
taining anything at all, even the simplest tunes. She stum-
bles over the most rudimentary exercises, and appears to

have no kind of ear for music. I think she is tone deaf! I apologise for my failure, milor'. I assure you that I have done my best.''

The Earl got rid of the music master after a while, and then sat deep in thought. It was must unlikely that anyone with as musical a voice as Perdita's would be tone deaf. And he was absolutely certain that she was very far from stupid. Was Champollion being unfair, even malicious? He could imagine Perdita growing impatient with the fussy little man. But then Madame d'Espery had said something similar last night. That Perdita was very slow. And the relationship between the girl and her chaperon was clearly cordial—even affectionate. What had the girl been up to? He was just on the point of going to look for her when the housekeeper came in.

''There is a note for you, Monsieur le Marquis, from Beau Lac. Shall I ask the groom to wait?''

''No, there's no need,'' said the Earl, quickly reading the note with a frown. ''Madame d'Harcourt has already departed for Paris. She will be away for some days. No, I will see her when she returns; there's no reply. Tell the messenger to go, but then come back here, *madame*. I wish to speak to you.''

Madame Lebrun went out, and he returned to his thoughts. Last night Perdita had seemed a different person—open and honest. She might not have answered Madame d'Espery's questions completely, but what she had said was true. Later he had been deeply moved by her innocent response to his kisses. Innocent? Yes, he had to admit it, he had thought her response innocent. Innocent? said the devil inside him. A pirate's lover and innocent? Come, now! It was true, it did seem ridiculous to think so...

Madame Lebrun returned in a few minutes, and he invited her to sit down. "How is my ward, *madame*?" he began abruptly. "Is she happy in the house?"

"I'm sure there is nothing that Mademoiselle Perdita could complain about," said the housekeeper, pressing her lips together. "The staff all do their duty as far as she is concerned." So the servants didn't like Perdita, thought the Earl. He wondered why. Madame Lebrun hesitated, then continued, "As for being happy...well, she looks for her amusement outside the house, not in it."

"I'm not sure I understand you," said the Earl. "What do you mean by that, Madame Lebrun?"

"If I don't tell you someone else will, Monsieur le Marquis," said the housekeeper, and continued not without a certain relish. "She slips out most afternoons. As soon as Madame d'Espery goes for her rest that girl is running out of these doors and over the hills. I don't know what she gets up to out there, but I can imagine."

"Be careful what you say," said the Earl coldly. "I will not tolerate malicious gossip."

"Oh, I'm not the only one to have seen her, *monsieur*. The others could tell you—"

The Earl interrupted her. "I do not propose to question the other servants, Madame Lebrun. I will speak to Mademoiselle Perdita myself. Thank you, that is all." As she reached the door he asked, "Why do you dislike my ward so, *madame*?"

"She's a wicked, cold-hearted girl, sir. She terrified poor little Colette. Locked her in a cupboard just because she found her in the house. I know Colette shouldn't have been there—I'm not defending the child—but that was a heartless thing to do."

"From what I've seen of Colette it would take more than that to terrify her. But, if what you say is true, then yes, I agree. It was heartless. Thank you, Madame Lebrun.''

The Earl rose from his desk and paced the room. What was he to believe? His old prejudices about Perdita were roused. The devil inside him was mocking him—innocent? You fool, you gullible fool! The strumpet looks at you with sapphire eyes and you'll believe anything! He rejected the voice. He would not condemn Perdita on servants' gossip. Neither would he question the servants about her. He would see her himself.

However, Perdita was not to be found in the house. One of the maids said she had seen her going into the woods some time before. The Earl returned to the library, suspicion wrestling with a determination to be fair to Perdita. Père Amboise was waiting for him there, and the Earl remembered he had arranged to see him. Annoyed with himself for having forgotten the *curé*, he apologised.

"Your excuses are not at all necessary, Monsieur le Marquis," the *curé* said sunnily. "I am glad to have an opportunity to examine your library. You have a fine collection of books here."

After some discussion of the needs of the village the Earl reluctantly asked about Perdita's work.

"She's a good child," Père Amboise said. "She listens so attentively. I fear I talk too long and test too little, *monsieur*, but she seems to understand. The writing is coming along slowly. She seems a little subdued in the house, but whenever I see her outside she looks happy enough."

The Earl asked slowly, "Alone, Père Amboise? When she is outside, is she alone?"

"Quite often. Her young friend is not always with her. But whenever it grows dark he always escorts her to the château. Or at least to its gates. I cannot say I have recognised him, but he is a handsome lad and I am sure he looks after her well. Monsieur le Marquis needs have no fear on that score.''

That the Earl finished the interview with the *curé* courteously and in no haste was a tribute to his iron self-control, for he was in a towering rage. He escorted Père Amboise to the door of the library, then returned to the desk, and with a violent gesture swept all his papers on to the floor. He stood in thought for a moment, then strode out of the house to the stables. The servants scattered as they saw him coming, and the grooms ran to do his bidding. His horse was saddled in the shortest possible time and he was off, urging the horse to a gallop as soon as he was clear of the buildings.

''Break his neck, he will, if he ain't careful,'' said one of the grooms.

''He don't look as if he'd mind, neither,'' said the other, shaking his head.

But when the Earl got to the trees he let the horse pick its way slowly along the bridle paths, while he listened and looked for Perdita. When he came out on the other side he turned to the left, towards the village. Only Beau Lac lay to the right, and since he knew the occupants of the house had left for Paris that morning there was no point in calling there. Anyway, the last place to look for Perdita was with his aunt and Linette. She would be seeking her excitement elsewhere.

He got back late in the afternoon after riding through the village and beyond without finding any trace of Perdita. The white heat of his rage had been replaced by a cold and deadly anger. During his ride the same thoughts had been churning over in his mind. He had begun to trust her, had even begun to wonder whether he should continue with his plan, since it involved her, and all the time she had been laughing at him, playing him for the fool he was. She would pay for it. He would catch her red-handed, and then she would pay!

PERDITA HAD TRIED TO SEE the Earl as soon as she had come downstairs but had been told he was occupied with his man of business. Too nervous to wait, she had gone to Beau Lac to take Madame d'Harcourt into her confidence and consult her on the best course to follow. But when she arrived at Beau Lac she found its occupants gone. One of the maids had a note for her.

"I am sorry not to have seen you before we left. The decision to go to Paris was taken very suddenly after our local doctor had examined Eliane. As you know, *mademoiselle*, Eliane is not robust, and I think it better that the specialist who treated her some years ago should see her now. We do not plan to stay longer than necessary in Paris. Eliane does not enjoy being in large cities, and I am sure she will miss your company—as I will."

Madame d'Harcourt finished the letter with her most cordial greetings.

Tucked inside was a shakily written note from Eliane. "Mademoiselle Perdita—I would be most obliged to you if you could find time to see Philippe. I did not have the chance to speak to him. Tell him I shall see him very soon. And I hope to see you soon, too, dear *mademoiselle*."

Perdita was seriously worried about her friend, but reminded herself of Madame d'Harcourt's over-protective attitude. She would have to wait, and hope that they would be back soon. Somewhat despondently she retraced her steps to the château and went up to her room, where she sat in troubled thought.

Shortly before dinner she was informed that the Earl wished to see her in the library. The moment of decision was upon her. Half hoping, half dreading the coming interview, she followed the maid downstairs. When she went in the Earl was standing at the window, looking out. Without turning round, he said, ''Where have you been, Perdita?''

She did not wish to start her confession to this uncompromising back, so she hesitated, then said, ''To the...to the woods, Lord Ambourne. They're very pretty at this time of year.''

''Just to the woods?''

His voice was cold and harsh. Was he angry because he had found out about her visits to Beau Lac? She swallowed and said, ''You told me I was not to go out of the grounds, Lord Ambourne—''

She was about to say more, but he turned round and demanded abruptly, ''So you met no one on your walk?''

Well, that question could be answered with a clear conscience. ''No, my lord,'' she said confidently. He stood there, a brooding look on his face. Finally he dismissed her, and she went with a last puzzled look at his silent figure.

The Earl was left with his thoughts. Obviously the girl was lying. He had searched the woods and found no trace of her. Where could she have gone? One thing was certain: he was going to find out, even if it meant following her himself!

That evening there was no pleasant dinner party. The Earl was not present when Madame d'Espery and Perdita had their meal. He took his late and retired to his room early. The two ladies chatted desultorily for a while in the salon, Madame d'Espery still amazed that Perdita had regained her speech, and then they also went to their rooms early.

CHAPTER SIX

WITH THE EXCEPTION of Madame d'Espery the whole household soon knew that Perdita was in disgrace. Madame Lebrun had wasted no time in spreading her account of the interview with Monsieur le Marquis, and most of the servants had witnessed his angry departure soon after. In the manner of a small community they gossiped about it and were eager to see what would happen. One thing they could all see for themselves—Monsieur le Marquis was polite to his ward but his manner was by no means friendly.

They were too well trained to make any comment in Perdita's hearing, but their sidelong glances as they passed her on the stairs or in the corridors of the great house made her uneasy. She was not quite sure why the Earl was so unapproachable—was it because of Beau Lac, or could it be that someone had told him of her walks with Colette? Surely not? He was autocratic, but not unreasonable. Such small offences could not have caused this change in him. Then she remembered his behaviour when he had first met her. Perhaps he was angry at her disobedience. She was worried, but could not bring herself to ask, and telling him her story was now out of the question.

When the Earl dined with them he addressed most of his remarks to Madame d'Espery, who was too delighted to have an audience for her stories to notice that Perdita was seldom included. Perdita was puzzled and unhappy, and at the same time angry with herself for being affected so strongly. Surely she ought to have learned by now that the only safe resource was herself? Just a few days ago she had felt ready to challenge life, to enjoy it again, and she admonished herself for being so feeble now.

Her preoccupation with her own misery made her clumsy and forgetful, provoking Madame d'Espery's strictures. Perdita was glad to escape from the dining-room as quickly as she could. She had no comfort during the day, either, for her tutors too were conscious of the Earl's disapproval and redoubled their efforts to improve her playing and dancing. Some perverse demon made Perdita all the more determined to refuse to learn. Père Amboise alone remained blissfully unaware of the trouble he had helped to create. His pupil seemed a little listless, without the eager attention she had previously paid to his lessons, but he only thought he was being more boring than usual and resolved to make the lessons more interesting for her.

Meanwhile Perdita had not forgotten that Eliane had asked her to get in touch with Philippe. She knew he would be unhappy at Eliane's absence, and sharing what news they had might cheer him up a little. But how was she to accomplish this? She knew where Philippe lived. His family had a small *manoir* beyond Beau Lac. If only there was someone who could take a note arranging a meeting—perhaps Colette knew of someone.

Since the Earl's return it had been more difficult for Colette to reach Perdita's room unobserved, for servants were constantly on the move around the house. However, she appeared one day at Perdita's door.

"Psst…*mademoiselle*! I'm here! How are you? Oh, *mademoiselle*, you look so sad. Have you missed me? Do smile, please dear Mademoiselle Perdita!"

Perdita was pleased to see the merry little face—it was

a change to see approval and affection directed at her! Colette spent a few happy minutes recounting what she had been doing, and then asked, "*Mademoiselle*, they say you talk now. Here in the house, I mean. Is that right?" Perdita assured her it was. "Oh, good, then you can talk to me as well! Why do you think Monsieur le Marquis is cross with you?"

Perdita had to confess she didn't know why they thought that. Perhaps Monsieur le Marquis *was* cross with her! "Well, never mind. I love you, *mademoiselle!*"

Perdita was touched by the little girl's loyalty, and wondered whether she was right to involve Colette in her problems. But Colette had no difficulty at all in thinking of someone. "My cousin Henri will do it, *mademoiselle*. He likes going to the Fourgets' house. He's got a friend there. Where's the note?"

Still doubtful that she was doing the right thing, Perdita wrote a short note, asking Philippe to meet her by the lake the next day. After checking that the Earl was at work in his library and Madame d'Espery had gone to her room, Perdita slipped out the following afternoon. She hurried to the edge of the wood, where she paused for breath and looked back. Except for the workmen still on the roof, the back of the château was deserted. The servants were probably at their own meal. She skirted the wood and ran down to the lakeside. Philippe was waiting for her.

"Mademoiselle Perdita, do you know how Eliane does?" was his characteristic greeting.

Perdita tried to reassure him about Eliane's state of health, reminding him of Madame d'Harcourt's obsessive concern for her daughter. He was not convinced, however, and indeed it was not easy for her to be convincing, since she knew so little herself. But she did manage to persuade him that Eliane's thoughts before she had left had been of him.

"She is an angel, *mademoiselle*, I assure you, but, alas, I fear she is not for me."

"Why ever not, *monsieur*? You are made for each other! Eliane is dear to you, I know, and she needs someone like you to cherish and protect her. It would be a perfect match."

"You do not understand, *mademoiselle*. The difficulty does not lie with Eliane and me, but with our families. You have not heard about my father?" Perdita shook her head. "My father, *mademoiselle*, is an enthusiastic Republican. Do not mistake me, he was not one of the rabble who caused the deaths of all those people at the guillotine in '93 and '94. But he believed in the Revolution and fought for it. When Napoleon became our leader my father thought a new age of equality had come into being. You can imagine how bitter he was when Napoleon in turn took the crown and made himself Emperor. He gave up a promising career in Paris to return to our estate here in Normandy."

"But it's very peaceful here. Could your father not have concentrated on his estate and forgotten his disappointment? And anyway, how does this affect you and Eliane?"

"The local landowners here regard my father—and his family—as traitors. Since the King was restored to power the old families have returned, and we are treated as outcasts."

"But, Philippe, Madame d'Harcourt doesn't treat you as an outcast! And, from what I have observed, she is no great landowner, either. She would not hold your father's defection against you, I'm sure!"

"Madame d'Harcourt has been very kind to me, *mademoiselle*. But she is not the only one who has a say in

what happens to Eliane. Surely you know that Madame
d'Harcourt belongs to the de Cazeville family? Eliane is
the cousin of Monsieur le Marquis."

"The...the Marquis?"

"Yes, mademoiselle. The Englishman—the Marquis de
Belleroi."

Perdita was stunned. She managed to ask, "But, Philippe, why should Eliane and her mother live so modestly
if what you say is true? So withdrawn from the great
world?"

"I think there is some tragedy in Eliane's past, *mademoiselle*. I am not sure what it is—they have never talked
about it. When they came back from England it was assumed they returned at the Restoration of the Monarchy.
But I think there was more to it than that. For more than
a year Eliane refused to see anyone. Even now, three years
later, she will only receive one or two—you, me, and Dr.
Grondet."

"I see," said Perdita thoughtfully. Though she would
not say anything to Philippe, she now knew something else
about Eliane. Her English family called her Linette.

"So you see, Mademoiselle Perdita, I have not much
hope of persuading Eliane's family that I am a suitable
husband for her," said Philippe gloomily.

"Philippe, you must not give up hope," said Perdita,
urgently clutching Philippe's arm. "I am convinced that
you are the very husband Eliane needs. She needs you,
Philippe. You must fight for her."

But Philippe was staring at a tall figure some distance
away. It was completely still, but there was a menacing
air about it. *"Le Marquis!"* he gasped.

Perdita turned to look, and her heart sank when she saw
him. If he caught them now he would not be content until
he had Philippe's story. He was sure to receive it unfa-

vourably in his present mood. "Philippe, has the Marquis ever met you?" she said quickly.

"No, never."

"Then he won't know who you are. You must go quickly—now, before he comes!" Perdita pushed him towards Beau Lac.

"But, *mademoiselle*—"

"Go, Philippe! I am not in any danger. And if you meet the Marquis now your chances of winning Eliane will be worth nothing. Go!"

Philippe was not happy at leaving Perdita to face the Marquis alone. But this last plea of hers persuaded him. He ran to his horse, tethered behind Beau Lac, and was off. Perdita turned to face the Earl. She jumped when she found he was upon her. His face was white and his jaw was set. "Lord Ambourne—"

"Who was he?" he bit out.

She could think of nothing to say. Her ready wit failed her. "W...wh...who?" she faltered.

He grabbed her arm, holding it so tightly that she almost cried out. "Don't push me any further, you slut! Tell me the name of your lover."

"The...the name of my lover?" she asked in disbelief. "I have no lover, Lord Ambourne. And you're hurting my arm."

"Don't put on your airs with me, you little wanton," he said, giving her a shake. "You've been meeting him for weeks, whenever you've managed to get away from the château."

"It's not what you think—" she started to say, but once again he didn't let her finish.

"Don't try your lies on me, Perdita. I'm in no mood to listen to fairy-stories told by a lying, deceitful, heartless jade!'' he said, giving her a shake with each of these last words.

She realised that he was deaf to any explanation she could give other than the one he expected from her. At the same time her own anger blazed up at this unjust treatment. She wrenched her arm out of his grasp and took a step back. ''Then I won't tell you any,'' she shouted. ''I won't tell you anything at all. Find out for yourself!''

''I won't need to; he'll soon come after you, like a dog after a bitch, when he realises you are not allowed to roam the fields any more! Or will he desert you when trouble threatens—like your previous keeper?'' She looked at him wildly and made as if to strike him, but he caught her wrist and pulled it back, forcing her gradually to her knees. ''You're coming back to the château with me, Perdita. There you will be kept like the chattel you are, until I am ready to make use of you. We have all been too lax. Leopards don't change their spots, nor do drabs become honest just because they're dressed up in fine clothes. You'll buy your freedom, Perdita, but not till you've worked for it.''

With that he pulled her to her feet and set off for the château, dragging her mercilessly behind him.

Though she was sure her undignified approach had already been observed by the people in the château, she attempted to release herself as they came to the building. He let her wrist go, but held her again by the arm. They passed Madame d'Espery on the stairs. ''Why, Mademoiselle Perdita!'' that good lady cried. ''We were looking for you...'' But she stared at them in amazement as the Earl strode on with Perdita close by his side.

Perdita was by this time fully as angry as the Earl. Six months before, when she was still with the pirates, she would have borne this rough treatment with stoicism. But now she had once again become used to life in a gentler society, a life in which respect for others played a major role. The Earl's treatment of her outraged her newly recovered self-esteem. As he opened her door she stood in stony silence, then she walked through into the room, turned and said, trembling with rage, "I will never forgive you for what you have said and done to me this afternoon, Lord Ambourne. You have made your low opinion of me quite clear. It does not begin to rival the depth of my opinion of you."

For a moment he looked surprised at the vehemence and confidence with which she spoke. Then he laughed sardonically. "My congratulations," he jeered. "But then we already know what an actress you are! Well, you're going to have plenty of time to rehearse your role. There won't be many distractions for you from now on, my little wanton. You won't have freedom to find them. I expect you down to dinner at the normal time. Take care to put your company manners on along with your fine dress!" With that he went out, pulling the door shut behind him.

Perdita threw herself on the bed and burst into a storm of angry tears. How dared he treat her in this manner? How dared he call her a liar? She'd show him! She'd throw his fine clothes and his stupid lessons back in his face. He could do what he wanted; she would not help him carry out whatever he had planned!

After a while she had cried herself out, and lay there in exhausted misery. As the afternoon wore on and the light began to fade other thoughts began to plague her. If she refused to obey him he might send her back to Algiers— he was angry enough at the moment. Her chances of escaping from her unhappy circumstances were much greater in France or England than in Africa. There was no guarantee that she could reach the Sheikh. When she was with the pirates she had tried several times to escape, but it had all been in vain, for the seaports were inhospitable places for anyone with no money and no friends. They had all been afraid of the captain of *Le Faucon*, and she had been unceremoniously returned to him. No, open defiance was not the best way to solve her problems. She must outwit the Earl—no easy task, for she knew that not much escaped those hard grey eyes. Of one thing she was certain: any attempt on her part to gain his sympathy by telling him her history would be greeted with jeering disbelief. She would not expose herself to that, and that in turn meant she must try to continue her deception.

A knock at the door startled her, but it was only a maid, who had been sent to help her dress. Her toilet was completed in silence; then she was escorted downstairs to the salon. She had always disliked this room—of all the rooms in the château it was the most imposing. Spindly chairs and sofas upholstered in dark green were arranged stiffly round its walls, the furnishings were of heavy damask silk and the walls covered in tapestries from an earlier age. Crystal chandeliers held hundreds of candles overhead, and tonight they were all lit. The windows overlooked the rigid formality of the drive.

She stood in the middle of the huge room, still uncertain of her course of action. Then, when the Earl greeted her, she put up her chin and went forward to the fire. "Good evening, Lord Ambourne."

"Playing the lady, I see," he said scornfully.

She looked at him coolly. "I do not perfectly understand why you should be surprised, Lord Ambourne. I thought that was what you wanted me to be."

"You could never be a lady, Perdita. I will be content if you can act like one—for longer than five minutes before dinner."

The gloves were off, then. "I agree it will not be easy.

It is difficult to sustain courtesy where none is met. I will do my best, however," she said, adding to herself, but not to please you, my lord!

He seemed to read her mind. "You dislike me for knowing what you are—that is natural," he replied. "But your games are finished, Perdita. This afternoon, while you were in your room, I thought long and hard about your future. I must tell you that I am sorely tempted to send you back to Algiers."

However hard she tried she could not prevent a shadow of alarm passing over her face. It was swiftly suppressed. The Earl continued abruptly, "But I have decided against it. Time is growing short, and in many other ways you are what I need. It will only be necessary to keep a closer watch on you when you are not actually in your lessons." He paused for a moment. "I have asked Madame Lebrun to assign one of the maids to your personal use. She will not be told that she is your keeper, but she will be expected to know where you are when you are indoors."

Perdita frowned resentfully. The Earl might not intend the maid to know, but Madame Lebrun would see that she did. The girl would know herself to be Perdita's warder. But the Earl was saying more. "It would, of course, be easier if we could confine you to the house until you are ready to go to London. However, I do not wish to deprive you of fresh air and exercise. You will be accompanied on your walks either by a groom or by me. Do not look rebelliously at me, Perdita. I assure you it is quite normal for a young 'lady' to be accompanied by a maid or groom when she goes out in London. Of course, we have learned from experience that in your case it is essential wherever you are."

"And Madame d'Espery?" Perdita asked stiffly.

"Madame d'Espery has been deeply distressed by your

behaviour. She has decided to return tomorrow to her own house in the grounds of the château. She believes herself to have failed in her commission to teach you how to behave.''

Perdita made a small movement of protest. "Madame d'Espery has nothing to reproach herself for, Lord Ambourne. She has been an excellent tutor—and a kind one.''

"Too kind,'' the Earl said harshly. "She allowed you to cozen her into approval and even liking. She knows differently now.''

"I do not wish Madame d'Espery to be punished because of me,'' Perdita persisted.

"You should have taken that into your reckoning before you embarked on your tricks. It is too late now.''

That Madame d'Espery was to be sent away for her pupil's shortcomings was too much for Perdita's composure. She turned away in distress and walked to the window, stumbling over a stool on the way.

The Earl looked at the figure gazing blindly out on to the drive, then added in a slightly softer tone, "Madame d'Espery is not in good health. She herself requested me to release her. I did not ask her to leave.''

"May I see her before she goes?'' asked Perdita.

"Of course. She will be down in a few minutes.''

At that moment Madame d'Espery came into the room. She was pale but very dignified. Her strict code of behaviour did not permit her to show how deeply she was hurt by Perdita's defection. She greeted her courteously and then talked about the weather, the state of the roads and the difficulties Père Amboise was having in the church. Her fund of anecdotes seemed to have dried up. Throughout dinner her manner was impeccably correct but bereft of any spontaneity.

Only now did Perdita realise how much the old lady had

come to mean to her, but she found it impossible to approach her. After dinner she tried to say how sorry she was that Madame d'Espery was leaving and to thank her for her patience and concern. Her chaperon listened carefully, then said, "I thank you for the sentiments you have expressed, *mademoiselle*. They are not at all necessary, I assure you. I regret that I was not able to help you more."

In the light of Madame d'Espery's wall of politeness Perdita could not ask her if she might visit her. She felt she knew what the reply would be, and wanted to spare herself and Madame d'Espery any further embarrassment. The Earl rang for candles early and they were escorted upstairs by a silent maid.

The next morning, while Perdita was with Père Amboise, the Earl took Madame d'Espery to her house on the other side of the park, and a new phase in Perdita's life began.

The first surprise came in an interview with the Earl. This happened a day or two after Madame d'Espery's departure. He had been busy and her walks had been supervised by an elderly groom, who was uncommunicative and disapproving. He clearly felt his proper work was being neglected and was only anxious to get back to it. He walked Perdita round the path the Earl had recommended as if she were one of the horses—and not a very valuable one at that. They were both glad to return. Indoors, her time was divided between her lessons, meals and her room. Rather than give the maid the satisfaction of re-porting her movements to Madame Lebrun, Perdita smuggled one or two books out of the library and spent most of her time reading in her room.

When the Earl finally sent for her he said, "There are several matters to be made clear between us, Perdita. Please sit down."

"I thought everything was perfectly clear," said Perdita. "We are working towards a goal known only to you, directed by decisions which are yours alone, enlivened by mutual antipathy."

He looked at her with a grim smile in his eyes. "That's exactly what I mean, Perdita," he said. "Where has a girl like you, apparently able neither to read nor to write, acquired a vocabulary more suited to a university dining table?"

Perdita thought hard and quickly. "Père Amboise?" she asked. "Of course, I don't always understand what the words mean—"

"I've warned you—don't try to play games with me."

The dangerous look in his eyes persuaded her to be prudent. She thought of her father and decided to tell the truth—at least partly. "I've always had a good ear, Lord Ambourne. I...I pick things up very quickly. And I once knew someone who loved books..."

"Another one of your lovers, no doubt. Who was he? And if he loved books so much why did he not teach you to read?"

"Teach me to read? Why?" she asked opening her eyes wide.

His lips curled in disgust. "I agree, it wasn't really necessary for what he needed from you. All the same, I think you do know how to read, Perdita. If not, why are there books from this library in your room?"

She jumped up. "You've had me spied on! How dare you? You've had my room searched!"

"Your room? You own nothing, Perdita. Not your room, not your dresses, not even yourself! Why should I not have any part of my house searched, if I so wish?"

"Would you search your servants' rooms?" cried Perdita angrily.

"No, but then I trust my servants."

With an exclamation Perdita swung round and made for the door.

"I have not yet finished what I wanted to say," said the cool voice behind her. She stopped with her back still towards him. There was a small silence. "There is little likelihood of either of us achieving our goals if we continue in this fashion," the Earl said eventually. "Sit down again, Perdita. If you will refrain from provoking me at every turn I will attempt to have more patience with your foibles. I do not refer here to your behaviour outside the house, but to your determined efforts to mislead all who come into contact with you. Sit down. Please."

She came back slowly and sat in the chair opposite him. She was puzzled, intrigued and slightly afraid.

"First I will suggest that from now on, when we are not in company, we speak English to each other." She looked at him in amazement. Was there nothing this man did not perceive? Seeing her surprise, he went on, "Your French is excellent, except for a few words of argot which are inappropriate to a young lady's vocabulary and which I suspect you learned with your pirate friends. Fortunately Madame d'Espery did not recognise them for what they are. However, though you speak French fluently and well, I have no doubt in my mind that your native tongue is English. Do you deny it?" Perdita shook her head. "What? No words at all? Not even French ones? I am curious to hear you speak English, Perdita. You have a voice which is pleasant on the ear, but the accent is also important."

He paused, but when she still did not speak he continued in English, "And that leads me to my second point—your failure to learn anything from Monsieur Champollion. Ah, a reaction—one of scorn. Why? Do you despise him so much?" He leant forward. "Is it because he was simply too easy to gull, Perdita? I refuse to believe that a girl with as musical a voice as yours has no gift at all for music. Did he offend you with his ready belief that you were stupid? Or was your game a deeper one?''

"You all assumed I was stupid," said Perdita, feeling a sense of relief at talking in her own language again. "I merely fulfilled your expectations."

The Earl sat back. "There, I fear, you're wrong. I never for one moment believed you lacked intelligence—merely any moral sense. But at the moment we are not talking of your behaviour. We are discussing your lessons. Have you, in fact, learned nothing from Monsieur Champollion?"

Perdita answered with a sense of satisfaction, "Not a thing!"

"That has the ring of truth. So why do I have the impression that you are prevaricating?"

Perdita shrugged her shoulders and the Earl got up with an exclamation of impatience. He came over to her chair and leaned on the arms, trapping her in it. "You block every attempt I make to establish some ground on which to work. I told you once before, Perdita, I know you for what you are. I bought you from the Pasha in Algiers because of what you are. It isn't necessary for you to attempt to hide the truth about yourself—not from me, at least. But why can't you tell me more? Who was this man from whom you learned to read? Was he the one who taught you such purity of diction? You have a lovely speaking voice, Perdita. I think he must have valued you." When she remained silent he continued, "What happened? Did you play him false? Did you drive him to selling you to the pirates? What parted you from him?"

Perdita closed her eyes in pain. "He…died," she whispered. "And then…and then…"

"Yes, what then?" the Earl asked, bending closer.

Perdita stared at him in an agony of doubt. Should she tell him the real truth about herself? Would he believe her? And, if he did, what would he do then? Send her away, probably. She did not believe he would insist on keeping her once he knew the truth—that she was gently born and bred. He was sure to send her away—and, it came to her in a flash of self-revelation, she could not bear that. She did not want to be sent away!

"Perdita?" The Earl's voice seemed to come from a long way away. But she must escape from him for the moment—she must have time to consider this new dilemma. With a quick sideways movement she slid out of the chair and walked quickly to the door.

"Lord Ambourne, you said recently that drabs cannot become honest, any more than the leopard can change his spots. Why are you asking me to tell you the truth? In your eyes it is not to be found in me. And now I hope you will excuse me; I have the headache. I will waste no more of your time." She slipped out of the door before he could stop her and ran to her room. She needed solitude to sort out the tangle of her emotions. She was glad to note that, though the Earl's face had darkened, he had not followed her.

In her room, she sat down by the window and gazed out. What in heaven's name was she to do? The obvious course, the sensible course, was to confess everything to the Earl. He was autocratic, but not unjust—except to her. And had she not deserved his lack of trust in her? She thought over their relationship. His first sight of her formed the background to everything he had learned of her since. Was it so surprising that he should assume the worst? She had done nothing, said nothing to disabuse him. Indeed, she had wilfully encouraged him in his original belief that she was an unlettered, ignorant wanton. She had enjoyed deceiving her tutors. It was a game in which she had pitted her wits against theirs—or so it had seemed at first. What she had really been doing, of course, was defying the Earl.

Then she remembered his arrogance when he'd informed her he was going to make her into a lady; when he had warned her that she was to behave and threatened her with the Pasha; the names he had called her—slut, jade, scum; his description of her as a tool... She grew indignant. He deserved everything she had done! But then...he had saved her life and brought her back into an environment she had thought closed to her forever. Whatever his motives, he had restored her will to live. Surely this was worth something? And, if her actions had been right and just, why was she now so unhappy? She shivered as she remembered the dreadful scene by the lake a few days ago, and its consequences. What could she have done? Tell the Earl about Philippe and perhaps ruin Eliane's chances of happiness? He probably wouldn't have believed her anyway.

There was yet another problem. What was she to do about the d'Harcourts? The Earl was bound to visit them as soon as they returned, and they were sure to talk about her. If the Earl remained in his present mood the fat really would be in the fire when he discovered how far she had been deceiving him about her abilities. He must then start questioning where she had acquired the attributes of a lady. And if he learned the truth he would send her away...

Her thoughts had gone full circle and she was no nearer a decision. One thing was undeniable: for whatever reason, she did not want to leave Belleroi and the Earl. She stayed in her room all evening. A tray was brought to her room, and, though she left the food, she drank the glass of wine that had been served with it. It enabled her to sleep. Her last conscious thought was of the Sheikh's words. "You have the courage and spirit to help Lord Ambourne. Use them wisely."

CHAPTER SEVEN

FOR HIS PART, the Earl was almost as confused as Perdita. He sometimes felt he could see right into Perdita's mind, and then a scene like their last one would leave him frustrated and angry, sensing there was something more he should know, yet unable to get it out of her. Why was she so reluctant to confide in him? Throughout the next day, whenever the business of seeing his tenants and discussing their needs with his agent left him time to think, his mind was exercised with this mystery. There were times when he cursed the day he had found Perdita. It should all have been so simple! Buy the girl, train her, and then use her to trap Piers Carston. The only difficulty he had envisaged was finding a suitable girl to act as his tool. And now, when his mind should be on the many problems the estate still faced, he was pondering about Perdita—not as a tool but as a human being with a personality all her own: her wit, her courage, her pride and grace, her concern for Madame d'Espery, the passion he sensed in her...and, on the other hand, her skill at deception, her lack of morals, her treatment of Colette... What was he to do with her? Use her? Or send her away? No, he didn't want that! With determination he banished her from his mind and concentrated on the business in hand.

When Perdita went back to her room after her lesson that morning she found Colette there, hiding behind the curtains. "Oh, it's you, *mademoiselle*! I was afraid it was Jeanne. She's your maid now, isn't she? Do you like her?"

"She looks after me well, Colette. Aren't you frightened of being found here?"

"Oh, they're all busy on the other side of the house. That's why I came. Can we go out? I want to go to the old castle. Henri says it's haunted."

"That ruin is dangerous, Colette. And anyway, I'm not able to come out at the moment…"

"I know. Georges has to be with you, hasn't he? Monsieur le Marquis told him to go with you whenever you went out."

Perdita's cheeks flamed. Did the whole household know? The answer was probably yes, for Madame Lebrun was no friend of hers. Why did the woman dislike her so much? She began to regret that she had never taken the trouble to find out. But when she had arrived at the château she had been indifferent to what anyone thought of her, and now it was probably too late.

"*Mademoiselle, mademoiselle!*" Colette was tugging at her skirt. "You don't have to have Georges with you if you don't want to."

"What? Of course I do. He doesn't let me out of his sight."

"I know, but he doesn't like taking you. He'd much rather be with the horses. If you didn't turn up at the right time he'd go back to the stables and he wouldn't bother telling anyone. Then you could come with me!"

Perdita was sorely tempted. Her walks had become penances—it would be wonderful to go into the woods once again with Colette. She badly wanted to see Philippe again, too, for he might have some news of Eliane. "I'll think it over, Colette," she said. "Meanwhile, you ought to go. Jeanne might come any moment."

"Please come, *mademoiselle*. I want to show you the castle."

"I'll think about the walk. It isn't easy, Colette."

"Course it is!" Colette replied scornfully. "All you have to do is be late for Georges. Bye."

She was gone. Perdita smiled—it was so easy for children. They didn't think of the consequences.

However, the fates seemed for once to be on her side. Two days later the Earl was called urgently to Paris. The household was in a bustle until he left, but he did not forget to check that Perdita would be properly supervised. In the rush to leave, however, he did not find the time to see Georges.

Soon after the Earl's departure Perdita seized her opportunity to see Philippe. Colette objected strongly to her decision to see him first, but Perdita refused to change her mind. She would not spend long with him, but she had to find out if he had any news of Eliane. She pacified Colette by promising to go out with her later in the week.

The day dawned bright and sunny, and Perdita was so full of anticipation that she had to laugh at herself. It was such a minor pleasure—her excitement was out of all proportion. It was not the prospect of seeing Philippe. She was, if anything, not looking forward to that at all. No, it was simply the freedom offered by a walk without Georges's gloomy supervision. All went as planned. Georges duly took himself off after waiting in vain for five minutes, and Perdita slipped out and made for the lake. She was pleased to see that Philippe was waiting for her, but when she drew near enough to see his face she was appalled.

"Philippe, what's happened?" she cried. "Have you had some bad news of Eliane? Is she very ill? She's not... she's not..."

"No," he replied heavily. "No, Mademoiselle Perdita,

Mademoiselle d'Harcourt is not dead. Though it would be better perhaps for her if she were.''

"What are you saying? Is she injured? Philippe, don't stand there making cryptic remarks—tell me what is wrong!''

Philippe looked at her. His cheeks, normally so pink and full of health, were white, and his eyes were dull. "I cannot tell you, *mademoiselle*. It is not fit for you to hear.''

Perdita felt like boxing his ears, but she clutched his arm instead. She was desperate to know what crisis had caused this change in Philippe's appearance. "Philippe, I am not a child. Please tell me what has happened.''

"*Mademoiselle*, you cannot imagine how distressed I was...how deeply distressed.'' He gave a shuddering sigh, then said, "The d'Harcourts have deceived me. Mademoiselle d'Harcourt is not the innocent I thought her. She has had an association with another man.''

"A love-affair!'' exclaimed Perdita. "When? Where?''

"In England. Before she came back here.''

"That's impossible! Eliane is innocent, I'd swear it.''

"*Mademoiselle*, there is no possibility of mistake. Before the d'Harcourts came back to France Mademoiselle d'Harcourt had an affair.''

"Who told you this? Why are you so sure it is true?''

"Mademoiselle d'Harcourt told me herself.''

"But when?'' cried Perdita.

"When you told me that Eliane was ill in Paris I decided that I must find out for myself how she was. I set off that same day. It wasn't easy to see her but finally her mother came and took me into her room. She was so pale, *mademoiselle*, and...and we were so happy to see each other again. Her mother saw how it was with us and promised to see that the Marquis gave his consent. Then... then...Eliane told me—what I have told you.''

"And now? You no longer wish to marry her? Is that it?'' asked Perdita quietly.

"Marry her? Marry a woman who has been with another man? I don't think you understand, *mademoiselle*. She wasn't married to him! She ran off... Oh, God, I can't bear it! Eliane, Eliane!'' Philippe turned away and a sob escaped him. At first Perdita's heart ached for him. He was so young and so full of ideals. He had put Eliane on a pedestal—an angel, he had called her—and now his world had crashed about him. But how had Eliane fared?

She waited until Philippe could speak again, then asked, "What of Eliane, Philippe? What did you say to her after her confession?''

"I...I don't remember. I ran out of the building and came straight back here. I never want to see her again!''

So this was the reason for the Earl's hasty departure for Paris, thought Perdita. She could imagine that Eliane might well have collapsed after Philippe's disastrous visit and that Madame d'Harcourt had sent for support. Poor, poor Eliane!

"Philippe, I can see why you should have felt like this in the first shock of discovery. But think of Eliane. What do you think she feels now, after you left her like that?'' Philippe shrugged his shoulders, but said nothing. Perdita said suddenly, "When did you say it happened? In England? But how old was Eliane then?''

"Sixteen,'' said Philippe sullenly.

"Sixteen! Only sixteen? She was only a child! Don't you know any more?''

"Nothing. Isn't it enough? That she's had a lover?''

Perdita lost her temper with him. She cried passionately, "No, it's not nearly enough! You can't judge Eliane on this. I've known Eliane for no time at all but I'll swear she is an innocent party. If she did have an affair, then she was duped into it. How long have you known her? Hasn't she always looked to you for protection? Hasn't she always been afraid of strangers, reluctant to meet new faces? You cannot desert her. Think about Eliane instead of yourself. She isn't a fallen angel, she's a girl who needed you, and you failed her.'' She gave an angry sob and shook her head. ''I'm sorry, I can't talk to you any more; I have to get back. Besides, there's nothing more to say. Goodbye, Philippe. You can reach me through Colette if you wish, but until you have reconsidered your attitude to Eliane I don't want to see you again!''

She spoke so forcefully that Philippe stared at her. However, he didn't say anything, and she turned abruptly and walked back in the direction of the house, brushing angry tears from her cheeks. Poor Eliane. Philippe's reaction was cruel but not unexpected. He was so young and inexperienced.

Her sad thoughts occupied her mind throughout the rest of the afternoon and evening. It was an ironic twist of fate that she and Eliane, two girls of the same age, should both have been so unfortunate. And who was to say which of them was the worse off? It was true that Eliane had a loving family round her now, whereas she had no one. But Perdita felt that Eliane was less well equipped to take the buffets life dealt out to her, that she could much more easily go under. She might well do so now. If only she could see her—perhaps telling Eliane her own story might help. She debated for a while how she might get to Paris, but finally decided this was impossible. She must hope that Eliane was brought back to Beau Lac. Would Madame d'Harcourt bring her here, where there were so many memories of Philippe? She went to bed with a heavy heart, thinking of her friend and wondering how she was.

Later that night she lay awake, remembering the con-

versation she had overheard in the cabin on the way to
Tangier. Tom had said something about Miss Linette,
about finding Miss Linette... That's right! And the Earl
had replied that he'd been thinking about finding her in a
'doxy's house in London'. He was going to 'teach someone a lesson' for doing it. It was Eliane they had been
talking about, she knew that. Then, from what the Earl had
said after that, he intended to use her, Perdita, to accomplish this. Was this why the Earl wanted a pseudo-lady?

Well, if it was reasonably near legal, she would help
him! She would willingly act as Eliane's champion, since
Philippe seemed to have failed her.

Life continued in the château. The Earl must have conveyed some of his scepticism to Monsieur Champollion
and Signor Calvi, for they were definitely suspicious of
her. So for the first time she worked properly, much to
their surprise and eventual delight. Here was a pupil any
tutor could take pride in! Père Amboise accepted the miraculous improvement in her writing without question, but
then he was used to living with miracles. The fact was,
Perdita no longer wanted to delay the Earl's plans. She
was burning to help Eliane in any way she could, and was
desperate to know how she was faring. When would the
Earl return?

The weather had turned cold and wet after Perdita's unhappy scene with Philippe, and it was impossible for her
to go out with Colette for nearly a week. They were both
eager for their walk. Perdita would be glad to exchange
her depressed thoughts of Eliane for Colette's lively company, and Colette was anxious to show *mademoiselle* the
old castle. When she did eventually manage to get out
Georges was less obliging than he had been on her previous outing. He waited for fully quarter of an hour before
he hunched his shoulders and went back to his horses.

When Perdita got to the edge of the woods there was no sign of Colette. Had she grown tired of waiting? Fifteen minutes might seem an eternity to a child. But she couldn't believe Colette would so easily abandon their plans. Where was she?

A faint cry was borne to her on the wind. Colette! She looked round, but saw nothing. Where had it come from? Again she heard it. It was coming from further round the hill, where the high road ran along the boundary. The castle ruins were in that direction! Full of foreboding, she scrambled hastily round to the pile of stones, which had once formed the original fortress of Belleroi. The cries were louder here—Colette must be in the ruins.

"*Mademoiselle, mademoiselle*, I'm here! Please come quickly. I'm going to fall."

"I'm coming," Perdita called. "But where are you?"

"In a hole in the ground. It fell in and I fell too."

Perdita found the place. It had been an old well or store, which had been filled in long ago. Now the top had collapsed and Colette was standing on a narrow ledge, clutching the fragile root of a small tree. Even as Perdita got down on her knees to see, Colette slipped a little further.

"Hold on; I'll get your wrists. You'll be safe then." Perdita lay flat, her arms over the hole, and caught hold of Colette's wrists. It was just as well that she did, for the root suddenly snapped. Trying to speak calmly, she said, "How on earth did you get into this predicament, Colette?"

"I didn't go in the ruins, *mademoiselle*. I was just on the edge. You were such a long time and I got a bit cold. I thought it would be warmer in the shelter of the big stones. But I hadn't got very far when I…when I…" Colette's voice had developed a wobble. Perdita finished the sentence for her.

"When you went tumbling into a hole that wasn't there. That's clever! How are your toes?"

"They're all right, I think. But it's not very comfortable, *mademoiselle*. Can't you lift me out?"

"I'll try. Come on!"

After several attempts, however, she had to give up. Colette's weight, together with the uncertain stability of the ground, made it impossible for her to get enough purchase. Perdita began to grow worried. She dared not let go of Colette's wrists, for the child was standing on a very narrow ledge, beneath which was a long drop. But, if she couldn't go for help, how would they ever escape? It was getting very cold and a mist was coming up from the lake—Colette would soon be chilled through. For the next half-hour she tried desperately either to lift Colette up, or to anchor her so that she could go for help, but all her efforts were in vain. Her feet slipped on the wet grass, and, once, the ground started to give way on the edge.

Towards the end of the period Colette was getting tired, cold and frightened. Perdita took more of her weight, and went through her repertoire of funny stories to cheer them up. By the end of the period she was exhausted. It was with heartfelt relief, therefore, that she heard voices in the wood, which proved to be a search party for Colette. By this time she was too weak to shout, and lay there laughing with relief.

"Hey you! What are you doing with that child? You wicked woman!" Colette was snatched up, and rough hands pushed Perdita aside.

"Take her back to her grandmother; she's frantic with worry. There, there, little one, don't cry! You're safe now."

They started off, Colette held in a burly stable-lad's arms, leaving Perdita on the ground by the well. She called after them, but they ignored her, except for one who turned as he went and shouted, "You should be in prison, you should! Or a madhouse! Treating a poor little motherless child like that. What sort of woman are you, thinking it's funny to lock her up in a cupboard and hang her over a hole? Unless you're a witch." He gave her a fearful look, crossed himself and scuttled off.

Perdita was left alone. She was so exhausted that she couldn't move for the moment, and lay there, weakly laughing. She didn't believe it! They'd left her here because they thought she had been tormenting Colette. Madame Lebrun had surely spread her poison wide. Not one of them had doubted that it was so, and Colette had been too far gone herself to say anything. Poor child, she had really been very brave up to the last few minutes.

Now she must pull herself up and make her own way to the château. But the mist had grown very thick and it was difficult to get her bearings. She walked doggedly forward in what she guessed was the right direction, but suddenly found herself on the crumbling ground by the well again. She halted and listened for any sound, but the silence was eerily complete. She shivered and felt a moment's panic, then made herself think calmly. The road must be on her left, so she set off again in that direction. It was now quite dark and the ground was rough... She tripped over a trailing bramble stem and fell heavily. For a moment she lay there, feeling dizzy, and when she tried to move again she found she was hopelessly caught up in a tangle of undergrowth. At least it was warm and dry here in the shelter of the trees and surrounded by leaves. She would have a rest and then try again...

PERDITA WOKE at first light, feeling curiously lethargic. The cold had penetrated to her very bones, though she was wearing her thick cape. She wondered why no one had come looking for her, for surely Colette had told the others the truth by now? Perhaps the little girl had fallen asleep as soon as she had got in and was not yet awake. But why hadn't Madame Lebrun organised a search? Not for love of Perdita, but from fear of the Earl! For whatever reason, she was on her own. She forced herself to her feet and considered what she should do. The way through the wood was shorter, but the road made for easier walking. Besides, though it was early still, she might just meet someone who would help her. She got to the road and set off along it. Her head ached, her arms ached—in fact, there wasn't much that didn't hurt! She must get to the château.

CHAPTER EIGHT

THE EARL HAD EXPECTED to return to Belleroi the previous evening, but a cast shoe had delayed him and he had been forced to spend the night at a villainously uncomfortable inn on the road from Bayeux. He had left before first light, thankful to escape from the place. With luck he would be at the château for breakfast. The pathetic figure limping along the road touched him—it looked so tired and so determined. She must be making for Belleroi, looking for work or charity. The kitchen staff would give her something. As he passed he slowed his horses to tell her to be sure to call. But the words died on his lips as he looked down into Perdita's weary face. "What the devil...?"

He had no time for more. Perdita smiled radiantly at him, said, "Oh, you're back!" then slid to the ground. He leapt down and, kneeling on the road beside her, lifted her into his arms. She was very pale, with dark circles under her eyes. After a moment she opened them and looked up at him. She made a vague fluttering movement with her hand and said, "I'm sorry...I couldn't help it. Don't be angry. Please."

"What is it, Perdita? What's happened to you?" he said urgently.

A small smile came to her lips. "You'd never believe me, Lord Ambourne. I hardly believe it myself." Then she gave a small groan as he lifted her more closely to him.

"Where does it hurt, Perdita? Tell me!"

"Everywhere, I think. But it's not serious. I'll get up in a moment."

It was clear she was in considerable pain. Her gallant spirit touched him as no tears could have done. He carefully lifted her into the chaise, settled her as best he could in a vehicle that was built for speed rather than comfort, and set off for the château. The way was short, but the Earl had some time to reflect. Curiously enough, in spite of what he knew of her, he did not doubt the truth of what she had said. Another instance of the gap between his head and his...his what? His heart? No, he dismissed that notion out of hand. The sooner he got Perdita back to the château the better. She needed care, and he...he wanted some answers! He urged his horses into a slightly quicker gait and they were soon bowling up the long drive.

They arrived to find the château in an uproar. Colette had woken up demanding to see *mademoiselle*. The servants soon discovered they had made a serious mistake in their judgement of their master's ward, and the men were frantically searching in the village and further afield. When the Earl arrived at his château there wasn't a groom to help him with his horses, and the rest of the servants were all in a highly nervous state. Their relief at seeing Perdita arrive with the Earl, however, was tempered by the knowledge of the trouble that lay ahead for some of them.

The Earl paid no heed to their greetings, nor did he listen to any of their stammered excuses. Brushing these impatiently aside, he carried Perdita up to her room and put her gently down on the bed. Then he told Jeanne to look after her. As he went out Perdita gave him a grin and said softly, "Aren't you going to throw me into the bath?"

The Earl avoided Jeanne's shocked look and said, "Get some rest now. I'll throw you in the bath when you're stronger. Look after her, Jeanne." He went downstairs to his distraught household, ordered one of the maids to bring at least some of the search party back to tend his horses, and requested Madame Lebrun to see him in the library in two hours. Then he went to his room to change. By the time he came down order had been restored to the household and breakfast was waiting for him in the small parlour. When he had finished he sent for Madame Lebrun.

"Now," said the Earl coldly. "Now I am ready to hear any explanation you can give me for what happened last night." The housekeeper shifted uneasily. What was she to say?

"I am waiting, Madame Lebrun," said the Earl.

"Monsieur le Marquis, we were all so anxious about Colette...Rosanne was out of her mind...and...and... We're so sorry for what happened, Monsieur le Marquis!" The housekeeper was so far removed from her usual imperturbable self that the Earl unbent a little.

"Sit down, Madame Lebrun. Now tell me first of all how it was that Mademoiselle Perdita was out alone. Where was Georges?"

"When *mademoiselle* didn't appear at her usual time Georges thought she wasn't coming. He had a lot to do with the horses so he...so he—"

"Forgot my orders and went back to the warmth of his stables. Right, that's one matter cleared up," said the Earl, making a note to take it further with both Georges and Perdita. "Where did Colette come in? I'm surprised she was with the *mademoiselle* in view of what you told me last time we talked on this head. I thought you told me Colette had been frightened?"

"Oh, *monsieur*, we were all mistaken there. Colette is a naughty girl. She kept her friendship with Mademoiselle Perdita completely secret. We had no idea that they went on so many walks together. That's why we..."

"Well?" asked the Earl.

"That's why we jumped to the conclusion we did. That Mademoiselle Perdita was tormenting Colette again, holding her over the well."

"Of all the ridiculous ideas! Didn't it ever occur to you that Colette might have fallen in by herself? Heaven knows she's been in enough trouble before. Well, didn't it? The stable hands might be stupid enough, but surely you knew better, *madame*?"

"I wasn't with the men when they found Colette, *monsieur*. I only saw them arrive, and by that time she was worn out with fright and cold. I couldn't question her then."

"How long was it before you decided to look for Mademoiselle Perdita?"

This was the difficult part for the housekeeper. She was aware that she had left it far too long before doing so. "We were so worried about Colette…and Rosanne, *monsieur*."

"When did you send the men out, Madame Lebrun?"

She swallowed and said in a low voice, "Some time after nine, *monsieur*—but we couldn't find her in the mist. We thought she had run away." His silence alarmed her and she said defensively, "We all knew you didn't trust her, and she wasn't very happy being taken for a walk like a dog every day, so we thought she'd gone. I didn't think you would mind very much…"

The Earl stood up. "Thank you, Madame Lebrun. That is all."

Madame Lebrun hesitated at the door. "I was wrong, *monsieur*, to do what I did. I will understand if you wish me to go."

"What you omitted to do was worse," said the Earl with grim humour. "You'll have to wait for my decision on whether you should go or not. I haven't yet heard the whole story. Thank you.''

The Earl threw himself into a chair by the fire. He'd have to see Georges, of course, though he knew what the groom would say. Why had Perdita been late, though? He fancied her part in this had not been totally blameless. But, from what Madame Lebrun had said, Perdita hadn't used her freedom to find her lover again. She had gone for a walk with Colette! Had the young man he had seen by the lake been frightened off for good? He hoped so. He stretched himself and sighed. He was weary, not because of the journey to Paris and back, but because of what he had found when he'd arrived there. Linette was like a little ghost. In itself her fever was not serious—a severe bout of influenza, no more—but she showed no inclination to fight it. Of course, removing her to Paris at the onset of the attack had not been wise, but his aunt had always been inclined to panic where Linette was concerned and had taken her to an eminent physician there. She would have been better left here in Beau Lac. Then, perhaps, the unpleasantness with the young man might have been avoided. Who was this Philippe who had followed them to Paris? The young puppy deserved to be whipped for his treatment of Linette—or Eliane, as he supposed he must now call her. She had grown hysterical when he had called her 'Linette'—Piers Carston had made much of that name. The Earl frowned. Piers Carston had not only destroyed Eliane's future. A whole happy childhood lay in ruins, too.

He got up impatiently. It was useless bemoaning the past; he must do something about Carston. It was time he suppressed his scruples about using Perdita, stopped her nonsense with her tutors, and prepared her for London. The sight of Eliane's misery had hardened his resolve. Besides, whatever else she was or had been, Perdita was undoubt-

edly a pirate's strumpet, and she was penniless—two qualities he had expressly searched for. No, he must dismiss
any scruples about her—he could not afford them.

As the Earl had thought, Georges was unrepentant. His
job was to look after horses, not silly girls who played
tricks and got themselves lost. He would have said more,
but the Earl sent him away. Georges was a genius with
horses and knew it. He had always made it perfectly clear
to the Earl that he let him ride his horses as a personal
favour, and was most unlikely to worry about dismissal.
Fortunately the Earl was fair-minded enough—and fond
enough of his horses—not to pursue the matter. He had
asked Georges to perform a task for which the man was
not suited.

When he went up to see Perdita he found the door open
and Colette sprawled on her bed, laughing at something
Perdita had said. They made a pleasant picture, and he
admired it for a moment from outside. As soon as she saw
him Colette scrambled off the bed, gave him a somewhat
inelegant curtsy and scurried out.

The Earl sat down in one of the rose chintz armchairs.
"Are you recovered?" he asked.

"I was never really ill. I ought to be up."

"It's a great compliment to the Sheikh's treatment that
you have survived a night out of doors so well," said the
Earl. "Am I right to assume it was out of doors?"

Her mouth tightened as she said, "You have made so
many assumptions about me, Lord Ambourne, that I am
sure you will assume anything you choose. I could show
you the clump of brambles, I suppose. But then you would
merely assume that I was lying, or you would assume that
someone was with me in the brambles. I assume you have
some doubt?"

He laughed and said, "Pax, pax, Perdita. I believe you.

Indeed, I can see the scratches on your face. Where was Georges?''

She hesitated and he could see her debating. Would she tell him the truth? Finally she said defiantly, ''I tricked him. It wasn't his fault—though he deserved it! Tell me, did you choose him for his stimulating conversation, or his courteous ways?''

''Neither. I chose him because he's good with horses.'' At her indignant gasp he said, ''When I engaged him initially, that is. He was the only one I could spare from the estate to walk with you. So you slipped the leash and ran off? Where?''

She looked at him for a moment as if she was assessing his question. ''If you are simply trying to find out what happened yesterday I will tell you. But I don't like the manner of your questions. There are too many animals involved. Do you wish to know what happened?''

A smile tugged at his lips. He was to consider himself rebuked! ''Yes, please,'' he said meekly.

She thereupon told him clearly and concisely what had happened in the castle ruins. The account was factual, but he could sense the fears and pain she and Colette had experienced. ''So I started walking to the château,'' she concluded.

He hesitated for a moment and then asked, ''Have you escaped from Georges on any other occasion, Perdita?''

''To walk with Colette? No,'' she said, not looking at him.

''So you've seen him again?''

''If you mean the man I was with when you were so angry, yes, I have,'' she said, lifting her chin and staring him in the eye. The Earl was conscious of a surge of disappointed fury, but he controlled it. In the light of his resolve to press forward with his plans for Piers Carston it was of little consequence if she had a hundred lovers. "I think you're making assumptions again," said a quiet voice from the bed. "My conversation with him—and that was all it was, Lord Ambourne—was short and unhappy. I doubt I will see him again."

"I doubt you'll have the time, Perdita. I wish you to be ready for England in a month. As soon as you are able to get up you will present yourself in the library. Things will be different from now on."

He got up and strode swiftly out of the room. As he went down the stairs he was frowning so heavily that little Jeanne pressed herself against the banister rail and prayed he would not notice her.

IN SPITE OF PERDITA'S brave words it was some days before she could go downstairs. The Earl had insisted on a visit from the local doctor, who had recommended that she should wait to the end of the week before attempting to get up. The Earl was all the more surprised therefore when Perdita presented herself in the library just three days after her experience.

She found him engaged once again with his agent. His trip to Paris had interrupted a programme of improvements to some of the farmhouses on the estate, and he was deep in discussion. When he saw her, however, he rose instantly and said, "Right, Etienne, see that it is all put in hand straight away. I don't want any more delays—I'd like to see it finished before I go back to England."

"When will that be, *monsieur*?"

"I'm not sure. In about a month, I think. It depends on *mademoiselle*, here. It won't be much later than a month, though, so don't delay! And Etienne—has the old well been properly boarded up? Good! Come and sit down, Perdita."

The agent looked curiously at Perdita as he went. He had heard strange stories about her, some of them contradictory. He hoped Monsieur le Marquis knew what he was doing.

When he had gone the Earl sat down again and contemplated Perdita. "Are you sure you're well enough to be downstairs? Dr. Grondet said next week..."

"I'm well enough, Lord Ambourne. My arms are still a little stiff, that's all. I'm ready for my lessons."

"Yes." He paused for thought. "Perdita, a short while ago I tried, and failed, to establish a working relationship between us. At that time I already knew you could read perfectly well. I established that you are a native English speaker, I learned a little of your history—though not nearly enough—and I attempted to find the truth about your lessons. As I told you, I did not believe you to be as stupid as your tutors suggested. Since my return from Paris I have had reports of amazing progress; one might almost call it miraculous."

He waited for comment from her, but when none was forthcoming he continued, "You already know I rescued you in Algiers with a specific purpose in mind."

"You bought me, Lord Ambourne."

"I prefer to say rescued, Perdita, but I am not about to argue the point; I haven't the time." Perdita stirred rebelliously, but her interest was caught. "I want some answers from you, Perdita. I do not wish to waste our time—yours, mine and that of your tutors—in trying to give you knowledge you already possess. I wish you to tell me without prevarication or evasion what accomplishments you have, and to what degree. I am ready to hear that now."

She felt as if a pistol were being held to her head. The moment of truth—some of it—had arrived. She got up. "Shall I play to you, Lord Ambourne?"

He rose and she led the way to the large piano in the centre of the music-room. She was nervous, but comforted herself with the thought of the hours of practice with the d'Harcourts. She played him a lively dance by Mozart and then, when he asked her to continue, she played part of a brilliant sonata movement by Scarlatti. Lastly, with Eliane in mind, she played a sad little tune from Lully. As the last note sounded she turned her head from him so he could not see the tears in her eyes.

There was silence. "You wicked girl," was the Earl's astonishing reaction. She turned back to him. "To have talent such as that, and to waste it playing tricks." He leant forward. "Why are there tears in your eyes, Perdita?"

Perdita shook her head, for she could not speak. What could she have said anyway? The Earl did not know of her friendship with Eliane, and she was not yet ready to tell him of it. "What about the rest? Of your gifts?"

"Madame d'Espery was right in one thing. I cannot sew. I think I know most of the rules of polite behaviour, though even when I'm trying I find it difficult to conform."

She had a sudden vision of her mother, shaking her head in exasperated affection and saying, "You are too impetuous by far, my love. A young lady always thinks before she acts and always acts according to the rules of society. When you go to London…"

She got up from the piano. Her impetuous behaviour had been the last link in a chain of disaster, but she must not think of that at the moment. What was the Earl saying?

"Perdita, are you all right? Come, I'll send for Jeanne. She'll take you upstairs."

"No, no. Thank you, I'm perfectly able to carry on. What else do you wish to know? As you probably suspect, I can write as well as read; I know the steps of most dances, but not the waltz; I have a knowledge of, though no talent for painting, but I think I will have little need for that in London. I have a basic knowledge of geography—especially of the Mediterranean,'' she added with a wry smile.

''Enough, enough,'' said the Earl, holding up his hand. ''You seem to be vastly better educated than any of the respectable young ladies of my acquaintance. Tell me, Perdita, where did a girl of your background acquire all these skills? Was it with your first…protector?''

A cloud passed over Perdita's face, but she only replied, ''Why did an aristocrat of your background acquire a girl like me? Isn't it time you told me, so that I know what you want of me, Lord Ambourne?''

The Earl was strangely reluctant to do this. Although she had not answered his last question, he had learnt more of Perdita during the last half-hour than ever before. He had the feeling that once he revealed his plans to her they would become strangers again. He said, ''I will, but not yet. There are matters that should be cleared up before we embark on our joint enterprise. I hope it will be a joint venture, Perdita. You have something to gain from this as well.''

''Yes,'' she murmured. ''A discreet establishment in one of the better quarters of London, perhaps.''

He looked at her sharply. She didn't sound grateful, yet to a girl of her history this ought to be the peak of her ambition. He didn't have time to think about that now, but he put it aside for later—part of the enigma that was Perdita.

He continued, ''But first I must decide what to do about Madame Lebrun. You could have been seriously ill through her negligence. Have you anything to say about her?''

''Only that I think she has been punished enough. She

must have been worrying for days about what was to become of her. I was certainly partially to blame for her antipathy towards me, and you yourself did not appear to value me very highly. The rest sprang from those two facts. Yes, she was wrong not to send out a search party sooner. But I am not much the worse for wear. And she has spoken very kindly to me since.''

''No doubt,'' said the Earl with a cynical smile.

''No, I think she is sincerely sorry. You must do as you think fit, of course, but she is a most efficient housekeeper and would be hard to replace.''

''So you think she should stay?''

''It is not for me to say. I should be sorry to see her go because of me.''

The Earl nodded his head but did not say anything for a moment. Then, ''Will you keep me waiting if I invite you to a walk this afternoon, Perdita? I must go over to one of the farms in the valley, and it is a pleasant afternoon's stroll. Will you come? We can talk on the way.''

Perdita's face lit up and was then controlled. ''Thank you, Lord Ambourne, I should like that. At what time do you wish me to be at the door?''

''I think two o'clock. That will give us time to walk in comfort before it gets cold. Are you sure you can manage it? You are not too stiff?''

''It will be good for me. Thank you.'' She went to the door, then paused. ''Lord Ambourne, am I to understand that your visit to Paris concerned your cousin?''

''Yes,'' he said uncommunicatively.

But Perdita persisted. ''I hope it was not bad news? Is she not well?'' She seemed to be waiting anxiously for his reply.

''My cousin had an influenza, which she found hard to

shake off. We are hoping the warmer weather will help her to recover. She is not strong.''

"Thank you, Lord Ambourne," said Perdita in subdued tones. "I will see you at two."

He followed her out and went back to the library, asking one of the maids to fetch Madame Lebrun as he passed. She came so quickly that he guessed she had been waiting for her summons. Perdita had said she must have been worrying for days about her future, and if she could be so generous to her late adversary then surely he could not lag behind? He would let the woman stay.

Madame Lebrun was embarrassingly grateful to be given a second chance. Without saying so outright, the Earl let it be understood that Perdita had influenced his decision for Madame Lebrun's reprieve. Madame Lebrun was as ready to tell the other servants about Perdita's magnanimity as she had been indiscreet about her unfriendliness on her arrival. Soon Perdita found herself generally approved of—in the servants' hall at least. This, together with the approval of her tutors, made for an atmosphere of sunny harmony, which was a novel and attractive experience.

The Earl proved to be a pleasant companion on the first walk and the others that followed. He used the opportunity to tell her about current London society. He had a well-informed mind, and his observations on the world he was teaching her to know were astringent and witty. Perdita grew to look forward to her outings, though she was never allowed to relax on them. He expected her to remember every name, every fact he gave her. He could be impatient, and they often came dangerously close to an argument when she thought he was being unreasonably demanding. The sense of exhilaration when her mind was stretched to the limit more than made up for these lapses, however.

On one occasion he took her to see Madame d'Espery, and after a difficult start to the visit Perdita was able to convey her genuine regret that she had upset her former chaperon. The company of the Earl no doubt helped to soften Madame d'Espery towards her, for he was at his most charming, listening to her stories and making her laugh. When Perdita came to go, Madame d'Espery said, "I have had great pleasure in your company today, Mademoiselle Perdita. I should like you to call again—even if that rogue there is not able to come with you." Perdita looked at the Earl in amusement, and thanked the old lady.

That evening the Earl announced that he was going to teach Perdita the waltz. If she was to be presented to London society as a young lady of wealth she would need this accomplishment.

"But why can't Signor Calvi teach me?" she asked, slightly startled by this suggestion.

"You disappoint me, Perdita. I thought you had a feeling for style. Surely you've realised by now that Signor Calvi, while no doubt excellent for country jigs and *boulangers*, hasn't enough elegance about him for the modern dances. You would be labelled in an instant as a country bumpkin. You wouldn't want that?"

"How do I know what I want?" muttered Perdita, who was decidedly nervous.

The next day Monsieur Champollion was asked to play for them, and the lesson began. For one reason or another Perdita had already had the Earl's arm around her several times, but this was different. Though she normally moved gracefully, she stumbled and tripped until the Earl, never the most patient of tutors, sat her down in a chair and demonstrated by himself.

"Now you do it!" he said, pulling her up and placing her in the middle of the floor. She performed the steps

with her usual grace. "I don't believe it!" said the Earl.
"Come, we'll try again." Once again she stumbled, and
he stopped where they were, demanding, "Are you playing
your tricks again?"

"No! I just don't seem to be able to concentrate when
you're holding...when you're holding me by the waist."

The Earl gave a roar of laughter. "That's rich! Come,
Perdita, stop play-acting and do it properly. Look up, girl!
Look up!" He took hold of her chin and pulled it up. The
gesture reminded them both of other occasions when he
had held her like this. For one heart-stopping moment the
Earl seemed on the point of repeating his kisses, and then
he gave a kind of groan and led her back to her chair. He
bowed and said lightly, "Perhaps it would be better if you
learned the basic steps from Signor Calvi. We can always
add a little town polish when we go to London. Thank
you, Monsieur Champollion; the lesson is ended. And
now, Perdita, if you will excuse me I have some work to
do in the library."

But by the time his agent came to see him two hours
later the Earl had achieved very little. He had been thinking long and hard about Perdita, about Eliane and about
Piers Carston. Pleasant though his interlude of walks and
lessons had been, it was time he told Perdita of his plan.
The next morning he sent for her.

CHAPTER NINE

"No, I WILL NOT DO IT! You cannot force me to, and I will never agree of my own free will!" Perdita stood before the Earl, her eyes flashing blue fire and her face white with rage.

The Earl was astonished at the strength of her reaction. It seemed such a little thing to ask of a girl with her experiences. "Perdita, did I not promise that once you have married the man, and we have made sure that the marriage is binding, I will provide you with the wherewithal to set yourself up as we agreed? What is wrong with that?"

"I do not recall ever having been asked, so how can I have agreed to anything? I have not agreed, my lord. I do not agree and will not agree!" She was so angry that her voice was trembling.

He looked at her and said, "I confess I do not understand this hysterical reaction. He may be a villain, but I do not believe he would mistreat you as you have been mistreated in the past. You have only to live with him long enough to validate the marriage. Then you will be free."

"And how is a marriage validated, my lord? Tell me that!"

The Earl turned away and stared out of the window. "I agree there will be a short time when you will be required to live with the man as his wife," he said shortly. "I am surprised this is distasteful to you. You are surely not claiming that your scruples would not permit it? You forget where and in what company I found you. This is not the time to claim any maidenly modesty—not to me, Perdita!''

She looked at his unrelenting back with something approaching despair. She would not do this thing he was asking, she knew that. But there seemed no way to reach him. The charming companion of the last weeks had turned into a monster. Surely love of Eliane could not have done this? "How will this plan of yours help your cousin?"

"Nothing will help my cousin," he replied, turning back into the room. "Her life is ruined. I explained that to you. But at least the man who destroyed her will live to regret it."

"But I don't understand how marriage to me will give him cause for regret. Other than the fact that I have nothing to offer him."

"He's an adventurer, Perdita. He lives on women. He ran off with Eliane because he thought she was rich, and abandoned her because she was poor. When the season opens in May he will be in London, looking for a rich heiress. He has to marry one very soon, or he will be thrown into Fleet Prison for debt. For the last two years he has been living off money he inherited in some way or other. Now that money has been gambled away and he is desperate for more. I will provide him with an attractive, modestly brought-up young lady with a rumoured fortune of thirty thousand pounds a year. He won't fail to take the bait. He would marry you if you squinted and had one leg. Your beauty will be a bonus."

He looked at her sombrely for a moment, then said, "By the time he realises that you haven't a penny to your name it will be too late for him. He will be ruined."

"But if you took me to London he would surely recognise you—if not your person, then your name. You can't do it, my lord; it's a mad scheme. And I won't help you.'' Her voice rose and she walked agitatedly to and fro.

The Earl was finding this interview more difficult than he had ever imagined. Perdita's distress perplexed and moved him, but he was none the less determined to carry his scheme through. ''You will not be presented under my aegis, Perdita. It would not do in any case, since I am a bachelor. I have a lady in mind to act as your sponsor in Society. She will do it for a fee, and she will act as your chaperon, too.''

He seemed to have considered everything. But however angry he might become he could not actually force her to marry this man. She went back to her original statement. ''I won't do it!''

The Earl turned on her angrily. ''I have waited for nearly four years to trap Piers Carston, Perdita. I am not going to be stopped now.''

She stood as if turned to stone. He thought she was going to faint and came to catch her arm, but she shook him off. ''Piers Carston? Is that his name?'' she said through lips that hardly moved.

''Yes. Perdita, I can see that this has been too much for you, and I think you should go to your room. But I warn you I will stop at very little to make Carston pay for what he has done to Eliane. Do you understand?''

''Yes,'' she said, making for the door. ''Yes, I understand. Please excuse me.'' She went swiftly out of the door and ran up the stairs as if pursued by the Furies.

The Earl, left in the library, sat brooding in front of the fire for some time. He had the feeling that he had just destroyed something precious, but did not know what it was. Then he thought of Eliane as she had been just before he'd left Ambourne to go to Vienna—a laughing, carefree girl, teasing him about his 'stuffy' work. That was the last he had seen of her until he'd found her in that filthy hole in London months later. Yes, he was right to act as he had planned. But why did he feel so out of sorts? He needed a hard ride round the estate to liven him up. As he got up to go, Sheikh Ibrahim's words came back to him: "...if, as I suspect, the 'weapon' is now lying sick in my apartments, then you must take care it does not rebound on you. To use human beings thus is dangerous."

Perdita reached her room, panting and dizzy, but she could not rest. She walked the length of the room and back again, to and fro, in a state of extreme agitation. Piers Carston! Piers Carston was intended as the victim of the Earl's plot! Even the name of Carston caused her to shiver with loathing, for the two men to whom she owed every misfortune were Piers Carston and his father, Frederick.

Memories that she had succeeded in repressing for years came flooding back to her—her gentle little mother, giving the news of her forthcoming marriage to Frederick Carston to her daughter. "You will see, he will be a new papa for you, my love. He's strong, and full of tender concern for both of us."

"I don't want a new papa; I loved the one I had, and I thought you did, too, Mama!"

"And so I did," her mother had said sadly, "but I have found life very difficult this last year. Taverton is a large estate and it needs a man's direction. I do not love Mr. Carston in the way I loved your father, but he is a good man and will look after both of us. Please don't be difficult, my darling. Life will be much more secure with Mr. Carston in charge."

Of course, that had been the trouble. Mr. Carston was not in charge, not really. Her father had left Taverton and all its rich acres in trust to his daughter, with a life interest for his wife, who would only own the estate outright if her daughter predeceased her. Perdita shuddered as she remembered the scene when Frederick Carston had discovered this. He had wanted to raise money by selling some of the land and found he could do nothing at all to the estate without the agreement of the trustees. He had bullied her mother mercilessly to attempt to have the terms of the trust changed, but this was one thing his gentle wife could not and would not do for him.

After that her new stepfather had changed almost overnight. Perdita had never liked him—his heavy white face and coarse features, his loud good humour and overbearing manners contrasted so sharply with her father's reserved charm. But now his good humour vanished except in the company of the London bucks he brought to stay, and he treated her mother with brutal contempt. Taverton was in Perdita's blood, for it had belonged to her family for generations. It now became a prison in which she could do nothing to help her mother, who was growing daily more fragile. The only solace in those dark times was Frederick Carston's son Piers, who was a frequent visitor and was everything his father was not. He had guinea-gold hair, frank blue eyes and a laughing, open countenance. He charmed her mother into an occasional smile, often made Perdita laugh and, whenever he could, bore the brunt of his father's ill humour. Perdita had reason to be grateful to him, looked forward to his visits, and was relieved and pleased when he decided to live at Taverton. When the crisis broke she readily turned to him for help.

A tap at the door brought her back to her room at Belleroi. "Who is it?" she asked, unwilling to see the Earl again until she had come to terms with this new and startling situation.

"It's me, Colette, *mademoiselle*. Can I come in?"

Colette probably wanted to go for a walk. Perdita had

been neglecting her recently because of her walks with the Earl. She went to the door and unlocked it.

"Why have you locked your door?" was Colette's inevitable question. But, without waiting for an answer, she went on, "It's a lovely afternoon, *mademoiselle*. Do come out. There are some bluebells in the wood I want to show you."

Colette's bright little face looking up so expectantly made Perdita's mind up. It would be better to give herself a respite from the emotional stress of the day, and a walk with Colette was just the thing. She found her pelisse and bonnet, and the two were soon outside and on their way to Colette's bluebells. These were duly admired, then they continued in the direction of Beau Lac.

In spite of Colette's chatter, Perdita was often lost in sad thoughts. Beau Lac looked forlorn in the spring sunshine, although some servants were certainly still there. Would Eliane ever return? Her mother might well decide that it held too many unhappy associations for Eliane to recover her spirits here. Where would they go? At the thought that she might never see Madame d'Harcourt and Eliane again Perdita grew even more melancholy. She caught Colette by the hand and said, "Come on, let's walk more quickly."

They went past Beau Lac and along a path winding away from the château through a small copse. Philippe was leaning morosely against a tree on the other side. Perdita didn't know what to do. She was still angry with him, but felt she could not ignore him. Colette would take in everything that was said, so serious conversation was out of the question anyway. Colette had no such inhibitions.

"Hello, Monsieur Fourget; how is Yvette? My cousin Henri says he's going to marry her. Have you heard the news from Beau Lac? Mademoiselle Eliane is dying."

Perdita felt as if she had had a blow to the heart. She cried, "Colette, where did you hear that? It's not true! It can't be!"

"Yes, it is! Grandmère said so," asserted Colette firmly.

Philippe was staring at Colette as a rabbit stared at a stoat. "No!" he said hoarsely. "No! It can't be true. It mustn't be."

Then without another word he ran wildly off into the trees. They could hear him crashing through the undergrowth.

"He's funny. Why did he go like that, *mademoiselle*?"

"When did your Grandmother say that, Colette—about Mademoiselle Eliane?" asked Perdita urgently, ignoring Colette's question.

"Oh, I don't remember... Yes, I do—it was before I fell down the hole. She said Monsieur le Marquis had gone to Paris because Mademoiselle Eliane was dying. There! So, you see, it is true, *mademoiselle*."

Perdita was breathless with relief. "That was a long time ago, Colette! And Mademoiselle Eliane is no longer in danger."

"Isn't she? That's good. Have you seen those ducks over there, *mademoiselle*? I think they're going to land on the lake. Can we go and see them?"

They spent some time looking at ducks, and then returned to the château. Perdita felt that the walk had not exactly fulfilled its purpose of calming her nerves, for Colette's bombshell had taken its toll. And poor Philippe now believed that Eliane was dying. He would soon find out his mistake, but meanwhile his reaction was most interesting. It hadn't been that of a man who genuinely believed she was better dead. She went up to her room, pondering on Philippe and Eliane. If only there was a chance, even the slightest, that they would find some happiness together.

That would be a far better outcome than any schemes hatched by the Earl. That thought recalled her own situation. What was she to do?

The meal that evening was a fairly silent one. Perdita was occupied with her own thoughts, and the Earl was reluctant to break in on them. He had asked her before the meal whether she had reconsidered her opposition to her part in his scheme, and she had replied briefly that she preferred to wait until the next day before discussing it. This seemed to be so much of an advance from her original position that he was content to let it lie.

Perdita sat at her window that night, thinking of Piers Carston. When she had first heard Eliane's story it had seemed strange that a gently bred girl, who had led such a protected life, should have acted so boldly in running off with the man who'd betrayed her. Now that she knew the man's name she understood perfectly. Piers Carston was a charming, smiling, plausible, ruthless villain—far more dangerous than his father because he seemed so trustworthy. With what sincere anxiety he had lied to her mother as she'd lain seriously ill! How protective he had seemed while he had been plotting to remove Perdita from the scene! Once again scenes from the past haunted her during the long night.

"My darling child, you must go away from here," her mother had whispered to her, clutching her arm and trying to raise herself.

"Mama, don't agitate yourself so. You must rest. How else will you get better?" Perdita had tried to put her back against the pillows but her mother had refused.

"I mean what I say; you must escape before it is too late! I am not going to get better, my dear. But you must go away from here before I die!"

"I can't do that, Mama. You need me here!"

"Your stepfather—oh, God, I can't say it. Your stepfather will do anything to inherit the estate—even murder!"

"That's not possible! He's not a good man, mama, but he's not capable of murder. No, I don't believe it!"

"His own son tells me so. If I die before you the estate will pass out of Mr. Carston's reach. But if you are dead, then he will inherit all through me. Now do you believe me?"

"Piers told you... How can he say this of his father?"

Her mother had lain back, exhausted, her face pale and her lips colourless. "He was very distressed. I felt such pity for him, but I believe him. You must go, my child. Piers will help you."

Perdita's eyes filled with tears as she remembered how her mother had pleaded with her. At first she'd refused to think of it, but then a coping stone from the roof had narrowly missed her as she'd walked on the terrace, the girth of her saddle had come mysteriously unfastened as she rode, and Piers had slowly convinced her, telling her that her mother would die in peace if she could know that her daughter was safe. Even now, three years later, Perdita could not bring herself to think of the parting with her mother, but she sat for a moment, clasping her hands in anguish, staring out on the moonlit garden.

Piers had suggested that he take her to his friends in Bristol, where she could stay for a while. Though neither of them had said it, they'd both known it would be until her mother's death. At least, that was what she had thought. He had been so considerate, had seemed so profoundly moved at her distress. The truth had never entered her head, not for one second, until they had got near Bristol and he'd drawn the chaise to the side of the road. It was nearly dark.

"I have a better plan," he'd said. "If we were to marry, you would be safe with me. I wouldn't allow my father to harm you."

She hadn't known what to say. It was the last thing she wanted, but she didn't want to hurt him by saying so. "You are kind, Piers, and I'm grateful for all you've done. But I can't marry you. I like and respect you as a brother…"

"But you could learn to love me differently," he said, smiling at her with boyish charm.

Her parting with her mother, the strain of the last weeks, had stretched her nerves to the limit. Though she tried for calm, her voice was impatient as she said, "No, Piers, I could not. I cannot marry you. I will not marry. I do not love you enough. Let us say no more on this subject. Please take me to your friends."

She should have taken warning there. Any normal man of honour would have heard the waver in her voice and taken pity on her. But he persisted.

"I don't believe you mean what you say, my sweet. It's only your inexperience that makes you talk like this. Can you imagine what it is like between a man and a woman? When they kiss and lie with one another and make love? Once I've taught you, my lovely one, you'll change your mind about me."

He tried to take hold of her and she struggled violently. She had never before been held so closely by a man, and his sudden attack put her into a panic. She hit out wildly, causing him to lose his balance, and he hit the side of the open chaise. He missed his footing, tried and failed to grab the rail, and fell to the road. While he lay there, dazed, she seized her opportunity, whipped the horses into action and drove them away in a frenzy of fear. She was desperate to get to a place of safety.

On the outskirts of Bristol she came to an inn. Trembling with cold and fear, she entered the parlour... It was like no place she had ever seen before. Living, as she did, in a remote corner of Somerset, surrounded by people she had known all her life, she had never seen the seamier side of life. Only desperation would have driven her into a strange inn now. This was a most unhappy choice. Even in the parlour the floor was covered with filthy sawdust. The settle in the corner may once have been red damask cushions, but now it sagged drunkenly against the wall, covered in greasy, greyish tatters.

A woman came into the parlour from the taproom. "Oh, la-di-da," she said in an affected voice. "Wot 'ave we 'ere? A *laidy*, no less!"

"Please...please, I need your help!" Perdita said.

"Wot's the matter, dearie? 'Ad a bit of a tumble, 'ave yer?" The woman gave a raucous laugh and summoned the men in the taproom to inspect the new mort come to pay a visit.

The girl now realised that she had made a very big mistake in hurrying in to the first inn she had come to. If only she had inspected it from outside! A more experienced traveller could have told her that inns on the outskirts of large towns, especially seaports, were seldom patronised by honest people. What better place to meet in secret than an inn near enough to the port for the smuggler or sea robber, near enough to the countryside for the highwayman or footpad, and far enough out of the town to avoid the unwelcome attentions of the watch?

She started to retreat to the door, but found her way blocked by a tall negro dressed in the loose trousers and striped shirt of a sailor. She moved away in terror as he grinned and mouthed words she did not understand at her. The rest howled with laughter, but suddenly fell silent as another sailor came in from the taproom. He limped slowly across to her, then turned to the others and said in a husky voice with a strong French accent, ''Where's Carston?''

Several voices assured him that they hadn't laid eyes on him.

''He's late,'' the Frenchman said, examining the girl with eyes that were almost black. ''Who's this?'' Anxiously the ungodly crew hastened to tell him they didn't know. He seemed to exercise some kind of power over them.

Perdita remembered how afraid she had been, and yet how proudly she had faced him.

''I am Miss Taverton of Taverton Hall,'' she said. ''I am on my way to Bristol to visit friends, and met with a...with a...an accident on the way. I see that there is no suitable accommodation here and I would like to be allowed to leave. Now.''

The crowd roared with laughter, conjuring each other to listen to her fancy speech. One of the women sidled over and caught her skirt.

''That's a nice dress, dearie,'' she said. ''I'd like that dress, I would. Perhaps yer'd like to give it me, ay?'' She started pulling at the dress, but the man with the limp put his hand on her shoulder. She gave a squeal of pain and scuttled away, rubbing the shoulder and looking resentfully at him.

''Leave her alone, Peg—until Carston comes. Then we'll know what to do with her. You can have the dress afterwards, if she doesn't need it any more.'' Once again the Frenchman boldly examined her. ''Though, if Carston hasn't a use for her, I know a thing or two I'd like to try...'' He turned and winked at the crowd, who responded with sly leers and obscene gestures. Suddenly he cocked his head. ''Someone's coming!''

In a flash half the occupants of the room had disappeared. The negro waited behind the door and the Frenchman stood facing it, his hand resting on a knife stuck in his belt.

Piers Carston appeared in the doorway, his clothing dishevelled and a bruise on his forehead. Three scratches ran down the side of his face. "Have you got her here?" he said menacingly as he came into the room. "Have you got her here, Legrand?"

But Legrand didn't answer straight away. He bared yellow teeth in a smile as he said, "What's happened Carston? Something has spoiled your pretty face for you. Was it..." he dropped his voice in an affected drawl "...was it Miss Taverton of Taverton Hall? Was the pretty boy unable to defend himself, then?"

He laughed, and sidestepped as Carston lunged for him. The girl, seeing the two men engaged, made a frantic dash to escape, but she was caught by the large negro at the door. Piers Carston whirled round and saw her. A look of fury made his face ugly for a moment, then a slow, cruel smile appeared.

"So you found my friends after all, my love. Let her go, Renard."

Though she was released, the three men surrounded her. She was sick with fear, but would not let them see it. Piers brought his face close to hers.

"Are you afraid, Miss Taverton of Taverton Hall? You should be, for I don't allow this—" he touched his face "—to go unpunished."

"We've got business to discuss. Leave the girl," said Legrand brusquely. "You can deal with her later."

"No!" Piers shouted. "She's going to pay now. I wasn't good enough for Miss High and Mighty, and she's going to pay for that too!" He gave the girl an almighty shove. She staggered, but was regaining her balance when he hit her. This time she went sprawling on to the filthy floor, hit her head on the leg of a settle and knew no more.

The gardens of Belleroi slowly grew visible in the early-morning light. Perdita could hear sounds in the kitchen—a new day was beginning.

CHAPTER TEN

PERDITA GOT UP and stretched herself wearily. In little more than an hour Jeanne would be coming in with hot water for her morning toilet, and she had not even been to bed. Reliving the terror of that fateful night had left her feeling drained, and in order not to upset her maid's susceptibilities she undressed and got into bed.

She smiled slightly as she thought of Jeanne. The little maid had become devoted to her mistress, forever coaxing her to try new ways of dressing her hair, and bemoaning the fact that Perdita was so indifferent to the way she looked. During Perdita's enforced rest she had been a constant companion, fetching small delicacies from the kitchen and bathing Perdita's temples with lavender water. Still thinking of Jeanne, she fell most unexpectedly asleep.

She woke later, feeling more refreshed than she would have imagined. Jeanne must have been in, for hot water was steaming in the jug on her wash-stand. She would return shortly to help her mistress to dress. Perdita leapt out of bed and busied herself. By the time Jeanne came she was standing by the window again, looking at the garden.

"As *mademoiselle* sees, it is a lovely day, but not, I think, yet warm enough for anything light. Would *mademoiselle* like to wear the blue merino today? Or the green wool?"

Perdita almost laughed at the expression on Jeanne's

face, for her maid made no secret of the fact that she considered Perdita's wardrobe woefully inadequate.

"I don't know, Jeanne. You choose."

Jeanne chose, as Perdita knew she would, the blue merino. She admired Perdita's eyes and was always looking for ways to enhance their dark blue beauty. After Jeanne had twisted Perdita's hair into a knot on top of her head, not without her usual plea for a more elegant style, Perdita breakfasted and went downstairs. The Earl was out with his agent, so she had a peaceful morning with Père Amboise, who had just reread the *Iliad* and had a new theory on the location of Troy.

The Earl had still not returned at midday, so Perdita ate a light meal alone in the small parlour. Then, after looking in vain for Colette, she went out for a walk. This time she decided to avoid Beau Lac with its shuttered windows, and went instead to the front of the château.

The advancing season was softening the lines of the flowerbeds and lawns, and the twin lodges had a hazy background of young green branches. After her sleepless night the fresh spring air was like champagne. She walked for some time, going out of the drive and through to the other side of the village. Finally she took a rest on a bench in front of a small country inn. The landlord's apple-cheeked wife came to ask her if she wanted anything and stayed to chat for a few minutes. She knew who Perdita was—her sister's husband's niece, Jeanne, was *mademoiselle*'s maid, and Colette was her husband's great niece. Perdita knew this kind of network of relationships from her own home in Somerset, and she and *madame* chatted amicably for a quarter of an hour.

It might have been that Perdita was more tired than she realised, or it might have been that the talk with *madame* had once again reminded her of the past, but for whatever reason the château seemed depressingly far away on the return journey. Perdita was lost in unhappy thought as she walked up the long drive. She was remembering the last time she had seen Piers Carston. It had been in the inn…

When she came to she was on the floor of the inn, and her hands and feet were tied so tightly that she was unable to move them. Piers and the Frenchman were sitting at a crude table, and she could hear the clink of money.

"That's the last, I think," said Legrand's voice.

"I like the pearl. I think I have a customer for that—how much do you want for it?"

"Not so fast, my dear friend. What about the shipping information? What have you got for me?"

"The *Isabel* is due in Bristol on the twelfth of May—she'll have a cargo of silks and spices from the Levant. She may even have some gold. But better than that is the *Fair Maid of Richmond*. She's carrying gold bullion out of Istanbul to London, calling at Marseilles on the twenty-seventh of next month. Can you do it?"

"Don't you concern yourself with that. You look after the information, and I'll catch the cargoes. What else do you have for me?"

"That's all I can do for the moment. We've been too successful, Legrand. So many cargoes have been pirated in the Mediterranean recently that the people at Lloyds are getting suspicious, and I'll have to tread very carefully for a while. What's wrong?"

"Your little termagant is awake, I think. I wonder how much she heard?"

The girl on the floor shut her eyes quickly, but it was too late. She heard him get up and come across; then cruel fingers were pinching her chin. When she opened her eyes the Frenchman was bending over her and the smell of his sweat was in her nose. "Very nice," he said. "Very nice!'' She tried to roll away, but he easily stopped her with his hand on her body.

Piers came over to join him. ''What are we going to do?''

''That's your affair, my friend. Tomorrow I'll be away from here and safe on the high seas again. But if you want to get rid of her I'll take her off your hands.''

''She's worth something,'' said Piers.

''She's worth a hanging to you, Carston, if she heard your talk back there and passes it on,'' said Legrand, smiling wolfishly.

This thought hadn't occurred to Piers. He said slowly, ''What'll you give me for her? What's more, can you guarantee she won't come back—ever?''

Legrand pushed the girl with his foot while he considered. ''I can guarantee that, sure enough. But what I'll give...let me see...''

The girl could not help herself. She looked at her stepbrother with terror in her dark blue eyes. ''Please,'' she whispered hoarsely. ''I beg you, Piers, don't send me with him!''

Piers stood by Legrand, looking down at her. His face was as handsome as ever, blue eyes in an open face, red-gold hair tumbling over his forehead. Only the three scratches and the dark bruise marred his looks. He smiled charmingly.

''Oh, Miss Taverton,'' he said softly. ''You should have married me when you could. I was willing to win the Taverton fortune by fair means. Now I have a double—no, triple reason to change my mind. If Legrand here will lose you for me there's a good chance the estates will eventually come to me, anyway—if your damned mother stays alive long enough. If you're allowed to tell others what you heard tonight I could hang. And...'' he fingered the bruise "...I really cannot let this go unpunished, can I? No, Miss Taverton, if Legrand pays me enough you will go with him. How much, Legrand? What about the pearl?"

"You're surely not serious? That pearl is worth at least fifty guineas."

"On the open market, perhaps. Not otherwise."

The girl struggled violently in her bonds. She screamed, "Piers, don't do it! Please don't! Oh, God, I beg you not to!"

"You should have counted my virtues before you said you wouldn't marry me, my dear. It's too late now. Gag her, Legrand; I can't think when she's caterwauling."

Legrand went to tie a dirty handkerchief round the girl's mouth. She renewed her struggles, kicking her tied feet, twisting her head and biting. When he had finished he wiped his fingers, looking down at her thoughtfully, and said, "I could enjoy taming this one... If you give me the girl and thirty guineas I'll let you have the pearl. But what are you going to tell her people?"

"Oh, I don't know. Some story of being knocked out by footpads—this bruise will help to make it convincing. Then when I came to she was gone. Give me her scarf— I'll put some blood on it. This was all I found of her— you wouldn't believe how distraught I'll sound. Her mother will feel almost as sorry for me as for herself. Where's the pearl? Goodbye, Legrand. Goodbye, Miss Taverton, and good riddance! Enjoy your voyage!"

With a mocking bow he was gone. That was the last she had seen of him. She was taken in a closed cart, still gagged and bound, held tight by the negro. They went on board a small fishing vessel, where she was released from her bonds and locked in the cabin. After three days she was transferred to a larger vessel, which was called *Le Faucon*.

The nightmare that had begun in a sleazy inn near Bristol went on for more than two long years. The second time she was brought back to him after trying to escape Legrand gave her two pieces of news. Her mother had died a month after her daughter had disappeared, and the Carstons were living at Taverton.

Perdita sat down suddenly on one of the ornamental seats on the side of the drive. She had no doubt at all that she was going to agree to the scheme the Earl had so carefully prepared. She could, and would, bring ruin to Piers Carston in her own time. It would not be quite as the Earl had planned, but he wouldn't know that until the last possible minute. If, after the closeness they had experienced on their walks together, he was willing to use her in such an ugly fashion, then she could use him to get her to London and give her a background until she struck. As she sat there weaving her plans, the Sheikh's words came to her:

"Hatred is destructive. You might or might not succeed in destroying the object of your hatred. You will certainly succeed in destroying your own happiness."

She jumped up and walked impatiently along the drive to the château. Her hatred for Piers Carston had kept her alive these past years. She would not relinquish it now. As for Lord Ambourne—he was uninterested in her courage and spirit. He merely demanded her obedience. Well, he would have it—up to a point.

She dressed carefully for dinner that night, allowing Jeanne to arrange her hair in a more becoming style. The blue jaconet muslin was a foil to her dark hair, and her precious cashmere shawl gave her warmth and colour. She found that the Earl had also dressed formally in dark blue tailcoat, black breeches and a diamond pin in his immaculately tied cravat. They could have been any couple in fashionable Society. The Earl talked of the work going forward on the estate, and Perdita mentioned her meeting with the landlady on the other side of the village.

"Ah, yes," said the Earl, "Masson's wife. Between them they're related to three-quarters of the village. I don't suppose you escaped under half an hour, did you?"

Perdita was relieved that he made no comment on her going out alone, and indeed, since the adventure with Colette, he had not insisted on her being accompanied when he was not with her. She amused him with her lively report of Madame Masson's conversation.

After dinner she and the Earl went into the library. He waited while she sat down, then he stood by the fire and asked, "Well, Perdita? Which is it to be? Do I have your co-operation? Or will I be forced to remind you of the alternatives? I am persuaded the Pasha would take you back with pleasure—especially if you are looking as charming as you do tonight. He might even keep you for himself."

She said calmly, "I do not believe you would send me back to the Pasha. However, I will admit I am loath to put you to the test!" One slender hand was clenched as she asked, "You have known me for some time now, Lord Ambourne. We have discovered in each other a similarity of taste and temperament, and I at least have found pleasure in our recent walks and discussions. Are you still resolved to marry me to a man you know to be a heartless villain, to force me to live with him as his wife, to ask me to withstand his fury when he first discovers we have tricked him?"

The Earl was pale and his face was set. "I have told you my reasons. I do not propose to abandon my plans because of...because of a certain sympathy that has grown between us."

He looked down at her bowed head and clenched fist, and said in a softened tone, "Perdita, believe me, I would not do this if there were any other way."

For a moment she hesitated, half wanting to reveal the truth, but then he turned to the fire and continued harshly, "But, since there is not, I must use you as I planned to use you from the beginning when I rescued you in Algiers."

"You *bought* me," she said bitterly. "But at least you thought I was worth a pearl."

"Don't speak like this, Perdita! I will protect you as much as I can from Carston's fury. Afterwards I will see that you have a home and a source of income. What more can I do?"

"Nothing," she said. "I will do as you wish, Lord Ambourne."

He was conscious of feeling a curious mixture of relief and disappointment. Now that he had achieved his goal he realised that half of him had hoped she would continue to refuse. This confusion of mind was totally alien to his keen and decisive intellect, and he was relieved when Perdita asked if she might retire early. He needed time to restore order to his thoughts. It was past midnight when he finally went to bed, but he had mastered his weakness and was once again calmly resolved. Perdita had agreed, and they would work together to achieve his goal.

THE NEXT TIME Perdita saw the Earl he was sitting behind his desk, writing a note. In front of him lay a letter, much crossed and recrossed, which had been brought that morning. He replied absently to Perdita's greeting, finished his note and addressed it, then stood up and said, "Forgive me; I was somewhat preoccupied with my letter. Have you slept well? No second thoughts in the night?" Perdita assured him of her determination to help him in his aim. He nodded, then said, "This is a devilish thing! My mother is in Paris with Eliane and my aunt."

Perdita looked surprised. "Is that not desirable? I should have thought your aunt would welcome any support the family can give her."

"It's not that," he said impatiently. "I'm glad, of course I'm glad that Tante Marguerite has my mother to look to. No, it's just that Paris is too near Belleroi, that's all. My mother is perfectly capable of taking it into her head to visit me here and, much as I love her, the last thing I want at the moment is the distraction of a visit. Hence the note."

Perdita thought she understood. It would be embarrassing if his mother found her at Belleroi. Perhaps she could stay with Madame d'Espery during the Countess's visit? She was about to suggest this when the Earl excused himself and left the room. She was left to her own devices.

He returned a short while later smiling with satisfaction. "She'll get that before she has time to think of coming here. Now it's time to tell you of the lady I have engaged to chaperon you in London. She's unusual, but socially very acceptable."

For the rest of the time they were together he carried on telling Perdita about the people she would meet, and the image he wished her to create. "Young, innocent, a little simple, even—but I'm sure your powers of dissimulation will be up to it, Perdita."

She realised he was being deliberately provoking, but did not rise to it. If Lord Ambourne wished her to be a tool, then a tool she would be. Her energies were now channelled into arriving in London with her own plans complete.

She spent the next morning with Madame d'Espery, and was pleased to accept an invitation to nuncheon.

"Just a small repast, *mademoiselle*. I dine early and do not take much at midday."

The "small repast" proved to be so filling that she felt in need of fresh air and exercise. She walked over the fields and through the wood before coming back to the château. After tidying herself she went to the music-room, where she played for half an hour or more, finishing with one of her favourite, rather mournful airs. Eliane had been much in her mind. How would she react if she knew what her friend and her cousin were planning? Perdita did not deceive herself. What she and the Earl were doing was meant to satisfy their own feelings towards Piers Carston. As the Earl had said, nothing they were doing could put Eliane's life back together again. She put her hands on the keys and sighed.

"Oh, dear," said a voice behind her. "Don't do that. You'll blow the piano away."

For an instant she thought it was Madame d'Harcourt, and whirled round to greet her in delighted surprise. But, though Perdita could see a resemblance, the lady sitting in the large armchair had an air of gaiety about her that Madame d'Harcourt had never possessed. And her dress of striped *Gros de Naples* silk, with its slightly lower waist and flounced skirt, her beautifully dressed pale gold hair, showed a consciousness of fashion very far removed from Madame d'Harcourt's sober attire.

"I'm Ambourne's mother," said the lady, smiling at Perdita's astonishment.

"Forgive me, ma'am. I…I…" In great confusion, Perdita got up and curtseyed.

As she rose, the Countess said, "I know, I know. I've put you all in a bustle by arriving so unexpectedly. It's good for you, don't you think? Life can be very dull if we always know in advance what is going to happen. I can't wait to see Edward's face! Do you know where he is?''

Perdita pulled herself together and thought. The Earl was visiting one of the outlying farms, but would be back shortly. She told his mother as much and added, ''Forgive me, ma'am, but did you not receive Lord Ambourne's note? Oh, how stupid of me, of course you couldn't have. He only despatched it yesterday.''

''I expect he told me not to come,'' said the Earl's mother complacently. ''That's why I set out before I could possibly get a reply to my letter. Besides, I have things to do at Belleroi and Beau Lac now, and Edward shan't interfere. You must be Mademoiselle Taver?'' Once again in confusion, Perdita acknowledged this to be true. ''My sister has told me a great deal about you. You were good for Eliane, *mademoiselle*—''

''Oh, ma'am, how was Eliane when you left her?''

The Countess smiled at Perdita's impulsive question, then grew grave. ''She is making a slow recovery. I have persuaded my sister to bring her back to Beau Lac soon. But don't stand there, child. Come and sit down beside me.''

''Lady Ambourne, I really ought not to be here,'' began Perdita bravely. ''Lord Ambourne will be distressed if he finds us together like this.''

''Rubbish, child! You're not his mistress, are you?''

Perdita gasped and shook her head vehemently.

''That's good, because, if you were, then, I agree, it wouldn't be quite the thing, would it? Imagine Edward's face!'' She went off into a peal of laughter. ''As for Edward being distressed...I'm sorry to tell you, my dear, but that I cannot imagine. Irritated, perhaps. Annoyed that his wishes have been ignored. But distressed, no! Besides, Edward has already told me about you.''

"Told you? He's told you? About me?" Perdita exclaimed in horror.

"Well, I suspect he hasn't told me quite everything. And anyway, he doesn't know all of it, does he? I don't somehow think my son knows of the existence of Miss Taver, for example."

The Countess watched in evident enjoyment as Perdita's face grew scarlet with embarrassment. Then she said, "You know, *mademoiselle*, I get very bored at home in Ambourne with nobody but the servants and a shockingly dowdy cousin of Ambourne's to keep me company. And I went to Paris out of a sense of duty to my sister. I really didn't expect such a delightfully intriguing set of circumstances as I have found here. I will not be satisfied until I have fathomed it all. How interesting it is going to be!"

Perdita said hollowly that she hoped the Countess would not be disappointed, but was saved from any further comment by the sound of the Earl's arrival. While the two ladies listened, one appreciatively, the other apprehensively, the Earl exclaimed, questioned the servant further and then came striding into the music-room.

"Mama, what a delightful surprise!" he said as he bent to kiss her cheek.

"Edward, you have the best manners of all the men in my acquaintance. I cannot imagine where you acquired them!"

"Come now, Mama, you do not do yourself justice. And, if your flattery is meant to distract me from asking you why you did not let me know sooner that you were coming, then I assure you it is not necessary. I am well aware of your reasons! How is my cousin?"

"She is well enough to be moved, and I have persuaded Marguerite to bring her back to Beau Lac. That's why I am here. But, Edward, you are very remiss. Have you not observed your ward? She looks delightful, does she not? Are you not going to introduce me?''

Perdita had moved to the window when the Earl had come in. He now turned and saw her there.

"If I know my mother, Perdita, she has already made a bosom friend of you. She does not normally wait for formal introductions. However, since it is her whim...Mama may I introduce Mademoiselle..." the Earl paused and his mother's eyes danced wickedly as he looked at a loss; but he regained his urbanity "...Mademoiselle Perdita, my ward. My mother, the Countess of Ambourne and Marquise de Belleroi, *mademoiselle*.''

As Perdita curtsyed for the second time she looked up at the Countess. Was she about to have her friendship with the d'Harcourts revealed? But no. The Countess said with a solemn face, belied only by the laughter in her eyes, "I am enchanted to make your acquaintance, *mademoiselle*. I have heard so much about you."

The Earl looked startled. He had surely not told his mother as much as that? Perdita's lips twitched. This was pure farce! Each of them knew something one or both of the others did not know. How long would the conjuring trick last?

CHAPTER ELEVEN

THE COUNTESS'S relationship with her son was a revelation to Perdita. She teased him, exasperated him, tested his patience to its limits with her impulsive promises to the tenants. But he always ended by indulging her, and was clearly devoted to her. Perdita herself was rapidly falling victim to her charm, and a warm friendship developed between the Countess and 'Miss Taver', as she was teasingly called whenever she and the Countess were alone. However, her tormentor soon tired of that, and in a surprisingly short time was calling her son's ward 'Perdita'.

The Countess was as musical as her sister, and she and Perdita frequently spent time together in the music-room. This was where the Earl found them one morning. The two ladies were seated side by side at the piano and were a sight to please the eye of the most impartial observer. Inside the high-standing collar of Perdita's blue merino was a saucy little ruff the Countess had insisted on giving her. The Countess herself was wearing lilac. Her son was unmoved by this picture, however.

"Mama," he said dangerously as he entered the room, "Mama, am I to infer from Masson's comments to me this morning that you have promised to have the roof of the inn repaired before next Tuesday?"

"Of course I have, dear. The rain is coming in."

"Perhaps you are unaware that Etienne has drawn up a careful schedule for re-roofing the houses in the village.

Large numbers of them suffered in the February gale, and Masson should wait his turn.''

''Oh, do you think I shouldn't have interfered? But Masson has always been so kind to us, Edward, and his daughter is coming back home to have her baby in a month. Masson's wife was most distressed. I really couldn't not promise, wouldn't you say?'' she said cajolingly.

''No, I would not, Mama. Etienne is going to have the devil's own job explaining it to the others.''

''I don't think you should use language like that in front of Perdita, dear. I, of course, am used to it. But I'm glad you've agreed about Masson's roof.''

He left the room with an exasperated groan and Masson had his roof by Tuesday.

This was not the only episode of its kind. Perdita marvelled that a man who normally had little patience for the foibles of others, and who was so disciplined in his own emotions, should be so indulgent with his wayward mother. When she expressed her surprise the Countess said, ''That's because he loves me, my love. He's just like his dear father. When I first met Charles he seemed the completely traditional Englishman—so cold, so...logical! But somehow, after really quite a short time, I found he was just the man for me. I defied my family to marry him, and I never regretted it. All his life people who did not know him as I did thought him cold. But with me he was the most loving, most indulgent husband a woman could ask for.''

The Countess wiped her eyes with a tiny lace handkerchief. ''I miss him a great deal. That's why I find Ambourne so depressing. And I think Edward will be exactly like his father; it's just that he hasn't yet found the right woman to be his wife. And since the trouble with Eliane he has been obsessed with punishing Piers Carston. He thinks he failed her when she was his responsibility. That's why he's so set on this wretched plan he talks of. I haven't asked for the details; I'm afraid to. He means to ruin Carston, so much I know. But Eliane has had enough to bear. She cannot stand any more notoriety. She needs peace!''

Perdita squeezed the small hand in hers. If the Earl hadn't told his mother what he proposed to do then she could not betray his confidence. She said what she could.

''If you are afraid of scandal, or even danger, ma'am, then let me reassure you. Piers Carston will not harm Eliane or any of your family again, I promise.''

''So you *do* know something of it. I suspected as much. And Edward means to include you in his scheme?''

Perdita withdrew her hands. ''You must ask your son that, Lady Ambourne. I cannot tell you. But, whatever he says, remember my promise. There will be no danger to you or your family. And now, may I remind you that you promised to show me the dresses you bought in Paris?''

They spent the rest of the morning looking at the Countess's wardrobe, which was extensive, and by tacit agreement their conversation in the music-room was not referred to again. But, while she admired the delicate muslins, the *Gros de Naples* and barège silk dresses and the velvet pelisses, Perdita was aware that the Countess occasionally looked at her with sympathetic speculation.

Since the advent of the Countess life had become at once more formal and more lively. She hated to be without company, and a dinner party that did not have at least half a dozen covers she regarded as a bore. She said as much one night at dinner. In tones of deepest gloom the Earl said, ''Alas, Perdita, we have failed in our attempts to entertain my mother. We must face the fact that we are dull fellows and not allow ourselves to be too cast down by it. But it is hard, especially for an only son!''

The Countess laughed and replied, "What rubbish you talk! How can I not enjoy my son's company? And Perdita is a darling. I must tell you, Edward, if she were my companion, instead of that boringly frowsty female relative of yours, I would not have to leave Ambourne so often."

The Earl raised his brows and protested, "Cousin Enid is a woman of sense and respectability, and well known for her charitable works. You ought not to be so unflattering in your description of her, Mama."

"There you are! As I said, the woman is a bore! Perdita, you surely agree with me?"

"Since I do not know the lady in question, ma'am, I cannot comment," smiled Perdita, holding up her hand.

"Yes, but would you describe me as a woman of sense and respectability? Ugh!" said the Countess, pronouncing the words as if they were insults.

Perdita laughed and said, "I think your son would be angry with me if I were to say you were not respectable, ma'am. And I am sure you have more sense than most people of my acquaintance!"

The Earl sat back, enjoying the exchange between the two women. They made a pleasant picture. His mother's face was alight with enjoyment, and the candlelight reflected the sparkle of diamonds at her throat and the sheen of her ruched wine-red silk dress. Perdita had laughter in her eyes too. She was wearing her pink silk, and, though she looked as lovely as ever, the Earl frowned slightly as he considered the simple way in which her hair was gathered on top of her head, and her lack of adornment. Was her maid incompetent? He must consult his mother.

His mother was observing her son with just as much interest. It seemed to her that Edward's eyes strayed constantly to his lovely...ward? Edward had told her a little of his plan for Perdita. He had sworn that he would see that she came to no harm, but how could he be sure? However, the Countess felt that Carston would find Perdita a more difficult prey than Eliane. Edward had not said a great deal about Perdita, but the Countess could see that she was no vulnerable child. Though there was an innocence about her, it did not stem from ignorance, and the girl had courage and intelligence. But why had Perdita not told Edward about her visits to Beau Lac? Her sister had talked at length of Perdita's kindness and charm, but Edward was not even aware that they knew one another. That was curious. How fortunate it was that she had come to Belleroi! Meanwhile she would insist that they did some entertaining. Apart from anything else she wanted to see Perdita's company manners. And she must talk to her son about clothes for the girl...

As a result of this Perdita found herself in possession of two or three very pretty dresses for the evening and a maid who was jubilant at being requested by no less a personage than Madame la Marquise herself to find new styles for Perdita's hair. Each evening from then on was enlivened by visits from the members of local society.

"And very tedious people most of them are, too," said the Countess one night after what had seemed a particularly long dinner. "I thought I should die of boredom during Monsieur de Sardet's eulogy of his estate—and especially his tale of the heifer. What on earth is a heifer, Edward?"

"It's a kind of cow, Mama. And you should not complain so of your guests—you insisted on inviting them. Most of them are only too glad to be back. After all, it's only three years since the monarchy was restored."

"There's another thing," said his mother. "Why do we have to have such a clod for a king? You may say what you choose about Louis XVI—he at least had style!"

"Style enough to get his head cut off, Mama. It's a new world we live in now, and Louis XVIII is doing his best. If the old aristocrats aren't able to change, then there'll be a second revolution. Let's hope it's less bloody than the first."

"Edward, why are we talking of such things? Perdita, I thought you looked particularly charming tonight; do you not think so, Edward? That jonquil muslin is very becoming. And Jeanne is growing skilful with your hair; I must tell her so when I see her. The flowers are an excellent idea."

Jeanne had parted Perdita's hair in the centre and, leaving a few curls to fall on her temples, had swept the rest back, twisted it and arranged it *à l'antique*. One or two tiny yellow roses were tucked into the back at the top. The Earl lazily admired this vision until Perdita moved restlessly and asked if they would give her leave to retire. The Countess looked disappointed, but Perdita left them in the salon and went upstairs.

Then came the news that Madame d'Harcourt and Eliane were returning within the week. The Countess immediately went down to Beau Lac to see that the house was suitably prepared.

"It's an old house, Perdita, and needs a great deal of heating up. I know—my family lived there in the old days."

"But, ma'am, I thought you lived at Belleroi!"

"Oh, no! My father was a younger son. All we had was Beau Lac. It wasn't until my uncle died that we inherited Belleroi, and there was no money, you know. I brought Ambourne a very poor dowry, but then he said all he wanted was me! My sister was not so fortunate, for her husband left very little. That's why—'' her face clouded over ''—that's why Carston abandoned Eliane. He thought she was rich, and she was not. But let us put these sad thoughts behind us, Perdita. Let us make Beau Lac so beautiful that Eliane will be happy to return! What is wrong? Why the sad face?''

''Eliane may be unable to enjoy Beau Lac, ma'am. I think she will be reminded of Philippe.''

''Philippe? Ah...I see. The young man from Paris?''

''Not Paris, ma'am. He lives quite close, at Vauvron. His name is Fourget.''

''Fourget? Fourget...not old Sansculotte Fourget's son? The Republican? I'd heard he was back in Normandy. Living in retirement, no doubt, the traitor!''

It was obvious that the Countess shared the prejudice of the local aristocrats towards the Fourget family, but Perdita decided to confide in her all the same.

''It is my opinion that Philippe still loves Eliane, ma'am. He found it impossible to face her when he learned she was not as innocent as he thought her. But when he thought she was dying he took it very badly.''

''Are you suggesting that Eliane might conceivably marry Fourget's son?''

Perdita replied bravely, ''If they can be brought together again I think it would be an ideal match. Philippe is really neither weak nor a fool. And, if he has discovered he loves Eliane in spite of what he knows, then I think he would look after her and love her in the way she needs.''

The Countess thought for a moment and then said briskly, ''Well, Perdita, what must we do to find out if Philippe has thought better? That seems to me to be the first step—and not the most difficult one. When I think of Eliane's state and my sister's reaction, my opinion of Fourget, not to mention my son's... What are you leading me into?''

"Perhaps Eliane's happiness, ma'am. At least we could try!"

However, Philippe proved to be away, so matters had to be left in abeyance till his return.

Meanwhile the Countess continued her social round in spite of her strictures on local society. Invitations to dinner were returned, and so it came about that Perdita and the Earl found themselves alone one evening. The Countess had been called for by what the Earl insisted was an old flame, which both annoyed and flattered his mother.

"You're a wicked boy to tease me so, but I confess he was quite particular in his attentions at one time—before I met your father, of course. But I forbid you to give so much as the batting of an eye when the poor man is here. He has put on a little weight since I last saw him, I must admit."

"Put on a little weight! That's rich. He can hardly get into the carriage, Mama!"

"You're very unkind, Edward, not but what you might be right..." At her apprehensive look the two who were being left behind burst into laughter, and the Earl assured her he would fetch her himself after dinner if her swain had eaten too much. He even offered to accompany her. "Oh, no," she said quickly. "Er—it would seriously discommode the Bonvilles. You forget, such an august person as yourself needs special attention. They aren't prepared for you. It might be too much."

He declared it a great piece of nonsense, but seemed content to stay. The Countess, in a swirl of pomana-green crêpe lisse, was eventually driven away by her gallant, and Perdita and the Earl were left.

It was some time since they had dined alone, and the Earl sensed that, though she was disguising the fact, Perdita was ill at ease. But she talked with cool self-possession on uncontroversial subjects throughout most of the meal. He was once more impressed with her manners. Wherever she had learned them, they were impeccable. As the meal progressed, however, she started behaving more naturally, and by the end she was talking animatedly of Père Amboise and his theory on the position of Troy. Her face was slightly flushed, her eyes sparkled in the candle-light, and the curls at the side of her temples bobbed as she spoke. She looked enchanting in her lavender silk dress, and the Earl found himself loath to let her go. Since Perdita had agreed to his plan she had been cool in her manner to him except in the presence of his mother. She was different this evening. So he took the opportunity of asking her to play for him.

They went to the music-room, where she played for half an hour before her hands fell from the keys.

"Don't stop," he said idly. "Play the tune you were playing the other day—the Lully thing."

The sad little melody filled the room, and once again Perdita thought of Eliane. The prospect of happiness seemed remote for her—as indeed it was for herself. Would she ever be happy, really happy again? She doubted it. She felt tears come to her eyes again, and bowed her head.

"Perdita! You're crying! What has upset you?" With a muttered apology she would have left the room, but he caught her. "No, don't go! Come her to the fire and tell me what it is. Has my mother upset you?"

She assured him between sniffs and gulps that this was not so. He passed her an immaculate handkerchief and recommended that she should wipe her eyes. After a minute or two she was herself again, except for a red-tipped nose. He found it utterly appealing and suddenly kissed it. She looked up, startled, and he found himself kissing her mouth, then gently pulled her to him and folding her in his arms, resting his cheek on her hair.

They stayed like this for some minutes, and then she removed herself and said firmly, "I am sorry, I was foolish. The music affected me. Please excuse me; it will not happen again." She was twisting his handkerchief round and round in her hands. He removed it, and led her unresisting to the chair by the fire.

"I will not let you go to your room while you are so unhappy, Perdita. Can you not tell me what is wrong."

She looked at the piano and said sadly, "I was thinking of Eliane..."

"Eliane?" he asked in astonishment. "You were so unhappy about Eliane?"

She looked at him helplessly. What could she say? He couldn't understand because he didn't know of her friendship with his cousin.

"I...I did not tell you before... Oh, it's complicated, but I found it impossible to tell you. I know Eliane already. And her mother."

"When did you meet them?" he asked with a frown.

"When I was out walking one day I met Eliane in the woods. She had hurt her ankle...and I helped her."

"So you know my cousin? Yes, well you probably saw how helpless she is. And how unhappy. But why didn't you tell me, Perdita? Am I such an ogre?"

Perdita saw that she was going to have to explain at least some of her deceit. "When I met her I was sorry for her. She was frightened, so I...so I forgot not to talk. It was before I started talking here at the château, so it was awkward..."

He sat back, an amused smile on his face, "You little

devil," he said. "So it wasn't the shock of the falling branch..."

"I didn't think you really believed that anyway."

The Earl laughed as he remembered the scene in the library the day he had returned from England. "You're right. I didn't. Tell me, when did you meet Eliane?"

She said in a small voice, "Before Christmas."

"Before Christmas...! So you were pretending not to talk for—how long, Perdita? Did you at any time find it impossible to talk?"

In an even smaller voice she said, "No...but in Tangier and for some time after I simply didn't want to. It wasn't until I met Eliane and Colette that..."

"Colette too? You talked to Colette? Was that why you kept your friendship secret?" She nodded without looking at him. Then he asked, "And the tricks with the tutors? When did they begin?"

"From the beginning. It started with Monsieur Champollion—he was so sure I was stupid. And of course there was you..."

"Yes, now we're getting to the interesting bit. What about me, Perdita?" he asked softly and silkily. She had heard that silken tone before. It was a danger signal, but she faced him bravely.

"I felt that I annoyed you by not speaking and by being so stupid, and that pleased me. You were in such a hurry to have me educated—no, not educated; you said trained, like a monkey—and by refusing to appear to learn I was defeating your purpose." She looked at him defiantly and he was disarmed once again by the frankness of those blue eyes.

"It was the episode of the bonnet on the boat all over again, was it not? Why were you so anxious to have the better of me, Perdita?'' Her hands were twisting in her lap and the Earl reached out and took hold of one of them.

"I had to, to keep some spirit alive in me. You were so... You made me feel degraded. You wanted someone who knew nothing, had no self-respect, was worth nothing..."

"You're wrong," he said, examining the slender hand in his. "You were worth a pearl to me..."

She cried out in pain and pulled her hand away. "Oh, yes, you paid a whole pearl for me! Well, you were cheated. The last one who bought me only paid half as much." She caught her breath. What had she said? He stiffened.

"Ah, yes, I was forgetting... How could I have? The Pasha wasn't the first to sell you. There was the gentleman who taught you to read. Or was it someone else? I won't ask you who it was, Perdita. I don't honestly wish to know." He stood up and walked over to the piano, absent-mindedly strumming the little tune. "I wish things were not as they are," he said sombrely. "And I am sorry if I have said or done anything to make you unhappier than you would otherwise have been. If the future career I have suggested is distasteful to you I am willing to arrange something else. Would you prefer to live in England, in the country? Or abroad, here in France, perhaps? No, not near here. Somewhere else. We will find something, Perdita. Try not to distress yourself."

She looked at him with eyes that were filled with pain, then she got up, curtsyed and left the room. After she had gone he struck the piano so that a great discordant note resounded through the room.

CHAPTER TWELVE

IT WAS TO BE EXPECTED that the Countess would notice an air of constraint between her son and Perdita the next morning, but she made no comment. Instead she startled them both with her latest idea.

"Belleroi is going to have a ball before we leave for England!"

"Are you mad, Mama?" said the Earl. "Whom would you invite? There are hardly enough couples in the whole of Normandy for a ball. May I remind you that the old days are gone? Half the estates have disappeared, or are owned by an absentee landlord making his fortune in trade in Paris! A ball indeed!"

"Well, a small evening party with dancing, Edward. No, I will not listen to any objections. My reasons are perfectly good."

"Dare one ask what they are?" said the Earl, somewhat disagreeably.

"I really think you should see Dr. Grondet about your dyspeptic condition, Edward."

"I do not believe I suffer from a dyspeptic condition, Mama."

"You must be suffering from some stomach disorder, Edward, otherwise you would not be so disagreeable. But if you are not, then you must cheer up and help me with my ba...my evening party. I think Perdita should have an opportunity, before she goes to London, to dance in public.

If she were at home in England she would have been to several small dancing parties by now, wouldn't you, my dear?''

Perdita opened her mouth to say she had in fact done so, before she suddenly recalled herself and stammered some disclaimer.

The Countess smiled and continued, ''Secondly, I think it is time the servants had something to look forward to…''

''Mama, you cannot pretend that it is not a great deal of work for the servants. How can they look forward to it?''

The Countess contemplated her son for a moment. ''Edward, dear, if you have not learned by now that servants enjoy the excitement of a ba…a small evening party as much as, if not more than, the hosts, then I despair of you. How are you going to manage your own household when you know so little about managing the servants? Think of the cachet they will have when Belleroi is *en fête*, and the vails and delicacies that will come their way.''

''Delicacies? I see no need for delicacies for the servants. And why will they have gratuities for a mere evening party?'' said the Earl impatiently. The Countess was exasperated.

''Well, of course, we must have a sit-down dinner party before the evening starts, and the servants always have a share of what remains, and naturally some of our guests will be unable to return home that night and will therefore stay here in the château. The servants will have vails from them when they leave. You are really being very tiresome, Edward. I don't think I shall tell you my third reason— you will only pour cold water on it!''

The Earl saw that his mother was seriously put out, and did his best to restrain himself. ''I'm sorry, Mama. Tell me your third reason and I promise to listen with an open mind.''

The Countess looked at him doubtfully, then decided he was being sincere. ''If we have a formal evening here at Belleroi...''

''Yes...?''

''...Eliane will have to come,'' she said in a rush. ''No, don't laugh at me, it's a very good idea. I'm sure Perdita will see that Eliane is properly cared for, they're such good friends— Oh!''

''It's all right, I know about Eliane and Perdita, though I wouldn't have said one meeting was enough to make them good friends.'' Here Perdita thought it prudent to explain to the Earl that she had met Elaine on several other occasions, whereupon he became quite annoyed. ''I don't know any longer who has done what, or when, or who knows about it! I learn last night that Perdita met Eliane once, I learn this morning that not only does she know her rather better than that, but that my mother, heaven knows how, also knows she does! My opinion about inviting Eliane to an evening party, Mama, is that it is an excellent idea—if you can persuade Eliane to come. Now I am going to find Etienne. Unless you have been visiting Masson again, I ought to know at least what is happening on the estate!'' He strode out, leaving the door wide open behind him.

''Lud, '' said the Countess, ''I've seldom seen him in such a rage about so trivial a matter. I wonder what has happened to upset him. Do you know what it can be, my dear?''

Under the discerning eye of the Countess, Perdita had difficulty in making her plea of ignorance convincing. The Countess seemed to accept what she said and continued to discuss her plans for the party. Despite the Earl's doubts, it was decided that twenty-five couples could be found from the neighbouring estates, and that about half of them would dine at the château beforehand.

From then until the day of the evening party the house was in a bustle. Servants scurried about the rooms, cleaning, dusting, polishing already immaculate surfaces. Madame Lebrun seemed to be everywhere at once, one minute chivvying the maids in the bedrooms, the next arguing with the steward in the wine-cellar. Even Colette was roped in to help her grandmother in the kitchen. A dressmaker came from Bayeux to refurbish one of the Countess's gowns for Perdita, since there was little time to find suitable materials so far from Paris. Since it was quite the loveliest dress Perdita had ever seen, she was content with this arrangement.

But through all these preparations, and however busy she was, Perdita found herself unable to forget her heartache. She upbraided herself for it, she tried to find occupation for her mind as well as her hands, she forced herself to maintain a cheerful appearance. All was in vain. When she woke in the morning the black cloud settled on her spirit, when she relaxed her guard for one second the blue devils appeared. Her love for the Earl seemed to have been growing without her noticing it for so long that she had no notion when it had begun. Yes, she had felt passion when he had kissed her before, but she could have overcome that with time. It was when he had held her so gently, so comfortingly in the music-room that she had realised that this feeling for him would not go away— perhaps not ever. She did not deceive herself. The Earl had felt something in return that night, she was sure. But he would never so far forget the duty he owed to his family as to marry her. And his mistress she was resolved not to be. So she busied herself more and more frantically until the Countess was forced to call a halt.

"Perdita! You must rest this afternoon. You look worn to a shadow, child. What will my sister and Eliane say when they arrive if you are in a worse state than Eliane? Come, up to your room." And she forced Perdita to lie on her bed with the shutters closed. She did not go away immediately, but sat on the edge of the bed. "Can you tell me what is making you so unhappy, Perdita? Or can I guess?"

Perdita tried desperately to find the detachment she had summoned to her aid in the past, but found it impossible. A sob escaped her and she found herself folded in a scented embrace and gently rocked.

"Perdita, Perdita, what are we to do? I feel in my bones that you and Edward might be made for each other, but he is too blinded by this stupid scheme of his to see where his happiness lies. What can we do? Must we wait till it is all over?"

Perdita released herself from the Countess's embrace and sat up. "No, ma'am, you mistake the situation. The Earl would never marry me—not even when the matter of Piers Carston is finished. I…I am not respectable enough for marriage to enter his head."

"Why not respectable enough, my dear?" asked the Countess, smiling slightly. "Are you a thief or a murderer?"

"No, ma'am, but I have associated with such. The Earl believes me to be a…a…"

"Really?" said the Countess, opening her eyes wide. "And yet he is in a fair way to falling in love with you? He must be more deeply affected than I thought." When Perdita would have protested she went on, "Though he tries to conceal it, he watches you constantly and is responsive to everything you say or do. This was my self-contained son! Your precise origins and the exact reason for your being here are unknown to me, though Edward assures me that you are his ward, and I have accepted that. But I have made my own observations and I know you are of gentle blood and have been carefully brought up. And I believe you know more about Piers Carston than Edward thinks.'' Ignoring Perdita's gasp, she went on, ''But have no fear, I will not tell Edward of my suspicions. You gave me a promise about Piers Carston and I trust you. Remember, if I can help you at any time you have only to ask. Now get some rest and come down with a bright face and a resolution to have faith—in yourself and Edward. Will you do that?''

Perdita assured the Countess that she would try to rest. Then she added, ''Thank you, ma'am, for your own faith in me. Until you know the whole, I think you cannot judge Lord Ambourne.''

''We shall see,'' said the Countess from the door. ''Eliane should be here tomorrow or the next day and that should provide a different problem for you. What has happened to Philippe, for example?''

She went, and Perdita was left alone. Though she could not see any happier outcome, her talk with the Countess had given her mind a more cheerful direction. She must try to see Philippe as soon as possible.

Accordingly she caught Colette that evening and commissioned her help in delivering a note. Perdita felt the need for secrecy was almost past, since the Countess approved her efforts to reunite Philippe and Eliane. Nevertheless, she wanted to avoid awkward questions from the Earl until she had established what Philippe's attitude would be. So, when Colette brought a reply early the next morning and gave it to her in an exaggeratedly secretive way, she smiled but did nothing to dispel the child's sense of drama. Unfortunately she was observed by the Earl. He guessed immediately that the note concerned the young man he regarded as Perdita's lover, and, though he despised himself for it, he watched Perdita when she later slipped out and hurried down to the lake. He would give them time to meet and then he would get rid of the young puppy once and for all!

Perdita was reassured by Philippe's appearance. He was still very pale, but looked calmer. He asked after Eliane.

"Good news! She is much improved. How are you, Philippe?"

"*Mademoiselle*, Eliane has never been out of my mind. You made me look at myself after I had been to Paris and I was ashamed of what I saw. I did fail Eliane. Do you think she would ever forgive me?"

Perdita answered honestly and carefully, "I don't know. She must have been hurt by your actions in Paris but your former friendship must have some value for her. If you really wish to be friends with her again you must ask her, Philippe. Am I to understand that you still would not want to marry her ever?"

"Mademoiselle Perdita, if Eliane could forgive me enough to marry me I would be the happiest of men. But how could she?"

Perdita smiled at his intensity, but said, "If Eliane loves you she will. Do you know she is coming back to Beau Lac soon? If you wish me to deliver a note to her, I will do so."

"*Mademoiselle*, when?" Philippe's face lit up and in his excitement he grasped Perdita's sleeve.

"You have spoken to my ward for long enough. Too long! Now take your leave and go, sir!" said a cold voice behind them, and the Earl appeared. Philippe jerked as if to go, but Perdita stopped him.

"No, stay! It's time to introduce you. Lord Ambourne, allow me to present Monsieur Fourget to you. He is—"

"Charmed as I am to have a name at last for yet another of my ward's secret acquaintances, I must request you to leave, Monsieur Fourget." Perdita would have interrupted, but he turned on her savagely. "I have had enough of your machinations, Perdita! You will be silent until this gentleman has departed." He turned to Philippe. "Be glad, Monsieur Fourget, that I blame my ward more than you for these encounters. However, I do not wish to see you on my land again."

Philippe began hotly, "If it is because of your prejudices—"

"You may call it that, Monsieur Fourget. Now goodbye."

Realising that there was little point in argument, Philippe shrugged his shoulders and walked stiffly away.

Perdita was walking tempestuously up the path to the house. The Earl easily caught her up, but she ignored him. He caught her by the arm and turned her round, saying bitterly, "I will say what I have to say out here in the grounds, Perdita. It is not fit for my mother's ears. I had begun to respect you, had wished there was not this barrier of your previous life between us. I even thought that you regretted your past as much as I did. But as soon as you have some freedom you are running off to your paramours. How can respect or trust survive this? Have no fear that I will behave as I did on the last occasion. If I am angry, it is with myself for the way in which I wilfully allowed you to deceive me. You have made a fool of me in my own eyes. I wish to heaven I had never laid eyes on you." He left her and started walking up the path again.

"Lord Ambourne!" When the Earl continued walking, Perdita ran in front of him and blocked his way. Her cheeks were scarlet and her eyes were blazing. "I have two things to say to you, Lord Ambourne. You will do me the courtesy of listening, or I will say them in front of your mother, and anyone else in earshot!" He stood there, expressionless. "Philippe Fourget is in love with Eliane, and hoped one day to marry her. You have probably just destroyed that hope forever. And the second is this—you cannot possibly wish more heartily than I that you had never seen me. I have reasons of my own for continuing on this scheme, otherwise, I assure you, I would go back to Africa tomorrow!"

She ran swiftly indoors and up to the safety of her room. She was trembling with fury, but at the bottom of the anger lay a deep despair. The Earl would never forgive or forget her situation in Algiers. He would find out his error on the question of Philippe as soon as he talked to his mother. But there would always be other doubts, other suspicions. Because of the circumstances in which he had found her he would never trust her completely. As she stood there fighting for control the Countess walked in.

"I came straight in because I knew that if I knocked you would deny me. Forgive me, but I am very concerned. I saw you and Edward out on the path, Perdita. What was happening?"

"You must ask your son, ma'am. He wrote the lines of the play."

"Well, as I saw it, Perdita, you seemed to have quite a lot to say, too! You looked like a little turkey cock! What has my son done now?"

Perdita turned desperately to the Countess. "Ma'am, forgive me, I cannot talk at the moment. I am too angry."

"I had noticed," murmured the Countess. "Well, I will go to see what Edward has to say."

"Why is he so unkind, ma'am?" burst out Perdita. "Why does he always leap to the very worst conclusions about me?"

"Yes," said the Countess. "You should ask yourself that, Perdita. My son has always been the most reasonable of men. Why should he be so unbalanced where you are concerned? It couldn't possibly be jealousy, could it? Surely not?"

She went, but a few minutes later Jeanne came with some cloths soaked in the Countess's own lavender water and a glass of the château's best claret. Then Perdita was left in peace. The comfort, the wine, and the exhaustion after losing her temper so thoroughly, gave Perdita the best few hours' sleep she had enjoyed for days.

She was woken by the sound of her name and sat up in confusion. Who was it?

"Elaine!" she cried and leapt up to hug her friend, who was standing at the foot of her bed. "Eliane, you're looking wonderful!" And indeed it was so. Eliane was flushed with the excitement of homecoming, her delicate features and pale gold hair were surrounded by a pretty bonnet, and her green velvet pelisse was in the very latest mode.

"Mademoiselle Perdita, it is very pleasant to see you again. I've missed you."

"When did you arrive?"

"Five minutes ago. We have not yet been to Beau Lac. I wanted to see you and Edward first. My mother is talking to him now. Aren't you pleased he is here, too?"

Perdita found this difficult to answer, but managed to evade the question by saying, "Your mother is here? I cannot wait to see her. Excuse me, Mademoiselle Eliane,

I will be downstairs before you can turn around." Eliane left and Perdita hastened to tidy herself.

Any embarrassment she might have experienced at seeing the Earl so soon after their altercation was lost in the pleasure of meeting Madame d'Harcourt again. If he had desired any evidence of his family's affection for Perdita he might have seen it in abundance that afternoon. Eliane constantly referred to her and Madame d'Harcourt grew quite animated as she told Perdita of the subscription concerts she had attended in Paris. Apparently the Earl desired no such thing. He stood morosely in the background until Eliane drew him forward with a laugh.

"Edward, you must join in! You are behaving very stuffily. Aren't you glad to see us?"

Perdita avoided looking at the Earl by observing Eliane. In repose Eliane's face was still sad, and one could see signs of recent illness once the excited flush had died away. But she was very much better than Perdita had feared, and in the company of the people she most trusted and loved she displayed greater confidence.

"Edward looks such a crosspatch. Whatever had happened?" whispered Eliane as she and Perdita went for Eliane's bonnet.

"I think he has made a mistake in his calculations," replied Perdita. The Countess, who had heard this exchange, wagged a finger at Perdita and laughed.

"Poor Edward," said Eliane. "He has so much bookwork to do." Perdita was ashamed of herself for misleading her friend, but explanations were impossible.

Perdita never knew what the Countess said in the interview with her son. He appeared when she was alone in the music-room and asked her, "Who is he, Perdita—the fellow in the park? My mother seems to think I have misjudged you."

Somewhat stiffly Perdita replied, "His father has an estate at Vauvron. His name is Fourget, Philippe Fourget."

"Then, if his interest is in Eliane, why the devil could he not approach me openly, instead of behaving in this havey-cavey fashion?"

"His father is not generally liked by the other landowners in Normandy so he didn't believe you would receive him kindly—and you have now given him every reason to believe this is so!" she added bitterly.

"Why should he...? Oh, of course—Fourget! The Republican. But why should he think I would blame him for the sins of his father? If being true to your convictions can be so described."

"You mean you would have listened to him? You wouldn't have shown him the door?"

"I am not so unreasonable, Perdita." Her face was eloquent of disbelief. He added with a trace of hauteur, "It was very natural I should have misunderstood the situation—"

"Forgive me, Lord Ambourne, but it was not!"

"Very well, very well, I was unreasonable! And I regret that I misjudged you." He looked at Perdita's unrelenting face, took her hand and kissed it, saying in a gentler tone, "I am truly sorry if I offended you, Perdita. Both today and on another occasion when I misinterpreted the evidence. My behaviour was totally ill-judged."

Perdita looked at him sharply but he was perfectly sincere. She responded in kind. "My behaviour was not without reproach on those occasions either, Lord Ambourne. I expressed sentiments which were excessive."

"You mean you would not prefer to go back to the Pasha?" he said with a slight grin.

"Algiers was not the part of Africa I was thinking of.

Sometimes I feel I would like to see the Sheikh again, but I know that is impossible.''

''I could arrange for you to go there after…afterwards for a visit, if you so wished,'' he answered swiftly. ''But I do not believe that to be your proper milieu for a longer stay.''

''I do not know what my proper milieu will be, Lord Ambourne,'' said Perdita, with a sad smile. ''But let us not, I pray you, broach that subject again. Perhaps time will provide a solution.''

''I hope so,'' muttered the Earl. ''I hope to God it will be so!''

They stood there at a loss for a minute or two. Then they both started a sentence and abandoned it in deference to the other. The silence that followed became painful to Perdita and she went to the door.

''Perdita,'' the Earl said, and when she turned he continued, ''Why did you not tell me earlier about Philippe Fourget? Was it to punish me, because I misjudged you?''

''Not exactly, though it would have been reason enough. No, the first time you saw us I was afraid that if I told you who he was while you were being so out of reason angry you would dismiss him without listening to him—or me.''

''I am far more likely to condemn him for making Eliane so unhappy in Paris. But why did you become so involved? Why not leave it to the two of them?''

''Because I love them!'' cried Perdita. ''I wanted them to have a chance of happiness and I thought I could help!''

The Earl moved restlessly and said, ''There is little chance of happiness for Eliane. I saw what Fourget's reception of her story did to her. No, don't go! There is something else I want to ask you. What did you mean when you said you had reasons of your own for continuing with our scheme?''

Perdita took a step back. She had forgotten she had said that in her rage. She thought rapidly and said, "I would like to see England again and I have only once been to London. I think its sights will be interesting."

"Not half as interesting as your real reasons for going there, I am sure. No doubt I shall learn them in time." He looked at her in silence, then said, "I wish I knew what it is about you, Perdita. You enchant everyone who crosses your path—the Sheikh, Tom, my aunt and Eliane and now my mother. What is it?"

"You are wrong, my lord. I know of at least one person in this house who has failed to be enchanted."

She curtsyed and left the room, but as she went she thought she heard him say, "Then I wish you would tell me his name, Perdita, for I do not know him."

CHAPTER THIRTEEN

MADAME D'ESPERY had been invited to dine before the party at Belleroi, and was as pleased and excited as a young girl. Perdita brought her a copy of the guest list and, as she had half hoped, Madame d'Espery gave her views on the company.

"Of course, the Bonvilles will be at the dinner, though in the old days Gaston Bonville would have thought himself fortunate indeed even to be included in the list for dancing. But there you are, *mademoiselle*; times have changed. So many of our friends died under the guillotine, and many others have never returned to France. It is difficult to maintain the old distinctions... I am pleased to see that the de Sardets have not been invited to dinner. The man has the soul of a peasant, though I have no reason to believe his mother played her husband false."

When Perdita gave a gasp of laughter, *madame* looked up from the list and said, "Oh, forgive me, child. I should not say such things—in front of you, I mean. I sometimes forget your youth." She looked at Perdita over her glasses and shook her head before she continued, "Now there's a name you should note, *mademoiselle*! I am surprised to observe that the Marantins are spending the night at the château, but then I suppose it is impossible for them to return home so late. I will not say anything more about them, but—" she bent forward and grasped Perdita's arm "—take care to lock your door firmly when Monsieur de

Marantin is in the château. I will protect you during the evening, but I cannot be there at night. The story I could tell you of his visit to the Château de Joignet... Of course, he said he mistook the door of his bedroom, but...I will say no more.''

The old lady finished the list with enjoyment, destroying the reputations of at least half of the guests on the way. Lastly she said, ''I shall enjoy meeting my old friends again, *mademoiselle*. It is always pleasant to exchange news. Tell me what you are going to wear.''

When Perdita explained that the Countess was giving her one of her dresses, Madame d'Espery said, ''Eugenie de Cazeville was a very pretty girl, *mademoiselle*, and a charming one. Her husband was a clever, strong-minded man, yet she could wind him round her little finger. She was one of the best dressed women in London or Paris— is still, I suppose, for he left her very well provided for, and her interest in fashion is unchanged. Dear me, I fear my tongue runs away with me. I am too much alone and it is agreeable to have someone to talk to. But I should not discuss your hostess with you. Forgive me.''

Perdita assured her that she was as charmed by the Countess as the rest of the world. After Madame d'Espery had told her what she was proposing to wear and had described in detail what had happened on the last occasion she had worn it they parted with expressions of mutual goodwill.

After a great deal of persuasion Eliane had agreed to come to the party. Curiously, it was the Earl who prevailed on her to be present. As she told Perdita, ''Edward represented to me how difficult it would be for Maman to be present if I were not. And Tante Eugenie would be disappointed if neither of us came.''

''I am delighted you are coming for whatever reason,

and think your cousin is quite right," said Perdita. "But could you not call me Perdita? If your aunt and mother do so, surely you could?"

Eliane smiled with pleasure. "I think Maman has caught it from Tante Eugenie, and I would be delighted, Mad...I mean, Perdita. It is so nice to have a friend again." Then her face clouded over, and Perdita knew she was thinking of Philippe.

"Eliane," she began tentatively, "have you...have you heard from Philippe?"

"He visited me in Paris, Perdita. I cannot talk about it yet. Perhaps later..." But Perdita knew that her time in France was now very limited and if she was to help her friend she must persist.

"I met Philippe after he came back," she said. "He told me something of what happened. No, don't go away, Eliane. It's important I tell you this. Please stay." She led her reluctant friend back to her chair and held both her hands. "Philippe regrets what he did—"

"And so he should!" cried Eliane. "I thought he was my friend!"

"Philippe did not regard you as only a friend, Eliane. He put you on a pedestal, thought of you as an angel, untouched and untouchable. That's why what he learned in Paris was such a shock to him." Eliane tried to pull her hands away, but Perdita refused to let her. "Philippe loved you and still does love you. He is bitterly sorry for the way he behaved. And I think you should forgive him."

"But how could he say those things—that he never wanted to see me again, and the rest...?" asked Eliane piteously.

"Because he is human and he was hurt. Listen to me, Eliane. Philippe still loves you. If he should write to you please read what he says. Will you?"

"Do you think I should?" Perdita nodded and Eliane said finally, "Well, if he writes I will read his letter. But I wish my cousin were not taking you to London. It will seem very quiet here without you. Could you not stay a little longer?"

Perdita was forced to disappoint her. Their departure date had been fixed for three days after the ball. The Earl had wanted to leave earlier, but the Countess had announced that she would travel neither on the day after the party, nor on a Sunday. This was not the only point of conflict, for the Countess wanted to stay for one or two nights at Ambourne before continuing to London, and the Earl refused to countenance it.

"I HAVE NEVER KNOWN Edward so short-tempered," said Marguerite d'Harcourt to her sister. "Is he not well?"

"I fear he is suffering from an incurable malady," replied the Countess solemnly. Her sister looked at her in concern, but when she saw the mischievous expression on her sister's face she, too, smiled.

"Oh, lies the wind in that quarter?" she asked. "What about the lady?"

"I should not have told you, Marguerite, for neither of them seems to know where they are. There's some mystery about Perdita, of course, and I'm afraid that behind it lies a serious obstruction."

"Edward would be a lucky man if Perdita found herself able to marry him," said Madame d'Harcourt. Fond as the Countess was of Perdita, no devoted mother could let this pass, and she pointed out to her sister that her Edward was one of the most eligible *partis* in England. He could, she said, have married any number of charming young ladies.

"But he has never shown the slightest inclination for any of them," said Madame d'Harcourt. "Indeed, till today I had never seen him display any strong emotion, other than his hatred for Piers Carston. And that," she said bitterly, "is an emotion I am forced to admit I share."

The Countess turned a troubled face to her sister. "You know he is about to do something connected with Piers Carston, and Perdita is included in his plans?"

"Yes," replied Madame d'Harcourt. "He told me when he first brought her here that she was part of a plan. What is it?" she asked, adding anxiously, "I hope it won't revive the old scandal. Eliane is wonderfully recovered, but any further stress would pull her down very quickly."

"No, no, there is no danger of that," said the Countess, quickly reassuring her nervous sister. "Edward would never risk such a thing, and Perdita has assured me of it, too. But pray do not repeat any of our conversation to him. He is difficult enough, without learning that we discuss him behind his back!"

THE DAY OF THE PARTY dawned. Flowers from the garden and succession houses had been put in huge bowls all over the house, the servants' uniforms and liveries had been brushed and pressed, the gardens raked and the lawns cut. Rosanne, in the kitchen with Colette and an army of helpers from the village, was putting the final touches to the food, and Madame Lebrun was inspecting the bedrooms to be used for the guests. Perdita noticed that Monsieur de Marantin's room was at the furthest corner of the château from hers. She wondered whether Madame d'Espery had spoken to Madame Lebrun, and pictured the scene with amusement.

Perdita herself was up early and out in the garden. She looked wistfully over the lawns, up the hill to the woods and to the right towards the lake. In three days she would leave for England, where the last scene of the drama that

had begun in an inn near Bristol would be played. She
wanted to be finished with it, wanted to start the next stage
in her life free of the hatred and misery of the past. Perhaps
when she no longer saw the Earl daily she would be able
to forget him, or at least learn to be content without him.
Perhaps. She sat for a while longer, enjoying Belleroi
while she still could, before going in to start the day.

The Earl had seen her sitting on a bench under the lime
tree, but had decided not to join her. The less time he spent
in her company, the more resolute he could remain. For
weeks now he had been in this unpleasant and unfamiliar
state of indecision. He had pursued his goal of ruining
Piers Carston for nearly four years. Now, when he should
have been rejoicing that he was so near its fulfilment, he
found himself weakening. But, he reminded himself, Perdita had been bought as part of his plan and must not mean
anything more to him than that. The sooner they got to
London the better. As for this scheme of his mother's that
they should break their journey at Ambourne—he would
oppose that absolutely. He would not have Ambourne
haunted by Perdita's presence as Belleroi was. Taking one
last look at the figure on the bench, he turned away from
the window.

The day wore on and evening approached without any
serious disasters. Colette dropped one of the jellies Rosanne had prepared, but a little adjustment of the other
dishes made up for this. Madame Lebrun found a snail in
the middle of the entrance hall, which had presumably escaped from one of the arrangements of flowers and plants,
and made three of the maids search every bowl lest there
should be any more, but none were found. Colette later
rescued the snail from the rubbish pail into which it had
been thrown and carried it out into the garden. At four
everyone started to dress, for the first guests would be

arriving at half-past five. Madame d'Harcourt and Eliane were to stay overnight and had arrived in the early afternoon. Eliane had whispered to Perdita that she had heard from Philippe, but when Perdita eagerly questioned her she merely said that she had not yet read his note.

"I have left it until I am alone, Perdita. I want to consider it carefully and slowly." Perdita was content to leave it so. The most important thing was that Eliane was prepared to read it at all.

When the four ladies assembled in the salon shortly before the guests were due, a prettier sight could hardly have been found in Normandy. At least that was what the Earl said, carefully avoiding looking at Perdita.

"In Normandy! You are too cautious, Edward. I dare swear you will not find a lovelier sight than these two young ladies in the whole of France!" The Countess had some justification for her extravagant claim. Perdita and Eliane each looked pretty in their spring-like dresses, but together they looked like something out of a painting by Botticelli. Eliane, in primrose-yellow muslin and fine lace, with her delicate beauty and pale gold hair, looked like a fairy princess. Perdita was in pale green silk embroidered with rosebuds, flowers in her dark brown curls. The formal clothes might have subdued her vitality, but her grace and beauty had never been displayed to greater advantage.

The Earl, himself very formally attired in dark red velvet coat and white breeches, bowed and said, still not looking at Perdita, "Nor a finer one than you and my aunt, Mama." His mother laughed and disclaimed, but smoothed the heavy gold silk of her own dress and glanced at her sister in silvery grey with a satisfied air.

"But, Edward, do you not think Perdita looks lovely? I do," cried Eliane.

The Earl was forced at last to look at Perdita, and his

face was expressionless as he said, "I congratulate you, Perdita. I predict you will capture all hearts tonight." Then he smiled down affectionately at his cousin and added, "Those that Eliane leaves untouched, that is!"

"Then I shall have a sad time of it, for I shall have none," said Perdita, looking warmly at her friend. The two sisters looked at one another, hardly able to conceal a smile, but they pulled themselves together when the first arrivals were announced.

"Monsieur Bonville and Madame! How pleasant that you arrive so promptly. Do you know my sister and her daughter?"

The Countess was in her element. As the guests arrived she moved from one to the other, introducing, reminiscing, mixing, but at the same time managing to observe Perdita and her son. Perdita's conduct impressed her. The girl's manner was apparently confident, yet modest. She bore with equanimity both the barely concealed curiosity of the polite and the impertinent questions of the less well-bred, and was able to disarm them both. She stayed close to Eliane until she saw her friend was happily engaged in conversation. Then she would leave her, only to return when Eliane was once again alone. Altogether a very nicely brought-up girl, thought the Countess.

The Earl was less pleasing to his mother. His manner was, as always, impeccably polite, and no one could have accused him of neglecting his guests in any way. But, to those who knew him, he seemed even more remote than usual, as if he was concealing his real person from the world.

Dinner was announced, and the Countess and her partner led the way in.

Perdita found herself next to Monsieur de Marantin, and conducted a harmless enough conversation with him until

his wine glass had been filled two or three times. Then the
tone of his conversation became less proper and she sometimes didn't quite know how to deal with it. On the one
hand, she was not shocked by what he said: on the other,
she knew that the sort of girl he imagined her to be—
young, unmarried, delicately brought up—would be painfully embarrassed by his insinuating remarks.

She saw the Earl's eye on her once as Monsieur de
Marantin laughed loudly at his own wit. Finally she leaned
forward and looked at Madame d'Espery, who was sitting
on Monsieur de Marantin's other side. That lady responded
instantly. She was a formidable sight in her black velvet
dress, which was twenty years out of date but had some
of the loveliest Mechlin lace carelessly pinned to it with a
large diamond brooch. She rallied to Perdita's rescue by
monopolising the unfortunate Monsieur de Marantin for
the rest of the meal, telling him stories of his father and,
when he would have turned back to Perdita, hinting in the
most delicate manner possible that she knew something of
the events at Château de Joignet. He was held in thrall by
the old lady till the end of the meal. Meanwhile Perdita
was able to talk to her other neighbour, a dull but harmless
young man, who was dazzled by her.

In London terms this was a very small ball indeed, but
to the provincial society of Normandy, still trying to settle
down again after the upheavals of the past thirty years, it
was the event of the year. Long after it was over they
would talk of the ball at Belleroi, and of Monsieur le Marquis and Madame la Marquise and their family. Eliane and
Perdita soon found they were much in demand for dancing,
and, since neither of them had had much opportunity before to be present at such an evening, they found to their
surprise that they were enjoying themselves.

Madame d'Espery, true to her word, had kept a severe

eye on Monsieur de Marantin, but during the supper interval she had unfortunately been carried off by the Countess. Perdita knew that Eliane had gone to find some fresh air and went in search of her. She found her in the music-room, struggling with an amorous Monsieur de Marantin. When Perdita arrived she could see that Eliane was becoming hysterical. How could she rescue her without causing the sort of scandal that would damage her friend? She hurried over and surprised Monsieur de Marantin into letting Eliane go by saying in enthusiastic tones, "Ah, *monsieur*! You too are a devotee of music. How charming! Eliane, your mama is looking for you. I think she is in the little parlour."

Eliane, with a grateful look at Perdita, ran out. Left with a befuddled adversary, who had imbibed too freely of the wine at supper, Perdita gathered her wits as she realised with a sinking heart that he was only too willing to transfer his attentions.

"A golden goddess departs and Pershephon...Perphesh... spring takes her place..." he said, making his unsteady way towards her.

She easily avoided him and went to the door, saying as she went, "Pray excuse me, Monsieur de Marantin. I should not be here alone with you, even for some music, which I adore." She turned to go, and ran into the Earl, who came storming in. He looked so murderous that she caught his arm, not only anxious for Monsieur de Marantin's safety, but also afraid that there would be the very scandal she had tried to avoid. "Monsieur de Marantin has been so kind as to express an interest in hearing some music," she cried, holding tightly on to the Earl's arm. "And I was just about to fetch your mother and aunt to play for him. He fully understands how improper it would be for me to remain here alone with him, is that not so, *monsieur?*''

Monsieur de Marantin was no expert on propriety, but he was fully aware of the Earl's anger and the tensed muscles under his elegant coat. He hastily agreed.

The Earl relaxed and Perdita let him go. He said smoothly, ''It is always pleasant to find a fellow lover of music, Monsieur de Marantin, but I fear the dancing is just about to recommence in the salon and my mother is fully occupied there. Perhaps you could indulge yourself on another occasion? Indulge your interest in music, I mean, of course.'' He held the door open for his discomfited guest and ushered him out.

Perdita turned to him, her eyes brimming with laughter. ''Oh, famously done! The poor man won't be able to look you in the face for a year.'' Then as she saw the Earl's serious look she said quietly, ''I did not encourage him. Whatever you may think, I did not encourage him.''

''I know,'' he said surprisingly. ''Eliane told me what was happening.''

''But Monsieur de Marantin—will he be all right? He was more than a trifle disguised.''

''To the devil with Monsieur de Marantin. I am more concerned for you. Did he hurt you, Perdita?'' She did not have time to do more than shake her head before he folded her in his arms, holding her tight as if he wanted to protect her against the world. ''It is as well for him!'' he murmured into her hair. ''Though you look delectable enough tonight to drive any man out of his senses.''

Though she knew it was an illusion, Perdita stood in the circle of his arms, feeling loved and cherished. It was a new and heady sensation. But after a short moment she stirred, moved away and, shaking out her skirts, said lightly, ''I was only trying to divert his attention from

Eliane. I was not prepared for such a lightning change of
heart—I think he was comparing me to spring and it went
to his head!''

The Earl grinned. ''He was in some difficulty with your
name, from what I heard, Persephone—or is it Perphesh-
one?''

Perdita laughed and said, ''You should not make sport
of your guests, Lord Ambourne, however badly they behave.''

With a brief return to his grim manner the Earl replied,
''If he had behaved any worse I might have done more
than make sport of him! Now, Perdita, may I escort you
back to the salon? We shall be missed.'' He held his arm
out to her and, taking it with a smile, she accompanied
him back to the ball. When they came into the room a
waltz was just striking up. The Earl turned to face her and
asked, ''May I?'' Then, without waiting for her flustered
refusal, he put his arm at her waist and guided her on to
the floor.

''I congratulate you, Perdita,'' said the Earl eventually.
''Your waltz has much improved since I last danced with
you. Now you should be able to look up at me and forget
about your feet.'' Perdita looked up and met his eyes smiling down at her. She missed a step and he said softly, ''I
absolutely forbid you to stumble! No, don't look down
again. Look up!''

His arm was about her waist and, though they were
dancing a strictly correct distance apart, they could not
have been closer in spirit. They moved as one, in a world
of their own, their eyes locked together and their difficulties forgotten in the enchantment of the waltz. They dipped
and swayed, turned and reversed without conscious effort,
lost in each other. When the music ended they stood quite
still for a moment, and the Earl's hand tightened round

Perdita's as he gazed at her in a bemused fashion. They
came to to find themselves an object of interest to three
pairs of eyes. Eliane was looking on in admiration, but the
Countess and her sister were unable to hide their sympathetic curiosity. The Earl looked slightly self-conscious as
he led Perdita to her chair, but by the time she was seated
he had resumed his remote air. He bowed and withdrew
without further conversation.

"That was wonderful! You both looked so graceful. I
should like to learn to dance like that," cried Eliane at
Perdita's side.

"I shouldn't," said Perdita sadly. "It's too dangerous."

"Oh, but it didn't look for a moment as if you would
fall," said Eliane. "Edward seemed to be holding you so
securely."

"That's what I meant," replied Perdita. Then she pulled
herself together, and to Eliane's puzzled query she would
only laugh ruefully and shake her head.

To Perdita's profound relief Monsieur de Marantin did
not approach her again that evening, but neither did the
Earl. Somehow, after the waltz, she found the zest had
gone from the ball and she felt tired. She was glad when
it finally came to an end and the guests had either departed
or were in their rooms. Eliane, too, was pale and heavy-
eyed, and worried them all when she almost fell at the foot
of the stairs.

"She is still not strong, Edward," Madame d'Harcourt
said. "I hope the dancing has not been too much for
her…"

Edward swung Eliane into his arms and started up the
stairs. "Send for her maid, Tante Marguerite. She will be
in bed in a very short time. And after we have gone to
England you can see that she does not exert herself unduly.
I cannot believe one evening's enjoyment can have a last-

ing effect." But when he returned to his mother and Perdita, who were waiting in the salon, he said, "It's this damnable business with young Fourget. I sent the Fourgets an invitation—"

"Edward!"

"Why not, Mama? It's time the old loyalties were forgotten. If the King would only realise it, France needs men of principle such as old Fourget. At present he's surrounded by sycophants and time-servers, men of the old regime, eager to restore their private fortunes." He sighed, then added, "But the Fourgets refused to come, and I cannot blame them. They would have had a cool reception from most of our guests. It would seem that Eliane must once again be unhappy."

"No!" cried Perdita. "I will not accept that. Philippe loves Eliane!"

"Oh, love!" said the Earl contemptuously. "That is a much overrated emotion, believe me. I am increasingly of the opinion that one should have a good dose of it in one's early years, much as one has the measles, and then it should be decently forgotten. Do you go to bed now, Mama? I will escort you upstairs."

The Countess rose wearily, and together with Perdita, preceded her son up the stairs. They bade each other goodnight and went their separate ways to their rooms. The ball was over, and all attention must now be on the voyage to England.

CHAPTER FOURTEEN

IT WAS A SUBDUED PARTY that set out three days later. The Countess was still tired after her exertions for the ball, and was as disgruntled as her sunny nature permitted at her son's adamant refusal to spend any time at Ambourne before going to London. He knew she was not a good traveller and, considerate son that he was, would normally have indulged her instantly in her desire to break the journey. But he had proved completely inflexible on this point. Hers was not a nature to repine, however, and she would have been in better spirits if she had been more sanguine about the affairs of the young people about her.

Eliane was far from happy, and her aunt was afraid that Philippe was proving to be a reluctant suitor. Then there was Perdita. The Countess considered the white face of the girl sitting opposite her in the chaise. Perdita was clearly distressed at leaving Belleroi. She had walked in the woods and round the lake and had visited Madame d'Espery and Père Amboise before she had left. The servants had been sorry to see her go, and Colette and Jeanne had been inconsolable. There was another thing! Edward had rejected her very reasonable suggestion that Perdita should take Jeanne with her as her maid. He seemed to want to cut all ties between Perdita and Belleroi.

She could not study Edward, for he had decided not to travel with them in the chaise and was riding alongside. But for a long time now he had been abstracted and short-tempered. What was he proposing to do about Perdita? The Countess feared that her son might be throwing away his chance of happiness in this pursuit of Piers Carston. But then, Perdita had said that even when it was over they could not marry. The Countess set her mind to think of something more cheerful, for she could do little enough for the moment about the problems the young were facing. At least they would have as comfortable a crossing as the Channel would permit. Edward had his yacht moored at Honfleur. She closed her eyes and tried to sleep.

Perdita too tried to rest. The last two days had been painful, and she had slept little at night. It was most unlikely that she would ever see Belleroi and the people in Normandy again. After the loss of her home in Somerset and the death of her mother there had been a large gap in her life, and during the last five months Belleroi had begun to fill it. Now she must forget it again. The future seemed dreary, and even the fact that she would at last face Piers Carston with his crimes failed to console her. With determination she turned her mind to what she would do in London.

As for the Earl—it was fortunate that he did not meet with any unexpected hazard on the way to Honfleur, for he was so deeply wrapped in his own thoughts that it was doubtful he would have coped with it. He dealt with the changes of horses, escorted the ladies into the inns on their way, but it was all done without real thought. To the casual observer he looked his normal authoritative self. But in fact he was still no nearer to recovering the calm certainty with which he had faced the world until such a short time before. Was there a way to ruin Piers Carston without involving Perdita in a distasteful marriage? But all his plans had been perfected with this in mind, and surely Perdita herself was not so squeamish? For all her dainty ways now, she must have lived roughly with the pirate gang. He thrust away the thought that, whatever Perdita's views on the subject were, her forthcoming marriage to Piers Carston was highly distasteful to him.

They arrived at Honfleur in the evening and wasted no time in embarking. Tom was there to help them on board and show the ladies to their cabins. The Countess retired immediately. Perdita would have helped her, but she said with a wan smile, "No, child. I fear I am very poor company on a sailing vessel, and my maid will do all I need. I shall see you again in Portsmouth."

Perdita was taken to a small cabin on the opposite side of the ship from the one in which she had lain ill six months before. Then she had been determined to reject all contact with others, to remain detached, not even bothering to communicate. Now she had just cut the ties of a whole web of relationships and involvement—Eliane and Philippe, Colette and Jeanne, Madame d'Harcourt and Madame d'Espery, and a host of others. She had a short time longer to enjoy the Countess's friendship, then that too would be gone. It hurt, and would hurt for some time, but she could not regret her friendships with these people. She avoided thinking of the Earl, for that was something different and had still to be resolved. A rocking motion told her that the ship had set sail and she lay down. Her tired mind gradually relaxed and she fell asleep.

THEY SPENT TWO NIGHTS on board and landed at Portsmouth early in the morning. It took some time to manoeuvre the yacht alongside and Perdita stood on deck watching the busy life on the quayside. This was England! In her darker moments on the pirate ship she had doubted that she would ever see it again, but now it looked as if she was home for good and she was grateful for it.

Tom came up to her. "Mind your dress on them ropes, miss. His lordship would have a fit if he saw them, they're that dirty."

"I'm not afraid of a bit of dirt, Tom," said Perdita, smiling slightly.

"Yes, well, things are a bit different now, aren't they? I mean, you're a lady now, and some of the things that happened in the past should be forgotten, Miss Perdita— if you'll forgive my saying so. Particularly baths and the like." Tom spoke severely, and his rugged face grew slightly pink. Perdita was sorry she had teased him, but she had forgotten his efforts when she was in the bath— she only remembered the way the Earl had dumped her into it.

"I'm sorry, Tom. I was wrong to mention it. But I was grateful for your care."

"Well, just you make sure you don't get into any more scrapes. I'm not sure how his lordship will take it, him being so out of sorts, like."

Perdita gathered that the sea voyage had not improved the Earl's frame of mind. She was glad; he ought to suffer a little. However, when he appeared a few moments later he spoke with his usual calm authority.

"I'd like you to stay below till we berth, Perdita. The less you are seen, the better. Perhaps you would like to join my mother? She seems to be recovered and would like your company."

Perdita went to the Countess's cabin. It was the one she had been in on her journey to Tangier, and she looked round it, remembering her fever and pain she had suffered.

"There you are, my dear! How have you fared on the voyage? I feel ashamed of myself for looking after you so badly. But it's always the same—Charles used to say that I felt queasy when I saw the lake at Ambourne!"

They heard footsteps approaching, but it was Tom who had come to collect the first valises. With a great deal of bustle the Countess's belongings were slowly taken ashore and loaded on the chaise. Then Perdita's bag was fetched, looking pathetically small by the Countess's pile of luggage, and in a very short time they were on the road to London. The last stage of Perdita's long journey had begun.

They spent the night at Godalming, where the Countess declared, quite without foundation, that the sheets at the inn were not properly aired.

"You are only annoyed, Mama, that we did not stay at Ambourne. The rooms at the King's Arms were very decently prepared."

"When I am in my bed with a rheumatic disorder you will remember, if you please, that I was not happy with them!" said his mother crossly, and then, as Edward smiled at the idea of his mother with rheumatics, she sighed in relief. It was the first time Edward had smiled in a fortnight.

They reached London at the end of the week, and, though they had travelled in comfort, they were all glad to reach Rotherfield House at last. This was a handsome building quite near Green Park in Arlington Street, Piccadilly. It had been built in the 1730s for the Earl's great-great-grandfather, when the barony had been elevated to an earldom. Though its style looked somewhat heavy to the modern eye, its large rooms and splendid central staircase were impressively grand.

The Countess shuddered as she came in, and hurried quickly into the small parlour.

"How anyone could live here in comfort I do not know. I was always asking Charles to modernise it or even to move to the other side of Oxford Street. There are some very pretty new houses near Portman Square and I quite set my heart on one of them, but Charles would not hear of it. He said they weren't big enough or some such nonsense, and would keep talking of family tradition and boring things like that. In most things I was able to persuade Charles into a more reasonable frame of mind, but not in this.''

While the Countess was talking she handed her cloak to a footman and settled herself on the day couch, which stood by the fire. Several other personages had appeared on their arrival, and these were now engaged in carrying luggage and clothing to the bedrooms.

''Now, Perdita, we shall have a little refreshment here; Purkiss shall see to it, won't you, Purkiss? And then we shall restore ourselves to good order in our rooms till dinner. You know London keeps late dinner hours, do you? We dine at seven.'' Perdita nodded, and watched Purkiss's stately approach to the door as the butler went to do the Countess's bidding.

''Can you imagine what it was like when I first came here, Perdita? You know how small Belleroi is. The salon there is its largest room, but it would fit eight times over into the ballroom at the back of this house. And Ambourne is even bigger! I was petrified, especially by Purkiss there. Charles's parents were the friendliest people imaginable and I was soon on good terms with them, but it took me three years to overcome my awe for Purkiss!'' Perdita laughed and said she could not imagine anyone taking three hours let alone three years to fall under the Countess's spell. ''You are a darling, Perdita. What shall I do without you?''

They both fell silent. The Earl had announced that Perdita could not stay at Rotherfield House for long, as it would rouse Carston's suspicion if she and the Earl were seen to be connected. When Perdita's chaperon arrived they would remove to the house he had engaged for them in Dover Street on the other side of Piccadilly.

The Countess's voice grew sad as she said, "Perdita, Edward says I must not visit you in Dover Street, so it is possible I may not see you again for some time. I have a small gift for you here. I hope you will remember your Belleroi friends when you wear it—it comes with our love and friendship. We shall think of you." A lump came into Perdita's throat as she looked down at the prettily painted box with the letter 'P' in gold on the lid.

"I need no souvenirs of Belleroi, ma'am. They are in my heart. But this gift means more to me...more to me than I can..."

"Come now, Perdita! It is a mere trifle. Open it and see what is inside," said the Countess in bracing tones.

Perdita took out a small gold brooch set with seed-pearls and sapphires. She went over and sat at the Countess's feet. "I shall never forget your kindness, ma'am. It's not just the brooch, the dress and the many other things you have given me. You have made me feel part of a family again..." She could not continue.

The Countess said warmly, "Well, of course you are! What sister could have cared more for Eliane? What daughter could have been better company? Don't thank me for that, Perdita—and please do not give us up! Wear the brooch when you come to see us again."

Perdita only smiled and nodded. How could she tell the Countess that her intention was to disappear once she had seen Piers Carston? Better by far that they part now while the Countess remained in ignorance of the ugly facts connected with her stepbrother.

Purkiss entered the room, so there was no time for more.

When they had drunk some tea they went upstairs to wash and change out of their travelling garb.

Dinner was a quiet meal, for the Earl had excused himself and was dining at his club. The two ladies were still tired and somehow low in spirits. They were glad when the tea-tray was brought in at ten o'clock and they could retire gracefully to bed.

The maid had gone, and Perdita was in bed, examining the brooch in the light of her candle, when she suddenly realised that she had left its box in the parlour. She leapt out of bed, threw on her wrapper and crept downstairs. The Countess had told the servants not to wait up for the Earl and they had all gone to their own quarters. The house was silent. A lamp burned in the hall, but the small parlour was in darkness except for the dying fire. She made her way over to the table, retrieved her box and started for the door.

"Perdita!" Perdita turned round with a jump. The box fell unnoticed to the ground as she became aware of the long figure sprawling somewhat inelegantly in the wing chair by the fire. "Perdita," he said again. She waited for more, but he seemed to have finished. She took a stealthy step towards the door but kicked the little box, and had to bend to pick it up. The Earl sat up and carefully focused his eyes on her. His cravat was loose and his hair slightly dishevelled. "Stealing the silver, perhaps?" he suggested, without any real conviction.

"No, Lord Ambourne. Rescuing a box given to me by your mother. I left it here earlier this evening. I did not expect to find you here."

"A box?"

"I have the brooch that was in it upstairs, but I would be sorry to lose this box. It is very pretty."

"Why did my mother give you a present?"

His tone annoyed her, and she replied sharply, "For reasons you could not possibly understand, my lord. It was a token of her affection, her trust, her friendship. And because I love her I shall treasure it."

A spasm of feeling passed over his face. He thought and then said, "In the best circles, Perdita, it is considered unsporting to kick a man when he is down. I had thought better of your sense of fair play. Show me this box. Please." A sudden suspicion occurred to her and it was confirmed as she came closer. There was an unmistakable aura of alcohol about the Earl's person. "Yes, I must reek of brandy. If it offends you you'd better keep your distance. But, Perdita..." There was a pause.

"Yes, Lord Ambourne?"

"Perdita, let no ignorant fool tell you that sorrows can be drowned in alcohol. It's an illusion, a myth, a chim...a chimera." He seemed to like the word, for he repeated it. "Yes, that's it—a chimera. I must have consumed more brandy this evening than I normally drink in a month, and here I am—stone-cold sober!" He emphasised these last three words by thumping the arm of his chair, and the small wine table next to his arm rocked dangerously. Perdita removed the brandy bottle to a safer place.

"Yes, my lord, I can see," she said, with only the faintest of smiles on her lips. "What sorrows have you failed to drown?" she sat down on the stool near by. At first his reply seemed irrelevant.

"Belleroi. Belleroi was always a happy place for me. The house, the woods, the apple orchards, the people. A place of peace...yes, truly a place of peace." He was so absorbed in his thoughts that he seemed to have forgotten she was there. "But, whenever I think of Belleroi now, I see Perdita running down the lawn to the house, Perdita limping along the lane, Perdita licking her fingers in the dining-room, Perdita in the music-room, in the library, at the ball…'' His voice died away.

Perdita could hardly breathe. Was he at last going to renounce his plan?

The disappointment when it came was bitter. ''But, try as I might,'' he went on in a sombre tone, ''I cannot forget those other pictures—Eliane at Ambourne on the threshold of womanhood, full of innocent gaiety. Eliane in London, half starved and cowering in a corner of the cellar. Eliane in Paris, indifferent as to whether she lived or died. I cannot let Piers Carston go unpunished.'' He covered his eyes.

Perdita got up. ''Of course,'' she said woodenly. ''Of course. I will wish you goodnight, Lord Ambourne.'' She walked wearily towards the door.

''Perdita, don't go!'' He leapt up from his chair, knocking the wine table over in his haste. ''Don't go yet.''

''I must. It is late and I should not be here dressed like this. If your mother or the servants—''

''Damn my mother, damn the servants, damn the world, Perdita! There's so much I want to say to you, so much we have shared…''

''I was of the opinion we had shared a great deal, too,'' she said sadly. ''But it is not enough to cause you to change your plan to marry me to Piers Carston, is it?''

''Perdita, I have explained to you why I cannot—''

''Then there is no more to be said. Goodnight, Lord Ambourne.''

''Can you not treat it as a game, Perdita? Can you not gull London society with the same impudent enjoyment as you gulled Champollion and the rest?''

''And marriage to Carston? Am I to treat that as a game too?''

''The stakes are high—and the rewards—''

"I beg you not to talk to me of jewels and dresses, establishments and rewards! You do me an injustice, Lord Ambourne! When this farce is played out I shall seek only peace."

He took her hand and said slowly, "Perhaps we could find peace together, Perdita?"

"And what part would I play in that idyll?" she asked, her lip curling in scorn. "Your mistress? Would the large discreet establishment be replaced with a small one, just for two? Or were you planning a modest retreat in the country? No, Lord Ambourne, I shall seek my own life in my own place. You will play no part in it!"

He let her hand fall. "You are right. I shall have no claim on you when the Carston affair is over. I shall see that you have your independence, Perdita, in your 'own place'."

"Thank you, my lord; I believe I can find one for myself."

He smiled ruefully. "Gallant to the last. But you will need some help. We shall see." As she got to the door he said, "Perdita, have you no gift for me? A final kiss—for consolation? I am persuaded that would help more than any brandy."

"I will not kiss you again Lord Ambourne. Not while I am destined to become Piers Carston's wife. Goodnight."

That night Perdita dreamt she was in a corridor from which there was no escape. As she went further along it she found herself moving faster and faster, unable to stop, and she knew that something grotesquely terrifying lay in wait for her at the end. She woke up in fright with tears on her cheeks, and lay shivering for a long while before falling asleep again.

The next day Mrs. Frith arrived. Perdita regarded her with interest, for this lady was to introduce her to London society and eventually lead her to Piers Carston. She was a tall, queenly woman with slender hands and feet. Her hair was almost hidden under a lace cap inside her grey velvet bonnet, but the little that could be seen was an unusual shade of dark red. Her face was dominated by her green, almond-shaped eyes fringed with dark lashes. She was soberly but fashionably dressed in French grey corded silk trimmed with bands of grey velvet ribbon. Her gloves and slippers were of fine kid, and a dark green cashmere shawl was elegantly draped over her arms. She regarded Perdita with a detached but kindly air, and greeted the Countess with cool amiability.

For the next hour Mrs. Frith sat in the salon at Rotherfield House, displaying considerable tact. The Countess had taken it into her head that Perdita should not leave her protection until she was satisfied she would be safe. It said much for Mrs. Frith's powers of persuasion that within a short time the Countess permitted it. No one, least of all the Countess, was unaware that Mrs. Frith had been engaged by the Earl, but as Perdita's friend she was determined to see that Perdita was going to be well looked after, even if her son was not there to see to it himself.

At the end of half an hour the Countess confessed herself satisfied, and Mrs. Frith smiled politely and rose to take her new charge to Dover Street. The moment of parting had arrived. Calling on all her lessons in deportment, and what was left of her self-control, Perdita took a fond but restrained farewell of the Countess. She must not betray by any undue emotion that this was probably the last time she could see her, for the Countess would be returning to Ambourne before Perdita's entry on to the London scene. Somehow she managed it, and she and Mrs. Frith entered the closed carriage the Earl had provided to make the short journey to Dover Street.

The house the Earl had hired was small, but beautifully furnished and decorated. It was in a highly fashionable quarter and was a perfect setting for Perdita's role as a rich heiress. Her mother might well have hired just such a one for Perdita's season if fate and Piers Carston had not intervened. The two ladies admired its airy hall and pretty parlour, its small library and well-proportioned drawing-room. It was already staffed with a butler, who was nearly as imposing as Purkiss, a housekeeper, two footmen and several maids, one of whom was for Perdita.

In the bedroom she found several dresses laid out for her inspection, and more in boxes on the bed. All the rest of a young lady's wardrobe was disposed in the drawers and cupboards round the room. She was gazing in wonder at this lavish display when she was disturbed by Mrs. Frith, who was standing at the open door of the bedroom.

"Miss Taver, if you wish my help in selecting some dresses I shall be happy to advise you. They will then be altered to fit you, since the modiste has worked only from one of your previous dresses."

Perdita could not be other than impressed by Mrs. Frith's low voice and quiet manner. But she was sure that there was more to this woman than that, for, apart from the red hair and green eyes, had she not seen her handle the Countess at her most wilful? With a promise to deal with the dresses the next day, Perdita persuaded Mrs. Frith to come down to the salon. She was determined to discover what lay behind this understated façade. She was embarking on a difficult, even dangerous, game, and wanted no hidden complications.

They met the housekeeper in the hall and Perdita exchanged a few words with her. Mrs. Frith watched for a short while, and then with a smile went into the drawing-room.

Perdita followed a few minutes later and said, "I have ordered some tea—I hope you will take some with me? I could send for chocolate, if you prefer?"

"I usually drink coffee Miss Taver, but tea will do very well. It is more refreshing, perhaps." Perdita was surprised, for coffee was not a customary drink during the day in an ordinary house.

"I lived for some time in Eastern Europe, where they drink vast quantities of coffee. I'm afraid I developed the habit—I am Hungarian by birth, Miss Taver."

"Your English is excellent. I would never have suspected it." The housekeeper appeared at that moment with the tea, and the two ladies talked generalities until she had once again left the room, shutting the door behind her. Perdita spent some time serving the tea, for she was trying to gather her thoughts. She finally decided to be frank.

"You will forgive me if I speak plainly, Mrs. Frith. I am not sure what Lord Ambourne has told you of me, but you have certainly observed that I am not a nervous seventeen-year-old just out of the schoolroom. I defer to Lord Ambourne's insistence that I have a chaperon because I myself see the need for one here in London."

Mrs. Frith smiled at this forthright speech and replied, "Am I to understand, Miss Taver, that you are happy if I confine my chaperon's duties to providing a socially acceptable background? While I am very willing for this to be the case, I ought perhaps to tell you that Lord Ambourne has given me some details of your past and was of the opinion that I could be of help to you—and himself."

"Lord Ambourne gave you details of my past...?" asked Perdita in astonishment.

Mrs. Frith put her cup down and said with a smile, "He knows he can have complete trust in my discretion. We have been friends for several years." When she saw Perdita stiffen, she said carefully, "Lord Ambourne and my husband were close friends and colleagues, Miss Taver. They acted as observers in a diplomatic mission to Vienna in 1814. It was not all simple diplomacy, I assure you, nor even simple observation! The Napoleonic Empire was being disbanded, and it was essential that England was in a position to protect her own trading interests. The three of us—Lord Ambourne, my husband and I—worked very well together to keep Lord Castlereagh informed. In times of stress and even danger, Miss Taver, one grows very close to one's companions—and, above all, one learns to trust them. That is why Lord Ambourne knows he can trust me."

This matter-of-fact statement intrigued Perdita beyond measure. What sort of woman was this who looked and spoke like a conventionally fashionable society lady, but who was Hungarian and mentioned so casually that she had taken part in dangerous activities? But she must find out how much the Earl had told her.

As if in answer to the question, Mrs. Frith went on, "I think he has told me everything he knows, including his plans for Piers Carston. I met that gentleman last season. I cannot say I admire him, for, apart from what I have heard of him from Lord Ambourne, I have had one or two indications from other sources of his character. I believe him to be an unprincipled villain." With that startling statement she picked up her cup, sat back and calmly sipped her tea.

"H-how...how do you propose to help me?" asked Perdita, somewhat daunted by this quiet Amazon.

"First and most obviously I shall introduce you to society. I have the entré to most circles—there should be no difficulty there. Then I shall see that Mr. Carston learns that there is a rich and charming heiress at large in London.

I think it would be better, Miss Taver, if you could manage to appear rather naïve—as much like a nervous seventeen-year-old as you can manage.'' She smiled, and Perdita was forced to respond to her charm.

She said ruefully, ''Lord Ambourne did not doubt my power of dissimulation for an instant.''

''Nor your intelligence, from what he has said,'' was Mrs. Frith's surprising response.

Though Perdita's curiosity about this Hungarian lady was still unsatisfied, she found it impossible to question her further. There was a certain air of detachment, which was difficult to overcome. Mrs. Frith had drawn up a list of the sights which might interest a young lady on her first visit to London, together with directions and where to apply. She had also made appointments for the modiste, the milliner and coiffeur to come to the house. She had arranged invitations for Perdita to visit some of the great ladies of London society...

Perdita grew increasingly impressed with Mrs. Frith's abilities, but did not know whether they pleased or frightened her more. A scheme in which this woman was engaged would be almost certain of success. But would Mrs. Frith see through Perdita's own plans? There was much to be done, including at least one visit of which the Earl was to remain in ignorance. She would have to exercise extreme caution with Mrs. Frith.

CHAPTER FIFTEEN

WITH ALL THE ACTIVITIES planned by Mrs. Frith, Perdita had little opportunity during the next day or two to find out more about her chaperon or to pursue her own interests. She was forced to exercise a great deal of self-discipline to hide her impatience to be free, for Mrs. Frith was sure to be curious, even suspicious, of such a desire. She tried, therefore, to enjoy the sights and sounds of a London that was still celebrating the end of the Napoleonic wars and the resulting growth in trade with new buildings, new entertainments and a lavish display of goods of all kinds.

They visited the Pantheon and the shops in Oxford Street, and they went one day to the City, to the older, more traditional shops on Ludgate Hill. After examining the splendid mercer's shops there, Perdita insisted on visiting some of the bookshops. Mrs. Frith could not reasonably deny her, though she did point out that, since Perdita's goal was to entrap Piers Carston, pretty dresses and shoes might be of use, but books certainly would not!

At no point did Perdita have any money. The Earl must have been explicit about this, for it would otherwise have been quite normal for Mrs. Frith to provide her with a little pocket-money. Perdita bided her time. Somehow or other she would find the means of seeing the lawyers at Lincoln's Inn.

They had just returned from one of their shopping expeditions, and were having tea and coffee in the salon, when one of the footmen announced that Perdita had a visitor, who was waiting for her in the parlour downstairs.

"Who is it?" asked Mrs. Frith swiftly. "The Countess of Ambourne, ma'am," replied the footman.

Perdita leapt up before Mrs. Frith could say any more and said, "Don't stand there, Forrest! Show Lady Ambourne up here immediately."

He turned to go, but was swept aside by the tiny figure of the Countess. She strode in imperiously, hesitated, then turned to look at the footman with a stony face. Perdita had never seen her look so like the great lady she was. Perdita dismissed the footman, and then turned to the Countess and said urgently, "Ma'am, Lord Ambourne said you were not to visit m—" But she was not allowed to finish.

"I have something I wish to ask you, Perdita. I would prefer us to be alone, if Mrs. Frith will permit?"

She stood while Mrs. Frith rose, looked quizzically at Perdita, then said, "If you have no objection, Miss Taver, I will return the sample silks to the modiste. It will only take me half an hour, and Lady Ambourne will be here to keep you company. You will be here when I return, Lady Ambourne? If not, I will take my leave of you now." She went out, not without a questioning look at the Countess, who stiffly bade her good afternoon.

Perdita invited the Countess to sit, but she refused impatiently and said, "Perdita, I cannot believe what my son has just told me, and I am here to hear you deny it. He is surely not going to marry you off to Carston? Tell me it isn't so!"

Perdita's face grew scarlet then white. She stammered that she could not deny it. The Countess had been told the truth.

"But surely you haven't agreed?" When Perdita stood in silence she cried, "I told Edward he was mad, Perdita! That, even if he had forgotten every decency, you would never agree to such a shameful thing..." She walked away from Perdita as if she could not bear to be near her, then turned on her. "What sort of monsters are you? I thought I knew you both, but I realise now that you are strangers to me. Up till this minute, Perdita, I would have sworn there was not a man in the world who had more integrity than Edward. And not a woman for whom I had more regard. I am sadly disappointed in both of you. My son to do this! My son..." Her voice trembled as she said these last words.

"Ma'am, you do not understand—"

"I understand very well, Perdita. I understand that Edward, who I would swear loves you, will see you married to Piers Carston, whom he hates. And that you, who love my son, will marry this...this...*salaud*, will live with him...I cannot speak of it." She turned away again, then cried, "But why are you doing this? It is insulting to suggest you are being offered money for this betrayal. But what else could have persuaded you to agree to such an infamous scheme?" When Perdita hesitated she said, "Oh, do not bother to tell me. Nothing could have forced you against your will, not even my son. You make a fine pair!"

There was a slight pause. Perdita was in an agony of indecision, but, before she could say anything, the Countess continued, "I loved you as a daughter, Perdita. I was foolishly taken in by your charming ways and your lovely face." She took a deep breath and said, "Now I never want to see you again. As for my son...it will be a long time before I will forgive him for his shameful plans. It is the worst thing yet that Piers Carston has done to our family." A sob escaped her.

Perdita cried, "He had his reasons, ma'am. It isn't as you think, I swear it!" Then when the Countess started to the door she made up her mind and said, quickly, "Ma'am, I beg of you, please wait here while I ensure we are not overheard. I know I can ease your mind on one point at least, perhaps more. Will you wait?"

The Countess stopped and turned round. What she saw in Perdita's face seemed to convince her that she was being sincere, and she nodded. Perdita hurriedly checked that the servants were all out of earshot and returned to the salon, where she found the Countess standing at the window.

"Ma'am, what I am going to tell you is in part known to your son, but only in part. I would like your assurance that you will not reveal to him anything he does not already know. Indeed, I think it would be better if you did not tell him that you had seen me at all... Will you promise?"

"I will not promise anything until I know what it is, Perdita," said the Countess coldly. "And Mrs. Frith is almost certain to tell him I have called. However, at the moment my son and I are not in communication. I have already informed him I am returning to Ambourne tomorrow, and I do not expect I shall see him again before I go. What is it that you have to say?"

"Will you sit, ma'am? It is a long story." The Countess reluctantly sat down and Perdita began hesitantly, "First, your son has good reason to believe that I would not regard marrying Piers Carston as abhorrent. I told you once that I had associated with thieves and murderers, and I do not think you really believed me. Lord Ambourne knows it to be true. For over two years I lived on a pirate ship in the Mediterranean." She went on to describe in detail the circumstances in which the Earl had discovered her. "You know of his determination to ruin Piers Carston, ma'am.

Believing me to be worthless, he bought me to be a tool, no more, to achieve that end. To his mind, my marriage and subsequent separation from his enemy was of benefit to me, for I would then have the means to escape from a life of cruelty and crime and...and...be able to live in comparative affluence. I beg you, do not blame your son for this. He may have developed some feeling for me, but he is determined to conquer it, for how could the Earl of Ambourne be associated with a pirate's...a pirate's whore? Forgive me if I have offended you, but I must speak plainly. It is important that you do not think so badly of your son.''

She waited, but at first the Countess was deep in thought. Finally she said, ''I still do not approve of his intentions, but I can understand them, at least. But what of you? I do not understand why you should have agreed, for, whatever the circumstances in which Edward found you, Perdita, I refuse to believe you would not in fact find marriage to Carston repugnant.''

''Now we come to the point at which I must trust you, ma'am, not to tell Lord Ambourne. Mrs. Frith, who is his associate in this matter, is out of the house, so she will not know anything. Can I trust you?''

The Countess considered Perdita's anxious face and said, ''If I can see my way of keeping Edward in ignorance I will, Perdita. Continue.''

Taking her courage in both hands, Perdita told the Countess the unhappy story of her family's involvement with the Carstons. She held nothing back, even giving her real name and the place of her birth.

The Countess was deeply shocked. ''The man is a monster! Indeed, I think Eliane was lucky to escape as she did.''

''Do you understand now, ma'am, why I have agreed

to help your son? I think if I had insisted he would have dropped this dreadful idea. Do not blame him too much, I pray."

"Well, I do still blame him, Perdita, for his willingness to expose the woman he loves to that kind of danger. It does not reflect well on him. But how will you go on? You will surely not pretend to marry Carston?"

"Oh, no, ma'am. All I have to do is reappear. If I could only get to our lawyers I could soon ruin Mr. Piers Carston, I assure you. The difficulty is that I do not wish to take Mrs. Frith into my confidence, for I believe her loyalty will lie with Lord Ambourne. And I have no money to go there myself—apart from the difficulty of escaping her vigilance."

"I am sure I can remedy that, at least. But, Perdita, why do you not wish my son to know what you have told me? Surely it would be much simpler if he knew?"

Perdita hung her head, then looked up defiantly. "I do not wish to make it simpler for him, ma'am. Though he is not the 'monster' you thought him, it is true that he is prepared to see me married to someone he hates in order to further his own plans. I know he could never marry me himself, but it has caused me some pain that he can contemplate such a thing. He does not deserve to have his path made smooth sooner than necessary."

The Countess regarded Perdita ruefully. "Oh, what a match that would be—you and Edward! Can it really not be so?"

"It is kind of you even to think of it, ma'am, but do not forget yours is an old and proud family. And I too have my pride. No, it cannot be."

The Countess thought for a minute.

"In one thing at least I can help you, Perdita. I can provide you with some money—enough and to spare for a hackney to Lincoln's Inn. Has my son really not given you any?''

"He does not trust me, ma'am," said Perdita sadly. "Not in London."

The Countess pursed her lips, but said nothing, while she considered. Finally she said, "We must make haste, Perdita. It cannot be long before Mrs. Frith returns, and we have to decide what you can do. Does Mrs. Frith always accompany you when you go out?"

Perdita nodded. "Always. But she usually rests in her room in the afternoon."

"Then you must slip out of the house unobserved tomorrow afternoon and take a hackney carriage from Berkeley Square. I can arrange to have one waiting for you if you tell me when you wish to go. And I'll make sure the driver is trustworthy."

The Countess was becoming quite her usual self in the interest of helping Perdita to outwit Mrs. Frith. By the time that lady returned they had arranged it all and were sitting amicably chatting in the salon. The Countess did not stay much longer, but thanked Mrs Frith for giving her this time alone with her son's ward. She had wanted, she said, to have one last cosy chat with Perdita before returning to Ambourne. Mrs. Frith was too well bred to express surprise or disbelief. She smiled slightly and said she hoped to see the Countess again—when she returned to London and had another cosy chat with Perdita.

ALL WENT AS THEY HAD planned. The following day Perdita slipped out of the house, her money wrapped in a handkerchief in the deep pockets of her cloak, and ran round to Berkeley Square. The Countess had not failed her, for as soon as he saw her a middle-aged, red-cheeked hackney driver came up and handed her into his cab. He already knew where he was taking her, and gave her a running commentary on London life as they bowled up Oxford Street with its numerous shops, through the dirt and misery of St. Giles, and into High Holborn. From here they turned into Chancery Lane and thence into Lincoln's Inn. Asking her driver to wait, Perdita hurried into the building.

When she entered the poky little ante-room the elderly clerk standing at a tall desk came over to ask rather testily what she wanted. But when he saw her face he clutched the side of the desk and said, "It can't be! Not after all this time. I don't believe my eyes! Who are you?"

"I'm Felicia Taverton, Burgess. Have you forgotten me?"

"Miss Felicia? Oh, Miss Felicia! Forgive me, what am I thinking of? Well, my goodness, I can't believe it...Miss Felicia, after all this time..."

He would have continued in this vein, but Perdita knew her time was limited. She asked, "Would you take my name in to Mr. Rambridge, Burgess? I should like to consult him on a matter of some urgency." Still muttering, the old man went into the inner room. Perdita heard more exclamations, and a white-haired gentleman came out in a most undignified rush.

"Miss Felicia! Miss Felicia Taverton! This is happy news indeed. Come in, come in. Burgess, fetch some wine. We must drink to this. But my dear young lady, where did you disappear to? What happened? We searched the country for you." Perdita was made to sit down with a glass of wine, and after more exclamations and questions, which she was not given time to answer, she finally managed to give him a short account of her adventures.

The lawyer already knew that Piers Carston was a villain, but was very shocked at his unbelievably callous treatment of Perdita. He kept interrupting to ask her to repeat what she had said, and shook his head each time in amazement and distress. When she came to the end, he said gravely, "And what do you wish me to do now? Of course, we can lay this information with the authorities. There can be little doubt that your evidence would incriminate him, though if he denied it it might be difficult for you... I suppose we might show what he had done with the estate..."

"I think I have a better scheme, Mr. Rambridge. But first tell me about my mother."

His face grew sad. "She died shortly after you disappeared..." Then he burst out, "I knew that young villain was lying, but your mother would have none of it. He couldn't say he had seen you die, though, so, in spite of what he implied, she was convinced you would return. Poor lady, she died believing in that ruffian. You know she left him to look after the estate until you came back? We could do nothing. Oh, we stopped him selling any of the land, but he has milked it dry, Miss Felicia. The tenants and workers are in a poor way; I don't know what you can do. There will be a great deal to repair and not many resources to do it..."

"After I have dealt with Piers Carston here in London," said Perdita, "I shall return to Somerset and do what I can. Meanwhile I want you to help me here." She went on to instruct Mr. Rambridge. He was very doubtful of the wisdom of her actions, but was forced to agree that taking Piers Carston to a court of law would be an uncertain business.

"As we all know," he said at last, "Carston is a plausible and attractive-looking rogue. He just might convince a jury you were lying, Miss Felicia. Perhaps you are right, after all. He might, if surprised, convict himself. Well, I will do as you say. Just send me word when you are ready." He renewed his expression of joy at seeing her alive and well and looking, "as pretty as a picture, Miss Felicia, if you will permit an old man to say so. Whatever you have suffered, it has not done your looks any damage."

He led her out to the hackney carriage and handed her in, telling the driver to take great care of her. She saw him standing at the gate until the carriage turned into Holborn.

Perdita asked the driver to put her down at Green Park, and when she tried to pay him he told her that her ladyship had already done so. She established that he would be prepared to take a message to Mr. Rambridge when called on. Then she went into the park. Thanks to the Countess's forethought, she now had a slender store of money to help her in any emergency. For a short while she watched the nursemaids and their charges, then went back to Dover Street. This enabled her to tell Mrs. Frith without a blush that she had taken the air in the park. That lady gave her a sharp look, but merely said mildly that she was surprised Perdita had not felt cold, and went on to tell her that her dresses had been delivered.

Perdita was glad of the excuse to escape upstairs to her room, and spent the time until dinner trying on her new wardrobe. Very soon now she would be launched. The first ball of the season was in two days' time at Glasham House. According to Mrs. Frith, Piers Carston was unlikely to be there. But at least it would start London talking about the new heiress.

IN ALL THIS TIME she had not seen the Earl, but he came on the night of the ball. When she entered the salon after dressing he was waiting for her, looking pale but very handsome in the dark blue tailcoat and white breeches. A diamond gleamed in his starched cravat... Her eyes closed as she suddenly remembered the evening at Belleroi after he had saved her when the branch fell. Madame d'Espery had been there too, and he had worn a diamond then. She remembered how it had sparkled throughout dinner. Then afterwards he had kissed her...

She came to with a start as his cool, well-bred voice said, "Are you quite well, Perdita? You look a little pale, though, as always, ravishingly lovely." The indifferent tone in which he uttered the extravagant compliment was like a slap in the face.

She rallied and said with deliberate malice, "You are equally pale, Lord Ambourne. I hope nothing has made you unhappy. Your mother is well, I hope?"

His indifferent air was lost as he said, "You know very well what has happened, Perdita, so don't sharpen your claws on me! My mother probably told you all—if she kept her temper with you long enough, that is. I gathered from her somewhat intemperate comments that you had an equal share of the blame in her eyes. Was the interview with her very bad?"

"Not at all, Lord Ambourne," said Perdita airily. "Your mother now knows me for what I am, and it is better so." He looked surprised, but did not comment. Instead he produced a thin box and passed it to her.

"This may be a bizarre come-out, but it is one, nevertheless. I wish you to wear these tonight, Perdita." She could not reply, for her throat was choked and her eyes full of tears. He had given her a long rope of perfectly matched pearls with a sapphire clasp. Its velvet-lined box, with the name of one of London's foremost jewellers on it, was exactly like the one her father had given her on her fifteenth birthday just before he'd died. The pearls then had been equally well matched, but that necklace had been a small one, suitable for a young girl. She wondered fleetingly what had happened to it...

"Perdita?" When she looked up he said roughly, "You're crying. Why on earth should you cry over this? You need not wear them if you do not wish to. Do not, for heaven's sake, give yourself a red nose and blotched eyes for a trumpery necklace. Was my mother very hard on you, Perdita?"

"No," she replied truthfully. "The Countess was very kind, but she went away quite soon."

"She has gone to Ambourne. I do not remember seeing her quite so angry before. Certainly not with me..."

For a moment he looked so unhappy that she longed to go and comfort him. But then she hardened her heart. His mother's anger might have distressed him, but it had not caused him to change his mind. He recovered his indifferent air in an instant, and asked if she was intending to wear the necklace. She sensed that her answer was important to him and did not have the heart to disappoint him.

"Thank you, Lord Ambourne. I will wear it with pleasure."

As he fastened it round her neck she felt his fingers tremble slightly, and then his hands rested on her shoulders. Their grip tightened as he said, "Perdita..." But when she turned round to him again his face was impassive. Only his eyes gave him away. "It is nothing."

Mrs. Frith came in at that point, looking elegant in brown silk, lace and emeralds.

"Ah, Edward, how nice to see you. Are you not pleased with your ward?"

She took Perdita by the hand and twirled her round like a doll. The dress to Perdita's mind was a trifle overdone, with its white lace robe over a pink satin slip, its pearl embroideries and knots of satin ribbons. A half-garland of

lace and small pink roses was tucked into her back hair,
and she was wearing white corded silk shoes and white
kid gloves.

The Earl looked at her through his glass and finally said,
"Perfect, my dear. Just the effect we want—lavish, rich
and naïve. Now, if Perdita can play her part, we shall have
Carston sniffing at her heels in no time."

With a sort of gallows humour Perdita decided to enjoy
this last act in her relationship with the Earl. She ignored
his last remark and said gaily, "Have you seen my pearls,
Mrs. Frith? Are they not splendid? I vow I have never seen
prettier beads in my whole life!"

Mrs. Frith examined the pearls with indulgence at first,
and then with real surprise. She raised one eyebrow at the
Earl—who, to Perdita's great pleasure, was looking outraged—and murmured, "Worth a king's ransom—or at
least a prince's! I am surprised you consider it necessary
to make the props so genuine, my friend. They are extremely pretty 'beads', Miss Taver. You must look after
them, for they will give you a rich old age!" Then she
looked at the Earl and Perdita with amused speculation in
her green eyes.

IT WAS OBVIOUS from the first moment that the Duchess
of Stockhampton's ball would achieve everything they had
hoped for. Mrs. Frith's information was sound—Piers Carston did not appear. But the rest of the polite world was
there, and Perdita's beauty, Perdita's naïve charm, and
above all, Perdita's apparent wealth were clearly about to
form the topic of conversation in most of the clubs and
houses that Piers Carston would frequent. No one doubted
her credentials, though no one could remember actually
hearing of the Taver fortune before. A few hints that the
family had connections with the East India Com-

pany...that the French wars had kept them abroad...soon put an end to any speculation. After all, who was going to question the origins of a lady sponsored by Mrs. Frith who, as everyone knew, was related to the Esterhazys and was a princess in her own right?

Perdita was soon pronounced to be a pretty, well-behaved girl who did not put herself forward in spite of her vast fortune. It was noticed by the observant that, though the Earl of Ambourne meticulously avoided any hint of gossip, never dancing with Miss Taver more than twice in one evening and never paying her undue attention, he seemed to be aware of her all the time. And any unfortunate young man who was unduly pressing in his attentions often found himself edged out of her presence by a grim-faced Earl. Miss Taver, for her part, seemed to treat her suitors with charming deference. They were all enchanted with her childlike innocence.

CHAPTER SIXTEEN

WORD FINALLY CAME that Piers Carston had reappeared on the London scene. Mrs. Frith's informant was certain that he would attend the ball to be given the following Tuesday at Lady Francombe's Palladian mansion in Berkeley Square. Now that the climax of her London season was so near, Perdita suddenly felt nervous. The feeling behind her conversation with Mrs. Frith when they heard this news was therefore unfeigned, though she would have pretended if necessary.

"I have been considering my initial meeting with Piers Carston, Mrs. Frith, and have some thoughts on the subject that might interest you," she began as they were sitting one afternoon in the drawing-room. Mrs. Frith looked up from her work and smiled encouragingly. "My suitors have grown to such numbers—drawn, no doubt, by the growing size of my reported fortune—that it might prove difficult for Mr. Carston to approach me as easily as he would like. I am seldom free of a crowd of admirers when I am in public."

"You think he will be frightened away by the size of your entourage? But surely the size of your fortune will outweigh that?" said Mrs. Frith cynically.

"I am sure it will. But it will take him time, and I would be happier if the business was settled as soon as possible. I do not find it easy to sustain this deception…" Her chaperon raised one eyebrow in elegant disbelief. Perdita said earnestly, "I assure you, I do not, ma'am. I am constantly in dread of being found out."

"I am sorry you find it such a strain, Miss Taver. I had thought you were enjoying it. So you would like to end the affair quickly? That would need some special thought, I agree. Let me think…"

Perdita sat there, crossing her fingers and praying for the right opportunity. She could hardly believe her good fortune when it came.

"How could Mr. Carston meet you away from your followers?" said Mrs. Frith slowly. "He would certainly be suspicious if you arranged a meeting alone with him too soon after making his acquaintance."

"Oh, I could not do that, ma'am. Nor would I wish to see him without your presence. If only there was someone who could offer to arrange such a meeting—perhaps even for a suitable sum? Is there anyone in your acquaintance who would act as a go-between?

"There might perhaps be just the person…" said Mrs. Frith. "I must speak to Lord Ambourne."

The result of Mrs. Frith's consultation with the Earl was everything Perdita had hoped for. Mrs. Frith herself would act the part of mediator, for it was not thought politic to introduce any other party to the scheme. Now that Piers Carston was actually in town they must practise extreme caution. Perdita joined in the planning of the deception with enthusiasm. If the Earl had been present he would surely have suspected her motives, but he was taking care to stay away from the house. Mrs. Frith, having no reason to doubt the truth of Perdita's anxiety, took her helpful suggestions at face value, and it was finally settled that Mrs. Frith would allow herself to be suborned by Carston into introducing him to Perdita in a private room at Lady Francombe's ball.

"Can you do that, ma'am?" asked Perdita.

"Oh, there will be no difficulty in persuading Mr. Carston that I can be bribed," said Mrs. Frith, "for he judges everyone by his own corrupt standards. Nor need you fear that he will suspect I put the idea into his head. Allow me some subtlety, Miss Taver." Once again Perdita reminded herself that Mrs. Frith was a dangerous woman. But she must continue.

"Do you know of a suitable room, ma'am? How will I know where it is?"

"After you enter Lady Francombe's house there is a great staircase in front of you, which rises up the centre of the hall. To the left of the staircase on the ground floor is an ante-room, followed by the library. This would seem to be an admirable place for you to meet. A small waiting-room opens out of the library on the far side, where Lord Ambourne can, if he wishes, conceal himself."

Perdita felt the Earl would like to witness this first meeting to see that his 'tool' was prepared to carry out his wishes. Well, he would see more than he bargained for!

"I should like that," she said nervously, "for I do not know how this Piers Carston will treat me. You have said he is a villain, have you not?" She thought she might have overdone it, but Mrs. Frith said gravely that he was indeed.

The next days passed swiftly. Perdita managed to send her message to Mr. Rambridge, and spent the rest of the time alternately worrying about her plans and her appearance. Woman-like, she wanted the Earl to see her at her best on this last evening, and she had saved her prettiest dress for the occasion. It was of white silk gauze woven with a thread of silver, and was worn over a white satin slip. Little ornament was needed for the material itself glinted and shone as she moved, but thin bands of pale blue silk caught the folds of the gauze round the bottom of the skirt, and were tucked round the white satin bodice at the waist. It was a triumph of lovely simplicity, and had cost more than any two of her other dresses together. With it she would wear her rope of pearls, wound twice round her neck, with the sapphire clasp at the front.

In her room on the night of the ball, while the maid arranged her hair and reverently put the dress on her, Perdita was as nervous as any débutante. It would not be too much to say that tonight would determine the rest of her life. Her heart was thumping as she came down to the salon, where Mrs. Frith waited. She hoped everything was done. If only Mr. Rambridge had done his part—and Piers Carston would do his—she would answer for the rest!

Mrs. Frith was standing in front of the large mirror to the side of the fireplace. She looked superb in dark green silk and diamonds, but Perdita sensed a most unusual excitement in her. Her green eyes were glowing like a cat's and her whole air was slightly feverish. She complimented Perdita on her appearance, and they were about to depart when the Earl was announced.

"Are you mad?" was Mrs. Frith's greeting. "What if Carston should observe you coming into this house?"

"He will not," said the Earl briefly. "I would like to speak to Perdita alone, Ludmila." Mrs. Frith looked from one to the other and then shrugged her shoulders.

"I'll wait downstairs, Miss Taver," was all she said before she went out.

As soon as the door had closed the Earl said abruptly, "Perdita, I have to speak to you before you meet Carston tonight. My mother was right. It is a vile thing I have asked you to do—you must not marry Carston. After tonight you are free to do as you please. If you wish to leave London and live elsewhere in England, or France, or even Africa, I will arrange for you to do so."

"But what of your wish to punish Carston? Have you forgotten what he did to Eliane?" asked Perdita in astonishment.

"No, I have not forgotten," was the terse reply.

"Then why do you wish to abandon your scheme? Is it because of your mother's anger?" Her eyes searched his face.

"No," he said. "She has merely crystallised my own feelings in the matter."

"Then why—?"

"Is it not enough that you no longer need to do something you have found so repellent?" he said harshly.

"No, it is not enough, Lord Ambourne. It is not nearly enough. After weeks of preparation you arrive here to tell me to abandon all our plans—"

"They are my plans, Perdita. Mine alone."

"Oh, I am fully aware that you have always regarded me as little more than your tool," cried Perdita angrily. "You have made that very clear from the first—"

"It isn't so, Perdita. I have come to have regard and respect for you—"

"Regard and respect! You do me too much honour, Lord Ambourne! What would a pirate's drab do with your 'regard and respect'?" Perdita was growing angrier by the minute. The unhappiness of the last weeks at Belleroi and the tension that had built up inside her in London culminated in a burst of rage towards this man. His plans had caused her so much heartache and anxiety, and now he wished to throw them all out of the window—for a caprice, as far as she could determine. "Are you afraid that your aristocratic friends will condemn you for associating with people like Piers Carston and me? A thief and seducer of young girls, and a strumpet from the Mediterranean? Is that it?"

"Be silent, Perdita. I—"

"I will not be silent! I am not an inanimate object to be used or rejected at your whim. And unless you can give me a better reason than your 'regard and respect' I will tell the whole of London what sort of girl you have foisted on all the ambitious mamas and their fortune-seeking sons!"

"Be quiet, you little termagant!" He snatched her to him and kissed her savagely. As she struggled and kicked he gave a short laugh and kissed her again, holding her so closely that she was lifted off her feet. "There's your reason! Mad though it is, I cannot tolerate seeing you married to Carston—or any other man!"

Shock held her still for a moment. Then she released herself from his hold, but still held on to his sleeve—she could not have stood otherwise.

Seeing how dazed she was, he led her gently to a chair and sat her down. Then he walked to the fire and gazed moodily into the flames. Still not facing her, he said, "I admit that when I set out on this enterprise I thought it would be simple. I would trap Carston with his own ambition and greed. You were merely the means by which I could achieve this. You seemed perfect for the purpose— lovely, abandoned and, as I thought then, depraved. But Sheikh Ibrahim warned me not to attempt to use you, and he was right. Believe me, Perdita, I have been well punished for ignoring his words. Can you forgive me?"

Perdita's thoughts were racing. There was so little time. She could not now abandon all her own carefully laid plans. And yet she must respond to the Earl's words. Should she tell him? She must! But at that moment Mrs. Frith came into the room, and the opportunity was lost.

"Edward, I must interrupt you. Miss Taver will arrive unpardonably late at Lady Francombe's. It is too bad of

you, after all our work. Come, Perdita, you must tidy yourself up a little before you are seen in public.''

Perdita looked at the Earl and said softly, ''I will meet
Carston tonight. We shall talk about my future after that.
You will be there?'' He nodded. She smiled at him. ''Then
I will not be in any danger.''

He started towards her but Mrs. Frith said sharply, ''Perdita!'' and with an apologetic glance at the Earl she followed Mrs. Frith upstairs to her room.

While Lucy fussed around her she stood lost in a dream.
Her chaperon contemplated her for a moment, then said,
not unsympathetically, ''Pull yourself together, Perdita.
You have much to do tonight. I cannot imagine why Lord
Ambourne could not have postponed the affecting talk he
has obviously had with you till another time. But men are
often incomprehensible creatures. They do not keep their
minds on the task in hand. Women are much more practical. Come, my dear.''

She took Perdita down to the waiting carriage, and they
were soon in Berkeley Square. When they entered the
house Mrs. Frith pointed out the library, and as they gave
their cloaks to the footman Perdita managed to remain
unobserved as she handed him a note and some money.
At the top of the stairs she was introduced to their hostess,
who was most gracious and chatted to her for some
minutes while the line of guests built up behind her. Then
they went into the ballroom. It was half-past nine.

Perdita was surrounded almost immediately by her
crowd of admirers, and Lady Francombe's affability was
explained when later a callow youth came up to her and
said, ''Your servant, Miss Taver. I am Gervaise Francombe. My mother has told me so much about you...''

THOUGH PERDITA DANCED every dance, the minutes till
eleven o'clock dragged and it was a relief when Mrs. Frith

came to her and it was time to go downstairs. With a pretty smile of apology to her waiting court, Perdita left the ball-room with her chaperon. She had not seen the Earl since arriving at Lady Francombe's, but trusted he was in his place in the writing-room. As she passed the footman he gave her a small nod. Good! Mr. Rambridge had arrived. She asked Mrs. Frith to wait for one minute outside the door, and then, forcing herself to look calm, walked into the library...

The man at the far end of the room had been examining himself in the mirror over the fireplace, and when he turned Perdita saw that time had started to take its toll of Piers's handsome face. His features had coarsened, the guinea-gold hair was fading, and his blue eyes were beginning to look bloodshot. A glass of brandy was in his hand and his face was flushed.

When he saw her the carefully practised smile vanished and his jaw dropped.

"Felicia!" he exclaimed in horror. "No, it can't be! How did you get here? You're dead. Felicia's dead!"

"Legrand brought me here, Piers," said Perdita softly.

"You're lying! Legrand is dead! He was drowned last year—and so were you!"

"Oh, no, Piers, I wasn't. As you see, I am here. And Legrand asked me to give you a present. Look!" He stared at the pearl held out to him in a slender hand. The soft voice continued, "I was worth more than the half-pearl he paid for me, Piers. And I've come back to give you this."

He backed away from her and said loudly, "I don't want it! Take it away! What sort of game is this? Legrand said he'd make sure you never came back..."

"What did you tell my mother, Piers? That you'd sold me to a pirate for half the price of a pearl? That you'd left me to be beaten and starved? That you'd given me into the hands of a twisted maniac? You surely didn't tell my mother that as she lay dying, did you?''

The tremendous shock that Carston had undergone had caused him to lose all sense of self-preservation. If he had kept a cool head he might have bluffed his way out of the trap Perdita had laid. But the shock, and the brandy he had drunk, made him reckless.

''Don't be so stupid!'' he said with a laugh. ''Of course I didn't! I was her golden boy! I had a damned sight better story than that, and she swallowed the lot—the blood-stained scarf, how bravely I fought…after all, I had been injured, hadn't I? You threw me out of the chaise, remember? No, I could wind her round my little finger—except that the stupid bitch wouldn't believe you were dead!''

''So I heard. So you couldn't sell the estate after all—Taverton, with all its rich lands and farms?''

''No!'' he said resentfully. ''And after my father died I found it damned hard to keep myself going with it, I can tell you. Those meddlesome fools of lawyers wouldn't let me sell off any of the land. I've had a rough time of it this last year.''

''Poor Piers,'' said Perdita sarcastically.

He took another drink of the brandy, gave her a calculating look, and carefully put down his glass. Then with conscious charm and an air of frankness he walked towards her, saying, ''Felicia, I know I behaved badly, and I'm sorry… Legrand frightened me and I acted in panic…''

''What about the pearl, Piers? Was I really worth so little?''

For a moment he stopped and thought. ''You made me angry,'' he said finally. ''You should have married me when I asked you.''

"My mother trusted you to take me to safety, not to try to force me to marry you!" Perdita cried.

"Yes, I know that," Piers said impatiently. Then he remembered his role and spoke charmingly again. "Felicia, can't we forget all this? Remember the good times we had at Taverton? Can't we go back to what we were? Even now, after all that you've been, I'm prepared to marry you. Come on, can't we kiss and be friends?" He was close to her now, and she could smell the brandy on his breath. He grabbed her roughly and she screamed.

In a flash three people came into the room. The Earl went straight for Carston, knocked him to the ground and stood over him menacingly, his face white with rage. Mr. Rambridge hurried from the ante-room, closely followed by Mrs. Frith, who took Perdita's hand and led her to the side. Carston groaned and tried to get up. The Earl pushed him back.

"You'll stay there, Carston, if you're wise. I'd be delighted to knock you down again!" he said. Carston lay back.

"I think you should let him go," said Perdita. "You can't keep him there all night, and he can't do any more damage."

"Let him go?" exclaimed Mr. Rambridge. "Let him go? My dear young lady, he should be handed over instantly!"

"Have you given the envelope to the magistrates? To be opened tomorrow?" Perdita asked.

"Yes, I have. I took it myself today. However—" But Perdita did not let him finish.

"Then tomorrow they will have a full list of his crimes, including the betrayal of shipping information—"

"But Miss Taverton, I still think he should be handed over tonight," protested Mr. Rambridge.

"I am giving him twelve hours' grace to enable him to leave the country. After that he will be a wanted man, but twelve hours he will have," said Perdita obstinately. "Lord Ambourne, let him get up, if you please." Reluctantly the Earl, who looked slightly dazed, allowed Carston to get to his feet. They watched in silence as Carston, without another look at any of them, went out.

"Perdita," said the Earl, "my love..." And he took her into his arms and kissed her passionately.

Mr. Rambridge gave a small cough, and when Perdita finally looked at him he said, "I cannot agree with your actions, Miss Felicia, but your clemency does you credit. There is much to discuss, and I'm afraid there will be many papers dealing with the estate to sign. Shall I see you tomorrow in Lincoln's Inn?"

Perdita hesitated, but refused to look at the Earl. Then she said she would be there at eleven. Mr. Rambridge, too polite to do more than glance curiously at the tall figure standing silently by his client, turned to go. He was immediately knocked aside by a frantic figure in a greatcoat. It was Piers Carston.

"You lied!" he shouted wildly. "You said you'd give me till tomorrow, but you lied! There are men out there—Runners! You lying devils! You did this, Ambourne!" He suddenly pulled a pistol out of the pocket of his greatcoat and pointed it at the Earl.

"No, Piers, no!" screamed Perdita and threw herself at him. There was a loud report, and Perdita staggered.

As she twisted round and fell she heard the Earl cry out, "Oh, God! Perdita!" But then his voice died and blackness overcame her...

WHEN SHE CAME TO she was lying on the couch and the Earl was bending over her. Mrs. Frith was in the background, and Mr. Rambridge was standing at the foot of her couch, looking very anxious.

"Thank God!" said the Earl as she opened her eyes. "No, don't try to get up. We've sent for a doctor."

"Did the men come for Piers?" she whispered.

He nodded gravely and said, "They arrested him immediately after he shot you."

"But who...?" Perdita struggled to sit up, but fell back with a cry as she felt a knife-like pain just below her shoulder.

The Earl swore under his breath and put her gently back on the couch. Then he said firmly, "You must lie back and rest, Perdita! Your wound is not serious unless you make it worse by your own unconsidered behaviour!"

He smiled at her to soften his words and got up to move away. But Perdita caught his hand and said, "No, don't go! It's better when you're here. But do tell me who sent for the Runners."

"They were not Runners, Miss Taver," said a calm voice behind them. Mrs. Frith came forward to the couch. "They were constables, hired by my friends at Lloyds. And I apologise. I should, of course, have called you Miss Taverton."

"From Lloyds? Well, bless my soul! I quite thought the magistrates had refused to wait till tomorrow to open Miss Felicia's letter," said Mr. Rambridge, his elderly face creased with worry as he regarded Perdita. "I must see that they are informed straight away. Will you excuse me, Miss Felicia? I think you are in good hands." He bowed to all of them and left.

"On whose authority did you send for these men?" demanded the Earl. Then, as Mrs. Frith remained silent, he said grimly, "We have a lot to discuss, Ludmila."

"And I will willingly tell you all you wish to know,

Edward, but not, I think, here and now. Miss Taverton needs some rest."

"Do not, I beg you, shut me out!" pleaded Perdita, faint but game. "I must know why those constables came to arrest my stepbrother."

"I will see that you know everything," promised the Earl, smiling at her. "But for the moment I must give way to the doctor, who is even now coming through the door."

There followed some extremely painful moments when the doctor removed the pads the Earl had placed over the wound and examined it. He advised Miss Taverton that the bullet was lodged in the flesh near her shoulder, and recommended that she should be carried carefully to her own home, where it could be removed.

"I'll take her," said the Earl quickly. "Ludmila, please make our excuses to Lady Francombe and follow us to Dover Street. I will arrange for a carriage to fetch you."

"Of course," said Mrs. Frith.

Throughout the excitement that was taking place in Lady Francombe's library the ball had continued uninterrupted. The music and chatter of the guests had drowned any untoward noises—even the sound of the shot—and the Earl, with Mrs. Frith's aid, was able to carry Perdita out with no other excuse than that she was feeling faint. This was no less than the truth. The pain of the last hour, together with the strain of the preceding interview, had drained all Perdita's resources. The doctor had not given her anything to deaden the pain because, as he kindly put it, she would need that solace later in the evening. In due course she found herself in her room, and the Earl was giving precise instructions to her maid. Then he went to escort the doctor upstairs.

"Oh, your dress, miss! Your lovely dress! What a shame!" was Lucy's contribution to Perdita's comfort.

Fortunately the doctor arrived straight away, and after an even more painful time the bullet had been removed and Perdita's shoulder bound up. No serious damage had been done, but Perdita was past caring. The doctor had given her some laudanum, and she was smiling sleepily when the Earl pushed a scandalised Lucy aside and came in to see how she had fared.

"Are you comfortable? You look it." Perdita tried to nod but her head felt too heavy. The Earl smiled and said softly, "Goodnight, Perdita. We shall see how you are tomorrow." As he left the room he bowed to the maid, who was staring saucer-eyed at the gentleman in her mistress's bedroom. And him an Earl!

CHAPTER SEVENTEEN

IT WAS NOT TO BE expected that Perdita would feel comfortable for the next day or two. The bullet had gone deep into her arm, and she dreaded the doctor's daily visit to examine and dress the wound. But on the second day she insisted on getting up in the afternoon, and the day after that she was downstairs as soon as the doctor had gone. Mrs. Frith protested once, and then helped to make her comfortable on the day bed in the salon. The Earl had not visited Perdita again in her bedroom, but had left a bottle of claret and some flowers. As soon as Perdita's admirers heard she was ill the house was besieged with callers, none of whom were admitted, and who left whole gardens of flowers, some with very fanciful notes.

"How nauseating!" was the Earl's response to a particularly effusive communication. He had been surprised to hear that Perdita was up and ready to receive him when he came round on his daily visit to the house that afternoon. On being invited into the salon he had examined one or two of the billets with an expression of distaste.

"You are not very kind," said Perdita, laughing.

"You will allow that this poem could not possibly help anyone to feel better. If one were not sickened by the sentiment, the quality of the verse would be enough to cause an instant relapse!" he replied. "And it has caused me to forget my manners—how do you go on, Perdita?"

Perdita assured him that she was almost better, at which he raised an eyebrow and asked her to raise her right arm.

"Well, that's a little difficult," she protested, laughing again. "It will be a while yet before I can use my arm freely."

"I don't think the services of the Sheikh are called for, are they?" he asked, smiling down at her.

"No, no. Time is all it needs, Lord Ambourne."

"As to that, I am charged with all sorts of messages from my mother, the gist of which is that you should come down to Ambourne as soon as Dr. Barnes pronounces you fit to travel."

"Amb...Ambourne?" faltered Perdita, looking doubtful. After all, the Earl had been very firm in his refusal to go there when they were travelling from France. She had thought that he didn't want to see Ambourne contaminated by her presence. "And what about you, Lord Ambourne?"

"I, too, would like you to come, Perdita. We have much to discuss, have we not?" said the Earl. "But now I think we should hear what Mrs. Frith has to say. Some of it I have already heard, but I insisted she wait until you were downstairs before she told us everything. Ludmila?"

Mrs. Frith came forward and sat down in front of them. For two days she had visited Perdita's bedroom constantly, but had always refused to discuss the events at Lady Francombe's ball. Now Perdita knew why. The Earl, as usual, had given his orders!

In her usual calm manner Mrs. Frith began, "First I should tell you both that I have known of Piers Carston's various activities for some time."

Perdita broke in to ask, "His various activities? You mean, not only about Eliane, but about his behaviour to me, too?"

"More even than that, Miss Taverton," Mrs. Frith said patiently.

"What—even the business of the shipping? But how?" asked Perdita.

"I think it is better if you let Mrs. Frith tell her story without interruption, Perdita," said the Earl, and Perdita subsided.

"I think I told you, Miss Taverton, that my husband spent some time working for the government at the Congress of Vienna. His special interest lay in routes for shipping and trade, and after the war he continued this work. Piracy was always a problem, though the situation improved after the Royal Navy bombarded Algiers, which was a centre for these criminals, three years ago. However, it came to my husband's notice that, though there were fewer pirate ships, the value of the cargoes lost—especially from ships registered with Lloyds—hardly diminished. He set out to discover why this was so. Unfortunately he died before his work was complete, and it has since been continued by others."

Mrs. Frith paused and pressed a small handkerchief to her lips. "I knew he suspected Piers Carston of selling information about shipping to a certain Michel Legrand. When Edward asked me to find someone to act as chaperon to you, Miss Taverton, I volunteered myself. His desire for you to meet and marry Mr. Carston seemed to provide me with an opportunity to get closer to the man."

Mrs. Frith's normally pale cheeks became slightly pink.

"I have to confess that I acted somewhat deviously. Though I did not inform Lord Ambourne, I knew more of your story than you suspected, Miss Taverton, and in particular I found what you had to say about the meeting that took place in Bristol between Piers Carston and Michel Legrand extremely interesting."

"How did you learn of that?" Perdita had to interrupt, even if it meant incurring the Earl's displeasure. When Mrs. Frith's colour deepened she exclaimed, "You listened! You listened at the door to my conversation with the Countess? But you were out!"

"I'm afraid returning the samples to the modiste was only an excuse to leave you alone. I knew you would not talk freely if I were present. In fact I stayed in," said Mrs. Frith calmly.

"But that was not honourable!" said Perdita in a shocked voice.

Mrs. Frith's tone was contemptuous as she replied, "I do not have this stupid English approach to honour. Piers Carston was a villain, and I wished to expose him."

The Earl gently pushed Perdita back against the cushions when she would have argued. "Let Ludmila finish," was all he said.

Mrs. Frith went on, "The evidence I gathered was almost enough to convict him—and Mr. Rambridge will now supply the finishing touches. You need not be involved at all, Miss Taverton."

The Earl leaned forward and asked, "Is that why you acted so precipitately, Ludmila—because you knew from Perdita's conversation with my mother that there would be only one meeting with Carston? You surely had very little time to arrange for the men to be there to arrest him."

Mrs. Frith's aristocratic lip curled in scorn. "I arranged that earlier than you think, Edward. For some time I had been doubting your resolve to carry the matter through to the end. I suspected that your feelings for Miss Taverton were becoming more important to you than your scheme to punish Mr. Carston. And I was right! Where would all my plans have been had I not anticipated this? But then, you always did allow sentiment to interfere with policy."

The Earl frowned, and Perdita wondered about their activities in Vienna. Had Mrs. Frith been as ruthless there?

"You and I have always differed on the rival claims of honour and expediency, Ludmila," he said in a cool voice.

Mrs. Frith drew in her breath and said sharply, "And I dare say we shall do so in the future, too, Edward. But I do not propose to argue old issues." With an effort she returned to her former calm. "Well, there you have it. Piers Carston will almost certainly be convicted of conspiracy with pirates, and I expect he will be at worst hanged, or more probably transported. My husband's work is vindicated," the quiet voice finished.

Perdita had always suspected that Mrs. Frith was not all she seemed, but she was appalled at the woman's ruthlessness. There was an awkward silence, which was broken by the Earl.

"It is time for Perdita to rest again—she is looking very pale." He paused and said deliberately, "I will wait down here while you see her to her room, Ludmila. Then we shall talk further."

Mrs. Frith rose and escorted Perdita upstairs. Neither of them spoke, and when Mrs. Frith merely gave her into Lucy's hands and returned downstairs almost immediately Perdita was glad. It was some time before she fell into a troubled sleep.

PERDITA NEVER KNEW what passed between the Earl and Mrs. Frith after she was safely upstairs. No one referred to it again. But when she came down the next day she discovered that the Earl had arranged to take her to Ambourne the following morning and that Mrs. Frith would not be accompanying them. She was slightly annoyed at this high-handed behaviour, but could not in all honesty find another solution. She was still too weak to be alone, and it would be some weeks before she could use her arm at all easily. So it was not difficult for her to acquiesce, and she merely asked Lucy to have her things packed and ready when the Earl should call. It was more difficult to know what to say to her chaperon. She had been kind in her way, and, though Perdita could not approve of her methods, her swift action against Piers Carston had solved a number of problems.

Mrs. Frith showed no consciousness of any awkwardness between them, and after luncheon settled herself in the salon by Perdita's couch.

"I have enjoyed our acquaintance, Miss Taverton," she began. "I seldom have the opportunity for close association with another woman, and it has proved interesting." Perdita stammered something, and Mrs. Frith, looking at her in tolerant amusement continued, "It is, of course, obvious that Edward is devoted to you. I have never seen him in love before—it has been a most enlightening sight. However, I hope you will not make the mistake I allowed my husband to make."

When Perdita asked her what that might be, she said, "I allowed him to marry me, knowing I was his social superior in every way. You know already that I am Hungarian. Do you also know I am a princess, closely related to the Esterhazys?" She looked at Perdita, who nodded. Then she said sadly, "I rarely allow my feelings to rule my head, Miss Taverton, but I would have walked barefoot to marry David Frith. I was passionately in love with him, and even now I am unable to consider any other man. But, though I never told him what I felt, I was never totally happy in our marriage."

Perdita said, "I don't understand. Did he not love you in return?"

"Oh, yes," was the reply. "As much as I loved him. Can you imagine what it was like, loving someone so much and yet always regretting what one could no longer have—the social position, the respect of one's equals, the status that one feels one is owed? I assure you, it was very difficult, especially as one could not share these feelings of resentment with the partner whose own inferior birth had led to the situation. I never became resigned to it."

Perdita caught a glimpse of the burning ambition which drove this woman. She had used the word 'vindicated' of her husband's work. It was more likely she was using the words of her own actions. Perdita felt pity for her, but Mrs. Frith's next words made her angry.

She continued, "I wonder if Edward is the same? Or will he tolerate what I could not?"

Perdita said coldly, "Mrs. Frith, what are you trying to imply? Any warnings you may be giving me against marrying Lord Ambourne are unnecessary, I assure you. But my birth is not inferior to his. He is the son of an Earl. My mother was the daughter of one, and my father's family have owned estates in the south-west since records began."

"And your reputation? Your life with the pirates? If that should become general knowledge, Miss Taverton, your noble birth would be of little consequence! Do not misunderstand me. I shall remain discreet—the polite world will never know from me where you have lived these last three years. But there is always the possibility that someone else will learn of your past..." Mrs. Frith spread her hands in a totally foreign gesture and shrugged.

Perdita restrained herself and said merely, "These warnings are totally unnecessary, believe me. We will say no more on the subject. If you do not mind, Mrs. Frith, I should like to stay in my room this evening. The journey tomorrow will need what strength I have. Will I see you tomorrow morning?"

"Oh, I think so, Miss Taverton. I shall depart after you, so we shall be able to say our goodbyes tomorrow. May I help you upstairs?"

THE JOURNEY TO AMBOURNE could have been one of unmixed delight for Perdita. It was a lovely day, sunny, but not yet hot, and the Earl's carriage was not only well sprung but had been loaded with cushions and rugs, so that it looked, as he remarked, like a scene out of the *Arabian Nights*. He swore he was afraid he would lose her among them all.

He was a charming travelling companion, and pointed out sights and scenes to amuse her on the way. They passed through several pretty villages—Brixton, Streatham and others—and the wayside was lined with may blossom, late bluebells, campions and the fretted network of cow parsley.

If only Mrs. Frith had not reminded her of her true situation she could have given herself up to enjoyment of the day. As it was, she did her best to let no trace of unhappiness show, but the Earl glanced sharply at her once or twice, and asked if she would like to stop, or if he could provide her with a more comfortable cushion. They took the journey at an easy pace and arrived at Ambourne in the middle of the afternoon. Before Perdita was out of the carriage the Countess was waiting for her on the wide steps in front of the house.

Larger than Belleroi, Ambourne Place had been rebuilt in the middle of the previous century by the second Earl. It was an imposing building with its many windows and spreading wings, but it was made beautiful by the colour of its rose-red brick and its lovely proportions. Perdita was to discover that the house was eminently comfortable to live in in spite of its apparent grandeur.

"Perdita, my poor child!" said the Countess, running down the steps to her visitor. She stopped short just in front of Perdita and said anxiously, "Will it damage you if I kiss you?" Perdita was tired and low in spirits, but she could not help smiling at this. She bent down slightly and the Countess gave her a warm greeting. "Now carry her in, but carefully, Edward."

"Ma'am, I don't need to be carried!" protested Perdita.

"Perhaps not, but Edward needs to carry you, Perdita!" said the Countess, with a wicked look at her son. The Earl glanced at the impassive footmen standing waiting on the steps, told them briefly to carry in the valises, and lifted Perdita gently into his arms.

"Hold on to me with your good arm, Perdita. My mother would disown me if I dropped you," he said.

The little procession wound its way through the marble entrance hall and into the guest wing. Here, a room facing south over the park had been prepared for Perdita. It was quite large, but very prettily decorated in soft blue and white, following the taste for chinoiserie in vogue in the previous century.

Perdita was put down on a day bed by the long windows, and, with a slightly concerned look at her wan face and dark-ringed eyes, the Earl withdrew. While her luggage was being unpacked and put away the Countess sat by her and told her something of Ambourne and its estate, but as soon as the other servants had gone she called the maid who had been assigned to Perdita and told her to get her mistress undressed and into bed.

"I am not an invalid, ma'am."

"Your face tells me differently, Perdita. Dr. Barker will come from Reigate tomorrow to have a look at your shoulder, but tonight you will rest here for an hour or two, and then we shall see whether you are to join us for dinner."

She went out, and the maid—a capable but rather solemn country girl—saw to Perdita, drew the curtains and left. It was fortunate that the journey, short though it was, had exhausted Perdita, and she slept soundly for two hours.

When she awoke she found she was able to come to a decision about her stay at Ambourne. She would enjoy it for what it was—a short interlude of happiness and recreation before she began with the hard work of renewing the Taverton estate. Mr. Rambridge had arranged to come down to Ambourne to see her soon, but she did not doubt for an instant that her heritage had been seriously damaged by Piers's depredations. For the moment, however, she would forget the problems waiting for her in Somerset. Mrs. Frith had suggested that the Earl would ask her to marry him, but she did not really believe that. He might be in love with her, but he would hardly commit the folly of marrying her. So for these two or three weeks she would live for the moment.

When the Countess came in to see whether she was awake Perdita was eager to get up and dine with them. She did not want to waste a single moment of the time left to her.

APART FROM A MORNING spent with Mr. Rambridge, which proved to be every bit as disheartening as she had expected, the days that followed were magical. Ambourne was an enchanted castle, where time did not count and all unpleasant thoughts were forbidden. They spent a great deal of their time out of doors, for the weather was perfect, too. At first Perdita could not walk far, and the Earl drove her round the estate in a light chaise, often in the company of the Countess. Under her benevolent eye the Earl showed Perdita the rudiments of fishing, argued with her over the merits of Byron's verse, taught her to play piquet and laughed as she recklessly gambled away several paper fortunes. He constantly watched over her for any sign of fatigue or pain. If he suspected she had done more than she should activities were instantly suspended and she would be ordered to rest. When she lost her temper at his high-handed behaviour he teased her into good humour again. On one occasion, when she had fished too hard and long in her efforts to catch a particularly large perch, he took note of her pale face and removed the fishing rod from her hand. Then he lifted her up and, in spite of her protests, deposited her on the garden seat near by. It took some time and all his skill to charm her into a good mood again.

"All the same, Edward, I think you are the outside of enough," she said eventually. "If I were a man you would not calmly remove me as if I were a parcel! And deprive me of my best chance to date of catching that fish. He was almost on the line!"

The Earl, stretched out on the grass before her, looked up, laughing, "If you were a man, Perdita, I would not now be prostrate at your feet, admiring the ridiculous straw hat on your lovely head and desperately longing for you to stop frowning at me. And why are you so sure it was the perch? It was probably an old boot." At Perdita's gasp of outrage he hastened to retrieve his position. "No, of course it wasn't. It was a giant of a fish, a champion swimmer. But aren't you secretly glad I saved his life?" Then his face lost its teasing expression and he grew serious. "As you saved mine—I believe I have not yet thanked you for that. What made you do such a foolhardy thing? You could have been killed."

All the things she wanted to say were forbidden, so she contented herself with saying lightly, "Your mother would never have forgiven me if I had allowed Piers to shoot you. Besides, you have saved my life more than once, I think. I still owe you two lives."

"It's not enough, Perdita," he murmured. "Two life-times is not enough." But at the sight of her puzzled face he only laughed. "Come, the sun is getting too strong. We must go into the shade."

"Edward, you more than anyone know that I am well able to support strong sunlight! Have you forgotten my past history?" She looked at him steadily, for she had not brought up the subject of her past by chance.

"How could I?" he said. "I am ashamed of the part I played in it. And it is my fervent hope I can help you to forget it all in time. I can only admire the indomitable spirit which enabled you to survive and thank God for it... But this is not a matter for a sunny afternoon. And we are moving into the shade all the same, Perdita. Think of my complexion, if you are indifferent to your own!''

Later, when she could move her arm more freely, she played to them in the evenings, while the Countess sewed and the Earl sat and watched them both. An idyllic time, one which she never forgot for the rest of her life.

It came to an end one evening after dinner. The rector had dined with them, and he and the Earl had disappeared into the library to discuss the matter of the church organ. The Countess had gone to her room for some more sewing silks, and Perdita was left alone. The long windows of the salon opened out on to a broad terrace, and she wandered into the soft June night.

She was beginning to feel it was time to leave Ambourne, and the thought was almost unbearable. It was not quite dark, but the moon had risen, bathing the lawns and trees with a soft radiance and laying a streak of silver over the lake. Ambourne looked incredibly beautiful, and Perdita felt she never wanted to leave it again. From the woods beyond the lake came the exquisitely unmistakable song of the nightingale.

The Earl saw the rector on his way, having convinced him of his interest, largely financial, in the church organ, and returned with relief to the salon. He caught his breath at the sight of the girl standing in the moonlight on the terrace, her head lifted as she listened to the nightingale's song. He was transported to Algiers, and the sight of the same girl in the courtyard of the Dey's palace. But this girl was now so infinitely dear to him that he could not envisage life without her. Ever since the night at Lady Francombe's ball he had been certain of his own feelings. But he had remained silent in order to give Perdita a

breathing space, time to get to know him in different circumstances, time to learn what sort of life she would lead
in the future with him here at Ambourne.

Suddenly he could wait no longer. He was as certain as
a man could be that she loved him, but he had to be sure.
He stepped forward on to the terrace.

They looked at one another, and somehow they had met
and were frantically kissing each other, murmuring little
terms of endearment and then kissing again. The Countess
came to the window and hastily retreated, unobserved by
either.

"My love, my darling, my lovely one," said the Earl,
somewhat incoherently. Perdita's answer was to pull his
head down to kiss him again.

"I love you!" she whispered. "I shall always love you,
wherever we are."

The Earl held her even more tightly, and then hastily
released her as he said, "Oh, God, I'm not hurting you,
am I? I'd forgotten your shoulder."

Perdita shook her head impatiently. "No," she said.
"Kiss me again!"

Lost in a world of delight, they stayed out on the terrace
for some time, until the moon went behind the hill and it
was dark. The nightingale's song still filled the air.

"We must go in, Perdita," said the Earl, stroking her
hair back from her forehead.

"No, please! Let's stay a little longer," pleaded Perdita.
"The night is quite warm and...and it's so beautiful out
here."

He smiled and they stayed for a few minutes more. Then
the Earl said firmly, "Perdita, has it not occurred to you
that my mother must have been looking for us long before
now?"

"The Countess!" gasped Perdita. "I had quite forgotten

her! I said I would meet her in the salon, and she will surely be wondering what I am doing!''

"I doubt that very much, my sweet innocent! My mother probably knows very well what you have been doing for the last hour!'' laughed the Earl, and at Perdita's self-conscious look he kissed her again. They were at the window by now, and a burst of clapping startled them. The Countess stood in a ring of lamplight, looking as excited and pleased as a child at Christmas.

"Famous!'' she cried. "Edward has lost all sense of propriety and is busy trying to seduce my guest under my very nose.''

"Then I must make amends and marry her out of hand, Mama,'' he said, gazing down at Perdita, a smile in his eyes. "How soon can you be ready, my darling?''

Perdita looked up, startled. "Marry you?'' she said. "You want me to marry you?''

Edward looked injured. "It's time you knew, Perdita, that, in spite of my treatment of you in the past, I am essentially a conventional man. If I kiss a young lady in public I expect her to marry me!''

He could hardly have used a more unfortunate phrase. Perdita stared at him. Conventional! What was conventional about her history?

The Countess saw her stunned distress and said hastily, "The poor child is worn out, Edward. All this emotion is very wearing!''

The Earl held Perdita's face in his hands and looked at her searchingly. "Sleep well. We have the rest of our lives before us, Perdita. Don't allow doubts to spoil it. Goodnight, my darling.'' He kissed her tenderly, infinitely sweetly, and then said, "But don't imagine for a minute I'm going to let you gamble my fortune away playing piquet with anyone else, my love! We'll keep your losses in the family!'' Then he lowered his voice and added, ''And I'll keep my wife's company to myself.''

Still in a daze, Perdita allowed herself to be led upstairs by the Countess. At the door of her room, the Countess stopped and said to her, ''I suspect you are more than tired, Perdita. Perhaps you are apprehensive about the future? You have no need to be. Edward will love you and cherish you, just as his father loved and cherished me.'' When Perdita would have spoken, she said, ''No, I won't hear of any objection. I truly believe that you and my son are made for one another. I beg you not to make any hasty decisions. Sleep now, and in the morning it will all seem very easy. Remember, you have the power to make Edward the happiest of men—and the unhappiest. Take care how you use that power. Goodnight, Perdita, my dear.''

What was the echo those words had aroused? The Sheikh! ''You have the courage and spirit to help Lord Ambourne. Use them wisely...wisely...'' The words echoed through her head all night.

In the morning she had decided what she must do...and two days later she was huddled in a corner of Lord Ambourne's carriage, being carried to an uncertain future far away from the two people she loved most and had hurt most.

CHAPTER EIGHTEEN

EVERY CARE had been taken for Perdita's comfort. The carriage was large and well sprung, and the Countess had sent Mary, the girl who had acted as Perdita's maid, to remain with her for the journey. Two of the Earl's best men, who would deal with accommodation and changes of horses on the journey to Somerset, were riding alongside. Perdita had nothing to occupy her mind other than the misery she had inflicted on herself and others. She tried to console herself with the thought that the Earl would eventually be grateful to her for his escape, but she could not persuade herself that this was the case. Throughout the long journey, with its tedious stops at posting houses and inns and its jolting progress along indifferent roads, her mind returned again and again to the scene the previous morning.

It had begun romantically enough with a note and a rose from the Earl, brought in by Mary. News had travelled round the great house that the master was at last intending to marry, and there was an unusual air of excitement about Mary's sensible person. Perdita's resolution was severely shaken when she read the note. The young men who had left their effusions in Dover Street could have learned much from the Earl, for it was everything a lover's note should be—romantic without being sentimental, and, though it was written with a light touch, it was full of the writer's happy anticipation of their future together. She went downstairs, reluctant but determined to put an end to these dreams.

She found the Earl with his mother at breakfast. He rose immediately and came over to her, bringing her hand to his lips and kissing it.

"Good morning, Perdita," said the Countess. Her tone was bright but her eyes were worried. "Edward, put Perdita down and continue with your breakfast, if you please." They smiled at her words and joined her at the table. After breakfast Perdita asked to see the Earl alone.

"Perdita," said the Countess urgently, but Perdita looked at her with stony determination and said,

"No, ma'am, I must speak to your son first." The Countess shook her head sadly and went out.

The Earl had observed this little exchange, and his mouth tightened slightly. He said nothing, but led Perdita into the library, where they would be undisturbed. Here he took her into his arms and kissed her. Then he held her away from him and said, "Now tell me what it is that is making you so thoughtful, Perdita."

There was no easy way to do this. "Lord Ambourne, I cannot marry you," Perdita said bleakly.

He looked searchingly at her for a moment, then said, "I thought as much. I find it hard to believe, but it's what I feared you would say. But how can you? How can you, Perdita?" Without waiting for a reply, he turned suddenly and went over to the window, where he stood gazing out at the woods. "I lay awake all night thinking of you, of what happened on the terrace, and of our future together, Perdita. It seemed to me that our understanding was so complete that nothing, nothing at all, could stand in its way. Why do you say that you can't marry me? Are you trying to tell me you don't love me? I won't believe you, you know."

She made a mute gesture of appeal, but he went on, "It's not just last night, Perdita, perfect though that was. It's all the other times—the excitement of being together, the laughter, the interest, the way the world becomes alive when we're with each other. No, I will never believe you don't love me." He swung back to face the room again. "So tell me why you can't marry me." His voice was calm enough, but his hands were trembling. If he had ranted or raved, if he had tried to persuade her differently by forcing her to kiss him, she could have borne it more easily. Her own spirit of resistance would then have been aroused and she would have fought him back. But this reasoned approach to the very heart of the matter disarmed her completely.

"We are not suited, Lord Ambourne," was all she finally said. But she should have managed something more convincing. He was at first astonished and then angry.

"Not suited, Perdita? Not suited? After the way you responded to me last night? Held me as closely as I held you, as reluctant as I was to part? Pray, do not insult my intelligence! Do you call this not suited?"

He strode over as he spoke and pulled her to him. He kissed her with no tenderness or restraint—and yet she found herself responding once again, not fighting him, but only wanting to assuage his anger and pain. Their kiss deepened and changed, and when after a long time they finally drew apart they were both breathing quickly. The Earl still held Perdita's arms as if he could not relinquish her completely. He rested his cheek on her hair.

"Perdita," he murmured, "you can't deny this. There is something which binds us together. This feeling has always been between us, from the moment I first saw you. I didn't recognise it immediately, but it was always there, right from the start. I think it will be with me for the rest of my life. I shall never forget it.''

''Nor shall I,'' she said quietly and sadly. ''But the circumstances of our first meeting are such that I can never agree to marry you.'' She gazed at him steadily. ''I must go away, Lord Ambourne.''

''You were on that pirate ship through no fault of your own, Perdita. No blame can attach to you for your imprisonment in the Dey's palace.''

Perdita pulled herself away from him and cried, ''It is not, however, a place in which to find the future Countess of Ambourne.'' She spoke with such desperate determination that he was stopped from further protest. He looked at her penetratingly, saw how she was trembling, and led her, protesting, to a chair.

''Sit there while I think for a moment. No, don't get up to go. I am not going to attack you again. It doesn't seem to help either of us,'' he said ruefully. They sat in silence for a full minute, then he said, ''You are really determined to give up all the happiness we could have? To bid farewell to me, and my mother, and Ambourne? In spite of anything I can say, you are resolved on this course of action?''

''I must,'' she cried, ''I must! I could not bear to see you turn away from me when you came to your senses again. I'm sure you love me now, but I must not let you make a dreadful mistake. You will be glad of it when you have had time to reflect!''

''And you, Perdita? Will you be glad?''

A sob escaped her, but she said valiantly, ''I must be— for your sake if not my own.''

For once neither her tears nor her gallantry moved him. He said slowly, ''I would have wished you to have more confidence in my love, Perdita. I have no doubts, and nor should you. But, since you will not be swayed at the moment, here is what I have decided.''

She looked at him in surprise. ''Decided?''

''Yes, why not? I reserve the right to have some say, too, in something that affects our happiness so greatly, Perdita. You may be prepared to cast it to the winds for a totally unnecessary scruple, but I do not have to acquiesce tamely—nor will I, by God!''

For a moment he looked so fierce that Perdita gave a gasp. He heard it and softened his tone immediately, picking up her hand and holding it in his. ''But I do in some measure understand your hesitation. It must be that you do not yet know me, or yourself, well enough. I thought three weeks here at Ambourne would be enough, but it is clear you need longer. It is not surprising. The events of the last three years have hardly encouraged confidence in your fellow human beings.'' He carefully put her hand back in her lap, and said, ''So you must go to Taverton, not, as I had hoped, with me, but alone. I will give you time to reconsider, to come to understand how real our bonds are, time to develop faith in me. I believe you will learn to trust me in the end. I hope to God you do, for I see a very unhappy future for all of us if you do not.''

''I will not change my mind, Lord Ambourne. I love you too well.''

''Perfect love has perfect trust, Miss Taverton. And you do not trust me well enough. But you will come to do so. I shall not let you escape. Come, we must find my mother—she will be sadly disappointed, but not, I think, surprised.''

At the door he turned her to him and kissed her again. The kiss was not passionate but deeply tender, each of them reluctant to end it. Perdita was saying a final farewell to her love, the Earl sealing his promise to seek her out again.

The Countess was sad, but she would not let it show. Her brave face tore at Perdita's heart, and her concern for Perdita's safety and comfort on the journey was only rivalled by the Earl's. Neither could supply the only comfort Perdita needed—the conviction that what she was doing was for the best. Indeed, the Countess's last words were, "You are so wrong, my child. And you are creating so much unhappiness. But you must promise not to be afraid to admit you have been wrong. I know Edward's affections will not change. Come back to him if you can."

OCCUPIED WITH THESE and other equally gloomy thoughts, Perdita found the journey unbearably long. Mary was not really amusing company, for not only was she normally rather a stolid girl, but she was also shocked and disapproving of Perdita's treatment of her master and mistress. Added to this was a tendency to coach-sickness. Perdita was glad of her company in the inns at night, but found her presence in the carriage during the day no comfort.

They spent the last night of their journey not far from Taverton at Warminster in Wiltshire. When she entered the inn she had a pleasant surprise.

"Why, I declare, it's Miss Felicia, isn't it?" The landlord's wife came up to her, half uncertain at first, then with a warm welcome. It was Abby, the Taverton coachman's daughter. She glanced curiously at the Earl's carriage in the yard, but made no comment. Instead, she led Miss Taverton up to a pretty bedchamber on the first floor, well away from the noises of the bar. A trestle-bed was found for Mary, and the two travellers were soon refreshed and ready for a meal. After supper Abby could restrain herself no longer and came to have a chat with Miss Felicia.

"It's a good day for Taverton when you come back, Miss Taverton. The estate has gone down dreadful since you've been gone."

"How is your father, Abby?"

"Oh, he's fair, Miss Felicia. He's living with my brother over at Sherborne now, you know. When he had to leave Taverton along with the rest he had a hard job to find anything else."

"Are there no servants at Taverton now?"

"Well, none that need money to live on. Old Joan and Samuel Lupton still keep an eye on the place. They keep theirselves going with the pigs and hens at the home farm. There's no others. They wouldn't stay, would they? Not for your stepbrother, they wouldn't—begging your pardon, Miss Felicia. But after your poor sainted mother died they didn't treat servants right at Taverton. Shouting and cursing, the old man was, and the son was not much better—except when he sweet-talked the girls. But where have you been all this while? We all thought you was dead."

Perdita gave her some sort of answer, which, though not very satisfying, at least stopped further questions. She and Mary went to bed not very long after supper, and as Perdita lay in bed, listening to Mary's adenoidal breathing, she wondered what she would find at Taverton the next day.

In fact she found desolation. Outside, the house looked much as it had for centuries. But what a scene of chaos greeted her inside—broken windows, invisible from the drive, shattered pictures, rooms empty of furniture, and bird droppings everywhere.

Upstairs, where the lead had been removed from the roof and fallen slates had never been replaced, the rain had run down behind the panelling and caused great patches of rot and decay. In her mother's bedroom, the huge bed was leaning drunkenly to one side, its curtains ripped and torn.

Numb with shock, Perdita wandered from room to room, each one worse than the one before. Old Joan followed her, her back bent with rheumatism, excusing, complaining, railing against the Carstons until Perdita could bear it no longer.

"Are there any refreshments for Lord Ambourne's people?" she asked. With much debate Joan decided she could produce some healthy farm fare, and Perdita asked her to feed Mary and the two men in the kitchen.

"The kitchen, Miss Felicia? You wouldn't feed the tinkers from Bartholomew's Fair in that kitchen! I'll take them to the farm. That'll do for them. But where are you going to live, Miss Felicia? You can't stay here. It's not fit!"

Perdita had to acknowledge this was true. Grasping Joan's arm, she said urgently, "Joan, you must not let those people see this house! Keep them away! And don't talk to them about the state of the house or the Carstons or anything, do you understand? I don't want the Earl and his mother to know what it is like here. I'll find somewhere to live, but can you put me up at the farm for tonight? We'll send Lord Ambourne's carriage back to Warminster. It's still early in the day and they'll be glad to be on their way." Joan tried to demur, but had to agree that there was nowhere for Miss Felicia to sleep tonight other than the farm.

After bidding farewell to Mary, who displayed a surprising disinclination to leave her, Perdita set the Earl's coach on its way. She gave the men some money from funds provided by Mr. Rambridge.

As the carriage disappeared she felt that her last link with the Earl and his mother had gone with it, and such a feeling of desolation overcame her that she was hard put to it not to cry in front of Joan. But she pulled herself together and asked Joan to take her to her room.

Still bemoaning the state of Taverton and the poor accommodation to be offered to its mistress, Joan tried to take her to the Luptons' own bedroom. This Perdita would not have, and in the end insisted on a tiny attic bedroom at the top of the farmhouse. It had the advantage of a small window, which overlooked the rolling Somerset countryside. At least the Carstons had not put their dreadful mark on that.

For the rest of the day she inspected the house and the buildings round it more closely. Apart from the walls and panelling on the upper floor, the damage was mostly superficial. Repairing it would take a great deal of work, but should not be beyond the resources of the estate. It was impossible, however, to replace the missing furniture— some of the chests and presses had been in her family for generations. She wondered what had happened to them, for they were only of value because they were part of the Taverton family history. She later found some of them in pieces at the back of the stables.

The next day she sent for the workers still living on the estate, and found that most of the young able-bodied men had left to work for better pay near by. Rescuing the estate seemed a daunting business, with few resources and hardly any men. She would have to sell some land, but which? Her experience in estate management was small, based on her early years with her father, but somehow she would have to learn!

The first evidence of the Earl's continued care for her welfare came two weeks after she had left Ambourne. With help readily given by the women on the estate, who were all unaffectedly glad to see her back, she had sorted out the kitchen, the breakfast parlour and a small sitting-room in the main house for her own use. Here she lived and slept. The conditions were by no means luxurious, but at least she was in Taverton Hall again. She laughed iron-ically—Miss Taverton of Taverton Hall, indeed!

She was sitting in her parlour one afternoon, worrying over the question of land, when Joan announced a visitor. She jumped up apprehensively, for she was expecting no one. In came a youngish, respectable-looking man with brown hair, the red cheeks of a man who was used to working out of doors, and a quietly confident air.

"Miss Taverton? His lordship sent me...Lord Am-bourne, I mean. My name is Seth—Seth Ashwood. He thought I might be of some use. Here's his letter."

He handed her a sealed letter, but, without opening it, she asked, "Why should Lord Ambourne think I need help?" Before he could stop himself Seth Ashwood looked round the room with its meagre furniture and patched-up furnishings. His open face was expressive, and Perdita's cheeks grew red. "I need no help," she began stiffly, but he said pleadingly,

"Please, Miss Taverton, read Lord Ambourne's letter. I'm sure he will explain. I'll sit outside, if I may. I like the fresh air."

The Earl's letter began abruptly, with no greeting.

Perdita—do not turn Seth away. He's a good man—one of the best I have. I trained him myself in helping to manage the estate and he has aptitude for it. You will say you do not need him, but, from what John the coachman told me, you most surely do. If you send Seth back I shall come to find out for myself how you go on. And even I feel it is too soon yet for

any substantial change in that obstinate will of yours.
My mother sends her love.

Ambourne

The businesslike tone of the letter did much to reconcile
Perdita to accepting Seth's assistance, and it was true that
his arrival was like a miracle. The women might have welcomed Perdita back, but their menfolk, fond as they were
of "Miss Felicia", were more doubtful of her ability to
cope. Seth proved to be like an answer to a prayer—tactful
with the remaining workers, knowledgeable about the
farms, a good manager of land.

She found herself leaving more and more in his capable
hands. At first she followed him, trying to learn from him,
but in the end she gave up. The men responded better to
Seth when she was not present, and anyway there was
enough work elsewhere to keep her fully occupied.

In a curious way it could have been enjoyable, this grad-
ual restoration of Taverton Hall to some of its former
glory, except that, wherever she was and whatever she was
doing, Perdita's thoughts returned constantly to the Earl.
Her unhappiness was like the toothache—she could numb
it for a while with hard work and the sleep of exhaustion
that resulted, but it never went away. No lovely view of
the Somerset hills, no exquisite birdsong, not even some
amusing incident on the estate could pass without a passionate wish to share it with him. Sometimes her longing
for him was so powerful that she was on the point of setting out for Ambourne. Then Mrs. Frith's words would
return to haunt her.

"Can you imagine what it was like, loving someone so
much and yet always regretting…?"

That was not for her! And she would return to work
even more frantically.

She was not without company. The neighbouring families, who had stayed away from Taverton for more than three years, gradually started paying calls. But Perdita was usually so tired that she seldom returned the visits, and when she did she found the somewhat restricted conversation left her cold.

So THE SUMMER CAME and went, and autumn had just started to change the countryside to gold. Perdita started to worry about the roof of the Hall. Where was she to find the money to pay for that? If she sold more land the Taverton estate would be diminished even further. The anxiety over this question and sundry other estate matters gnawed at her mind until she could no longer sleep, however tired she was. She walked the house at night like a restless ghost, and, like any other ghost, she mourned her love. The last time she had heard from the Earl had been several weeks before, when he had sent her an account of Piers Carston's trial. Her stepbrother had been sentenced to transportation for life, so they would not see him again.

But since then there had been silence. She was afraid now that she had, after all, achieved what she had set out to do in the library at Ambourne in June. The Earl had come to his senses and was forgetting her. She was forced to call on all the strength of character she possessed to withstand the pain of this thought.

MEANWHILE, AT AMBOURNE, the Earl was finding the enforced wait a strain. He had done what he could to make sure that Perdita had arrived safely at Taverton, and had provided her with some much needed help on the estate. To a man who wanted to cherish her for life and to give her the world, this was a woefully inadequate substitute.

The strain showed in his manner, and his mother was often reminded of the difficult time at Belleroi when Ed-

ward's temper had been equally uncertain. Her heart ached
for her son, and she was quite relieved when he decided
they should go to Normandy for a while. On his return,
however, he was even more restless. He threw himself into
the work on the Ambourne estate with such vigour that his
agents wished he had remained in France with his mother!
Finally, unable to bear Ambourne with its echoes of Perdita everywhere, he went to London. The capital was almost empty of people he knew. The season was over, and
most of them were enjoying the late summer and autumn
in the country, or at Brighton, Bath or some other watering
place. But he did find Mrs. Frith, who was preparing to
leave England and return to Vienna.

"Edward, I am glad to see you before I go," she said
coolly. "I did not enjoy our last parting. You were unnecessarily harsh."

"I cannot believe that anything I said has had a lasting
effect, Ludmila, but I too am pleased to be able to wish
you well in your future life. I think you are right to rejoin
your family in Vienna, but is there a special reason for
doing so?"

"I have finished what I had to do in England," she said.
"Mr. Carston's trial and sentence have put an end to my
ambitions here. But tell me, how is my protégée, the little
Taverton girl? She must have been gratified at Piers Carston's end."

"I am not in her confidence, but I do not believe that
Perdita would think of it like that, Ludmila. If you remember, she would have given him time to escape elsewhere,
which you denied him."

"If I had been as sentimental as she he would no doubt
be cheating and lying his way to another fortune at this
very moment. God help Australia if he ever gets free, is
all I can say. But have you, then, parted with Miss Tav-

erton? I congratulate you. You have more strength of mind that I would have credited. Or did she take my advice?''

The Earl suddenly grew alert. ''Advice? What advice?''

''Oh, come, Edward, surely you can see for yourself that, however besotted you were at the time, her somewhat lurid past would certainly have caused you embarrassment in the future? Even if it did not become public. I merely pointed this out to her.''

There was a silence while the Earl regarded Mrs. Frith with growing anger. Finally he asked in clipped accents, ''May I ask what I have ever done to arouse such malice, Ludmila?''

''You are wrong. I did not dissuade Miss Taverton from marrying you solely out of malice. You have been very discourteous to me and I was angry with you, it is true. But I also sincerely believed it would be wrong for you to marry her. You forget how I felt in my marriage to David.''

''You ruined David, Ludmila. You ruined him, though I know you loved him. He could have been a brilliant diplomat—was on the way to becoming one—but you destroyed him with your empty ambition and consciousness of position, your scorn for honour and your lack of principle. Did you really think you kept your true feelings hidden from him? In the end he took himself, at your valuation, as inferior and unworthy.''

She was white with rage. ''Take care, Edward! The story of your dealings with Miss Taverton would entertain London society for months if I chose to reveal it!''

''Do you think I care? I will not discuss my feelings for Miss Taverton with you, Ludmila, for I do not think you could possibly understand them. But if she marries me, then I will count myself more fortunate than I deserve. I think we have said enough to each other. For David's sake

I will wish you a happier future in Vienna. Goodbye, Ludmila.''

The Earl turned and left her standing there. For a moment her face was a tragic mask, then she resumed her normal expression of calm indifference. She went back to her packing and set off for Vienna that afternoon.

The Earl also left London that afternoon. At last he could understand why Perdita had been so determined to refuse him, so reluctant to trust his constancy. That coldhearted woman had done her best to destroy something infinitely precious. Well, she wouldn't succeed. Perdita was his; there would be no more denials, no more hesitation. When he got to Ambourne news was waiting for him from Normandy, which, if he needed one, gave him the perfect reason to go to Taverton. A few arrangements had to be made, and then he set off early the next morning.

CHAPTER NINETEEN

EDWARD ARRIVED at Taverton late in the afternoon. The Hall lay in its valley, the warm gold of its stones glowing in the autumn sun. He met Seth Ashwood at the gates, talking to an elderly lady who was introduced to him as Mrs. Lupton.

"Sam's wife, isn't it?" She curtsyed and smiled and looked flustered. He went on, "Is Miss Taverton in the house?"

"Yes, sir...my lord. She'm be having a rest, sir. She works too hard, does that poor maid."

"Thank you. I'll see myself to the house, Mrs. Lupton. You stay here and keep Seth happy." He strode up the drive, half expecting Perdita to appear at any moment, but the house lay silent and still in the sunshine. When he came into the parlour he could see why she had not heard him. She lay in a chair, fast asleep, her cheeks brown but thin, and her whole body expressing unutterable weariness. He walked softly over to her and kissed her. The dark blue sapphire eyes flew open and once again he was lost in their magic.

"Edward," she murmured, smiling sleepily. "Oh, Edward, my love." He kissed her again, but she pushed him away and sat up. "Lord Ambourne, why are you here? I have not changed my mind!"

He sat back on his heels. He was going to enjoy this.

"I haven't come to ask you to, Perdita my darling," he said.

She looked at him suspiciously. "Then why are you here?"

"To ask you to come to France with me," he said, his eyes dancing.

"Come to France with you?" She stared at him in amazement. Then an expression of understanding came over her face. "I see. You don't want to marry me, yet you're asking me to come to France with you—as your mistress, I suppose? I am not yours to command now, Lord Ambourne!"

He replied ruefully, "Believe me, Perdita, if that was the only way I could persuade you to live with me I would. But my intentions in this instance are perfectly, boringly honourable. My mother wishes you to come. Eliane needs you."

She flew out of her chair and grasped his arm. "She's not ill again, is she? Oh, poor Eliane!"

He put his hand over hers reassuringly. "No, but she needs you. You will see. Are you coming with me? I will engage to behave admirably."

"Of course. But what about Taverton?"

"I think Seth can manage Taverton in your absence. He seems to be on good terms with Mrs. Lupton. Are you satisfied with him?"

"I cannot thank you enough, Lord Ambourne, for sending him. He has been the saving of Taverton."

"I could wish he had saved you more," he murmured. "What have you been doing to make such a wreck of yourself?"

"Working," she said briefly. "Are you sure you wish to take a 'wreck' like me to France?" She was hurt, but she would not show him, nor would she tell him that sleepless nights were more to blame for her appearance than any amount of hard work. Besides, though she wasn't going to say so, he looked a bit worn himself!

He looked at her with a smile in his eyes. "I can't console you in the only way I should like," he murmured. "But I do want you to come to France with me. Please come, Perdita."

In a surprisingly short time Perdita was ready to leave, and in two days they were on their way to Portsmouth. The Earl had stayed at the local inn and spent the intervening time viewing the work Seth had done on the estate and inspecting the house. After an argument with Perdita he had persuaded her to accept help with the re-roofing of the Hall. He found it strange to meet people who had known Perdita in her early years. They all called her Miss Felicia, of course, and he asked her one evening whether she would prefer him to call her by her original name.

"After we have been to France you will have no need to call me anything, Lord Ambourne. 'Perdita' will do till then."

He saw her looking at him to see how he was taking this provocation, but kept his face impassive. Her attitude provided him with no little amusement. He was now in no doubt that Perdita would marry him, whatever she was saying at the moment, but he refused to rise to her challenges. Perdita was no longer as determined as she had been, he was sure. Those dark-ringed eyes, her thinness, and above all her reaction at his arrival—all told their own tale. But at the moment she would welcome a chance to put him down. She was not going to have it, not if he could help it.

Again they travelled together in the Earl's coach, but he confined his attentions to ensuring she was comfortable and to making light conversation. Once he caught her looking at him, when she thought she was unobserved, in a puzzled and wistful fashion. He longed to take her in his arms there and then, but instead, exercising severe self-control, he said, "You are looking tired, Perdita. Perhaps you would like a short sleep. There is little of interest on the journey."

Convinced that the Earl thought she looked a hag, Perdita turned away with a suppressed sigh and tried to do as he suggested. Memories of the loving care he had taken of her on their journey to Ambourne and the laughter and interest they had shared kept her awake, however, and when she did fall into an uneasy slumber the lurching of the coach woke her again. Finally she let herself fall over to lean on the Earl. She felt an immediate sense of well-being, which was cut cruelly short when he gently but firmly put her back against the squabs on her own side. The journey to Portsmouth seemed very long to Perdita.

They had a good crossing with a following wind, but this time Perdita was thankful to stay in her cabin. The carriage that waited for them at Honfleur was comfortable but small, and the Earl elected to ride alongside in order, he said, to give Perdita more room to rest. It was with relief that she saw the chimneys of Belleroi on the horizon.

Colette was waiting at the gates, and ran up the drive by the carriage until Perdita ordered the coachman to stop and let her in. Madame Lebrun had been warned of their arrival and was waiting in the entrance hall. It was an indication of the change in Perdita's status that Madame Lebrun curtsyed and greeted her formally as an honoured guest. She also apologised for Colette.

"That child has spent hours waiting at the gate for the last three days, *mademoiselle*, but she shouldn't have been so importunate. I'm afraid her behaviour doesn't improve with time. May I show you to your room?"

Perdita followed Madame Lebrun to the foot of the stairs, but here she was detained by the Earl, who had just come in from the stables.

"Georges wishes me to convey his pleasure at your return, Perdita." She turned and smiled at this sally, but he went on, taking her hand and kissing it, "Welcome to Belleroi, Felicia Taverton of Taverton Hall. All your Norman friends are very happy to see you here at last. My mother is at Beau Lac at the moment, but by the time you are downstairs again she will be back. I'll escort you to your room."

At the door of her room he handed her over to a smiling Madame Lebrun and an excited Jeanne, and left her.

As soon as he had gone Jeanne cried, "Oh, *mademoiselle*, I'm so happy to see you again! Look at your room!" Madame Lebrun made a small sign of disapproval at this undisciplined outburst, but Perdita smiled and greeted Jeanne warmly. The girl dragged her into a room that was full of flowers and messages—less pretentious perhaps than the notes in Dover Street, but much more welcome. Her eyes filled with tears at this evidence of the affection that waited for her here, but she was soon laughing at Jeanne's insistence that she remove her bonnet and allow her to arrange her hair. Madame Lebrun gave Jeanne a warning glance and excused herself, then Jeanne set to work, talking all the time. It was clear that the girl was bursting with news that she was not allowed to pass on. Several times she began a sentence that she cut short, until Perdita's curiosity got the better of her.

"What is it, Jeanne? What are you hiding?"

"Oh, it's wonderful news, *mademoiselle*! But I can't tell you. Madame la Marquise could be angry with me if I did. But you'll be pleased, I know." Perdita refrained from testing the girl's discretion any further. She would have to wait till the Countess told her. If it was what she hoped, then it would be joyful news indeed.

The Countess came into the house with a flurry of silk skirts, demanding to see Perdita and the Earl immediately. She swept into Perdita's room and embraced her enthusiastically.

"My child, my dear child, it's wonderful to see you here again. Heavens, you're so thin, Perdita! You've been working far too long and hard, child. No matter, Rosanne's cooking will soon remedy that, and then we shall see you as you were. How is your arm?" She accepted Perdita's assurance that her arm was as good as ever and went on, her face alive with happiness, "We have such good news for you, Perdita—and but for you it might never have happened. Eliane is about to marry Philippe! Is that not wonderful?"

Perdita's reception of this news was as rapturous as the Countess had hoped. To have such a happy end to a story which had begun so miserably was all she could have wished for her friend. "But, ma'am, what about Monsieur Fourget? Does he agree?"

"Oh, yes, though I should think he would be relieved to have the entrée once again to decent society, the traitor! Oh, but I forget—Edward says I mustn't call him that any more. Monsieur Fourget is about to become an important man in politics here in Normandy. I don't really think that is a great improvement on his former position, but Edward seems to think it is, and he has spent a great deal of time with Monsieur Fourget. So all is forgotten and forgiven, and Eliane and Philippe are going to be very happy together."

Perdita exclaimed without thinking, "So that is why I heard so little from your son! He was in France."

"Did you think he had forgotten you?" asked the

Countess. "Oh, Perdita, when will you learn? Edward's feelings will not change. You should know that by now. Why are you so cruel to him, so cruel to us all?"

"But, ma'am," cried Perdita, "you do not understand. He might come to regret marrying me if my story becomes known and he is ostracised for it! What love could stand that?"

"Edward's!" said the Countess promptly. "Do you mean to say, Perdita, that you are making Edward so unhappy for this reason? I could be angry with you, I think. You claim to love him, and yet you know him so little."

"I do love him, ma'am. I want to spare him pain."

"No, you want to spare yourself pain, Perdita. You're prepared to sacrifice any hope of happiness for yourself or Edward because you won't risk the pain of losing him. I don't call that love—love is not so selfish! Of course you might lose Edward—you might lose him in a riding accident, you might lose him, as I did my husband, through a sudden illness, you might die yourself at an early age. These are all risks we take when we love someone enough to marry. But you will not lose Edward's affection because of some trivial question of social position. How dare you even think it?" The Countess got up to go. "I thought you had more spirit, Perdita. Think of the courage Eliane and Philippe have shown. You are not the only one to have an unhappy past. But are you ready for an unhappy and lonely future? It is certainly not what I wish for my son."

She went out, leaving Perdita deep in thought.

Outside, the Countess paused and looked back at the closed door. She smiled and crossed her fingers. Then she went downstairs to greet her son.

"Edward, dearest boy. Have you seen Masson's new grandson? He's a delightful baby. They are so taken with him that they have persuaded their daughter and her husband to live with them. Of course, Masson will need more room and I have told him you will see to it. How was your journey? I congratulate you on getting Perdita to come, at least."

"Mama, poor Etienne will have to deal with Masson, but I'm sure he'll manage. I must tell you something I learned in London before I came over…"

By the time Perdita came down, still thoughtful, the Countess knew of Mrs. Frith's intervention in the Earl's affairs. She was both furious and relieved.

"So that is why Perdita is such a coward!" she exclaimed.

"Perdita is no coward, Mama," said Edward swiftly. "You forget how badly life has treated her."

The Countess laughed. "I should have known better than to say anything about Perdita to you, Edward. Perdita is perfect in your eyes."

"No, not so. She is often perverse, sometimes obstinate, and can be completely maddening," he said with feeling. At this interesting point Perdita walked into the room.

"And at the moment I look a wreck, too," she said composedly.

"You devil, Perdita! You were listening!"

"I cannot emulate Mrs Frith's talents in this respect," she said demurely, "but when something is said so loudly that the household now knows I am maddening I cannot avoid hearing it, too."

The Earl came over to her and took her hand. "My apologies. I should have said 'maddeningly lovely.'"

"A maddeningly lovely wreck, perhaps?"

"That is enough, Perdita. You refine too much on what I said in Taverton. You are already looking a great deal better than you did. It was your health, not your beauty, I was concerned with."

The Countess regarded this exchange with deepest satisfaction. Perhaps, after all, there would be two happy couples at Belleroi this autumn.

A few minutes later Eliane came running in. Perdita gasped when she saw her, for she was transformed. The hesitant, melancholy air had vanished, and Eliane was brimming with happiness. She looked more beautiful than ever, in her pale green muslin dress.

"Perdita! I'm so happy to see you. Have you heard? Philippe and I are to be married quite soon. Oh, I must thank you for acting as our good angel."

Perdita looked sharply at the Earl, who was murmuring, "An angelic, maddeningly lovely wreck…"

"Rubbish, Eliane," she said, leading her friend away from the sound. "I am sure you would have made it up in time. You're made for each other…" The two girls sat down at the far end of the room and chatted together.

The Countess said, "Are you going to manage it this time, do you think?"

"Manage what, Mama?"

"Don't be so annoying, Edward. Manage to persuade Perdita to marry you, of course."

"Perdita will be given no alternative, Mama. But I need your help…"

THE PREPARATIONS for Eliane's wedding took three weeks. Perdita enjoyed every minute of being back at Belleroi, seeing her friends again, being jealously looked after by Jeanne, living in the comfort of a large, well-run house. She found it all the more pleasant because it was such a contrast to the gruelling time she had been having at Taverton. Jeanne exclaimed over the state of her hair and hands, and set to work to recreate the beautiful *mademoiselle* who had left Belleroi. Strangely, she was sleeping better too, and she was soon pleasing her friends by looking as lovely as they remembered her. With one exception they all said so, but the fact that the Earl made no reference to her improved appearance piqued her. He remained a charming host, engaging her in conversation at dinner, showing her improvements in the château, but never again referring to their relationship. It was true that Eliane's marriage seemed to be taking a great deal of his attention— almost an excessive amount for what was to be a very quiet wedding. But Perdita reminded herself that in France a marriage was a civil contract first and a love-match second. No doubt there were details of dowries and jointures to be settled. She accidentally broke in on one such discussion shortly after she arrived. The Earl was in earnest conversation with Eliane and Philippe in the library when she went in to look for a book.

As she entered she heard the Earl say, "I have spoken to your mother, Eliane, and she has no objection if you agree. Do you?"

Then she saw Eliane throw her arms round the Earl and say, "Edward, it's a wonderful idea! Don't you think so Philippe? Do say you'll agree to it, Philippe, please."

Philippe kissed his bride-to-be on the nose and assured her he would be very happy to agree. Eliane danced round the room in excitement, but stopped dead when she saw Perdita hesitating at the door.

"Ah, Perdita," said the Earl. "Er—you don't yet know perhaps—Eliane and Philippe have agreed to live here at Belleroi after they are married. They will be doing me a great service—Belleroi needs more attention than I can give it at the moment, and Philippe will learn all about managing the estate from Etienne in order to take over from him in due course. And our two love-birds will still be near their families. Will you not congratulate us?"

Perdita hastened to say how happy she was for all of them. It gave her a pang, all the same, to see how close these three were—Eliane was gazing at her cousin in open admiration, and Philippe was smiling broadly. They talked for a short while, but Eliane seemed rather distracted and soon went off to see her mother, taking Philippe with her.

The Earl also seemed slightly abstracted, and Perdita went to collect her book and go.

"Perdita," he said suddenly, "come for a walk. I'm sure you need some air, and I must see Georges. Then I'll take you to visit Madame d'Espery."

She agreed immediately and ran for her bonnet. It was a particularly fetching one of Leghorn straw trimmed with forget-me-nots and dark blue ribbons. Jeanne had commented that they were just the colour of her eyes, but no such comparison appeared to occur to the Earl. As she followed him out to the stables, Perdita was full of gloomy thoughts. He thought she needed some air...hadn't noticed her bonnet...was more interested in Georges than he was in her! He was probably taking her to see Madame d'Espery out of kindness to the old lady. The Countess was wrong—the Earl had lost interest in her. He had fetched her from Taverton only because his mother wished her to be here for Eliane's wedding. And it was no more than she deserved—she had had her chance and had thrown it away.

Georges was walking a handsome black Arab horse round the stable-yard. When the Earl saw the horse he drew Perdita back to the gateway and told her to stay there.

"This one is wicked," he said. "He runs like the wind, but is full of nasty tricks. Look at him there—butter wouldn't melt in his mouth, but he's had me off more than once, and even Georges can't do a thing with him. You have to watch him all the time. He's a killer."

"Can nothing be done?" asked Perdita. The Earl shook his head,

"We've had him gelded—that usually works, but it hadn't changed this one's nature. There are horses like that—you can't do much with them. Pity, he's a handsome brute."

"I don't like him," said Perdita with a shudder. "I feel he's evil. He reminds me of Legrand."

Even as she spoke the horse suddenly reared up, and if Georges hadn't been on his guard it would have kicked him with its flailing hoofs. The Earl waited to see that Georges was in control of the brute, and then took Perdita away.

They spent a pleasant afternoon with Madame d'Espery, who was delighted to see her *"mademoiselle"* again. Naturally they talked of Eliane's wedding, while the Earl sat looking relaxed and slightly bored.

"Of course, you will be Mademoiselle Eliane's attendant. What are you wearing?" When Perdita told her madame nodded her head in approval. "Very pretty! I do not approve of the new idea of wearing white for bridals. Such a dead colour. It's fitting for royalty, of course, but the old way of dressing in pastels is much more flattering. And *'Rêve d'Automne'* has such a pretty sound, *mademoiselle*. Is Mademoiselle Eliane wearing the same? I heard her dress was ivory."

Perdita corrected her, "It's called *'Rêve d'Or'*, madame. She is wearing ivory roses in her hair…"

Finally the Earl rose and announced it was time to return to Belleroi.

"You have failed me, Madame d'Espery. I had hoped for some reasonable conversation from you. Belleroi is swamped in silks and laces and the set of a sleeve or the placing of a bow has become more important than the state

of the nation! However, in two weeks it will be over, and
Belleroi will become a fit place for a sensible man again.
We shall see you before then, no doubt. Come, Perdita,
you will miss your fitting with the modiste, and I shall be
in Coventry for the rest of the month with all four of my
ladies.''

There was a measure of truth in what the Earl said.
Belleroi was a hive of activity, and the two weeks flew by.
Though the wedding was to be quiet, Père Amboise and
the notary came and went, the neighbouring families were
invited to dinners and evening parties, and the people on
the two estates were invited to a huge gala in the park.
Rosanne was in her element, and the girls of the village
had never worked so hard before.

Finally the last preparations were done, the last ribbon
sewn on the dresses, and Belleroi was *en fête* again, every
room polished to perfection and all the ground floor
decked in flowers. It seemed rather excessive to Perdita.
No guests were staying the night, and the Earl was taking
the Countess and herself back to England the following
morning.

The wedding-day was an Indian summer day—mellow
sunlight shining on trees turning gold to copper, clear blue
skies, and just a hint of autumn crispness in the air. The
ceremony was to take place late in the morning to enable
the few guests to make their way home in daylight, but
there was plenty of time for Eliane to get up late and dress
at her leisure. Perdita, on the other hand, rose early and
walked to the lake. She might come again to Belleroi—to
see Philippe and Eliane—but the likelihood was not great.
How different it would have been if she had now been
married to Belleroi's owner!

As she stood watching the water rippling over the lake
and thinking of Eliane and Philippe, of the happy ending

of their story and the dismal future that awaited her, she was startled by a voice behind her.

"Are you remembering your past, Perdita? It was here you met Philippe, was it not?" It was the Earl. He came and joined her at the lakeside. She smiled, but made no answer. He waited a moment; then he said, "Do you love me, Perdita?" Then before she could say anything he added hastily, "I'm not asking if you will marry me. You have said you cannot, I know. But, if things had been different, do you love me enough to have married me?"

She nodded, looking sadly away from him. Was he about to ask her to be his mistress? What would she answer? The last months had taught her that living with the Earl, on whatever terms, could not be as bad as living without him.

He turned her round gently, lifted her chin, and gazing into her eyes, he said, "You fool. You idiotic, quixotic fool, Perdita," and kissed her. Then he said briskly, "Come, we have a great deal to do before Philippe is finally made the happiest of men. I like him, Perdita. I believe Eliane will at last be happy as she was born to be. And old Fourget is a very decent fellow when you get to know him…"

They returned to the house, where the Countess met them with a curious look and scolded Perdita for being up so early.

The dresses were laid out in each girl's bedroom, ready to be put on. The modiste and her assistant, who had been brought from Paris for the occasion, first dressed Eliane and then Perdita, but only after a slight contretemps with Jeanne. Both dresses were to be worn over ivory slips, both were made of a delicate butterfly silk, based on ivory and shot with another colour. It had been specially woven in Lyons, and a piece of the same material was later put in the museum there as a supreme example of the weaver's art. Eliane's dress was shot with pale gold, Perdita's with a kind of copper-rose, and in the depth of each fold was a delicate shadow of colour. Brussels lace edged Eliane's dress and covered her hair. Jeanne had arranged Perdita's hair in a simple topknot, with a few tiny curls escaping at the side. Over this she had placed a fall of Honiton lace anchored with a cluster of copper-pink roses.

The Countess and her sister had tears in their eyes when they saw the two girls. And indeed it would have been hard to find a more exquisite sight. When the four came down the stairs the assembled household gave an audible gasp of admiration.

Perdita didn't hear it, didn't see the crowd in the hall, for she had eyes only for the Earl. He looked pale, she thought, even rather grim. He led Eliane into the flower-decked salon, where Philippe waited, together with Père Amboise and the notary. Everyone present at the ceremony that followed was moved by the simple sincerity with which the young couple exchanged their vows. Then, after the civil formalities had been completed, they were surrounded by a crowd of well-wishers, and for a while the salon was filled with laughter and noise. This did not please the notary, who was a self-important man, determined not to be overwhelmed by his aristocratic clients.

He stepped forward fussily, clapped his hands, and cried, "*Messieurs*! *Mesdames*! Please!" When the noise grew less he said, "I understand there is a second couple to be married here today. Where is the lady, Monsieur de Belleroi?"

A puzzled murmur grew among the guests, and the servants, who had crowded outside the salon to see Mademoiselle Eliane married, looked at one another questioningly. The family, on the other hand, waited in happy anticipation as Perdita's startled gaze met the Earl's. As if in a dream she allowed him to lead her forward.

"This is the lady who will be my wife. Is that not so, Perdita?"

All her doubts, all her fears, melted away in the love shining from those steadfast grey eyes. Secure at last, she looked at the Countess, smiling encouragement, at Eliane's delighted face, felt surrounded by the warmth and friendship of the others—Madame d'Harcourt, Madame d'Espery, Père Amboise and the rest. How could she reject all this? Her eyes returned to the Earl, who was still holding her hands firmly in his.

"Edward, I will marry you, and love you all the days of my life," she said.

Under the shocked gaze of the notary, she was seized in the Earl's arms and passionately kissed. The guests recovered from their astonishment and applauded loudly. The notary had some difficulty in restoring order to these unconventional proceedings. This was not the way business was conducted in the town hall at Bayeux!

In spite of the notary's disapproval, Edward and Perdita were duly married, and at the enormously successful feast that followed Eliane laughed at the dazed look on Perdita's face.

"I was sure you would guess," she said. "Did you really think Edward was telling us about Belleroi when you interrupted us in the library? He was asking us if we objected to sharing the wedding, you goose! We've known about Belleroi for ages! Oh, Perdita, I could burst with happiness—married to Philippe and having you for my new cousin... Isn't it wonderful?"

AT LAST THE GUESTS had departed, the Countess had taken a slightly tearful Madame d'Harcourt to Beau Lac, Eliane and Philippe had gone to their room, and the Earl and Perdita were walking in the grounds.

"Tomorrow I take you to Ambourne, my love, where we shall be undisturbed for as long as we wish."

"And the Countess? I thought she was coming tomorrow."

"My mother is far too tactful, Perdita, my darling. She will stay here for a while to console my aunt. And now, my wife, shall we go in?"

"Edward, there's something I ought to tell you, but I don't know how…"

He smiled down at her anxious face and raised an eyebrow. "More secrets? Can't it wait?"

Perdita said desperately, "No, it can't. That's just it." She took a deep breath and said in a rush, "That gelding you have in the stables—Legrand was like that. He…he…he made me sleep in his cabin to fool the other men on the ship. He didn't want them to know what he was like. But…but…he couldn't…couldn't…I mean, he beat me and burned me instead of…instead of anything else." Her face was scarlet when she had finished.

The Earl said, "Are you trying to tell me that Legrand was impotent, Perdita? That you are, strictly speaking, untouched?" She nodded and then jumped as the Earl let out a great whoop of joyous laughter. Then he picked her up in his arms and whirled her round. "Oh, Perdita, Perdita!" he shouted. "You wonderful, wonderful girl!"

"Put me down, Edward! Put me down, I say. You'll have the whole château out here asking what is wrong!"

"Everything is perfect! And I don't mind if the whole world knows it," said the Earl, keeping firm hold of his bride.

"Well, I do," said Perdita. "It's not the sort of information I want to share with anyone but you. Now there's one more thing I want you to do. Will you promise to do it?''

''Anything, anything, my angel—you've just made me feel ten feet tall.''

She whispered in his ear as she lay there in his arms. He laughed again and took her indoors and upstairs. The next morning the scandalised staff of the château heard from Madame Lebrun how the Earl had taken his lovely new Countess and dropped her, in her shift, into the bath in his dressing-room. But no one ever said what happened after.

Raven's Honour
by
Claire Thornton

Claire Thornton grew up in Sussex. It is a family legend that her ancestors in the county were involved in smuggling. She was a shy little girl, and she was fascinated by the idea that she might be distantly related to bold and daring adventurers of the part – who were probably not shy! When she grew up she studied history at York University, and discovered that smugglers were often brutal men whose main ambition was to make money. This was disappointing, but she still feels justified in believing in – and writing about – the romantic and noble heroes of earlier ages. Claire Thornton has also written under the name of Alice Thornton.

Chapter One

Spain, November 1812

'Come on, Belinda, don't give up on me now!' Honor urged.

The donkey baulked, her ears flicking nervously at the sight of the angry, fast-flowing waters of the River Heubra. Ahead of them, soldiers of the 52nd Regiment of Foot were jumping down the steep banks of the river, then fording through almost shoulder-deep water. Many of the men were holding on to each other to save themselves from being swept away by the current.

Honor couldn't blame Belinda for her reluctance to plunge into the river, but the delay was dangerous. She could hear musket and rifle fire behind her as the rearguard of the Light Division skirmished with the advancing French. Honor gritted her teeth and urged the donkey forward. She'd always kept up with the column, ever since she'd first arrived in the Peninsula over three years ago— she wasn't about to become a French prisoner now.

'*Come on*, Belinda!'

The donkey still wouldn't budge. Honor was just won-

dering whether to slide off her back and lead her into the
water when the decision was taken out of her hands.

She heard a dull thwack behind her—then Belinda
bolted forward, half-jumping, half-falling into the rushing
water. The shock of icy water knocked the breath from
Honor's lungs. The current hammered and sucked at her
legs, plastering her shabby skirt against Belinda's struggling body.

The little donkey was already losing the fight against
the wild-tempered river. She could barely keep her head
above the foaming water. Her eyes rolled with fear and
panic.

Honor had no breath to reassure her. The river tossed
the donkey like a dead leaf, dragging Honor beneath the
surface of the water. Her skirt was caught. For long, desperate moments, she fought to free herself from Belinda's
foundering body. Her lungs burned. She could hear nothing but the water roaring in her ears. The current pounded
around her head, hard as a clenched fist, battering her
bruised body. She forced her head up, sucked in a quick,
painful breath, and finally found some leverage against
Belinda's side. She tore her skirt free. Relief surged
through her that she was no longer anchored to the failing
donkey. She made one last effort to get to Belinda's head,
to save the donkey and her possessions. It was too late.
She was already too tired, and the donkey was too far
gone. Just saving herself was going to take all her strength
and determination.

She tried to ride the current, to use it to reach the river
bank. She'd been swept too far downstream for any of the
infantry crossing the river to help her. She was numbed
by the heat-sapping cold. Blinded by the stinging water.
Choking and drowning…

She slammed up against something hard and unyielding.

What little breath she had left in her body was knocked out of her. A strong arm plucked her unceremoniously from the water to lie across the high pommel of a Hussar saddle. She was draped face down, like a sack of corn, her breasts pressed against a muscular leg.

Honor gasped and coughed uncontrollably. She tasted bile in her mouth and was suddenly afraid she might throw up in this undignified position. By an effort of sheer determination, she reasserted some control over her shivering, battered body. Honor blinked water from her eyes and turned her head to one side. She was aware of her hair hanging down towards the ground in sopping rats tails.

She was lying across a tall black horse, her body resting on the hard thighs of its rider. His body heat penetrated her sodden dress, warming her in a shockingly intimate way. The virile, masculine strength of her rescuer stirred a response deep within her—but then she deliberately pushed aside her inappropriate awareness of him.

She focussed her attention on his mount instead. She knew this stallion. Even from her limited viewpoint the horse was unmistakable. But then she'd known from the first moment the identity of her rescuer—and the horse possessed the same fierce courage as his rider. She felt the stallion's hindquarters bunch as it thrust up the river bank. The wild current which had taken her poor Belinda troubled the black no more than a gurgling summer stream might have done.

'Corvinus,' she whispered hoarsely.

'As you say,' said a dry voice, from far above her.

The black stood patiently as strong hands lifted Honor and lowered her to the ground. Her legs were so weak she would have fallen if she hadn't grabbed the front of the saddle and hung on tight.

'Steady.' Her rescuer had released her, but now he

caught her upper arm again, supporting her while she collected herself.

Honor shook her dripping hair out of her eyes and lifted her head to peer up at Major Cole Raven.

He was leaning over her, his face only inches from hers. She'd never been so close to him before. She gasped as she met his fiercely probing gaze, almost as shaken by his proximity as she had been by her plunge into the Heubra. Raven's ice-blue eyes were shockingly vivid in his wolfish, stubble-darkened face. Beneath his shako his tawny hair had been bleached by the sun until it resembled the brindled pelt of a wolf. He must have been born with those deep-set eyes, strong cheekbones and square jaw—but years of campaigning had intensified the dangerous edge to his personality.

He was a consummate soldier. His big, rangy body had been hardened by long marches in freezing snow or scorching heat, and tempered by the battles he'd survived. The men joked he had a bayonet for a backbone and ice water for blood. Even now, after two days of forced retreat, most of it in the pouring rain, without food because the Commissariat had gone by a different route, Honor could see no sign of fatigue or distress in the Major's lean face. Only the thick stubble on his usually clean-shaven face gave any indication of his situation.

Honor normally tried to avoid the man. Whenever she was near him she could sense, beneath his controlled demeanour, currents as deep and wild as the river from which he'd just saved her. Her instincts warned her of danger, so she tried to keep her distance.

Right now her instincts were screaming, but his firm grip on her arm meant retreat was impossible.

She shivered slightly as she met his penetrating gaze. She was numb with cold and shock from her disaster in the river, but this quiver of nervousness was purely in response to Cole Raven's undivided attention.

'Thank you, sir,' she said, as steadily as she could.

He nodded a brief acknowledgement of her thanks. She tried to pull away, but his grip on her arm tightened. A shiver of alarm coursed through her.

'Have your legs stopped shaking yet?' he asked, his neutral tone belying the searing intensity of his gaze.

Her irrational panic receded as she realised he was simply concerned she might fall if he released her. Since she still had a death grip on his saddle with her other hand, it wasn't an unreasonable assumption.

'Yes, thank you, sir,' she said again.

She tried to prove her words by releasing the saddle and stepping away from him. He'd already wasted enough of his time rescuing her. Now she was safe, he had more important duties awaiting his attention.

She was dimly aware of the constant sound of rifle fire as the 95th engaged with the French—but then the shock of what had nearly happened hit her like a wall of freezing flood water. Fear of recently past danger temporarily overwhelmed her awareness of the imminently approaching threat. Instead of letting go, she moved closer and clung tighter for a horrible, desperate, heart-stopping moment.

Corvinus swung his head around to sniff curiously at the bedraggled woman standing by his shoulder. Honor felt his velvet lips mumble against her wet, muddy hair. Then he snorted disapprovingly and straightened his neck, shaking his head vigorously.

Honor's mood broke. She laughed and stroked the stallion's smooth, glossy neck.

'Show off,' she said, unaware of the note of affection in her voice as she spoke to the horse. 'Just because *your* mane's in such fine, untangled condition...*I* haven't got a lady's maid to pick the twigs out of *my* hair every—' She broke off, embarrassed to be caught talking like that to Corvinus in the presence of the stallion's master—particularly in the current, precarious circumstances. The shock of nearly drowning must have unhinged her mind.

She forced herself to look up at the Major, but to her relief he was looking beyond her.

'Your wife, Corporal,' he said curtly.

'Thank you, sir.' The relief in Patrick O'Donnell's voice was heartfelt and unmistakable.

Cole Raven released Honor into her husband's arms and rode away, rapping out quick orders as he did so.

'I thought I'd lost you, girl.' Patrick hugged her.

'Not me, just poor Belinda—and all our belongings.' Honor replied, hugging him back, grateful for the safe, unalarming warmth of his embrace.

She was missing one shoe. Her shabby skirt was ripped almost to her knees. She'd taken off her coat to make it easier to cross the river, and now it was lost with all their other possessions. She was covered in mud, her sodden hair dripped cold water down her back, and she couldn't control her bone-aching shivering—but at least she was still alive.

Patrick shrugged out of his greatcoat and insisted she put it on.

'But you're just as cold and wet as I am,' she protested, reluctant to take it from him. Shabby though the coat was, it was both warm and dry because Patrick had folded it and carried it across the river tied to the top of his knapsack.

'I'm dry from the shoulders down, girl,' he pointed out cheerfully, 'you look like a drowned rat.' He thrust the coat into her arms before hurrying to do his duty.

Honor wrapped herself gratefully in the coat and

squeezed as much river water from her hair as she could. She smiled ruefully as she fell into step beside the marching men. She and Patrick had been through some difficult times in the past, but they'd never before been reduced to only one coat between the two of them. When she was warmer, she would insist Patrick took his turn wearing it.

The battalion had been ordered downstream to defend the ford at San Muñoz. Cole rode beside the column, his outward demeanour as calm as ever, and tried not to remember his horror when he'd seen Honor disappear under the dark surface of the Heubra.

She had been a married woman—not only that, but a loyal, devoted wife—for as long as he'd known her. She'd done nothing to attract his interest, yet he desired her more than any other woman he'd ever known. When Honor was nearby Cole always knew where she was and what she was doing. He could sense her presence with every fibre of his being. He knew all the expressions on her fine-boned face. He'd been intensely aware of her even before he'd joined her husband's regiment—though he was damn sure that hadn't influenced his decision to seek promotion into the 52nd.

He'd watched from a distance as the sun bleached her golden blonde hair until it was nearly white. He'd watched her naturally slim body become almost painfully thin as she'd adapted to the rigours of army life. He'd seen her smooth skin darken to a rich golden brown under the Iberian sun. In her own way, she was as seasoned and battle-hardened as any of the troops around him. Yet her large hazel eyes were bright and expressive. And she possessed an inherent grace which was never eclipsed by the shabby clothes and clumsy shoes she wore.

Cole told himself he didn't approve of women submit-

ting themselves to the brutality of war. He told himself
that Honor had unsexed herself when she'd followed her
man to the battlefield, marching beside him with no shoes
on her feet and her skirt ripped in tatters almost to her
knees. He told himself fiercely that Honor O'Donnell was
a married woman—and he reminded himself almost daily
that he had a fiancée waiting for him in England. But nothing he told himself altered the fact that, every time he
looked at her, he wanted her.

The most important consequence of his inner battle was
that, until today, he had taken great care to keep a physical
distance between them. The moment when he'd hauled her
out of the swirling water was the first time he'd ever
touched her in the two years or more she'd been destroying
his inner peace. He could still feel her slim, shivering body
laid across his thighs, her slight breasts pressed against his
leg. Despite the cold discomfort of his present situation,
fierce heat flooded him at the memory of holding her so
intimately against him. She was too thin, he thought, and
there would be nothing for her to eat tonight. She didn't
even have a blanket—it had been lost with the donkey in
the Heubra.

He savagely damned the Quartermaster-General for
sending the supply train by a different route from the
troops, and himself even more savagely for acting like a
lovesick fool over a woman he could never have. She had
a husband to take care of her. Cole had seen the expression
in Patrick O'Donnell's eyes when he looked at his wife.
No doubt he was more than willing to keep her warm on
a cold night.

'Damn!' Honor slipped in the mud and nearly fell over,
cursing the quagmire even though she had reason to be
grateful to it. A shell hit the ground near her, burying itself

in the mud and throwing up a shower of clay that half-blinded her, but didn't otherwise hurt her.

They'd reached San Muñoz just in time to be caught up in a skirmish with the French artillery.

She saw a soldier in Patrick's company hit and crawled over to him. There was blood mixing with the mud on his arm, but he was bright-eyed when he looked up at her.

'Shouldn'a' spooked the donkey,' he said jerkily, slurring his words. 'Di'n' mean to drown you, Miz O'Donnell.'

'I know, Danny,' she said, smiling at him through a mask of mud. She ripped a strip off her wretched skirt, tying it round his arm to slow the bleeding. 'It's not your fault Belinda wasn't much of a swimmer.'

Another shell landed close by. She leant over Danny, protecting him with her body from the shower of sticky clay. The sound and smell of battle were overwhelming.

A hand grabbed her shoulder and dragged her backwards.

'For the love of God, get to the rear!' a voice grated in her ear.

Before she could respond, Major Raven had gone.

'Best follow orders, ma'am,' Danny Thompson croaked.

Honor lifted her head, pushing her filthy hair out of her eyes as she sought out Patrick. It was very unusual for her to be this close to him when he was fighting. It was a complete accident she'd been caught up in the skirmish.

Just as she found him, she saw him stagger and fall into the soft ground, his musket still clutched in his hand.

'Patrick!'

She stumbled to her feet, slipping and sliding through the mud to reach him. She tripped over a wounded man and sprawled headlong in the glutinous mud. Gritty clay oozed through her fingers and covered her from head to toe. She pulled herself up, staggered a few more yards and fell down beside her husband, ignoring the other men around them.

'Patrick?' She tugged desperately at him, barely noticing the cold rain which had begun to fall.

He drew in a deep, unsteady breath, coughed, and pushed himself shakily onto his hands and knees, his head falling forward as if it was too heavy to lift.

Honor threw her arms around him, supporting his weight against her slender body as he recovered his senses.

'It's a scratch, sweet lamb, just a scratch,' he said hoarsely, his soft brogue more noticeable than usual, as he finally sat up unsupported.

'Oh, God!' Honor was so relieved he could talk coherently that tears burned her eyes.

She blinked them back because tears were certainly not what Patrick, or any one else, would expect from her. As she did so, she realised that the French firing had stopped. They were no longer under attack, but now it was pouring with icy rain.

'Damn the weather, damn the French, damn the Commissariat!' she muttered like a chant.

Patrick was trembling from shock and cold. They'd all been cold, wet and hungry since they'd left Salamanca two days ago. First the torrential rain, then the river, now the rain again.

'Let me see,' she said, gently opening Patrick's jacket. He'd been wounded in the side by a piece of case-shot. It was a long, shallow gash. She'd seen men recover from much worse injuries—and die from apparently less serious wounds. She knew of a woman who'd died simply because she'd pricked her finger on a pin which had fastened a bandage around an infected wound.

It was the first time Patrick had ever been hurt and

Honor was afraid for him, but she couldn't let her fear show.

'Just bind it up with a strip of your petticoat and I'll be fit for another day's march,' Patrick said bracingly.

'Yes, sir!' Honor snapped, anxiety putting an edge on her voice. 'Clean? clean?' she muttered, glancing around. 'There's nothing clean in this whole damn world.'

The relentless rain plastered her hair to her face, her clothes to her back. Dirty water ran down Patrick's body and mingled with the blood seeping from his wound.

'Honor, girl, I don't like to hear my wife curse so freely,' Patrick chided her gently.

'I'm sorry.' Honor bit her lip. She'd never felt so helpless, or so worried. She would have given everything she possessed for clean water, clean linen and a dry place to tend her husband's wound. Unfortunately, everything she possessed except the clothes on her back were lost in the river.

Before she had time to do anything further a clean, dry handkerchief was thrust into her hand. She instantly pressed it against Patrick's side, leaving it up to him to thank the donor, who'd already moved on.

'Hold this,' she commanded, putting Patrick's hand against the handkerchief, hiding her fear beneath her brisk manner.

Her petticoat was in no better shape than her skirt. She had to tie three strips together before she had a makeshift bandage long enough to go round Patrick's body. When she was finished she helped him to his feet. There was no provision for the wounded on this march. If he couldn't keep up, he would be left for the enemy. Of course, everyone believed the French treated wounded enemies with humanity, but neither Patrick nor Honor wanted to put that belief to the test. She was relieved to see that he seemed quite steady on his feet, though still somewhat dazed.

'Give me your musket,' she said. It weighed more than ten pounds, a heavy burden for anyone to carry, much less an injured man.

'I can carry my own weapon,' Patrick protested.

'Then give me the rest,' Honor countered. 'I've carried more, and now I have nothing to carry.'

Patrick hesitated, then let her take his knapsack, haversack and even his water canteen. He started to protest when Honor made him take back his greatcoat, but his objections faded when he saw her strip the coat from one of their fallen comrades.

'He doesn't need it any more,' she said quietly. She touched the dead man's face gently. 'Poor Samuel,' she said sadly. She checked to see if he had any personal belongings she could save for his family.

Then she stood up and put on the coat. It was tattered, muddy and stained with blood, but it still provided some protection from the weather. She distributed Patrick's equipment about her person and then she was ready to march beside him in the column. Normally she followed at the rear of the battalion, with the other womenfolk and camp-followers—or even went ahead to prepare the camp for the men's arrival—but today Patrick needed her. She wasn't the first woman to help her man on the march.

Danny Thompson was near them in the column, his arm held in a crude sling. They'd lost several good men in the brief skirmish, including the two senior officers of Patrick's company. Honor was inclined to think the whole retreat had been mismanaged, but grumbling wouldn't help. All she really wanted was a dry billet and a chance for Patrick to rest.

* * *

A dry handkerchief. In this whole, Godforsaken world, all he could give Honor was a dry handkerchief to ease her misery. Cole turned up his collar against the sleeting rain and cursed his helplessness, while mud sucked at Corvinus's hooves with every step the stallion took.

This retreat was a grim business. The Light Division hadn't lost a battle. They'd marched into Madrid in triumph in August and, along with the Third Division, had been comfortably quartered in the vicinity until October. Wellington had left the Fourth Division at Escurial and marched north with the First, Fifth and Seventh Divisions. He'd laid siege to Burgos in September, but a month later the fortress was still in enemy hands, and the French and their allies had had time to gather their forces. Wellington had been forced to retreat from Burgos, while the Divisions he'd left behind had retreated from Madrid under the command of General Hill. The Allied army had reunited at Salamanca, the scene of its victory in July, but this time there'd been a stand-off between the French forces and the Allies, and now Wellington's army was in retreat.

As a member of the Light Division, Cole hadn't taken part in the siege of Burgos. Privately, he thought it had been a badly mismanaged affair—both the siege train and the provision of trained engineers had, by all accounts, been laughably inadequate—but he preferred to voice his opinions only when they might make a difference. Right now his first priority was to ensure the safety of his own men.

The country between Salamanca and Ciudad Rodrigo was a flat, wooded plain. The road was criss-crossed with rivulets of water which in wet weather turned the route into a muddy quagmire. The road was littered with the carcasses of dead horses and oxen. Cole had seen an exhausted Portuguese soldier buried so deep in the mud he couldn't pull himself out. There had been no help for it but to leave him behind. There were many sick, weary men on the march. O'Donnell could still stand, he could still walk—he was not the worst of them.

With curt words of encouragement, and the occasional black joke, Cole put heart into the wet and disheartened men of his regiment. But even under these conditions he would not tolerate even a hint of insubordination from the hard-used men.

There was no warm billet that night, and nothing to eat but acorns. Honor tried not to think of poor Belinda, who'd carried their remaining rations away with her on the bitter waters of the Heubra.

Most of the ground was ankle-deep in slushy mud, so the men congregated in groups on the higher ground around the roots of trees. There was only green, wet wood to burn, but they managed to light a smoking fire. When Major Raven's servant, Joe Newton, brought her a blanket, Honor accepted it with gratitude. Joe and Patrick had become friends soon after Raven had joined the 52nd. They were united by their love of good horseflesh—a love Honor shared. She knew the Major's black stallion well, although she'd always avoided Cole Raven when she and Patrick visited with Joe. She wasn't surprised by Joe's kindness to them, and it didn't occur to her to wonder whether Cole Raven had had any hand in the matter.

Beyond the small circles of light cast by the struggling campfires the night was cold and unfriendly. In the distance, hidden by the black, dripping tree trunks, wolves howled. Honor shivered at the eerie music. So many fallen horses and men meant easy pickings for the beasts.

'Sing for me,' Patrick urged.

He was lying on the ground, his head on her lap, wrapped in the blanket Joe had given them.

Honor hesitated. In all the time she'd been in the Peninsula, she'd done nothing to remind others of her life before her marriage. She was Mrs Patrick O'Donnell, the respectable wife of a steady, dutiful man. She'd left Honor Meredith, toast of the fashionable London stage, far behind her. Patrick had never questioned her behaviour, and never before asked her to do anything which might compromise her relationship with the other men or wives. She was surprised by his request, but she had no thought of refusing him.

She began to sing softly, choosing one of Thomas Moore's Irish melodies which she knew Patrick particularly liked. If she closed her eyes and concentrated, she could almost imagine they were back in London. She was onstage in a crowded theatre, trying to hold the attention of an audience which was more interested in gossiping than in watching the performance. It had required courage as well as talent and persistence for Honor to establish a career under such circumstances.

Now, singing for Patrick in a dark, alien landscape, Honor imagined she was back in the gaudy, fantastical world of the theatre, where the forbidding black trees were only painted on to a flimsy backcloth, and when the performance was over they'd wash off the blood and eat a comforting meal in a firelit room.

She tried to put the cosy warmth she imagined into her voice, but tears seeped beneath her closed eyelids. It was so hard to drive the cold away.

Cole returned from checking the picket and paused in the shadows of the dank trees, listening to Honor sing. He'd never heard her do so before, though some of his fellow officers claimed to have seen her perform in London. She'd been a fêted actress before her marriage. He could only assume she loved Patrick O'Donnell very much to give up a pampered life to follow the drum.

Her clear, musical voice was husky with weariness, but it conjured happier, warmer times. When she stopped, someone asked her to sing again. Her voice pierced the cold and darkness which isolated them all in this miserable corner of existence.

Cole's heart twisted with foreboding. Honor had never sung before. He wasn't given to fanciful ideas, but her song seemed prophetic. Even the wolves had ceased their own song to listen. *Not a swan song. Please God, don't let it be a swan song,* he thought. *Not for Honor.*

The next morning, as usual, the men stood to their arms an hour before dawn. Honor watched Patrick anxiously in the uncertain light, but he seemed fit enough. She danced from foot to foot and hugged herself in a vain attempt to get warm as they waited for the orders to move off. The French were not far behind and the delay seemed inexplicable to her.

She snooped around a little and overheard a conversation between some officers which indicated that the Light Division couldn't move until the First Division had done so—and the First Division couldn't move because its officers didn't have a guide and they were lost.

Honor bit her lip and hid discreetly behind a tree trunk as Cole Raven stalked past, a scowl on his face. The Major had transferred to the 52nd Foot a year ago from the 16th Light Dragoons. According to stories she'd heard, while he was in the cavalry, he'd often acted as an intelligence officer for Wellington. It occurred to her that a man whose previous duties had not only included leading patrols deep into enemy territory, but also sketching accurate maps of Spain and Portugal during his first months in the Peninsula, was unlikely to be impressed by the excuse that an entire Division was lost!

Unfortunately, Honor's own sense of direction was so poor she didn't feel able to criticise the officers of the First Division as freely as she might have liked. If she'd known where Luis was, the goatboy who often acted as her own guide, she could have offered his services—but Luis, like the Commissariat, had disappeared along another route.

One of the Light Division officers provided the First Division with a guide, and finally the Light Division itself was able to move off. Honor listened anxiously for any sign of pursuit by the French. She knew her companions were equally eager to avoid a confrontation. In the present situation there could be no victory, only unnecessary losses.

The sun shone, which was a relief after the endless rain of the previous day, but the roads were still swamped with mud, which hid potential hazards from the unwary. Honor bit back an exclamation of pain as she stubbed her bare foot against a buried tree stump. Her feet were already so numb from cold that it didn't hurt as much as it might have done, but she was afraid of doing real damage to herself. She wouldn't be able to keep up with the column if she couldn't walk, and then she wouldn't be able to help Patrick.

She was keenly aware of every movement he made. He seemed well enough in the morning, but when they set off again after the midday break he was obviously having more difficulty. He stumbled several times, before he finally allowed her to take his musket, concentrating all his strength on putting one foot in front of another.

When they eventually halted for the evening she looked

at Patrick's wound. At the sight of it, she swallowed tears of fear and anxiety. It was far worse than it had been when he'd first been hit. She did her best to tend it, then huddled against Patrick, wrapping them both in the damp blanket, trying to keep them warm and alive through the cold night. She was too exhausted to stay fully awake, but too anxious and uncomfortable to rest properly. She dozed fitfully, nightmarish images chasing each other through her mind.

The next morning they tried to set off with the others, but it was soon clear that Patrick could barely stay on his feet, much less keep up with the column. The rest of the men in the company were too weakened and weary to offer more than verbal encouragement. Honor struggled to keep Patrick moving for a while, her arm around his waist. In the end it was too much for both of them.

'If you wait here, you may be able to get a ride on one of the wagons that are following us,' said Lieutenant Gregory, harried and anxious.

The death of the Captain and the other Lieutenant had given him added responsibilities under particularly difficult conditions. He wanted to get all his men to safety, but there was not much he could do for one who couldn't walk. Especially since his own mare had foundered the previous day and he was compelled to march beside his men.

'I'll wait,' Patrick wheezed. 'Take Honor with you, sir,' he begged.

'No,' said Honor flatly. 'I'm staying with my husband.'

The Lieutenant hesitated, meeting Honor's unwavering gaze. He was barely twenty years old, and not long in Spain, but he knew a lost cause when he saw one.

'Mrs O'Donnell will do her duty as she sees fit,' he said stiffly. Honor knew he didn't want to leave them behind, but he had no choice.

'I'll be looking out for you tonight,' Maggie Foster told Honor sharply. She was the wife of one of the other soldiers, a raw-boned, harsh-voiced woman who often fell foul of the military authorities. 'The Corporal could have ridden on my donkey if the Provost Marshall hadn't shot it!' she continued belligerently, flashing a hostile glance at Lieutenant Gregory.

It was the Provost Marshall's business to prevent women and other camp followers from impeding the progress of the troops—or plundering the surrounding countryside. In extreme circumstances he might even shoot a woman's donkey—and Maggie's had been shot the previous day.

The Lieutenant flushed, but refused to be drawn into an argument with the formidable woman.

'Thank you,' said Honor, genuinely grateful to Maggie, who'd often looked out for her since Patrick had joined the Regiment. 'We'll manage.'

'I'm counting on it,' said the older woman. Her eyes were hard, but her brief grip on Honor's hands was painfully tight.

She nodded grimly to Honor, then stepped back and ordered her children to get up from the muddy ground. When she walked away two little girls were clinging to her skirts, while an older boy kept pace beside her, carrying some of their belongings.

'God be with you both,' Lieutenant Gregory said, his voice cracking. He spun on his heel, and Honor and Patrick watched in silence as the company marched away.

They sat beneath a tree on some relatively dry ground. Honor huddled against Patrick. She'd wrapped him in the blanket and loosened the uncomfortable leather stock from around his neck. Occasionally cold drops of water splashed down on them from the branches above. Their surroundings seemed to be composed only of stark, monochrome shades. Patrick drifted between delirium and brief moments of consciousness. He was far too ill to talk to her or to share any of the responsibility for their predicament. Honor had never felt so alone in her life.

She was cold and scared and hungry. The cold numbed both her body and her mind. Despite the extreme danger of their situation, her thoughts became lethargic and detached, with the surreal quality of dreams. Her mind ranged over many unrelated people and subjects. She thought of her mother, who'd never been daunted by any of the enormous obstacles she'd had to overcome in her life.

But thinking about her mother made Honor feel inadequate and unhappy. Annie Howarth would never have allowed herself to fall into such desperate straits. Honor knew her mother wouldn't be at all impressed by the mess her daughter had made of everything—so she thought about Major Raven instead. Thinking about Cole Raven warmed her. When she summoned his image into her mind her body inexplicably responded. When she remembered how the furnace-like heat of his body had burnt through her clothes after he'd rescued her from the river, her cold, turgid blood once more flowed hotly through her veins. She knew she shouldn't think of him like that but, just briefly, she allowed herself to indulge in the strangely comforting memory.

She hadn't seen either the Major or Joe Newton since the previous evening. She wondered where they were. Joe Newton was a good friend to Patrick. She would have asked for his help if she'd had the chance. Now there was no one to help them.

Honor and Patrick waited for hours on the dreary, inhospitable road. No wagons came.

'Leave me,' said Patrick, during one of his brief moments of coherence.

'No,' Honor replied. She bit her lip, shaking herself out of her cold-induced apathy. She looked up and down the road, searching for a solution to their problem. If only she still had her donkey. She cut off that line of thought before bitter frustration overwhelmed her.

'You have to,' Patrick insisted, more strongly. 'If you stay here, I will die and you will be at the mercy of any man who comes—French, Spanish, deserter.' He broke off, breathing quickly. 'I didn't marry you in London to let you suffer a worse fate in Spain,' he gasped. 'Honor, girl, you have to leave me.'

'Would you leave me?' she demanded.

''Tis different,' he protested.

'Hah!' Honor forced her cold, numb body into activity. She divested herself of everything she'd been carrying except the musket, ammunition pouch and canteen. Then she twisted the musket until it was hanging diagonally across the front of her body. It wasn't comfortable, but if she adjusted it carefully it didn't impede her legs.

'Now get up,' she ordered Patrick.

His eyes widened at the steel in her voice.

'You sound like your mother,' he said, astonished, and not quite approving.

'Get up, damn you!' She hauled him to his feet, using her anger at being compared to her mother to give her the strength she needed for the task ahead. She didn't want to be unkind to Patrick, but somehow she had to find the strength of will and courage to save them both. If the only way she could do that was to call upon the spirit of her sharp-tongued, fierce-tempered mother, then so be it.

As soon as Patrick was upright she turned her back on him and dragged his arms over her shoulders, holding on tight as she bent forward and lifted his feet clear off the ground.

'Help me!' she gasped.

He locked his arms around her neck and she managed to jerk him a little higher up her body, until she could get her arms beneath his legs. He grunted with pain when she jolted his wound, but it was impossible to be gentle. They had to make some adjustments before Honor started walking. At first, Patrick's arms pressed the musket into her body so hard she could barely breath; but soon she was ready to plod after the long-gone column of men.

Cole snapped his telescope shut with an impatient gesture. He'd spent the past twenty-four hours checking on the position and movements of the French. Normally he enjoyed the opportunity for independent action. He was an experienced outpost officer. At different times he'd worked with both the regular Spanish army and the guerilla bands. But since joining the 52nd Foot his activities had been more circumscribed. He should have relished this chance for a little more freedom of action. Instead he'd been irritated rather than pleased when he'd received his current orders. He hadn't wanted to leave the battalion as it struggled towards safety. He was concerned for the well-being of all the men who served under him, but he couldn't deny that the gnawing anxiety he felt for the O'Donnells—for Honor—was particularly intense.

But now that Cole was satisfied that the French had no intention of pursuing them any further, his task was completed. He was free to rejoin his men as soon as possible.

He glanced at Joe Newton. His servant had been ill at ease from the moment they'd left the column; now he was positively fidgeting with impatience.

'We're going back, sir?' he burst out.

'Yes, we are.'

'Thank God for that.' Joe didn't waste a moment in turning his horse towards Ciudad Rodrigo.

Cole frowned, briefly puzzled by Joe's uncharacteristic vehemence. But since Cole was equally keen both to rejoin their comrades and to reach a comfortable billet, he didn't question him.

Honor walked steadily, keeping to the least rutted part of the road, taking every step with care, fearful of stumbling over a mud-covered obstacle. She was a tall woman; at five foot four, Patrick was actually an inch or two shorter than his wife. That made it easier. So did the fact that he was a skinny, wiry man, without a spare ounce of extra flesh. But he was still a heavy burden, and she was already tired and undernourished.

The light was fading and she knew they wouldn't reach safety by nightfall. Her awareness shrank to the next few feet of muddy road. To look ahead and see how far she had to go would have invited despair. Perhaps that was why it took her so long to realise she wasn't alone on the road. She couldn't hear anything, she certainly hadn't seen anything—but she slowly turned around and looked straight into the amber eyes of a wolf.

The wolf was so close she could see its breath misting on the cold air. There were two others, circling behind it. 'My God!' She exhaled in shock. 'Patrick, let go.'

All she could think was that she couldn't fire the musket with him hanging around her neck. But Patrick was barely conscious. He was clinging on by instinct, unable to respond to her desperate request.

The wolf padded closer, head outstretched towards her, golden eyes focussed on Honor.

'Patrick, let go!' she screamed. He tumbled off her back. The wolf shied away, snarling at her sudden screech.

Honor fumbled with cold, unresponsive fingers in the ammunition pouch. A moment ago she'd thought she was too tired to care what happened to them, but now anger stirred her numb limbs. She was damned if they were going to survive so much, just to become some damned dog's dinner! She tore off the end of the paper cartridge with her teeth, primed and closed the pan, then rammed the powder, torn cartridge and ball into the muzzle of the musket.

Don't fire away the ramrod, she reminded herself a little hysterically. She thrust it into the ground by her feet and lifted the musket to her shoulder. At least the wolf couldn't shoot back. Patrick had to do this under enemy fire.

She aimed at the nearest wolf. The musket kicked so hard her shoulder went numb, but she was too frightened and excited to notice. She was more concerned about the brief interval of blindness when the sudden flash and cloud of smoke obscured her vision.

Had she hit the wolf? Would she feel its teeth in her throat at any second?

The smoke cleared and she saw the wolf was either dead or so severely wounded it would never hunt again.

Excitement surged through her and she gave a hoarse, wordless shout of victory. One of the remaining wolves turned tail at her loud cry. The other sniffed cautiously at its fallen companion and bared its teeth at her, its head low to the ground.

Honor reloaded the musket with shaking hands.

'Mangy cur!' she raged at the wolf. 'Eat the dead meat! That's all you're fit for!'

She fired again. This time she missed, but the solitary wolf had had enough. It disappeared into the trees and Honor was suddenly alone with Patrick. It was only then that she realised two horsemen were approaching. She lifted the unloaded musket instinctively, afraid she was going to be ridden down by French cavalry, then she recognised the leading horse—and his rider.

'Corvinus,' she whispered. The musket was suddenly too heavy to hold and she dropped it, falling on her knees beside Patrick.

Cole heard the first shot before he saw Honor in the failing daylight. When he saw the wolf she'd shot, his heart lurched with admiration for her courage and resolution.

By God, she was a woman among women! he thought exultantly.

Then Honor collapsed beside her husband's hunched body, and the sight chilled his triumphant mood.

He leapt to the ground and seized Honor's arms in an urgent grip.

'Are you hurt?' he demanded fiercely, all his cool composure forgotten.

Beside them, Joe Newton crouched over Patrick.

Honor stared at Cole blankly, as if she didn't recognise him. Her hazel eyes were red-rimmed and sunk in deep, dark circles. Her face was so thin it twisted his gut to see it. Her cheeks were streaked with mud, her hair so matted it was impossible to tell its true colour.

'*Honor!*' Her name ripped from his lips.

'Patrick,' she whispered, staring past him towards her husband supported in Joe's arms. It was as if Cole's presence had barely registered with her.

Cole released her, feeling a kick of jealousy, because her only thought was for her husband. That emotion was quickly followed by self-disgust and shame at his wildly emotional response to the situation.

'O'Donnell?' Cole bent over the sick man, his voice expressionless, but his touch gentle as he pressed the back of his hand against Patrick's forehead.

'Take care of Honor, sir,' Patrick croaked. His eyes were clouded by sickness, but no sign of confusion when he met Cole's guarded gaze.

Cole's conscience pinched. Did the man have any idea how he felt about his wife? He glanced at Honor, but she was kneeling in the slush like a statue, her face devoid of expression or response, as if the last of her reserves had finally been exhausted. Joe Newton waited woodenly for orders from his master.

The stallion nuzzled Honor's shoulder gently, then nudged her back with his head a few times, in an almost human gesture of affectionate impatience.

'Corvinus.' Honor turned her head and focussed on the black. 'Come here, boy.' Her voice was utterly flat but, to Cole's amazement, the stallion obediently took a few steps forward.

Honor took hold of the stirrup and hauled herself to her feet. Her stoic determination was so mesmerising that, by the time Cole recollected himself enough to help her, she was already on her feet.

She looked at him directly for the first time.

'We can put Patrick on Corvinus,' she said. It was a statement of fact, not a supplication to an officer.

'Yes, ma'am.' Cole was startled to realise that he'd just given her the same response she often elicited from the privates in her husband's company. Honor didn't seem to notice. Unseen by either of them, a brief smile lightened Joe's sombre expression.

'I intend to put you both up,' Cole said drily, reasserting his authority. 'You first. I will lift...your husband up to you.'

Honor barely acknowledged his words, but she allowed him to help her on to the stallion's back. Cole cursed himself for his momentary hesitation. Why was it so hard to call the man her husband? Cole had always known they were married.

Perhaps his emotional turmoil now was the result of being forced to see, at first hand, the depth of devotion Honor felt for Patrick O'Donnell. She would do anything to keep her husband alive.

He took Patrick from Joe's supporting arms, steadying the man's feverish body briefly before he hoisted him on to Corvinus.

'She carried me.' Patrick's voice was little more than a hoarse whisper against Cole's shoulder. 'No wagons—so she carried me. I was meant…to take care…of her…' His words faded to nothing on the frosty evening air.

The man's words only intensified Cole's self-disgust, but he kept his face expressionless as he lifted Patrick into Honor's arms. Then he turned to Joe.

'Ride ahead, find us a billet, and inform the surgeon he will be needed,' he ordered harshly.

'Not the hospital.' Honor said flatly. 'I'll take care of Patrick.' Her voice sounded rusty and unfamiliar in her ears. 'Don't take him to the hospital.'

She'd seen the conditions in the hospitals. Two or more men crowded in one bed, in airless, filthy wards. A man could go into hospital with a broken leg and die of the fever he'd caught from his unfortunate bedmate. Some of the medical staff were conscientious, but too often the men were left in the care of hospital mates who were ignorant and inattentive to their patients. While Honor still had breath in her body, she would not permit Patrick to be submitted to such an ordeal.

'No, not the hospital,' said Cole, his steady voice inviting her trust.

'Good.' Honor nodded, accepting his assurance. She wrapped her arms around Patrick, holding him in place on the stallion's back as Cole began to lead his little party towards Ciudad Rodrigo.

Patrick was barely conscious, but he'd been around horses all his life. Deep-rooted instincts kept him in the saddle—and Honor did the rest. She'd thought many times that, if Patrick had to be a soldier, he might have been happier in the cavalry—but it had been an infantry recruitment party which had finagled him into the army.

She was hardly more alert than Patrick. From the moment she'd seen Corvinus—and the unmistakable broad shoulders of his master—her relentless determination had begun to unravel. Raven would save them. She had no doubt of it. She closed her eyes, letting him lead them where he chose. Just before her weary, overburdened mind lost all coherence, a stray thought drifted to the surface. What luxury, for once in her life, to be able to rely on someone else's strength and determination.

Chapter Two

The regiment was bivouacked outside Ciudad Rodrigo, but Joe Newton and Maggie Foster met Raven's bedraggled little group as they approached the fortress. Joe led them into the suburbs. Honor was too tired to wonder what he had arranged, she was simply grateful that they had somewhere to go.

The next few days passed in a blur. Later she was able to remember only a few random incidents from that time. She had been billeted with Patrick in the house of an elderly Spanish gentleman and his two sisters. Their hosts were discreet and remarkably tolerant of being burdened with a very sick man. Honor expressed her gratitude to them, but she was too distracted to pay much attention to her surroundings, and too worried about Patrick to question the unexpected comfort of the billet Raven had arranged for them.

Joe was frequently in attendance. Honor never wondered what his master thought of his long absences from his duties. Maggie Foster left her children in her husband's care and helped nurse Patrick. It turned out that Joe had met her trudging back along the road to look for Honor and Patrick, and had told her they'd been found.

The O'Donnells' Spanish hosts brought a priest who made little impression on Honor, though she thought his presence comforted Patrick. Lieutenant Gregory came to see them, grateful that they had not died on the road, sorry that Patrick was so ill.

Major Raven visited, bringing with him the battalion surgeon, but otherwise saying little.

Patrick received the best care available—but it wasn't enough.

He rallied briefly, then his condition deteriorated. Most of the time he was too weak or confused to speak to Honor. She remembered only two things he said to her.

'You're a good wife,' he whispered once, when she lifted his head to help him drink.

For a while his memory drifted back to his childhood in Ireland, and Honor could do little more than guess the correct response to his ramblings.

'You must make peace with your mother,' he said suddenly, his voice surprisingly strong. It was the last thing he said to her.

He died the next day. Honor prepared his body almost mechanically. She was too weary to cry, or even to grieve. Then she lay down beside him, knowing only that her long struggle to take care of him was over and she could finally rest.

Cole found them like that half an hour later. His first, appalled thought was that they were both dead.

'Honor! My God!' He pulled her into his arms. Her head lolled on to his shoulder. Then she sighed, an effortful breath, and relief thudded through him.

He tightened his hold on her. She was too thin. She weighed nothing in his arms. Her hair and her clothes were clean, but she looked more waif-like than ever. He hadn't realised quite how much the fierce determination of her will counterbalanced her fragile appearance. With her eyes closed it was hard to associate her with the woman who'd moved Heaven and earth to bring her husband to safety.

Then he saw that Patrick was dead, his body laid out for burial, and a chill invaded Cole's soul. Was Honor's life so bound up with her husband's that she no longer believed she had a reason to live?

'Honor!' he cried, fear edging his voice.

'Mmm.' She moved slightly in his arms, pillowing her cheek against his scarlet uniform. She drew in another deep breath. 'Tired,' she mumbled on an exhaled sigh. The rhythm of her breathing changed. To Cole's amazement, he realised she'd fallen into a peaceful sleep in his arms.

'Honor?' he murmured, an unfamiliar calm soothing his anxiety as he cradled her against his heart.

He didn't move—he couldn't. He could not bear to lay her down. She felt so warm and trusting in his arms. If he lowered his head, he could brush his lips against her sun-streaked hair. The temptation was overwhelming. He stroked a stray tendril back from her face. Her skin was soft and smooth, her fine bones as delicate as a bird's.

That brief, gentle touch was the only liberty he allowed himself to take with her. She was so vulnerable in her sleep that it stirred an ache deep within him. He could not protect her from the pain and grief she would feel when she woke and realised that Patrick was dead. She needed this interlude of unburdened rest.

She was still asleep when Joe Newton arrived. Shrewd eyes observed the care with which Raven held Honor, but the servant didn't comment. Cole didn't say anything either. His angular face was typically expressionless as he watched Joe briefly examine Patrick.

'She laid him out?' said Joe, a question in his low voice.

Cole nodded. Honor had been alone when he'd found her. He doubted anyone else had performed that chore for her.

'Her last duty,' said Joe. 'She ploughed her furrow to the end.' His eyes softened as they rested on Honor's sleeping face. 'No one could have asked more of her than that—not Patrick O'Donnell, at any rate.'

Honor slept for hours. Cole carried her out of sight of curious eyes while Patrick's body was removed, held her in his arms while Newton set the small room to rights, and then—reluctantly—put her gently down on the crude bed. He sent Newton away, knowing his own actions had betrayed him, but trusting the man's loyalty and goodwill would keep him silent.

Cole didn't leave. Honor was alone and unprotected in a strange place. She needed him.

Honor woke slowly and reluctantly. She ached in every bone and muscle of her body, which had become normal. She was also warm—which was a miracle. And she had a nagging, aching awareness that something was dreadfully wrong.

Patrick!

She turned her head, but he wasn't beside her. She thrust upward, staring wildly around. Patrick was gone—but she wasn't alone.

There was a candle burning on the table, and she saw Cole Raven sitting in the dim light. His presence shocked her, but somehow it didn't surprise her. He'd been a constant—though distant—presence in her life for a long time. Her first, instinctive response was to feel comforted by the familiar sight of his broad shoulders.

At her sudden movement he turned his head towards

her. The hard planes of his face could have been carved from teak, they showed so little expression. His deep-set eyes were hidden in shadows and unreadable. He didn't speak. Suddenly his presence didn't seem quite so reassuring. He was too powerful, too inscrutable, too much at ease in the darkness which surrounded them. Terrifying images crowded into her mind as she recalled the traditional association between ravens and the battlefield—ravens and the dead. Was Raven here because Patrick had died? A human emissary of death?

Honor shuddered and put her face in her hands. Her imagination had always been as much a curse as a blessing. Normally she tried to conjure only warm, positive musings, but tonight all her defences were down. She took a deep breath and tried to clear her thoughts. She had no idea what time it was or how long she'd been sleeping. Why had Raven watched her sleep?

'Do you remember what happened?' he asked after a few moments.

'I know Patrick is dead.' Her voice was muffled by her hands.

Grief welled up inside her for her husband, but she choked it back. She was acutely aware of Raven's scrutiny. She didn't understand what he was doing beside her, but she was determined not to give in to her emotions while he was watching her. Her mother's teaching had been unequivocal in that respect. Annie Howarth firmly believed that one should be rational, practical and, above all, *businesslike* on all occasions.

'There is food if you are hungry,' Raven said. 'You must be hungry. You've been asleep for hours. God knows how long it is since you ate.'

Honor swallowed her tears and lifted her head. She wouldn't allow herself to grieve for Patrick until she was alone. In the meantime, although she didn't feel hungry, she knew Raven was right, she needed food. She pushed back the covers and discovered she was still dressed, although her shoes were on the floor beside the bed. She put them on and drew in a deep breath, light-headed from the mild exertion.

'Here.' Cole put a plate of food into her hands.

There was only one chair in the room and Raven had it, so Honor sat on the side of the bed to eat.

Garlic sausage, cold pork and bread. Real bread, not the weevil-infested biscuit which was the staple of army rations. Despite her wariness over Raven's intentions, she was touched that he'd given her food. She couldn't remember the last time she'd eaten food she hadn't been responsible for providing.

She ate slowly, doing her best to ignore Raven's watchful presence, focussing instead on her meal. She seldom had the opportunity to enjoy the sheer pleasure of eating good food. If there turned out to be a price for this meal, she would conduct the negotiations with the food safely in her stomach.

'Brandy?' Cole poured her a glass from the bottle on the table.

She accepted it wordlessly and took a cautious sip. The strong liquor burned her throat and she handed it back to him immediately. Gin had been the undoing of the normally abstemious Patrick. She had no intention of letting her own wits be clouded by drink.

'Or tea?' Cole smiled faintly, and she saw a tin kettle sitting on the hearth.

She waited while he made the tea, not surprised at his competence. The food had strengthened her, and now she had the energy to notice things that had previously eluded her.

She was wearing a warm brown skirt and jacket, just like so many of the local women. There were good, square-toed shoes on her feet. There was a black shawl lying across the foot of the bed. She barely remembered the moment when Joe Newton had given her the new clothes; she'd been too tired and too preoccupied with the task of nursing Patrick. Now she had time to consider the implications of those gifts. Joe had presented them to her, but he hadn't paid for them.

She accepted a cup of tea from Major Raven, and saw that he'd poured one for himself as well. She studied him carefully, refusing to be daunted by his cold reserve, as she tried to remember everything she knew about him.

He was a big man with enormous physical stamina. She'd heard he had been wounded while he was still in the dragoons, but he'd survived both injury and the tortuous medical treatment he'd received. He was a head taller than Patrick, and Honor had noticed that tall men often suffered most on the march, but Raven seemed immune to the discomforts of campaigning.

He also possessed a forceful personality. After the bitterly costly siege of Badajoz earlier that year, all discipline had been lost among the British soldiers. They had rioted drunkenly in the streets of the town. Raven had been among the few officers who could still exert any control over his men. Patrick had told Honor how the Major had saved a Spanish girl from rape, relying simply on the strength of his personality. No sane man, looking into those crystal blue eyes, would willingly cross him.

Honor was grateful for Raven's help, but she was wary. Experience had taught her that most interactions with other people involved negotiations of some kind. She preferred those negotiations to be as unambiguous as possible.

'What do you want from me?' she asked quietly.

Cole's eyes narrowed as he studied her intently.

Honor met his gaze steadily, refusing to be cowed by his keen-eyed inspection.

'Nothing,' he said at last. He finished his tea and set the cup down on the table.

His denial puzzled Honor, but she didn't let her confusion show.

'I will pay for the clothes as soon as I can,' she assured him. 'There will be work I can do.' There was always work—mending, washing or cooking for different officers.

'That's not necessary,' said Cole brusquely.

'It is for me.' Honor lifted her chin stubbornly. 'I don't accept charity.'

He held her gaze with his hawk-like blue eyes for a long, tension-filled minute. Her heart rate increased as she realised more fully the hazards of crossing his fierce will. The Major did not tolerate any form of insubordination.

To her relief he broke eye contact first, glancing sideways at the shadow-filled room.

Honor drew in a deep, steadying breath. 'Thank you for all you did for Patrick,' she said.

'He was a good man.' Raven moved his long legs restlessly.

Was. Honor swallowed back her flash of anger at Raven's use of the past tense. She did not like the idea that Patrick's life could be dismissed in a few brief words.

'Yes,' she agreed raspily.

There was a heavy silence between them for several minutes, then she roused herself to speak once more.

'Patrick told me you saved his life at Badajoz,' she said.

Raven shrugged impatiently. 'In the heat of battle, who can be sure of such things?' he said, disclaiming responsibility for being considered any kind of saviour.

'God! You're a stubborn, contrary man!' Honor exclaimed, surprising herself as much as Raven with her un-expected outburst.

Raven's eyebrows quirked ironically. '*I'm* stubborn?' he said, a gleam in his eyes. 'I'm sure you could give me lessons, Mrs O'Donnell.'

'At least I say what I'm thinking!' she said forcefully. 'Talking to you is like debating with a baggage mule. You don't say what you want, but you're bound and determined to do things your own way! Hah!'

She grabbed the plate and chomped down on another piece of bread, suddenly ravenously hungry.

Raven blinked at the force of her attack then, to her amazement, grinned. The expression completely trans-formed his angular face, making him seem both younger and far less threatening.

'What do you think I want?' he enquired blandly.

Honor was momentarily startled to see a rakish smile hovering on his lips, but the unexpectedly suggestive gleam in his eyes fuelled both her suspicions and her grow-ing annoyance.

'That's what I'm talking about!' she snapped, hastily swallowing the mouthful of bread, and waving her hand at him crossly. 'Answering a question with another ques-tion. If you can't say anything to the purpose, go away.'

Raven chuckled softly, apparently not offended by her bluntness. 'You don't mince your words, do you?'

Honor ate some more sausage, glowering at him, trying not to acknowledge the small thrill of pleasure she got from sparring with him. She might be playing with fire—but at least the flames warmed her, driving away her mem-ories of the recent endless cold.

'What will you do now?' Raven asked, his expression sobering.

Honor wasn't ready to face that question. Instead of answering directly, she instinctively went on to the offensive.

'Me, me, me!' she exclaimed. 'Why is this whole conversation about *me*? I want to know what *your* part in this is. Why were you sitting beside my bed when I woke up, with a plate of food and a bottle of brandy at hand? Exactly what kind of bamboozling game are you trying to play with me?' she demanded recklessly.

Raven's expression darkened.

'In case you've forgotten, I saved your life,' he said icily, all humour wiped from his dark face.

'I *know*!' Honor leapt to her feet in agitation. The candle flame danced in response to her hasty action, sending long shadows plunging around the room. 'The question is, *why*? This is the third time you've come to my rescue. Why did you fish me out of the Heubra? Why did you give me these clothes? What do you want in return?'

She stood over him, her hands on her hips as she fiercely confronted him with his own actions.

Raven flushed, tilting his head back to look at her. 'Don't you know better than to look a gift horse in the mouth?' he growled furiously.

'Why? Have you got plaster teeth?' she threw at him.

'Try me.' He bared his teeth at her in a silent snarl.

Honor froze. She was pitched back to the moment on the road when she'd stared into the amber eyes of the wolf. Raven's eyes were blue, but the expression in them was as dangerous and unfathomable as the wolf's. Despite the fact that Raven was still sitting, while she stood over him, the feral, masculine power in his lean body threatened to overwhelm her. Tension crackled in the air between them.

She stepped back slowly, never taking her eyes from Raven's face. She had an irrational fear that, like the wolf, he might spring at her if she dropped her guard for an instant. But she knew she must never let him see she was afraid. She clenched her hands to hide the fact she was trembling.

'I...I am grateful for all you have done for us,' she said, unsteadily. 'I have no wish to insult you by questioning your motives. But I prefer to know exactly what I'm dealing with. I am sure you understand that...sir.'

The last word was not said in a disrespectful tone, but to emphasise the difference between them. Raven's generosity to Patrick was not unprecedented. His personal attentions to her were...unusual...to say the least—unless he had a very specific role in mind for her.

He scowled at her. Her throat was so dry she couldn't swallow. Her ribs ached with tension when she tried to draw a breath—but she didn't dare take her eyes off his face.

'I will arrange for your return to England,' he said abruptly.

'*What?*' Honor's jaw dropped in amazement. She was so surprised she forgot her nervousness. 'In what capacity?' she exclaimed, finally recovering her wits.

'Dammit, woman! I'm not trying to make you my mistress. I'm simply trying to ensure your safety,' he snarled at her impatiently. 'That *is* what your husband wanted, isn't it?'

'Patrick?' She was bewildered by his reference to her husband.

'"Take care of Honor", that's what he said to me on the road,' Raven reminded her savagely. 'I wonder if he knew just how difficult you'd make it?'

'You're here because you feel some sort of obligation to *Patrick*?'

Honor's legs were suddenly too weak to support her. She flopped down on the bed, staring at Raven in bewilderment. Somehow his attentions to her had seemed a lot more personal than that. Had she completely misread the situation?

'What else?' He glared at her. 'Let me tell you, Mrs O'Donnell, your opinion of my morals is insulting, to say the least. I do not customarily take advantage of grieving widows.'

The lash in his voice stung. It was an indirect criticism of her own conduct since waking.

'Would you have preferred me to collapse in tears at your feet?' Honor demanded, in a low, shaking voice. 'You are *not* the arbiter of my conduct. You did *not* need to watch me sleeping—like a vulture gaping for the feast. Your intentions could just as well have been conveyed to me by Joe later, when I was in a state to consider them. Not now, in the middle of the night, when I'm alone, tired and confused.'

Raven's hands clenched into fists. He was pale beneath his tan. His face might have been chiselled from granite as he stared at her in the flickering candlelight.

'I have seldom witnessed anyone less confused—or more calculating and suspicious in their response to dis-interested kindness,' he grated. 'No doubt O'Donnell is giving thanks for his merciful release.'

Honor's lips parted wordlessly. All colour drained from her face. She was stunned and bitterly hurt by his cruel accusation.

'Patrick,' she whispered. Tears blinded her.

'Honor? My God!' Raven was suddenly on his knee before her. 'That was unforgivable.' He seized her hands in his. He sounded as shaken as she felt, but she was al-most too distraught to notice.

'Go away,' she whispered. 'Please. Go away.'

'Honor.' His hands tightened over hers.

She turned her head away.

'I did not mean what I said.' His voice was strained and ragged. 'Forgive me. No man could have wished for more from his wife.'

She didn't reply. She couldn't trust herself to speak.

Raven stood up.

'We will discuss your return to England at a more suitable time,' he said grittily. 'Goodnight, Mrs O'Donnell.'

Honor sat like a statue for several minutes after he'd gone, fighting for self-control. At last she reached a shaking hand for the glass of brandy and swallowed it down. It seared her throat and she coughed, fresh tears stinging her eyes. But these tears had a physical cause and she was not afraid of them. She was afraid of the grief which threatened to consume her. She clutched the glass against her chest, realising suddenly that she had nothing left from the last few years—not even her wedding ring. She'd traded it for necessities when Patrick's pay had been late and their funds were low. She was penniless, possessionless, and alone. This bleak room in an alien country was certainly not the place to surrender her self-control. If she gave up now, she would betray Patrick, as well as herself.

Cole stood in the street, leaning against a wall as he struggled to discipline his raging emotions. He'd known Honor was a determined woman, but he'd never expected to be on the receiving end of her temper. Always before she'd treated him with the courtesy and deference his rank required. Now she treated him as an equal. It was a novel sensation for Cole. Very few people were prepared to challenge him head on.

He was furious with her suspicions. He'd only been concerned for her safety, yet she'd accused him of being some kind of foul scavenger, preying on her misfortune. He clenched his fists angrily.

Damn Honor. Damn his own soft-minded weakness where she was concerned. He hadn't considered how she would interpret his presence by her side when she woke, he'd only known he couldn't leave her alone when she was so vulnerable.

If he'd expected anything from her awakening in such circumstances it had been grief, confusion—or even gratitude that he'd considered her plight and would protect her. But she'd gone from sleep to wakefulness with a campaign-hardened efficiency that would have done any soldier proud. That was not how Cole wanted to perceive her. He ran a hand through his dishevelled hair. If he had any sense, he'd leave her to fend for herself. She was clearly more than capable of holding her own against anyone.

Within a day of Patrick's death, Honor received marriage proposals from four of the men in his company. It was usual for widows to remarry quickly. Without a man, and with no easy means of getting home again, a woman was very vulnerable. Sometimes a woman could be married and widowed more than once within a few months. Honor turned all the proposals down, careful not to offend any of the men.

She also received considerably less respectable proposals from a couple of officers. She turned them down as well. She had no desire to become any man's mistress. She knew Raven's offer to send her safely back to England was intended to save her from such indignities, but she wasn't ready to leave Spain—and when she did leave, she would make her own arrangements. In the meantime, with Maggie Foster's help, she found employment as the maid of the Spanish mistress of an officer in the 43rd Foot.

The Light Division was to spend the winter in various villages around Ciudad Rodrigo. Honor was relieved to discover that her new employer, Captain Arthur Williams, was quartered in a different village from Major Raven. The empty cottage assigned to Captain Williams and Dolores, his mistress, consisted of two mud-floored rooms. The outer chamber was intended for the use of both pigs and people, while the inner was divided into sleeping chambers around a central sitting room. The bedrooms were dark or light depending on whether the small windows were shuttered or left open. The fire was in the middle of the floor, the smoke was supposed to escape through a hole in the roof.

Honor threw herself into the task of making the place habitable for herself and her new employers. Within a short space of time she'd had a hole knocked in a wall and an outside chimney built, cleaned the rooms, and even found crockery and wall-hangings to make the place more comfortable.

She welcomed the hard work. Sooner or later she would have to think about the future, but for now she preferred simply to live from day to day.

'A woman of many parts,' said Captain Williams appreciatively, a week after she'd started working for him. 'With a gift for making a hovel into a gracious home.'

'Thank you, sir,' said Honor.

'Most remarkable,' he said. 'I saw you perform as Rosalind at Drury Lane a few years ago. Captivating performance. Tried to offer my compliments later—but couldn't get near you for all your other admirers. Now, here you are cooking my dinner in Spain. Quite a turn-up, hey?'

'Yes, sir,' said Honor calmly, her heart sinking as she heard the satisfaction in his voice.

'Well, well,' said Williams jovially. 'They must have been heady days. I don't suppose you ever thought you'd end up here, did you?'

'I don't think any of us can predict with certainty where we will be in a few years' time,' Honor replied. 'Even during peacetime.'

'Why did you marry O'Donnell?' Williams burst out. 'You could have had every luxury. Pampered, privileged... Selhurst would have given you anything you asked for! Instead you threw yourself away on—'

'Unfortunately the Duke of Selhurst didn't have anything I wanted,' Honor interrupted crisply. 'I'm glad you find my work here satisfactory, Captain. But I must inform you, I'm not willing to discuss my personal life. If that is not acceptable to you, then let us terminate this arrangement forthwith.'

'B-but what will you do if...?' Captain Williams's startled response faded into silence in the face of Honor's unwavering gaze.

Her heart hammered in her chest, but she didn't reveal her agitation by the merest flicker of an eyelid. She was angry at the Captain's disparaging reference to Patrick, and she wasn't willing to discuss her personal history with anyone. On the other hand, she needed both the money and the relative security that this job gave her. She didn't want to alienate her employer unnecessarily.

'Come, sir,' she said, offering Williams a friendly smile. 'Surely we can agree that the past is done with, and hardly worth the effort of discussing?'

Williams frowned at her attempt at conciliation. Honor held her breath and tried to project an aura which was both respectful and respectable.

'Dolores likes the way you do her hair,' said the Captain at last.

'She has beautiful hair,' said Honor, grateful the Spanish girl wasn't present. She thought Williams might have been less willing to tolerate the minor challenge to his authority if his mistress had witnessed it.

'Very well.' Williams came to a decision. 'You may continue as Dolores's maid. But if I detect the slightest impertinence in your behaviour you will be dismissed immediately.'

'Yes, sir. Thank you,' said Honor, bowing her head slightly to show her acceptance of his terms. 'I must fetch some water.' She wrapped her black shawl around her head and shoulders and hurried out of the cottage before he could say anything further.

Once outside she picked her way carefully over the uneven, rocky road. The wet, slippery stones beneath her feet were uncomfortable to walk on, and for a few minutes she focussed all her attention on taking each step.

At last she took a deep breath and tried to relax the tension in her muscles. Everywhere she turned she seemed to face obstacles. She wasn't comfortable with Captain Williams. She didn't like his casual dismissal of Patrick, and she didn't care for the way he seemed to derive pleasure from the reversal in her fortunes. Had he employed her simply so he could boast about how the one-time darling of Drury Lane had been reduced to working as his mistress's maid?

She'd wanted a few months' peace while she considered her future. She still hoped that might be possible, but she would have to be careful of the Captain. She didn't want any more trouble.

She looked up and saw Cole Raven riding through the village towards her. His unexpected arrival startled her.

Her heart thudded with apprehension. She hadn't seen or spoken to him since the night she'd woken to find him sitting beside her bed. Her first impulse was to run and hide. She even glanced about, looking for an escape route—then she realised such an attempt would be futile.

Instead she braced her shoulders against the wind and stood still, waiting. It was possible he wasn't coming to see her—more than possible. It was highly likely he had other business in the village. Strangely, she didn't find that idea as consoling as she should have done.

She watched as he came nearer. He was riding Corvinus. The big black tossed his head proudly and she heard the jingle of the bridle carried to her on the cold wind. Despite herself, she had to admit that man and horse made an impressive sight. Corvinus was sure-footed on the rocky ground: powerful muscles moved easily beneath his shining black hide. Raven was completely at home in the Hussar saddle he still favoured. A consummate horseman. He and the stallion were so closely attuned to each other they almost seemed to be two parts of a single entity.

Raven looked straight at Honor and inclined his head in a brief acknowledgement. He continued to look at her as he rode straight towards her. Even over a distance of several yards she was aware of the intensity of his scrutiny.

She clutched her shawl tighter, hating how easily Raven could reduce her to nervous uncertainty. She'd wondered if Raven would seek her out again. She wasn't sure if she'd hoped for or feared their next encounter, but with her heart beating up into her mouth she would be lucky if she could talk at all when he greeted her.

At last Corvinus closed the distance between them. Honor tipped her head back to look at the man high above her. Last time they'd been in a similar situation—when Raven had fished her out of the Heubra—he had bent over her, reducing the difference in their heights. Now he towered more than four feet above her head. For a few long moments they stared at each other, the tension thick between them—then Corvinus nudged Honor's shoulder impatiently.

She gasped and immediately turned her attention to the horse, grateful for the distraction. She petted him, murmuring soft words of praise as he tossed his head, his black mane flying.

'You speak as old friends,' said Raven. His voice sounded gravelly. 'I noticed it before.' He dropped lightly to the ground and stood beside Corvinus's shoulder.

'Ah, yes.' Honor looked up at him warily, unable to read anything from his tone or his expression. 'Patrick was Joe's friend. And we both—Patrick and I—we both love good horses.'

'I see,' said Raven. He removed his shako and tucked it under his arm. Honor noticed how the black feather plume brushed against his sleeve. All her senses were fully alert, trying to interpret Raven's intentions towards her. She'd never been so close to him when they were both standing. He was taller even than she had imagined. The scarlet of his uniform jacket contrasted dramatically with his sun-browned, angular good looks. His silver epaulettes drew attention to the breadth and power of his shoulders.

At five foot six inches, Honor was used to looking most of the men in Patrick's old regiment in the eye. Raven was over six feet tall. She felt dwarfed in his presence—almost intimidated by his size and the controlled masculine energy which radiated from his person. Apparently the cold wind didn't bother him as much as it bothered her.

She took a deep breath, determined not to let herself be overawed by the formidable major.

'Joe always puts the interests of the horses first,' she

said, belatedly afraid she might have caused trouble for the servant.

'Not always,' Raven replied coolly.

'He does!' Honor fired up immediately on behalf of the absent Joe. 'I assure you—' She broke off as Raven raised a hand to silence her, a slight, enigmatic smile on his lips.

'I have no quarrel with his priorities,' he said calmly, taking the wind out of Honor's sails. 'Is there somewhere we can talk?'

'I really don't—'

'I fully intend to talk to you—in the wind or out of it,' Raven interrupted her again without apology. 'But I'm sure Corvinus would appreciate a more sheltered location.'

Honor pressed her lips together, annoyed at the way Raven had manipulated her.

'This way,' she said shortly. 'There are two empty barns further up. Captain Williams keeps his horses in one of them. I'm sure Corvinus will be comfortable in the other.'

'Good. Lead on.'

Honor disliked the peremptory note in Raven's voice. It clearly hadn't occurred to him that she might not obey his command. She told herself that the only reason she was doing so was from simple courtesy—she still owed him a debt of gratitude for his help with Patrick—but she was also uncomfortably aware she preferred to avoid arousing his displeasure.

She'd woken in the night from disturbed dreams about Patrick, Raven and the wolf she'd shot, only to realise that she really was listening to the eerie, terrifying howls of a wolf pack as it circled the village. For a few seconds, images of Raven had been indistinguishable from the savage eyes of the wolf. She had no doubt that, in some ways, the man was more dangerous than the wild beast.

But she'd had other dreams associated with Raven that

made less sense to her—of warmth, comfort and peaceful rest. Could a dangerous predator also be a protector?

She listened as Corvinus's hooves struck the hard ground behind her. Raven walked without making a sound. How could such a large man move so silently? She turned abruptly to check he was still following her. He was less than two feet behind her.

He raised his eyebrows in a wordless query.

'Here we are,' she exclaimed, hating the breathless quality of her voice. Hating the way Raven seemed to tower over her.

'Good.'

The stone-walled barn had been damaged in one of the many skirmishes that had taken place in the area. There was a hole in the roof and in one of the walls. Rubble lay in one corner of the floor, but the building still offered reasonable shelter from the cold wind.

Raven efficiently tended to Corvinus, then turned his attention to Honor.

She wrapped her black shawl firmly around her head and shoulders, her hands tucked safely inside. She didn't want to risk the possibility that he might see them tremble and think he had gained an advantage over her.

'I've come to arrange your return to England,' he said bluntly.

'Thank you,' she said tautly. 'I appreciate your concern—but I will make my own arrangements, Major.'

'Don't be ridiculous,' Raven said curtly. 'If you had the means to arrange your return home, you wouldn't be skivvying for Williams and his doxy. Pay attention. I will shortly be making a brief visit to Lisbon. You will accompany me. In Lisbon I will select someone suitable to travel with you on the packet boat to Falmouth and thence to London. I'm assuming you wish to return to London?' He cocked a questioning eyebrow at her. 'All I require from you at this moment is the name and direction of the individual in England into whose care I will be delivering you.'

'Why? So you can check their references?' Honor demanded, too stunned by his announcement to consider her words—or even to feel indignation at his high-handedness.

Raven flushed. 'This is not a subject for levity,' he growled. 'The name and direction, if you please.'

Honor walked around him to stand beside Corvinus. She patted the stallion's shoulder affectionately. He swung his head round to mumble his lips at her shawl. He snorted disapprovingly and, despite herself, Honor laughed. She pushed the shawl back to reveal her sun-bleached hair and moved to stand at Corvinus's head. She knew that stallions could be dangerous and unpredictable creatures—but Corvinus had always been exceptionally good-mannered with her.

She always enjoyed her encounters with the fine black horse, but on this occasion she was simply giving herself a little time to think. Raven's plans for her, not to mention the autocratic way in which he'd conveyed them to her, dumbfounded her.

'Aren't you handsome?' she murmured, threading Corvinus's forelock gently between her fingers, then gently drawing her hand along his silky black ear.

Corvinus nodded and nudged his head against her chest, pushing her back a couple of steps.

'Be careful!' In a couple of strides Raven was beside her, seizing the bridle in his strong hand. 'He's not a child's pony.' With his other hand on Honor's shoulder, he moved her firmly away from the stallion.

Corvinus snorted in annoyance and pulled against his master's controlling hand on the bridle.

'I know he's not a pony,' Honor said in exasperation. 'He's a great big dangerous beast who could stomp me into the ground if he wanted to—but he's not going to. He's always been a complete gentleman whenever we've met.'

She sensed the swift glance Raven threw in her direction, but she kept her attention on Corvinus. She could still feel Raven's touch on her shoulder, even though he'd released her immediately. She had no doubt that he'd moved to protect her—just as it seemed he wanted to send her back to England for her own safety.

She had very mixed feelings about that. She didn't want Raven interfering in her life—but it was a long time since anyone had tried to take care of her so competently.

'Mrs O'Donnell, kindly tell me the names of your friends in England,' Raven said impatiently.

'I really don't see why you need that information,' Honor demurred, looking sideways at Raven. 'Even supposing I might be willing to accept your help getting back to Falmouth, I certainly don't need anyone else's help to take the stagecoach back to London.'

'Your husband asked me to take care of you,' he replied grittily. 'To my mind that includes making sure you do *have* somewhere to go once you arrive back in England.'

'Somewhere suitable, you mean?' Honor couldn't help teasing him, despite his glowering expression. 'You *do* want to check the references of my friends. If they aren't up to your exacting standards, what will you do?'

'Dammit, woman! I don't have time for this!' Raven threw up a hand, jerking it impatiently through his dishevelled hair. 'The name, if you please!'

For some reason his frustrated gesture both amused and reassured Honor. She thought perhaps Raven wasn't quite as sure of himself, or the situation, as he wanted her to believe.

'What if I don't have anyone to return to in England?' she asked curiously.

'I know you have,' he replied curtly. 'You send and receive letters regularly.'

'Have you been spying on my correspondence?' Honor demanded, disturbed that he should know so much about her.

'Of course not! But not many of the men—let alone their women—have regular communication with England,' he pointed out.

'I see. So now you want the name of my correspondent. Since you obviously believe that I *do* have somewhere to go once I reach England, why are you so determined to find out where? Surely you don't think you have a right to know my personal business—simply because Patrick asked you to take care of me?' Honor challenged him.

Even in the dim light of the barn she saw Raven flush.

'I have no wish to intrude in your personal affairs,' he denied grittily. 'I will be more than happy when I can transfer responsibility for your care to someone—'

'Responsibility for my care!' Honor interrupted hotly. Her initial shock and mild amusement at Raven's overbearing attitude had now given way to annoyance. 'I've been responsible for my own care since I was seventeen years old. I do not need or want your help, Major. I will make my own arrangements when I am ready.'

'You are impertinent and ill disciplined,' Raven said icily. 'I will inform you when it's time to leave.'

'The only way I'll leave here with you is against my will!' Honor declared fiercely. 'Abduction, sir! What will that do for your reputation—if it becomes known you forced a dead soldier's wife to go with you against her will? Bathsheba to King David…'

Raven reared away from her as if she'd struck him; his expression dark with anger. His hands, held rigidly at his sides, were clenched in fury at her insult. Every muscle in his powerful body was taut with barely contained rage. Honor's breath stuck in her throat as the terrifying currents of Raven's wrath swirled around them. Corvinus danced backwards, edgily responding to the highly charged emotional atmosphere in the barn.

'For God's sake!' she gasped, stunned by the violence of Raven's reaction to her biblical allusion.

Bathsheba had been the wife of one of the officers in King David's army. The King had made Bathsheba pregnant, then given the orders which had led to the death of her husband in battle. After that the King had taken Bathsheba into his harem.

Honor didn't think the story of Bathsheba and King David bore any resemblance to her relationship with Raven. She'd only mentioned it because, in her exasperation with Raven's dictatorial manner, she hadn't been able to think of a more appropriate retort. But it seemed as if Raven had taken her words as a mortal insult.

'Surely…?' Her voice faded away as she stared at him, trying to decipher the cause of his fury.

His blue eyes seared her with the ferocity of his emotions. She thought she saw hatred and disgust as well as anger in their stormy depths.

She started to tremble uncontrollably, appalled at the hostility she had unwittingly aroused.

'You think I'm the kind of man who could order another man to his certain death—just so I could take his woman?' Raven demanded, his voice low and throbbing with outrage.

'*No!*' Honor stared at him, struggling to regain her own composure. 'No, of course not.'

'You as good as said so when you first woke after O'Donnell died,' Raven said, with harsh contempt. 'Now you've repeated the accusation. You overrate yourself. The sooner you're safely away from here, the better. You'll be informed when it's time to leave for Lisbon.'

He lead Corvinus out of the barn into the cold dusk and mounted in one easy movement. He didn't look back at Honor as he rode away through of the village, his back ramrod straight.

'Oh my God,' Honor murmured, shaken to her core. She staggered back and leant against the rough stone wall of the barn. Her trembling legs were too weak to support her unaided.

Raven had indeed taken her hasty words as a mortal insult, though she'd never intended them as such. She remembered the fleeting impression she'd received of disgust—even hatred—in his eyes, and shuddered. Did he really have such a low opinion of her?

She found the idea deeply distressing—so hurtful that a physical pain clutched at her midriff. She bent forward, wrapping her arms protectively around her body as she waited for the first intensity of her distress to subside. At last she straightened up and resolutely squared her shoulders. She had no intention of letting Raven dictate her actions—but nor could she allow him to believe she thought so badly of him. She took a deep breath, trying to calm her apprehension at the thought of facing Raven again.

Chapter Three

'Mrs O'Donnell wishes to see you,' Joe Newton said expressionlessly.

Cole looked up, startled by his manservant's announcement. It was two days since his confrontation with Honor in the barn and he still couldn't think calmly of the incident. She'd accused him of lusting after her, of manipulating events—perhaps even hastening Patrick's death—so that he could have her. Her reference to Bathsheba and King David had been far too apposite. The Old Testament story of the King's sinful action had never been far from Cole's mind over the past few weeks. So Honor's accusation had cut like a whiplash across his already tormented conscience, laying bare his guilt and precipitating his wild fury.

'She's here?' he said sharply.

In future he intended to discuss nothing with Honor except for the essential, practical details of her journey home. Under no circumstances did he want another, gut-wrenching, emotionally devastating argument with her.

He was just about to send her away when it occurred to him that perhaps Honor wanted to see him for the same reason. She'd obviously realised the wisdom of leaving

Spain and wanted to talk about the arrangements. Bolstered by that possibility, Cole stood to greet his uninvited guest.

'Show her in,' he said brusquely.

'Major Raven.' Honor stopped just inside the door, briefly meeting his eyes before glancing nervously around at the sparsely furnished room.

As always when he saw her, Cole's heart leapt with a combination of fierce, conflicting emotions. She was always beautiful to him, whatever she was wearing, but it pleased him that she was dressed in the warm new clothes he'd given her.

He instinctively checked her countenance for signs of fatigue or illness. She was still too thin, and far too fragile for the brutal life she'd been forced to lead—but she no longer looked as if she was on the brink of exhaustion.

Her slender fingers clutched her shawl tightly. He saw that her expression was both wary and resolute. He'd always admired her courage, but he was filled with self-disgust when he realised that today she was afraid of him. No doubt she saw him as some kind of ogre who lusted after another man's wife without a thought for the feelings of others.

'Mrs O'Donnell.' He stopped, uncertain what to say next. He cleared his throat and started again. 'I have not yet made all the arrangements for the journey to Lisbon—'

'No, no,' she interrupted him quickly, 'that's not why I came.'

'You wish to tell me the name of your friend in England?' he asked hopefully, though he tried to keep his voice businesslike.

'No. I didn't come to talk about my return home at all,' she said firmly.

'We have nothing else to discuss,' Cole said roughly,

his stomach clenching at the prospect of a more personal conversation.

'Perhaps not to discuss,' Honor agreed, looking at him warily. 'I mean, I came to tell you something...'

'I have no interest in your self-willed opinions,' Raven said, his harshness prompted simply by his need for self-preservation. 'I promised your husband I would take care of you. I fully intend to do so—with or without your co-operation.'

He saw Honor take a deep breath and press her lips together before she replied. He realised he'd angered her—as he so often seemed to—though that hadn't been his intention. All he wanted was to bring this interview to an end as quickly as possible.

'I came to apologise,' Honor said grittily.

Cole stared at her in silence.

'I should not have accused you of such a dishonourable thing—even in jest,' she said tightly.

'You were not jesting.' He wasn't mollified by her attempted apology. He found even the most oblique reference to his feelings for her extremely painful.

'No, but I spoke in haste.' She clutched her shawl tightly as she watched him across the width of the room. 'I was angry...' He saw her take another deep, unsteady breath. 'You can be very free with your orders, Major.'

Cole gritted his teeth together as he stared at her through narrowed eyes.

'I'm very conscious of your kindness to Patrick before he died,' Honor continued. 'And your kindness to me—'

'I don't want your gratitude,' Cole growled.

She blinked at him in confusion and he wished he could recall his hasty words. He could almost see the question forming in her mind—if he didn't want her gratitude, what did he want?

'Patrick O'Donnell was a good man. It is not a hardship to carry out his dying wish,' Raven said quickly. That much was true, and he could say it with a clear conscience.

'Or it wouldn't be if I weren't so damned contrary,' Honor replied wryly.

Her smile took Cole by surprise. It transformed her face, hinting at the sense of humour he'd almost forgotten she possessed. He'd first been drawn to her, even from a distance, by her laughter and the good humour with which she faced the discomforts of army life.

His own mood lifted in spite of himself. He liked seeing Honor smile. He wanted her to be happy.

'If you know that, why are you so determined not to co-operate?' he asked, his tone warmer than before. 'There would be no need for any of this if you would simply—'

'Do as I'm bid?' Honor finished for him. 'I am not biddable, Major.'

Cole couldn't help uttering a wordless, but emphatic, grunt of agreement with her statement.

She raised her eyebrows slightly in response, then smiled and pushed her shawl back from her pale hair.

'I respect your determination to keep your word to Patrick,' she said, 'but I really think you should also take my preferences into account.'

'You prefer to work your fingers to the bone for Williams and his—'

'She's a very nice, kind girl,' said Honor quickly, before Raven could make a disparaging reference to Captain Williams's mistress. 'Dolores. Her family were killed by the French. She really doesn't have many options available to her—and Captain Williams is kind to her.'

'I see,' said Cole. He ran a hand through his hair, wondering how the devil he was going to deal with Honor. Even when she wasn't flatly contradicting him she was as difficult to get to grips with as a greased eel. 'Nevertheless, however considerate your employers, your life here is hardly a sinecure,' he pointed out.

'Life is never a sinecure in my experience,' Honor retorted. 'May I sit down—or would that be an affront to your views on military discipline?'

'I'm surprised no one has strangled you yet!' Cole exclaimed, thoroughly exasperated, as he gestured towards a chair.

'No doubt they've considered it,' she said, seating herself with annoying composure.

'May I offer you some refreshment?' Cole offered, doing his best to impersonate a genial host, since that was the role she'd apparently chosen for him.

'No, thank you.' Honor folded her hands primly in her lap. 'I simply wanted to clear up a few points of confusion between us.'

'I am not confused,' Cole stated baldly.

'Then the confusion must be all mine,' she replied equably. 'I'm sure you'll be generous enough to clarify things for me.'

'Are you, indeed?' Cole said drily.

'Oh, yes,' said Honor. 'You're a very generous, honourable man, Major. There is no doubt about that.'

Cole's sharp riposte died on his lips as he saw the sincerity in her hazel eyes as she looked at him. He glanced away, shaken by the possibility that maybe she did believe him to be an honourable man. If so, her judgement was sadly lacking. An honourable man didn't desire another man's wife.

'We were discussing your confusion,' he said rustily.

'We were discussing your determination to eject me from Spain before I'm ready to leave,' she corrected him.

Cole's familiar temper rose at her persistent stubbornness—but then it occurred to him to wonder why she was so resistant to leaving.

'Why don't you want to leave?' he asked.

Honor hesitated, her eyes narrowing as she gazed into space, and he realised she was choosing her words carefully.

'I'm not ready to go,' she said at last.

'That's hardly an answer,' he said impatiently. 'Why not?'

'Patrick has not yet been dead two weeks,' she said. 'I haven't become accustomed to…to…'

'You can become accustomed just as easily in England as you can here,' said Cole roughly.

Honor lifted her eyes to meet his. 'Why are you so eager to get rid of me?' she asked curiously.

'I'm not!' he replied angrily, guilt sharpening his response. Despite his determination to send her away, he didn't want her to leave.

'Perhaps we can find a compromise,' she said after a few moments. 'When I'm ready to leave, I will allow you to help me with the arrangements.'

Cole raised his eyebrows at her terminology. 'You will *allow* me to help you?' he repeated sardonically.

'I am not one of your men,' she reminded him.

He resisted the urge to tell her how he would have dealt with her if she had been.

'And when do you suppose you'll be ready to leave?' he asked drily.

'I don't know,' she replied. 'I will tell you when I am.' She stood up and he did likewise.

'You haven't told me the name of your friend in England,' he reminded her.

'No, I haven't,' she agreed. She looked up into his eyes and surprised him by smiling. 'Were you planning to write to them in the hope they might use their powers of persuasion on me?' she asked.

He gritted his teeth, unwilling to admit that what he'd really been seeking was the assurance she did have somewhere safe to return to in England.

'Will you go back to the stage?' he asked instead.

He didn't like the idea of her putting herself on public display once more. He'd never enjoyed the theatre himself, but he'd heard enough comments by his fellow officers to know how they viewed actresses. Even Honor's status as a devoted wife had not saved her from being the subject of several lewd remarks during her time in the Peninsula.

'You don't approve of actresses, Major?' Honor asked him.

'I don't approve of the life they must live,' he said stiffly.

'Ah.' She went very still, studying his expression intently. 'I see. No wonder you are so impatient to fulfil Patrick's wishes. Your approval of him does not extend to me.'

Cole's ribs expanded as he dragged in a deep breath of air. 'I don't disapprove of you,' he said grittily.

Honor continued to hold his gaze for several more seconds and he forced himself not to look away. There was nothing else for him to say. He could hardly tell her how much he admired her courage, or how much he desired to hold her slight body in his arms.

'You may have some time to…accustom…yourself to your change of circumstances,' he said hoarsely. 'Then I'll arrange your journey.'

'I had no idea you had such a passion for administrative tasks,' Honor remarked, walking to the door. 'I always imagined you were more at home leading patrols deep into enemy territory.'

'I am now in the infantry,' Cole reminded her.

'I know.' She smiled slightly. 'But don't you miss the freedom your previous duties allowed you? Joe told us so much about your exploits in the dragoons.'

'Joe wasn't with me then,' Raven said brusquely. 'He only joined me shortly after I transferred to the 52nd.'

'You mean the stories aren't true?'

Cole was startled to realise that Honor was gently teasing him. 'Since I have no idea what Newton told you, I'm not in a position to say,' he replied gruffly.

Honor smiled. 'Goodbye, Major.' She held out her hand to him. 'I am grateful—'

'I'll have Newton escort you back to your billet,' he interrupted her. 'Goodbye, Mrs O'Donnell.'

A few minutes later he closed the door on her and wondered why the devil he'd let her talk him into allowing her to remain in Spain. The only honest answer he could come up with was that, in his heart, he didn't want her to leave.

He walked over to his writing case and took out the most recent letter from his fiancée, Miss Bridget Morton. They had been betrothed for four years. If not for the fact that Bridget's mother had died shortly after their betrothal, they would have been married for over three years.

Cole had left for Spain before Bridget's period of mourning had ended, and had not returned to England during the intervening years. As soon as he did so, he and Bridget would be married. He read Bridget's letter and tried to conjure an image of her in his mind—but the only face he could see was Honor's.

He set the letter aside with a raw curse and hit the table with his clenched fist, filled with anger, frustration and guilt at his unruly desires.

'Now, why won't you let the Major send you home?' Joe asked, as he escorted Honor back to her billet.

'I'm not ready to leave yet,' Honor replied, wondering how many times she would parrot the same answer to that question.

'Why not?' Joe asked reasonably. 'There's nothing to stay for—is there?' He shot her a sideways look.

Honor sighed. 'It's not so much what there is to stay for,' she said reluctantly.

'And what do you mean by that?' Joe challenged her, when she didn't continue. 'Are you saying there's someone in England you're trying to avoid? The Duke of Selhurst, perhaps?'

'Oh, no!' Honor exclaimed, before she could stop herself. She hadn't given the Duke a thought but, if she'd been more alert, he would have made a good excuse for her foot-dragging, at least as far as Joe was concerned.

'Then who?' Joe persisted. 'Surely your mother would welcome you home again?'

'My mother disowned me when I married Patrick,' said Honor, unable to hide her bitterness. 'I don't think she'll be waiting with open arms.'

'Ahh.' Joe nodded wisely. 'But people change. Perhaps she's thought better of her action since then.'

'Oh, I dare say she'd take me in,' Honor agreed wearily. 'She told me I'd beggar myself if I stayed with Patrick. If I go home now—if Major Raven delivers me to her like a piece of lost property, as he seems to intend—she'll think she was right. I couldn't bear to hear her tell me so.'

'Hmm.' Joe pursed his lips together. 'Not so good. I see your point. But she's not the only person you know in London. Isn't Lady Durrington still writing to you?'

'Yes, she is. But I'm not turning up on her doorstep like a stray mongrel either. Whatever would she think?'

Although Honor enjoyed corresponding with Lady Durrington, she'd never quite understood why the older woman had sought her friendship. Her ladyship had approached Honor quite soon after she'd become the latest rage of Drury Lane. Honor had been surprised. At first she'd been polite but wary, but it hadn't taken her long to decide that Lady Durrington was sincere.

Honor liked the older woman immensely, but it had always been a purely private friendship. Honor had never met Lord Durrington, though she'd heard a lot about him, and she'd never been introduced into the Durringtons' social circle. She had wondered whether her marriage to Patrick would change things, but Lady Durrington's friendship had remained steadfast. She'd even offered her husband's influence to extricate Patrick from the army, but both Patrick and Honor had been too proud to accept such help.

'If she's a true friend, she would be pleased you thought of her in your hour of need,' said Joe robustly.

'I'm not in need!' Honor protested immediately, hating to be cast in such a pitiful role.

'Ah well, then, if you're too proud to go back to London with your tail between your legs—you'll just have to stop here, and battle it out with the Major,' said Joe phlegmatically.

'I don't wish to battle with anyone,' Honor said, frustrated. 'Least of all Major Raven. I never met anyone so high-handed—'

'Didn't you?' Joe interrupted, sounding startled.

'What? Oh, you mean Mother?' Honor couldn't help grimacing. 'Patrick must have told you about her. I hadn't noticed any similarities between them before. Actually...' She frowned, considering the situation. 'Perhaps you're right. My experience with Mother does make me resistant to being told what to do. But Major Raven has no business giving me orders. I'm not his daughter—nor one of his men.'

'I think he knows that,' Joe remarked, suppressing a small smile.

'I beg your pardon?' Honor was still preoccupied with Joe's earlier comment and didn't notice his expression.

'Nothing important. Here we are.' They'd reached Honor's billet. 'I'll visit you in a day or so,' Joe told her.

'Thank you.' Honor impulsively hugged him. 'You're a good friend.'

'That's all you know,' said Joe gruffly, briefly and awkwardly returning her embrace. 'You're a good needlewoman. Who else will I get to do the Major's mending once you've left?'

Honor laughed. 'I might have known you'd have a mercenary motive,' she teased him.

'You can be sure of that.' He took his leave of her.

Honor watched him go, but her thoughts were with Raven. She'd been sick with anxiety before her meeting with him—so nervous that she hadn't been able to sleep the previous night. But the encounter had been less distressing than she'd feared.

Raven *had* been brusque and autocratic, but he'd tacitly accepted her apology, and he hadn't ridden roughshod over her wishes as she'd anticipated. She'd even seen a brief lightening in his mood, though he hadn't let her thank him for his kindness towards her.

He was, she thought, a very difficult man. He was so unpredictable in his responses that every time she opened her mouth she was afraid she might inadvertently provoke his temper. Talking to him wasn't a relaxing experience— but it was certainly invigorating.

It was a cold, foggy evening and she hugged herself in her shawl. She had an elusive memory of being held in warm and comforting arms, but the comfort wasn't at home in England, it was here in Spain—and it had something to do with Cole Raven.

Honor shook her head, wishing she didn't have such a fanciful imagination. There was nothing about the fierce, hard-muscled Major that was the least bit soft or comforting.

She sighed. She knew she'd have to leave Spain soon, and when she did she'd have to face her mother. But the memory of her mother's rejection still chilled Honor's heart. She needed more time before she would be brave enough to confront Annie Howarth.

Cole Raven came to see Captain Williams the next day. When Honor first saw his broad shoulders in the doorway her immediate thought was that he had come to see her— but beyond offering her a brief greeting, he devoted all his attention to the Captain.

Honor felt relieved, disappointed and curious in varying amounts. As far as she knew, the two men had not formerly been friends, but Raven made himself at home in the Captain's billet as the two talked endlessly about various masculine pursuits.

She served them with a hearty stew made from local pork, and wondered in bewilderment how anyone could have such an inexhaustible interest in fox-hunting, hare-coursing or shooting woodcock. Dolores obviously shared Honor's feelings, because shortly after she'd finished eating she murmured something about being tired, and disappeared into her room.

Honor dealt with her domestic duties as inconspicuously as possible. When she was finished she lingered, trying to appear busy without drawing attention to herself. She knew she ought to leave the two men alone, but she liked listening to Raven talk, even when she had no interest in what he was talking about.

She glanced up, and realised his intense blue eyes were watching her. She knew instantly that he'd seen through her little charade. She flushed with embarrassment and caught up her shawl. She hurried out of the cottage with a muttered comment about firewood before either Raven or Captain Williams could say anything.

Once outside, she tried to regain her composure. Almost inevitably she was drawn to the barn where Raven had left Corvinus. It was a long time since she'd had the opportunity to see the horse without his master also being present. Corvinus was pleased to see her and she made a fuss of him, comforted by his undemanding company.

She'd been controlling her emotions from the moment she'd woken after Patrick's death. For the first couple of days it had taken an effort of will not to succumb to her grief. After that she'd been too emotionally numb even to want to cry. Then she'd been distracted by her argument with Raven.

But now she was alone with Corvinus. He was warm and solidly comforting. She leant against his shoulder, her face pressed against his glossy black hide, and finally allowed her guard to drop. Hot tears scalded her eyes and burned her cold cheeks. She clung tighter to Corvinus as she cried out her pain, loneliness and uncertainty.

Raven had visited Captain Williams because he wanted to ensure the man treated Honor with appropriate respect. He allowed the conversation about hunting to continue for a few more minutes, then he came straight to the point.

'Mrs O'Donnell's husband was a good soldier,' he said abruptly. 'When he was dying he asked to me take care of his wife.'

'How did he expect you to do that?' Williams enquired, raising his eyebrows in mild amusement.

'I am arranging for her safe journey home,' Raven said curtly.

'And deprive Dolores of her maid!' Williams exclaimed. There was an edge to his humorous tone. Raven was aware that the other man didn't like the interference in his domestic arrangements.

'Mrs O'Donnell was devoted to her husband. She is still strongly attached to his memory,' said Raven evenly. 'At the moment she is reluctant to leave the place where he died. I am sure she will continue to perform her duties while she comes to terms with her loss.'

'She'd come to terms with it soon enough if she had a better offer,' said Williams cynically. 'Not much left for her in England now, I don't suppose. But if—' he broke off as he met Raven's cold gaze.

'Mrs O'Donnell is under my protection,' said Raven, his voice soft but deadly. 'If she wished it, I would arrange for her return to England immediately. Currently she prefers to support herself, rather than accept any form of charity. While she is working for you, I will hold you responsible for her safety.'

'If you want the woman, take her!' Williams exclaimed, flushing angrily. 'She's nothing to me.'

'Good,' said Raven. 'I trust Mrs O'Donnell will remain secure while she works for you.' He stood up, ready to leave. He'd made his point. He had no desire to antagonise the Captain unnecessarily. 'Thanks for your hospitality. I hope you enjoy some good runs after the hounds this winter.'

'I'm sure I will,' the Captain replied. His anger had been replaced by a speculative expression as he watched Cole's face. 'It will be interesting to see which of us enjoys the better sport.'

Cole didn't bother to reply. He inclined his head in a brief gesture of farewell and left the cottage. He'd known all along that his warning was likely to arouse Williams's curiosity—but he didn't give a damn what the other man thought of him. As long as the Captain allowed Honor to do her job in peace until she returned to England, Cole would be satisfied.

It was late in the day, and dusk was falling. Cole paused briefly, wondering where Honor had gone. Despite himself, he wanted to see her before he left the village. Then he smiled, guessing where he was likely to find her.

She was indeed with Corvinus, but he was amazed by the sight that confronted him.

Honor was leaning against the stallion, one hand on his withers, her other arm curving beneath his proud neck. Her face was buried in the black's shoulder—and when Cole heard her pain-racked sobs he realised she was crying.

He froze in surprise, both at the intensity of her emotion and the stallion's patient response to it. For the most part, Corvinus was a good-tempered beast, but neither Cole nor Joe Newton took liberties with him. Yet here was Honor treating the stallion like an old, familiar friend.

He'd seen this connection she had with the horse before but, although it still surprised him, he was too concerned about her to give it much thought.

Honor's distress was very real, and it disintegrated the last of his anger with her. He'd always admired her fortitude, but he had thought her unwomanly when she'd restrained her grief so ruthlessly immediately after Patrick's death. Now he wondered how he'd ever thought he had a right to judge her behaviour.

He hated to see her in such distress but, strangely, her

obvious grief helped ease his own crushing sense of guilt. The fact that Honor had not cried in his presence, nor turned to him for help when she clearly needed comfort, somehow reassured him that his unruly desires had not sullied the purity of her devotion to Patrick.

Cole was able to console himself with the thought that she really did regard him only as one of her husband's more overbearing, interfering officers. That was not how he wanted her to respond to him in his undisciplined dreams—but it was certainly what he hoped for in his rational mind.

He hesitated, unwilling to intrude upon Honor's private grief. Then he heard men talking as they approached the barn. He stepped outside and recognised several of his fellow officers. He raised his own voice in a loud, cheerful greeting, and stood talking to them for several minutes. By the time he finally entered the barn, Honor had gone.

Cole didn't see Honor again for over a month. He knew Joe visited her every few days, and he trusted his servant would tell him if she needed anything.

Wellington, who'd set up headquarters at Frenada, seventeen miles from Ciudad Rodrigo, went to Cadiz for several weeks over Christmas. The rest of the army and its camp-followers settled into their winter quarters and entertained themselves as well as they could.

Cole took his shotgun out after woodcock, hiking for miles through the rugged countryside. He enjoyed the physical challenge of pitting his strength and endurance against the wild terrain. The mournful howls of the plentiful wolves in the region didn't trouble him; instead, their song stirred a desire within him to explore their wild kingdom.

He relished his solitary forays into the wilderness, but he was restless. He wanted to see Honor again.

Towards the end of January he gave in to his craving and rode Corvinus over to her village. It was time to see whether she was ready to go back to England. He was determined that, however obstinately she protested, she would leave Spain before the next campaign season began.

He dismounted outside the barn, then paused at the sound of voices coming from within. He recognised Honor's voice immediately. She was talking to a man, though he couldn't immediately place the fellow.

'Lawyers!' she exclaimed energetically. 'I hate lawyers!'

'Nay then, we will not wait for their lingering forms,' her companion assured her earnestly. 'But instantly procure the licence, and—'

'The *licence*!' Honor was clearly incensed at the suggestion. 'I hate licence!'

'Oh, my love! Be not so unkind! Thus let me entreat—'

Cole was first stunned, then furious at what he'd overheard. Some jackanapes was forcing his attentions on Honor! He strode forward—then stopped short as Honor spoke again.

'Pshaw! What signifies kneeling, when you know I *must* have you?' she demanded scornfully.

'Nay, madam, there shall be no constraint upon your inclinations, I promise you. If I have lost your heart—'

Cole had heard enough. He stalked into the barn, determined to put an end to this nonsense. As long as he was there to protect Honor she didn't *have* to do anything— certainly not submit to the whims of...

...*Lieutenant Gregory?*

Cole recognised the younger man immediately. Patrick O'Donnell and the lieutenant had both served in the same

company. Cole knew Gregory had thought well of
O'Donnell, but that was no excuse for him to take advantage of his widow.

'What the devil are you doing, Lieutenant?' Cole rapped
out, his blistering gaze sweeping over Gregory's flushed
countenance.

'M-Major Raven!' Gregory stammered. 'W-what…?'

'Good afternoon, Major,' Honor said smoothly. She was
as shocked as the lieutenant by Raven's unexpected appearance, but she recovered her wits more quickly.

Her heart raced, partly from sheer surprise, but mainly
from excitement at seeing Raven again. He was as tall and
formidable as ever. And right now he was furious with the
unfortunate Gregory. One look at Raven's grim expression
and she knew exactly what he thought was happening. She
didn't have time to wonder how she felt about his fierce
response—her immediate instinct was to save him from
unnecessary embarrassment.

'I didn't know you were such an exacting theatre critic,
Major,' she said lightly. 'I thought the lieutenant's performance was very convincing.'

'Th-thank you, Mrs O'Donnell.' Gregory's face flushed
with gratification, though he still watched Raven warily.

'Performance?' Raven said wrathfully.

'I'm sure you recognised that scene from *The Rivals*,'
Honor said, walking over to lay her hand on Raven's arm.

She touched him without a thought except to calm him,
but she was instantly conscious of the tense, corded muscles beneath his sleeve. For a moment she forgot everything except the impact of his powerful masculinity upon
her senses.

He stared down at her, his eyes searing her with their
intensity. She caught her breath, disturbed by the way her

whole body leapt in response to that limited contact with him. She forgot what she'd meant to say.

'I didn't recognise the scene,' Raven said baldly, ignoring her attempt to spare his embarrassment. 'I've never had much time for the theatre.'

'But surely you'll attend *our* performance?' Gregory burst out, sounding both shocked and disappointed that Raven could be so boorish.

'The Light Division's performance of *The Rivals*?' Honor explained breathlessly, seeing that the lieutenant's hasty comment had only caused Raven's already thunderous expression to darken even more ominously.

'Are you taking part in this entertainment?' Raven demanded, ignoring Gregory as he pinned Honor with a diamond-hard, disapproving stare.

'Of course not!' she exclaimed. Her stomach fluttered nervously at his fierce gaze, but she was also exasperated by his high-handed attitude. 'I was simply coaching Lieutenant Gregory in his role.'

'I'm playing Lydia Languish,' Gregory offered, clearly anxious to placate his senior officer.

'You did not sound as if you were playing the part of a female,' Raven said, his blistering gaze sweeping over the discomfited young man.

'He took the part of Jack Absolute so he could see how I managed Lydia,' Honor said impatiently. 'I had no idea you were so straitlaced, Major. No doubt you think it's a pity the theatres were ever reopened after the puritans closed them.'

'It's an indisputable fact that playhouses are a hotbed for every kind of depravity,' Raven said inflexibly.

'*Depravity!*' Honor forgot everything except her outrage at Raven's insult. 'How dare you accuse me of being depraved!' She prodded Raven's chest with a furious finger.

'I've put up with all kinds of snide innuendo from others—but you're the first man to call me depraved to my face. Who the devil do you think you are?'

'I did not call you depraved!' Raven shot back at her, his brows drawn down in a forbidding frown. 'Misguided and ill disciplined—yes. But I did not call you depraved!'

'Well, I'll just…I'll just…um…excuse me,' Lieutenant Gregory muttered, edging past them and escaping from the confines of the barn, his battered script clutched to his chest. Neither Honor nor Cole were aware of his departure.

'But that's what you think of me,' Honor said hotly. 'You've alluded to your disapproval of me several times.'

'I do not disapprove of you,' said Cole grittily.

'But you disapprove of the life actresses lead—and therefore of the life I led before I married Patrick,' Honor challenged him. 'And you just called me *misguided* and *ill disciplined*. You really don't have much opinion of me, do you, Major?' Her voice cracked on the last few words. She dashed a quick hand across her cheek and abruptly turned her back on him.

Her heart hammered in her chest. She was both angry and upset. Her throat ached with unwanted tears she was too proud to shed. She'd endured all kinds of criticism in her life, but Raven's condemnation hurt far more deeply than most.

'You said Patrick was well rid of me,' she whispered, barely aware she'd spoken aloud as she remembered what Raven had said the night she'd woken after Patrick's death.

She heard Raven draw in a rasping breath, then she felt his hands rest tentatively on her shoulders. She held herself rigid, but she didn't pull away from his touch.

'I don't disapprove of you,' he said hoarsely. 'I think Patrick was a fortunate man to be blessed with you as his wife.'

Honor stared straight ahead at the stone wall of the barn. Tears filled her eyes until she couldn't see. She knew if she blinked they'd overflow on to her cheeks. She swallowed, pressed her lips together and tried to control her overwrought emotions.

Raven's hands tightened on her shoulders, then his grip relaxed, but he didn't release her. She was acutely aware of him standing behind her. She could feel the virile energy radiating from his powerful body. She could hear his quickened breathing. The tension between them was almost suffocating in its intensity.

'I don't...disapprove of you,' Raven repeated. He rubbed his hands stiffly down her upper arms, then moved them back up to rest them on her shoulders.

Honor ducked her head, swallowed again, trying to regain her composure. 'You think I am misguided and ill disciplined,' she whispered. She hated that his opinion meant so much to her, but she couldn't prevent herself from saying the words.

The silence between them lengthened.

'You are not ill disciplined,' Cole said at last. 'Misguided...yes. You would be safer in England.'

'You're so sure of that?' Honor murmured, a little wearily.

Cole gripped her shoulders tighter for a couple of seconds, then spun her round to face him. 'Why would you not be safer in England?' he demanded sharply.

Honor gasped, startled by his sudden action, then she looked down, unwilling to meet his searching gaze.

Cole waited, but she could feel his barely curbed impatience at her continued silence.

'What the devil am I going to do with you?' he exclaimed, his frustration audible.

'You don't have to do anything with me,' she retorted, finally managing to step away from him.

She missed the warm strength of his hands on her shoulders, but she welcomed the opportunity to brush her own hand across her eyes. She refused to let Raven see her cry.

'I can't help you if you won't let me,' he said roughly.

'I don't need your help.' Her denial was automatic and unthinking. She kept her head averted from him.

Cole didn't reply, and a few moments later she heard him walk out of the barn. She spun around to stare after him, pressing her hands against her mouth in dismay. Uncomfortable though she'd found their encounter, she hadn't wanted it to end so unsatisfactorily.

But then Cole came back into the barn, leading Corvinus. 'There's no need for him to stand in the wind while we debate this,' he said brusquely.

'Of course not.' Honor went straight to the horse, finding comfort in him as she always did. She wished she could lean her head against his shoulder, but she wouldn't do so in front of Raven. Instead she confined herself to stroking Corvinus. She couldn't even speak to him because she was afraid her voice would betray her.

She was surprised that Cole remained silent for several minutes, long enough for her to find some emotional balance.

'You'll have to leave before the campaign season starts,' he said at last. 'And if there is nowhere in England you feel comfortable returning to—we will have to arrange something else for you. We can discuss it another time. I'm going to see what adventures Williams has had with his hounds since I last spoke to him.'

'Major.' Honor stopped him just as he reached the door. 'Do you enjoy spending hours talking about hunting?' she asked, hating the uncertain waver in her voice, but wanting to delay Raven's departure.

He hesitated. 'Perhaps not for hours,' he replied, after apparently giving her question serious consideration. 'Why?'

'I…just wondered,' she said, and saw a glimmer of amusement in his blue eyes. Suddenly she didn't feel quite so bad.

'I cannot help you if you resist me at every turn,' he said quietly.

'I didn't ask for your help,' she reminded him, but without heat.

'Your husband did.'

'Poor Patrick.' Honor sighed.

'You miss him very much,' said Raven. It was a statement, not a question.

'We were married for more than three years,' said Honor softly. 'And I'd known him since I was a child.'

'He was several years older than you,' said Raven.

'Eleven years.' Honor focussed her attention on Corvinus, but she was acutely aware that Cole had moved a couple of steps nearer to her as they spoke—and that he was watching her closely. 'Patrick was driving the London-Bath mail the first time I saw him.'

'Impressive fellows—coachmen,' said Raven stiffly. 'Every young buck wants to emulate their skill with the ribbons.'

'So did I!' Honor said, a hint of amusement in her voice.

'He didn't let you?' Cole sounded scandalised.

'Of course not!' she exclaimed. 'He was very responsible. Besides, Mother—'

'Mother what?' Raven prompted, when she didn't continue.

'Nothing. I forgot myself.' Honor watched Raven warily out of the corner of her eye.

'Why did you become an actress?' Cole asked, surprising her with the change of topic.

'Because I was good at it—at least, I thought I was,' she said after a few moments. 'It was a way for me to earn an independent living without...'

'Without what?'

'It was more exciting than being a governess,' Honor said a little defiantly, risking a brief glance at Cole.

'I dare say,' he replied drily. 'Was that the only alternative?'

'Not the only alternative,' said Honor carefully. 'But it was the only one I was prepared to consider.'

'What do you mean?' Cole frowned at her evasive answer. 'What of your family? I have never understood why they allowed you to take such a disreputable course of action,' he added, a note of censure in his voice.

Honor turned her back on Corvinus so she could look directly at Cole. The horse rubbed his chin on her shoulder and she lifted her hand absent-mindedly to pat his neck.

'What exactly do you mean by that?' she asked.

'You have the manners and speech of a gentlewoman,' Cole said bluntly, after only the briefest hesitation. 'You don't belong among the camp followers of an army—nor on the public stage. I can only assume your family suffered such a serious reversal you had no choice but to seek your own fortune.'

Honor gazed at Cole. 'I'm not sure if I should take that as an insult or not,' she said at last.

'Will they welcome you when you return—or did they disown you after you went on the stage?' Cole asked.

Honor gasped, stunned by how accurately Cole had assessed her situation.

'You think my family have disowned me—for joining the theatre?' she exclaimed.

'Or...perhaps for your marriage?' Cole said softly, his tone carefully neutral, though he watched her intently.

Honor started to laugh out of sheer, shocked surprise. 'You think I was disowned because I married Patrick?'

'I was obviously mistaken,' Cole said stiffly, withdrawing a couple of steps in the face of her laughter. 'Your reluctance to act reasonably invites speculation—but I did not intend to pry.'

Honor was too shaken by his unexpected perspicacity to challenge his insult to her reason. 'You seem to have given a lot of thought to my situation,' she said wonderingly.

'Certainly not!' Cole retorted immediately, frowning at her. 'I have considered the matter only in relation to fulfilling your husband's last request to me. Had you been less obdurate, I would have been spared considerable inconvenience.'

'How flattering!' Honor responded instantly to his disapproval. 'I'm sure if Patrick had known you would regard me as a disreputable inconvenience he would never have burdened you with his request.'

Raven drew in a deep breath and exhaled slowly, obviously struggling to retain both his patience and his good temper.

'This is a fruitless conversation,' he announced with finality. 'We will discuss your departure when you are in a more amenable mood.'

He moved purposefully towards Honor. Her heart leapt into her throat. She swallowed back her nervous anticipation at what he intended to do—but he reached past her to take Corvinus's reins.

Honor stood aside, feeling a sense of anticlimax as Raven led the stallion out of the barn.

'I thought you wanted to see Captain Williams,' she said.

'I have changed my mind,' said Cole briefly. 'Good day, Mrs O'Donnell.'

'Goodbye, Major.' Honor watched him ride away, struggling with the conflicting emotions he had aroused in her. His perpetual assumption that he knew what was best for her aggravated her beyond measure. His sweeping condemnation of the theatre offended her. She still wasn't sure how favourably he thought of her—but it was clear that he *had* thought about her a great deal.

She knew it was utterly foolish, but she liked the idea that Cole Raven thought about her in her absence. She just wished he was less pig-headed and more open to compromise.

She sighed, remembering his firm grip on her shoulders. She'd welcomed the wordless reassurance of his touch. But it had stirred a yearning in her for things she would never be able to have.

Chapter Four

The Light Division's performance of *The Rivals* was staged in an empty chapel in the village of Gallegos.

Despite his lack of enthusiasm for such entertainment, Raven was in the audience. Wellington, who'd returned from Cadiz, attended with his staff. Cole glanced around to see who else was present. He immediately spotted Honor sitting a short distance away beside Captain Williams and his mistress, Dolores.

Honor looked poised and serene as she waited for the performance to start. As Cole watched, she inclined her head to hear something Dolores said to her. She nodded and smiled in response, then she turned to the officer sitting on her other side who also wished to speak to her. A few moments later she smilingly replied to his comment. She seemed completely at ease.

Cole's jaw clenched as he tried to control the surge of undisciplined emotions he always experienced in Honor's presence. Seeing her, without touching her, was an excruciating pleasure. It required all Cole's self-control not to thrust aside the impertinent young officer who was talking to her, then sweep her off to a more private location. He had plenty of unfinished business with the obstinate Mrs O'Donnell.

Since abducting her from the chapel would only create the kind of scandal he'd been trying so hard to avoid, he turned his frustrated attention to the stage. It didn't take him long to conclude that he'd never witnessed so much unmitigated nonsense in his life.

'I wrote a letter to myself, to inform myself that Beverley was at that time paying his addresses to another woman,' Lieutenant Gregory declared from the stage, in his role as Lydia Languish. 'I signed it "your friend unknown", showed it to Beverley, charged him with his falsehood, put myself in a violent passion, and vowed I'd never see him more.'

Raven frowned. In his opinion Lydia Languish deserved a severe dressing down for her romantic follies. Instead her suitor indulged her preposterous fancies without protest. He wondered if Honor had once shared Lydia's ridiculous fantasy that living in poverty was intrinsically more romantic than living in comfortable circumstances. Was that why she'd married a coachman? If she had made that mistake, she'd certainly discovered her error, Cole thought grimly.

He was distracted from his reflections by an unusually long silence from the stage. He realised one of the actors had forgotten his lines. Despite his jaundiced view of the entertainment, he felt sorry for the man making a fool of himself in front of his brother officers, not to mention the Commander-in-Chief.

Fortunately, before the situation became too embarrassing, Wellington himself stood up and began applauding.

'Bravo, bravo,' he called.

Raven sensed the release of tension in the audience around him. Wellington's encouragement also helped the actors to relax, and the rest of the performance passed without a hitch.

The play was followed by a selection of comic songs. Cole sat back, stretching out his legs, and glanced around the makeshift theatre. He noticed immediately that, although Captain Williams and Dolores were still present, Honor had left.

Cole's limited interest in the entertainment vanished. With a muttered apology to the men sitting next to him, he stood and made his way out of the chapel.

'You were very good,' Honor assured Lieutenant Gregory.

'Thank you, Mrs O'Donnell. Your opinion is very important to me!' he exclaimed, still euphoric from his success.

Honor had slipped outside to discuss the lieutenant's performance with him. She had guessed how excited he would be after the show, and she thought he would probably welcome the opportunity to talk about it. In truth, she was proud of the way he'd responded to her coaching.

She had been prepared for a detailed postmortem of the play, but the Lieutenant surprised her. After only a few questions about his performance, Gregory changed the subject.

'Mrs O'Donnell...ma'am...that is to say...um...' he stammered, and fell silent, a flush spreading over his face.

Despite the brutalising experience of war, he was very young, Honor thought indulgently, his chin still quite smooth. In that respect, he'd been a good choice for the part of Lydia.

'I believe my prospects are quite good,' he said hurriedly. 'I hope to be promoted as soon as I am eligible, and my father has promised to purchase a Captaincy if necessary—though, as I say, I hope to succeed through my own efforts.'

'I'm sure you will,' said Honor, encouragingly, a little puzzled by the lieutenant's choice of subject.

'You must know how much I admire you!' he announced desperately. 'You have such courage, such grace...so beautiful...' He got stuck in the middle of his sentence.

A muffled roar of laughter from inside the chapel filled the painful silence. The audience was obviously enjoying the comic performance.

Honor gazed at the Lieutenant, hardly able to believe where he appeared to be heading. She hoped he wasn't about to ask her to be his mistress—but surely he couldn't be considering marriage?

'I wondered...that is...would you marry me?' he gulped. 'Mrs O'Donnell? Ma'am?' He stared at her, his anxious eyes pinned on her face. She'd never seen anyone look quite so nervous or hopeful.

'Lieutenant...' She hesitated, momentarily at a loss.

She had never envisaged such a proposal from the young officer, and she wasn't sure how to reply. She didn't want him to feel patronised or humiliated by her rejection. It would be cruel to remind him that he was five years younger than she was, and that she was probably his first serious infatuation.

'I know that you cannot possibly love me,' he said, with desperate persuasiveness. 'But I have seen that your situation is not...not *comfortable*.' He flushed painfully. 'And I would take care of you. You may have thought I was backward in protecting you before. But I assure you—'

'Protecting me?' Honor echoed, bewildered. 'I don't understand...'

'You have been much...much *harried* by some of our

officers,' Gregory stumbled over his explanation. 'I am sorry I was not more...that is...I was taken by surprise by...by Major...but I assure you in *future* I would—'

'I understand entirely,' Honor said soothingly, as she realised he was referring to the incident in the barn, when Raven had interrupted their rehearsal. She'd forgotten the junior officer had witnessed any of her conversation with Cole. 'Really, sir, you have no reason to feel...' She hesitated. She didn't want to hurt his feelings. 'Lieutenant, your good opinion means a great deal to me,' she said honestly. 'Far more than I can say. And I am proud that you think I'm worthy to be your wife—but I can't marry you.'

She saw him swallow violently.

'Any man would...' he began.

'No, not any man,' she corrected him gently, 'and you know that as well as I do. But that's not why I can't marry you. I can't marry you because I loved my husband. I'm still grieving for him. You deserve much more than I could offer you.'

'I...if you change your mind...' Gregory's throat worked.

'If I change my mind,' she agreed, knowing that on this matter she never would. 'Lieutenant, I am so sorry to disappoint you.'

He gazed at her for several seconds, seeing the finality of her refusal in her face. Then he spun round on his heel and strode away, stumbling slightly on the rocky ground. She suspected he wasn't seeing too clearly. Later he would probably be grateful he hadn't tied himself, so early in his career, to a woman of dubious reputation and no influence—but not yet.

'What was that all about?' a voice growled in her ear.

Honor gasped with surprise. She was so startled her

heart seemed to leap into her mouth. She pressed her hand against the base of her throat, trying to calm her agitated nerves.

'For God's sake!' she exclaimed, when she finally found her voice. 'You nearly frightened me to death!'

'Really? I didn't think you were afraid of anything,' Raven replied, arching a mocking eyebrow at her.

Honor drew in several quick breaths. Although her initial surprise at Raven's sudden appearance was receding, her heart still beat faster than usual. She was far too conscious of the virile energy radiating from his broad-shouldered frame—not to mention the gleam of satisfied masculine amusement in his eyes as he enjoyed her discomfiture.

'I didn't say I was afraid of you,' she retorted crossly. 'Just that you surprised me. What are you doing, skulking around out here?'

'I wasn't skulking.' Cole corrected her mildly. 'I'm hardly to blame if you were so engrossed in your conversation you paid no attention to your surroundings.'

'The play was good, wasn't it?' Honor said, trying to change the subject. She didn't intend to discuss Lieutenant Gregory's proposal with Raven, but nor did she wish to argue with him.

Cole grunted disparagingly. 'Preposterous nonsense! I never heard such foolishness.'

Honor opened her mouth indignantly, then closed it again as she realised that what Raven had criticised was not the performance but the play itself.

'You would have preferred a morally uplifting tragedy?' she enquired, unable to resist teasing him a little.

'There is nothing uplifting about tragedy,' Raven said trenchantly.

'I never thought so,' Honor agreed.

Cole looked at her sceptically. 'From my limited experience of young females, they enjoy nothing better than imagining themselves at the centre of a melodramatic tragedy,' he observed. 'Certainly the play we've just seen supports my view.'

'Lydia Languish is not the only character in the play who acts foolishly,' Honor pointed out, refusing to let Raven bait her. 'Some of the male characters, Faulkland in particular, are hardly paragons of sturdy common sense.'

'Popinjay!' Cole muttered, in what she took to be agreement with her. 'Do you *enjoy* acting?' he demanded explosively a few seconds later, studying her face intently. Clearly he found the idea inconceivable.

'Yes,' said Honor, bracing herself for his castigation. She refused to lie about something which had once been so important to her.

'Why?' he demanded.

'Why?' she repeated gazing at him in momentary uncertainty. It wasn't what she'd expected him to say. 'For the freedom it gave me,' she said at last.

'Freedom?' He frowned. 'To flout convention and flaunt yourself before an audience of strangers?'

'No. *No*! Not that at all!' Honor pulled her shawl over her head, hurt and angered by Cole's assumption. She started to walk away from him, but he stopped her with a hand on her arm.

She stood stock still, her heart pounding at his unexpected touch.

'What then?' he asked.

'It would make no sense to you,' she said unsteadily, keeping her face averted. She was acutely conscious that he was still holding her arm. His grip was strong yet gentle. He didn't touch her often but, whenever he did so, it was always the same. Somehow his hands conveyed a message to her that he'd never put into words.

'Then you will have to make allowances for my faulty understanding,' he said, his voice deeper than usual.

She hesitated a few seconds, then turned to face him. 'It's an opportunity to escape from one's self,' she said, watching him warily. 'To be someone else, free from the limitations and expectations of everyday life. No doubt you consider that the height of folly,' she added defensively, lifting her chin as she spoke.

He studied her so searchingly she felt as if his eyes were probing the depths of her soul.

'Do you intend to return to acting?' he asked in a low voice.

'I'm not sure that's any of your concern,' Honor said coolly. She stepped back, trying to create a more comfortable distance between them. He was crowding too close to her, physically and emotionally.

'I was...curious, that's all,' he replied. Honor could see the fire smouldering in his eyes.

'No,' she capitulated suddenly, tired of sparring with him. 'I don't want to go back to the stage,' she added, making her preference absolutely clear.

Cole relaxed perceptibly at her words. It seemed strange to her that he was so concerned about what she did in the future.

'I've been thinking about your situation,' he said. 'Since you are reluctant to return to...your family, I have been considering alternative arrangements.'

'Oh?' Honor stared at him. Her heart rate speeded up again. She felt breathless. She wasn't sure if she was waiting for Cole's explanation with apprehension or anticipation.

'I've recently had a letter from Malcolm Anderson,' said

Cole, taking her hand and slipping it through his arm. He began to stroll away from the chapel. A few other members of the audience had come out for air. Several officers were looking at Raven and Honor with open curiosity.

'Malcolm Anderson?' Honor prompted him, wondering whether to withdraw her hand from Cole's arm. She could feel the strength in his lean muscles, even beneath his sleeve. She enjoyed touching him, but she wasn't sure if she was wise to indulge herself in such a way.

'Malcolm is my uncle. He took care of business on my father's behalf for years. Now he does the same for my brother,' Cole explained briefly.

'I see,' said Honor. She didn't, not entirely, but she was eager for Cole to get to the point. What plans did he have for her?

'My family has estates in several counties,' Cole continued, watching the ground ahead, rather than looking at Honor. 'I know you do not care for the position of governess—and in truth I don't think any member of my family has young children—but there are a number of other possibilities.'

'There are?' Honor swallowed back a rush of disappointment. When Cole had first talked about other arrangements she'd foolishly wondered if he'd meant something more personal. But it seemed that his suggestion for her was going to be both practical and businesslike.

'For example, Great-Aunt Dorothea.' Cole stopped walking suddenly and turned to face Honor. 'She's lonely—according to Malcolm. In need of a companion...'

'You want me to be her companion?' Honor gazed up at him in disbelief.

'It occurred to me as a possibility,' Cole replied. He didn't look particularly happy at his own proposal. 'No doubt there are others. Malcolm will know better than I.

He will take good care of you. This seems to me a good compromise,' he added, looking directly into Honor's eyes.

'You want to send me to your uncle, so he can take care of me?' she said, her voice echoing unfamiliarly in her own ears. This was the last thing she had ever expected Cole to say.

'Yes,' he replied brusquely.

Honor gazed at him, ignoring the cold wind whipping tendrils of her hair around her face, as she tried to understand what motivated his offer. As always when she was with Raven she could sense fierce, unreadable emotions concealed just beneath the surface of his rigid self-discipline. She was confused by his suggestion, not sure exactly how she felt about it—but she was comforted by his continuing concern for her well-being.

'My safety means that much to you?' she said softly.

She almost thought he flinched at her words, but the expression was so transitory she decided she must have imagined it.

'I promised your husband,' he said roughly.

'So you keep telling me,' she said, suddenly realising she had only Raven's word for that.

'Don't you believe me? He asked me to take care of you at the same time he told me you'd carried him,' Cole said harshly. 'Did you carry him on your back? I didn't see that. He was lying in the mud when I found you.'

'I carried him,' Honor whispered. Her thoughts turned inwards and she shivered at the bleak memories Cole had called to mind.

'Honor?' Cole gripped her shoulders. 'You are safe now,' he said, his rasping tone at a variance with the reassurance his words—and hands—conveyed. 'I will keep you safe. Think about the future—not the past.'

She focussed on his face, seeing a mixture of concern, frustration and regret in his fierce eyes. And other emotions she couldn't decipher. Then she realised he had just made her a promise. He had told her he would keep her safe.

She drew in an unsteady breath. From the way her ribs creaked with the effort it seemed like a lifetime since she'd last breathed.

Patrick had once made her the same promise. But Patrick O'Donnell and Cole Raven were two very different men. And Patrick had tried to keep her safe by marrying her—Cole wanted to send her away from him to the protection of his uncle.

'There has to be a better way,' she murmured, unaware she'd spoken aloud.

'I beg your pardon?' Cole frowned at her. 'I assure you that Malcolm—'

'No, no.' She reached out instinctively to touch him, her fingertips brushing over the scarlet cloth of his uniform. 'That's not what I meant.'

She laid her hand flat against his chest, feeling the solid strength and heat which emanated from his virile body. He tensed, his muscles flexing at her touch. It excited her to be so close to such fierce masculine energy. It hurt too. Because he was sending her away.

'I will think about what you've said,' she told him.

'Good.' She thought perhaps he wanted to say more, but he left it at that. 'You've been standing in the cold long enough,' he informed her briskly. 'Do you wish to return to the chapel, or shall I escort you back to your billet?'

Honor choked back an unwary laugh. Her hands were rough from the manual work she'd done since she'd arrived in the Peninsula. She was currently performing the combined duties of lady's maid, housekeeper and cook,

yet Raven treated her as if she were a fine lady—at least
when he wasn't issuing her with peremptory orders. She
wondered if he was aware of the contradictions in the way
he behaved towards her. Did he understand them? Because
she certainly didn't.

In March, Lord Wellington decided to hold a ball in
Ciudad Rodrigo. This was partly to honour the Spanish,
who'd made him a duke of the city, and partly to provide
him with a formal opportunity to invest one of his generals
with the Order of the Bath. There was to be a grand dinner
for various important dignitaries, both Spanish and
English, followed by a ball and supper. Cole received an
invitation to the ball. He had no particular desire to attend,
but no good reason not to go. He decided to make the best
of it.

The ball was held in the largest house in Ciudad
Rodrigo. The band of the 52nd Foot was playing when
Cole entered the room. There was a noticeable chill in the
air, and he glanced around sardonically. The ceilings and
walls were hung with splendid damask satin drapes which
made the room look rather like a large yellow tent—and
disguised the fact that a cannon-ball had punched a hole
out of the roof when the city had been under siege. There
was also a sentry standing guard next to a carpet which
had been placed over a gaping hole in the ballroom floor.

He smiled faintly, wondering what Honor would say if
she could see the decorations. But this was not the kind
of occasion Honor could attend, even though the gentleman outnumbered the ladies by more than three to one.
He was grateful for the uneven numbers, which fortunately
reduced his obligation to dance.

'A fine spectacle, isn't it?' said Captain Williams enthusiastically, as he joined Cole. 'A pity there aren't more ladies.'

'A great pity,' Cole agreed drily, watching the Captain inspecting several of the female guests with an eager eye. Dolores had not received an invitation.

'Everything done in the grandest fashion!' Williams exclaimed. 'The supper was half-cooked in Frenada and brought here in waggons, so I'm told. Nothing but the best for his lordship.'

'As you say.' Cole located Lord Wellington in the throng, dressed up in his best uniform, glittering with all his orders, dancing with the wife of one of his Colonels. Wellington enjoyed a party.

Raven circulated, ate sparingly in the damask-hung supper rooms, and wondered how soon he could leave. He'd never enjoyed this kind of affair. He was a poor hand at small talk and he was an indifferent dancer. He tried not to think about how Honor would have shone at such an occasion. He was sure she was a graceful dancer, and he knew she could be charming company when she wasn't being unreasonably obstinate.

He sipped his champagne, thinking of his last meeting with her. She hadn't yet agreed to go to Malcolm Anderson, but nor had she dismissed the suggestion out of hand. Cole was sure it was only a matter of time before she fell in with his plans. He was relieved, because soon the army would be leaving its winter quarters, but he also dreaded her departure—because once she had gone he knew he could never risk seeing her again. When he himself returned to England, it would be to marry Bridget Morton.

He'd known Bridget for most of his life. Their families' estates adjoined each other in Oxfordshire. Their fathers had been close friends and the marriage had been planned while they were both still in the schoolroom. George Morton had considerable property, but no male heir. As the younger son of an influential family, Cole Raven had a name and useful connections, but a limited inheritance.

George Morton and Sir Edward Raven had planned the marriage between them. As part of the marriage arrangements, Cole would receive the Oxfordshire estate, which would in due course be united with the Morton property. Thus Sir Edward provided for his younger son, and George Morton for his only offspring.

It was to be a union of families and land. Cole had not enjoyed being the make-weight in such an arrangement, and he had resisted a formal betrothal for several years. But at the age of twenty-five he had realised two things: the first was that he had never yet met a lady who fired his blood enough to overthrow the long-standing arrangements; the second was that, since Bridget's family already thought of her as being promised to him, her chance of finding happiness elsewhere was non-existent. While he kicked his heels, she simply grew older and more anxious about her future. So he'd made a formal offer for her.

Two weeks later her mother had died unexpectedly. It was clearly necessary for them to delay the marriage while her family was in strict mourning, and then he'd been posted to Portugal. Four years later, he was twenty-nine and Bridget was twenty-eight, and her prospects were even less rosy if he jilted her. Not to mention the breach it would cause between their families, and the possible lawsuit against him if he reneged on his obligations.

He wondered what Bridget expected from him? Just his name and his protection—or did she want more than that? His wider experience of women was limited. His own mother had died when he was in shortcoats, and he had been in the army since he was eighteen. With the exception of his feelings for Honor, his liaisons had been brief, and focussed on the mutual exchange of physical pleasure. He was sure that Honor would not be prepared to accept a marriage in name only so, if he took her as his yardstick, he could only assume Bridget wouldn't either.

Cole's mood darkened as he contemplated marriage to a woman whose face he could barely remember. He was tired of the merriment around him. He shouldered his way out of the ballroom, into the frosty night air. There was a silver moon in the sky. He could see his breath in front of his face. The music and laughter from the ballroom sounded muffled and distant. He stepped into the street, intending to find Corvinus and go back to his quarters.

'Major?' A soft-voiced shape detached itself from the shadows.

'Honor?' He was dumbfounded to see her there. 'What—?'

'I came to see the spectacle,' she said softly. 'I peeked earlier, when they were setting everything up. So beautiful—and so theatrical, don't you think. All that yellow satin to hide the holes—just like the backdrop to a play. Anything could happen in the middle of a magical illusion like that. You should be inside, dancing.'

'I don't dance,' he said briefly, gazing down at her.

She'd pulled her shawl up over her head to protect herself from the cold. Her eyes glowed in the moonlight. She looked beautiful and ethereal—Cinderella, waiting for her fairy godmother to send her to the ball. Cole wished he could take her back into the ballroom, let her experience the magic which had made so little impact upon him.

'But you could still enjoy the spectacle—watching everyone else dance,' she said, smiling up at him. 'Didn't you?'

'No.' He stared at Honor. She was so delicately beautiful he felt like an inarticulate clod in her presence. 'I fear I'm too dull.'

'Major!' Her hazel eyes twinkled teasingly at him in the moonlight. 'No one could call you dull.'

'Indeed?' He wanted to ask her what she *would* call him, but he didn't. 'I'm sorry you could not attend the ball,' he said. 'You would have outshone all the ladies present.'

Her lips parted in surprise at his compliment, and he saw her draw in a quick breath. Her mouth looked soft and inviting. He wanted to kiss her so badly it hurt. His own breathing quickened as he fought to control his rising desire. Her eyes widened as she looked at him. As he watched, he saw the focus of her gaze shift to his mouth and she moved almost imperceptibly towards him. He put his hand on her arm, drawing her a little closer, and bent his head...

A couple of loud-voiced officers suddenly emerged from the house behind Cole, obviously in a state of good-humoured inebriation. Their unexpected appearance jolted Cole back to reality.

'I'll take you home,' he said gruffly. He caught Honor's hand in his and drew it through his arm. 'You're miles from your billet,' he scolded her, as they began to walk along the street. 'How did you intend to get back?'

'I thought maybe I'd find someone going my way,' she replied breathlessly. 'Possibly Captain Williams. If not, I could always walk.'

'Dammit, woman!' Cole exploded, finding an outlet for his frustrated desire. 'Haven't you got any common sense?'

'Well...' Honor hugged his arm as they walked. 'I found you,' she pointed out teasingly. 'And you're taking me back to my billet.'

Cole was about to give her his unabridged opinion of

that piece of folly when it occurred to him that perhaps she'd been waiting for him all along. She must have known he'd never leave her unprotected in Ciudad Rodrigo. He almost asked her if he'd guessed correctly, but then he thought better of it. His dealings with Honor were already too complicated for comfort.

Honor had assumed Cole would either put her on a spare horse, or take her up behind him. He did neither. He held her in front of him on Corvinus, resting sideways in the cradle of his arms.

Honor thought it was the most romantic thing that had ever happened to her. She didn't dare comment on the arrangement in case he changed his mind and made her sit behind him. She was completely dependent upon him for her security in the precarious position. She didn't feel in the slightest bit nervous about her safety, but she did feel a continuous flutter of excitement as she savoured every aspect of her situation. She was in Cole's arms, protected from the cold air by the heat of his powerful body. She rested her head against his broad shoulder and allowed herself to relax. Whatever he had—or hadn't—said to her, the way he held her communicated its own message.

Corvinus walked unhurriedly out of Ciudad Rodrigo, over the Roman bridge that crossed the Agueda river, and through the chilly countryside. Moonlight glistened here and there on the white frost which hardened the road and decorated the dark trees.

'See?' she murmured, rousing herself a little. 'The moonlight makes the whole world look magic.'

'I'm afraid I'm too prosaic to believe in magic,' Cole replied gruffly.

'Oh, no.' She tipped her head back a little to look up at

his strongly delineated features. 'Believing in magic is what makes life bearable.'

'Is that how you've survived this country?' he asked curiously.

'Perhaps.' She laid her hand against his shoulder and pillowed her cheek against it. 'It's a beautiful country. I wouldn't have missed these last four years, not for anything.'

'Except for the way they ended,' Cole said roughly. She felt a sudden increase of tension in his arms. 'I did not mean to remind you of painful memories,' he added, in a low, regretful voice.

She stroked his shoulder in a soothing gesture, accepting his apology. After a few moments she sighed.

'Poor Patrick,' she murmured. 'He didn't like being a soldier, but he made the best of it, poor sweetheart.'

'How did he come to be a soldier?' Cole asked stiffly.

'A recruiting party took advantage of him when he was drunk,' she replied bleakly.

'I didn't know he drank.' Cole was surprised. In an army where drunkenness was endemic among the soldiers and most of their wives, the O'Donnells had been notable for their restraint and sobriety.

'He didn't usually, that's why he was such an easy mark for them,' Honor replied.

Cole caught an odd undercurrent in her voice, almost as if she blamed herself. He didn't know how to ask her that question directly, or even if he should ask it at all.

'But you stood by him,' he said carefully. 'You came to Portugal with him.' He hesitated. 'You loved him very much,' he added steadily.

Honor was silent for several minutes as Corvinus paced proudly along the road.

'I did love him,' she said, so quietly that Cole had to

bend his head to hear her, 'but he deserved so much more than I ever gave him.'

'How can you say that?' Cole demanded, shocked. The stallion halted in response to his rider's unthinking command. 'No one could ask more from their wife than you gave Patrick. You cannot blame yourself because you couldn't save him from—'

Honor reached up and laid her fingers gently over his lips.

'Shush,' she murmured. The moonlight silvered her hair and the curve of her cheek. 'That's not what I meant.' She smiled slightly. 'Are you indignant on my behalf or Patrick's?' she teased him gently.

'I…' He tried to reply, but he couldn't think. Her fingers were delicately exploring the contours of his face.

'If you had a choice,' she said softly, 'would you rather have a wife who could nag a harpy into submission—or one who trembled in your arms?'

Cole was stunned by her words. Did she mean…? What did she mean? The intimacy of the moment was both intoxicating and terrifying.

'Didn't you?' he said hoarsely. 'Didn't you tremble in his arms?'

He saw the moment when a mixture of shyness and shame suddenly overcame her. She flushed and drew her shawl up, turning her head to hide her face in his shoulder. Her embarrassment was incredibly endearing, because in her confusion she'd turned towards him, not away from him. Cole felt as exulted as if he'd just seized a French eagle all by himself. She hadn't trembled in her husband's arms!

He urged Corvinus forward again, giving Honor a chance to recover her composure to the steady rhythm of the stallion's hooves.

'Why did you marry him?' he asked at last, when the excitement blazing through his body made it impossible to stay silent any longer. He did his best to keep his voice as calm as possible.

'I did love him,' she repeated, as if it was important to emphasise that fact. 'I was very fond of him. I'd known him since I was a child, long before I was successful. I knew he was devoted to me—God! I shouldn't have been so weak-minded!' she reproached herself abruptly, stirring restlessly in Cole's arms.

'Shush.' It was his turn to sooth her. He was overwhelmed with pleasure that, after so many months of resisting his help, she was finally confiding in him. 'What happened?' he asked gently.

'The Duke of Selhurst,' she said tensely. 'I got so tired of it all. Every time I turned round he was there—or one of his minions—flattering me, pawing at me. He had… plans…for me I didn't care for.'

Raven held her fiercely, anger raging through him on her behalf.

'Damn him!' he swore.

Honor stroked Cole's cheek, immensely gratified by his protective fury. 'He came to a mortifying end,' she consoled him.

'He did? How?' Cole demanded.

'I…well, um, it wasn't very ladylike,' she said uncomfortably.

'What did you do?'

'I…um, I kneed him in the groin,' she said blushing hotly. 'He sort of…collapsed. I thought I'd killed him. I was only twenty-one.'

'Honor!' Cole burst into delighted laughter, holding her close.

Honor was amazed. She'd never realised he was capable

of such uninhibited light-heartedness. She laughed too, intoxicated by his good humour.

'What a virago!' he exclaimed, planting a celebratory kiss on her forehead.

She gasped, her laughter dying, and gazed up at him searchingly. She felt his breath catch. His face hovered above hers for a heart-stopping moment, then he brushed his lips against hers.

'Oh-ohhh.' Honor's sigh was long and soft.

Again, he touched his mouth gently, almost hesitantly, to her parted lips. She reached up to rest her hand on his high collar. His lips were firm, warm, and tantalisingly tender against hers. He tasted her delicately, exploring the sensuous curves of her mouth. She was wrapped in a golden cocoon—protected and cherished. It felt so good when he kissed her. She wanted more. She pressed up towards him almost impatiently. He groaned softly, and deepened the kiss. His tongue teased her lips, kindling fires deep within her, then thrust boldly into the warmth of her mouth.

She was briefly stunned, then an answering passion surged through her, firing her blood. He wanted to be inside her. She could feel it in the fierce gentleness of his embrace. His lips and tongue plundered her soul, then he withdrew slightly, tempting her to her own exploration. She followed his example, her own tongue flickering tentatively, almost shyly against his firm lips, learning the new game he was teaching her with all the passionate eagerness of which she was capable.

He shuddered in response and groaned. He kissed her cheek then pushed back her shawl so he could explore her warm tender neck. His lips were hot, clever and moist against her sensitive skin. He sucked, drawing heat to the surface, claiming her. She melted against him, fluid in her responsiveness.

'I have you now!' he whispered, hoarsely triumphant in her ear. 'Are you trembling, Honor?' he demanded fiercely.

'Y-y-yesss.' She exhaled a long-drawn out hiss of breath. She rubbed her face against his shoulder like a cat, only wanting to be nearer still to him.

'Honor, Honor.' He rubbed his cheek against hers. She felt the rasp of his whiskers against her soft skin. She wanted more, but he held her quietly until the urgent tempo of their passion gradually slowed. At last he lifted his head and signalled Corvinus to move forward.

Honor was amazed. She'd been married for several years. She'd lived in conditions which had made it impossible for her to remain either naïve or innocent, yet she'd never fully anticipated how devastating Cole's lovemaking would be. He could turn her inside out with a single kiss. She was shaken to the core.

So was Cole. He'd promised himself to keep Honor at a distance, yet here she was in his arms. His heart was still thudding with unresolved desire, his body uncomfortably aroused. Honor's passion had matched his—and she'd trembled in his arms! By her own admission, she'd trembled in his arms! He wanted to give a primitive shout of conquest. He was so fired up with pride and excitement he could have defeated the French single-handedly. A pity Wellington was too busy partying to make use of his new secret weapon.

Raven tried to cool his passion, knowing he was heading them both for disaster. Wanting Honor was completely different from being able to have her. Nothing had changed—he was engaged to a virtuous woman he'd known since childhood. He was unable to make Honor any kind of offer that would be worthy of her.

'We left the Duke of Selhurst writhing on the floor,' he said, when he finally trusted himself to speak.

'What?' Honor had been floating in a magical world all her own. The Duke was the last thing on her mind.

'What happened next?' Cole prompted her.

'Oh.' Honor would have preferred another kiss, but she was too shy to say so. She roused herself to answer his question instead.

'I was frightened,' she admitted. 'Decommissioning a peer of the realm is...unnerving. Righteous indignation can only take you so far—I was afraid of his revenge. And I was tired. I enjoyed playing different roles on the stage, but I'd never anticipated how complicated my life would become away from the theatre. I'd known Patrick since I was fifteen. He was eleven years older than me. I think he loved me for a long time, but he was so patient about it. Then I burnt my bridges with the Duke—and Patrick was there when I needed him. He was safe and kind...but I should never have married him. I took advantage of him.'

'Did he ask you to marry him?' Cole asked carefully.

'Of course!' Honor exclaimed. 'I know I'm as brazen as an eight-inch howitzer, but I'd *never* have pushed myself on Patrick if he hadn't wanted me!'

'I know.' Cole brushed his lips tenderly against her forehead. He could feel her distress. He had never before realised just how sensitive she could be beneath her battle-hardened exterior. 'I was just wondering...' He hesitated, not sure if he should voice his thoughts.

'What?' she prompted him.

'You were frightened and tired,' he said slowly. 'And Patrick was eleven years older than you. He seemed safe in a hazardous world. Perhaps he took advantage of your weakness to—'

Honor moved restlessly and he broke off, half-expecting her to launch into a passionate defence of her late husband, but she didn't immediately say anything.

'I don't know,' she said eventually. 'I had a stronger personality than Patrick. Overbearing is the kindest thing that's been said about me. Termagant, vixen…virago,' she reminded Cole, smiling a little. 'I was wrong when I married him. I was too…forceful—and he was too proud not to mind. I cared about him a lot. I tried very hard to be a good wife and not shame him in front of the other men.'

She turned her face into Cole's shoulder, and he realised she was close to tears.

'He knew that,' said Raven gently, unbearably moved by her admission. 'He was proud of you, Honor. When I found you that day, when I lifted him up onto Corvinus and he told me you'd carried him, he was proud of you. And all the years before that, anyone could see how proud he was to call you wife, how…honoured…he was.'

She started to cry in earnest.

'Ah, sweetheart, you've been so battle-tossed,' Cole murmured, pressing his cheek against her hair.

After a few minutes she pulled herself together, drying her face on her shawl. It was too cold to cry.

'I'm sorry,' she said, somewhat defensively. 'I'm not usually this, this…droopy and limp-minded.'

Cole chuckled deep in his chest.

'Ohh!' She thumped him in exasperation, though it was really only the lightest of taps.

'Your boxing skills aren't on a par with your marksmanship,' Cole teased her.

'I thought I should learn to fire the musket,' Honor informed him with dignity. 'Patrick was dubious…he said I reminded him of my mother,' she added uncertainly. 'When I made him get on my back.'

'Don't you want to sound like your mother?' Cole asked. He was extremely curious about Honor's family.

'No. I don't know,' Honor stirred restlessly in his arms. 'It was because of Mother that Patrick got drunk and the army got him!' she burst out in anguish. 'Or because of me. I don't know. Mother doesn't approve of marriage.'

'She doesn't!' Cole exclaimed. 'Good God! Does she think it's a sinful state?' He could only imagine that Honor's mother was so strictly religious she condemned all human unions.

'Oh, no, she just doesn't believe any woman with a modicum of wit ought to waste her time and energy on propping up a man,' Honor explained matter-of-factly.

'Good God!' Cole said blankly. 'Is she a disciple of that Wollstonecraft woman?'

Honor giggled unexpectedly. 'Mother wouldn't dream of being anyone's disciple,' she asserted. 'She's very independent and strong-minded.'

'She disapproved of your marriage to Patrick,' said Cole, assuming Honor's mother's disapproval of marriage was actually rather more specific than Honor had implied.

'Oh, yes,' Honor agreed immediately. 'But she wouldn't have approved, whoever it was. I told you, she—'

'Doesn't approve of marriage,' finished Cole. 'Your father...' he began, pausing with unusual delicacy.

'I don't know who he is,' said Honor quietly. 'Mother...' She hesitated, took a deep breath, then plunged on. 'Mother has never *been* married,' she said steadily.

In the silence that followed, Raven realised she was waiting tensely for him to pass judgement on both her mother and her.

'Tell me,' he said gently, and felt her relax again at his lack of condemnation.

'I don't know who my father is,' she said in a low voice. 'I know...she was a maid in a nobleman's house. The son taught her to read. He must have had a genuine affection for her, don't you think?' she asked, lifting her head to look at Cole with almost painful shyness. 'The Duke never offered to teach me anything—useful, that is.'

'I'm sure he had affection,' said Cole, guessing that was the answer his tough, self-sufficient Honor needed to hear.

'Yes.' Honor rested her head against his shoulder again, drawing little circles around one of his silver buttons with her finger. 'I used to like to think of them sitting together over the books and ink well—learning a little, flirting a little. Then of course he had to send her away. He gave her as much money as he could. He pawned his pocket watch and the snuff box and signet ring he was bequeathed by his godfather. She never saw him after that. She had to make a life for us all by herself. Mama is *very* brave and strong-minded. *She* never gave in, in a moment of weakness, and married a man she didn't truly love.'

What a legacy, Cole thought, imagining the child Honor must have been, weaving consoling stories about her father's affection for her mother, to assuage her hurt at his abandonment.

'Did she love your father?' he asked, wondering if perhaps the woman's hostility towards marriage was caused by her bitterness towards one particular man.

'Oh, yes,' Honor replied without hesitation. 'She says he is a man of honour and integrity'—Cole could tell she was quoting something she'd heard many times—'who never shirked his obligations to his name or his family. That's why she called me Honor. They were very young at the time,' she added. 'Mama was sixteen, and my father was nineteen.'

'Sixteen!' The woman had been left to fend for herself and her child with only the value of a few trinkets to save them from oblivion when she was sixteen.

'I was seventeen when I went on the stage,' said Honor defensively.

'Did she force you into it?' Cole demanded.

'Of course not. She didn't approve at all,' Honor exclaimed.

'Her favourite tune,' Cole muttered.

Honor laughed, warmed by his unmistakable partisanship. 'You don't approve of me either,' she reminded him. 'And you're so sure you know what's best for me. Sometimes you remind me of her.'

'God forbid!' Cole sounded appalled.

'She sent me to a seminary in Bath, when I was sixteen,' Honor said, smiling. 'For young ladies of quality. Miss Goodwin said I was a corrupting influence. I was no such thing!' Indignation burned in Honor's voice. 'Just because I took a small part in a play in the public theatre—for a wager. She'd praised me for my performance in private, amateur theatricals.'

'So you left in disgrace?' Cole said in a carefully neutral voice. Despite himself, Honor's indignation was amusing.

'Certainly not,' she said imperiously. 'I went to London and became the toast of the Town. Actually, it took me a couple of years to become an overnight sensation, but it was very gratifying.'

'I'm sure it was,' Cole murmured. 'What did your mother have to say about it?'

'Oh, she said when I left the seminary, if I was determined to go to the Devil, I'd better get on with it my own way,' Honor said airily.

'Very maternal,' Cole commented drily. 'How did you manage?'

'Susannah, Mama's cousin looked out for me—brought me up really. Even she doesn't know who my father is,' said Honor, revealing what was clearly a continuing gap in her life.

He'd said she was battle-tossed, Raven thought, and he hadn't known the half of it.

'Sometimes,' she said, patting his chest uncertainly, 'sometimes, I am too much like my mother. I am too obstinate, and I am too sharp-tongued,' she said with difficulty. 'I say things that hurt, but I don't mean them to.'

'Sweetheart.' He couldn't stop himself, he had to kiss her again.

She slipped her arm around his neck, surrendering to him completely. He dimly realised that, in telling him the truth about her parentage and her marriage, she had given herself to him more completely than if she'd simply given him her body. Her trust overwhelmed him, because life had not taught her to trust easily. He wondered if she would regret her honesty—and sincerely hoped not.

'You don't have to worry about me,' she whispered. 'I know Patrick asked you to take care of me. But I also know better than anyone that a woman doesn't need a wedding ring to survive. I will manage.'

'Honor.' He buried his face in the hollow of her shoulder. 'It will be past dawn before I get you back at this rate,' he said, when he lifted his head.

'I've...enjoyed my ride,' she said, feeling shy again, worrying that she'd said too much.

'So have I.' His grip tightened reassuringly.

Corvinus tossed his head and snorted.

'He agrees with me,' said Raven.

'No, he's just frustrated with our slow rate of progress,' Honor teased.

'I can't think why!' Cole retorted. 'It seems to me we've progressed quite fast.'

Chapter Five

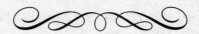

Honor went about her chores in a daze. In the mundane light of day, it was hard to believe her ride in the moonlight with Cole had been any more than a dream. But if she closed her eyes, she could feel his arms around her, and his lips on hers.

It was a wonderful memory, filling her with tingling warmth and the kind of happiness she'd rarely experienced. Now and then the fugitive thought would creep into her mind that she loved Cole. But every time she became aware of the thought she chased it away again.

She didn't know what Cole had meant by his actions—and that made her nervous. The last time he had spoken of her future, he'd been determined to send her to England, to the safe care of his uncle. He'd even suggested she might become companion to one of his elderly aunts. Honor had a sinking feeling that two moonlight kisses wouldn't have changed his mind about that.

Perhaps he'd simply been carried away by the magic of their surroundings. She had good reason to know that men often succumbed to lust without feeling love or even affection for the object of their desire. Perhaps next time they met he would be autocratic and distant, and simply order her back to England.

She wished she'd been more guarded in the things she'd told him. She flushed with embarrassment as she remembered telling him she hadn't trembled in Patrick's arms. She should never have told him that! How would she ever face him again?

She wielded the long-handled brush vigorously, wishing she could sweep out her worries as thoroughly as she swept the cottage floor.

Raven's temper was atrocious.

'If you've got no orders for me, I'm going to watch the wrestling match in the village, sir,' said Joe Newton, eyeing his master warily.

'Very well,' Cole replied curtly.

Joe looked as if he might have said something but, whatever it was, he thought better of it.

When he was alone, Cole slammed the edge of his fist down onto the table and bounced a newspaper, an ink pot, several loose sheets of paper and a pen onto the floor.

He cursed and bent to clear up the mess. A sealed letter fell out of the newspaper and he stared at it blankly for a few seconds.

'Mrs Annie Howarth, Belle Savage, Ludgate Hill.'

He knew of no one by that name and wondered briefly how the letter came to be on his table. Then he remembered Joe corresponded regularly with home and propped the letter up for his servant to find.

He ran his fingers through his hair and cursed again. What the hell had he been thinking of when he'd kissed Honor?

She believed in dreams and magic. Now she was sure

to think those kisses meant more than they ever could. He wondered if she was even aware of his betrothal.

He stood up, pushing his chair back so violently it crashed to the floor. He'd allowed a situation to develop which was dishonest and profoundly unfair to Honor. All because he hadn't been able to control his desire for her. He had to explain things to her as soon as possible. And he had to make her to go back to England.

Honor finished cleaning the cottage. She left the door open to let the light in and started the stew for supper. Then she wrapped her black shawl around her shoulders and sat down to write a letter to Lady Durrington. It was hard not to think of Cole, but she managed to describe the splendid, yellow-satin ballroom in Ciudad Rodrigo without mentioning his name. She only looked up when her light was obstructed.

Raven's tall, broad-shouldered frame blocked the doorway. He had to duck his head to come into the cottage. He was holding his shako in one hand. His back was to the daylight, but Honor thought his expression was unusually grim.

Her heart rate accelerated. She felt breathless with anxiety. She'd imagined their next meeting over and over, but she hadn't been able to decide what she should say or do. She stood up, and realised her knees were weak.

'Major Raven,' she croaked.

'Hon—' He cleared his throat. 'Mrs O'Donnell,' he greeted her.

He stood frozen to the spot, staring at her. Honor was mesmerised by his vivid blue eyes. She wasn't sure which one of them was more awkward but, as his hostess, she decided it was up to her to put him at his ease.

'I'm...glad to see you,' she said shakily. 'How are you?'

'Very well,' Cole growled.

'And Corvinus?' Honor enquired at random, daunted by his ferocious expression.

'You can see for yourself if you wish,' said Cole brusquely. 'I rode him over.'

'Oh. Er…would you like some tea?' Honor enquired desperately.

'I won't trouble you.' Raven shook his head. 'I'll be on my way shortly.'

'You will?'

'I came to discuss the arrangements for your journey,' he said flatly.

'Oh.' Honor felt a hot wave of shame and disappointment roll over her. She tried not to let her emotions show in her expression but, from the look in Cole's eyes, her efforts weren't very successful.

'Dammit!' He came closer to her, dropping his shako on to the table. Then he hesitated, looking around the cottage. 'Where are Williams and…?'

'They went to Frenada,' she said, trying to control her bitter sense of mortification. 'To shop and hear the gossip.'

'Good.' Cole pressed his lips together, his eyes hard with regret as he looked at Honor. 'I'm sorry,' he said curtly. 'I had no business to behave as I did last night. It was inexcusable.'

'Why?' Honor demanded, unbearably hurt by his rejection. 'Surely I'm *just* the kind of woman to dally with in the moonlight. You're not the only officer to think so—'

'What?' Cole seized her upper arms in a fierce grip, staring down at her with blazing eyes. 'Who's mistreated you? Williams? I warned him—'

'*Warned him?*' Honor gasped, shaken by Cole's feral expression. 'What…? No.' She suddenly decided it was more important to calm Cole than to question him. 'Cap-

tain Williams has always treated me well,' she said breathlessly. 'He is a gentleman. Besotted with Dolores...
Please...' she begged, urgently. 'Please.' Cole's hands
were still locked on her upper arms, but she was able to
lift her forearms to touch his chest with her fingertips.

'No one has mistreated me,' she assured him unsteadily.

His grip relaxed a little, but he didn't release her. 'If not
Williams, then who?' he demanded tautly.

'It doesn't matter,' she said, trying to smile. It was silly
to feel reassured by Cole's fierce partisanship when he was
so intent on sending her away—but she couldn't help it.
'It's not important. They simply asked—and I said no.
That's all. It's not important. Please.'

Cole's gaze locked with Honor's for several long moments before the rigidity in his powerful body eased a few
degrees. He was still far from relaxed, but she thought he
was no longer on the verge of hunting down her unwanted
admirers.

She was so shaken by the incident that tears welled up
in her eyes. One minute Cole was starkly telling her she
must leave—the next he seemed to be on the brink of
starting a war on her behalf.

'Don't!' he exclaimed, sounding as tormented as she
felt, when he noticed her shimmering eyes. He started to
pull her towards him, then set her abruptly aside and turned
away from her.

Honor wrapped her arms around her body, in desperate
need of the comfort he refused to offer her.

'Do you know that I'm betrothed,' he asked, without
looking at her.

'I...betrothed?' Her voice wavered. 'I don't remember.'

'I am. I have been these past four years,' he said harshly.

Honor's throat was so tight with tears she couldn't swallow. She stared at his rigid shoulders, unable to say anything. The painful silence extended…

Raven turned to face her. His jaw was clenched with tension, but the wild tempest of emotions he was fighting so hard to control seemed to fill the cottage.

'Do you…?' Honor whispered, but she couldn't finish the question she wanted so much to ask. 'You would never betray your fiancée,' she said instead.

'I would never betray you,' he replied, his eyes fixed on her face. 'And I have nothing to offer you that is worthy of you.'

'Worthy of me?' she exclaimed bitterly. 'Have you forgotten what I told you last night?'

Raven gestured impatiently. 'Your father's sins are not yours,' he said fiercely. 'You have to go back to England. There's nothing for you here.'

Honor recoiled as if he'd slapped her. Then her shock turned to anger.

'How dare you dictate to me!' she flung at him furiously. 'I didn't stay for you. And you have no control over my actions. I'll leave when I'm ready. Not when you order me to go!'

She picked up his shako and hurled it at him. 'Get out! Get out!' Her voice shook with rage and unshed tears.

He stepped back a pace, but didn't leave.

Frustrated beyond measure, she spun round and grabbed the broom from its place in the corner. She swung the bristles downwards, ridiculously intent on sweeping him out of the cottage.

Raven twisted the broom out of her grasp, wrenching her wrist in the process, and threw it aside with a clatter.

Honor winced. She instinctively wrapped her fingers around her aching wrist, holding both hands against her chest as she bent her head over them. She bit back her tears, but she couldn't stop herself from trembling.

She heard Cole exhale a long, unsteady breath, then she felt his hands on her shoulders, gentle this time.

'Dear God!' he murmured. He sounded as anguished and shaken as she felt. 'I'm sorry.' He pulled her into his arms, holding her against his chest. 'I'm sorry. I'm sorry.'

She held herself stiffly, unwilling to accept his comfort. She felt his lips brush against her hair, his hands gently stroking her back. She wanted to let him comfort her so badly it took all her will power not to lean against him.

But she couldn't lean on Cole. He'd made that agonisingly clear. He wanted to send her away from him. He'd been trying to do so for months.

She forced herself to step away from him. It was one of the hardest things she'd ever done, not made any easier because his arms tightened around her before he reluctantly released her.

'Captain Williams and Dolores will be back soon,' she said, not looking at him. 'I have work to do. Goodbye, Major.'

'We'll talk again when we are both…calmer,' Cole replied, after a few moments. 'I will do everything in my power to make sure your life is comfortable. That you are not…harassed…in any way.'

'By sending me to your uncle,' Honor whispered.

Cole didn't reply. He bent to pick up his shako, then walked out of the cottage.

Honor covered her face with her hands, struggling to hold back her tears. The Captain and Dolores really would be back soon and she couldn't bear the thought of them discovering her in such distress.

She brushed her hands across her eyes and set about making a cup of tea for herself before her employers returned. It was just another role to play. She would think of her life in those terms, and never admit how much she hurt inside.

'You should come to the dance tonight,' said Dolores as Honor finished dressing the Spanish girl's hair.

'The dance?' Honor was startled out of her introspection by the unexpected suggestion.

'In the officers' mess.' Dolores nodded firmly. 'All the girls from the village will be there. You should come too.'

'Oh, no,' Honor protested instinctively.

The officers had established a regimental mess in a barn, and once a week they held a ball to which they invited the ladies of the village, but Honor had never attended such an affair. As Patrick's wife it had been impossible for her to socialise with officers and, as his widow, she had to be even more careful in her conduct.

'I think you should come,' said Dolores, twisting in her chair to take Honor's hand. 'You are sad. There will be music, and you can dance.'

'I really don't think I should,' Honor replied, smiling. 'But thank you for asking me. You're very kind.'

'I will be your chaperon,' Dolores informed her. 'And now I will do your hair. You will be the belle of the ball. You are so fair and dainty.'

'Thank you.' Honor hesitated, torn by indecision.

All her common sense told her it would be stupid to attend the dance—but she was tired of being sensible. She was tired of being practical, respectable and dowdy.

'I will come!' she exclaimed. 'I will.'

Dolores laughed happily and hugged her. The relationship between the two women had never truly been one of mistress and maid. Dolores had been wary of Honor at first, afraid she might be a rival for Captain Williams's affections. But as soon as she'd realised that the Captain and Honor had no interest in each other, the Spanish girl had treated Honor with genuine kindness.

'I must have taken leave of my senses—but I will dance tonight!' Honor declared recklessly. She picked up her skirt and took several light dance steps across the room.

Dolores applauded and Honor responded with a graceful curtsy, just as Captain Williams arrived.

'Honor is coming to the dance with us tonight,' Dolores informed him buoyantly.

'Is she, indeed?' Williams glanced at Honor assessingly. 'I look forward to an entertaining evening,' he said, a glint of anticipation in his eyes.

It was nearly eight o'clock when they entered the officers' mess. Honor gazed around the converted barn, fascinated by everything she saw. She'd never attended such an event before, and she knew she never would again. She was hiding a grievous pain deep in her heart, but tonight she sought temporary release in the gaiety of the party.

She intended to leave for England in the next couple of days, but she wouldn't ask Cole Raven for help. She'd once told Cole that she had been paying her own way since she was seventeen, and that was quite true. Just as importantly, she'd always been frugal with her earnings. Patrick had been too proud to let her spend her money on him, so she'd left it untouched during their marriage. During the last few years her financial affairs had been managed by her lawyer in London. A few days after Patrick's death she had written to the lawyer, asking him to send a portion of her money out to her in Portugal. She'd received his reply towards the end of January. Once she'd visited the bank in Lisbon she would have the cash she needed to pay for her passage home.

Her presence at the party caused quite a stir. It wasn't long before she was surrounded by several officers. Cole wasn't among them. Her eyes automatically sought him out, even though she told herself she was glad he wasn't there.

There was a small orchestra composed of a clarinet, a fiddle and a drum. An officer asked Honor to dance and she let him lead her out onto the hard clay floor. That dance was followed by another. She sat out the next dance on a bench beside the wall as yet another officer brought her some wine. It was a long time since she'd received so much flattering attention. She laughed, waved her fan in front of her overheated face, and tried not to think of anything but the pleasure of the moment.

Cole entered the mess just in time to see Honor spinning around on the dance floor, her cheeks glowing with colour as she laughed up at something her partner said to her. The hem of her skirt was coated with dust thrown up from the floor, but she danced with the grace of a princess at a grand ball.

Cole stared at her, stunned speechless to discover her in such a setting. For a few seconds he could not drag his eyes away from her. Her blonde hair had been dressed in fashionable curls and framed her face like a golden halo in the candlelight. Her hazel eyes glowed with life. Her lips were pink, soft and slightly parted as she smiled at the man dancing with her.

Cole forced himself to look away from her and realised almost every man in the room was watching her either openly or surreptitiously. Several of them wore expressions of undisguised desire. There were many pretty girls in the room—Dolores was beautiful—but they were all dark-haired. Honor was the only one who shone like an ethereal, golden angel.

Cole's shock gave way to burning anger. He was furious that Honor could display herself so wantonly in public. He clenched his fists, overwhelmed by a raging desire to knock her smirking dance partner through the wall, then turn his fury on the men watching her with such open lust. Only years of strict self-discipline prevented him from acting on his first impulse.

As the immediate shock-wave of his anger receded, Cole realised it was not his fellow officers who were to blame for the situation—it was Honor. She was the one who was shamelessly provoking the men around her to act like rutting stags.

He strode towards her. He was dimly aware that the music had come to a discordant end. He was acutely aware of the men around him and the intentions their body movements signalled to him. He was less sharply aware of Honor's shocked expression as he closed the distance between them. He would deal with her later.

He seized her wrist and pulled her towards the door, not bothering to say anything. As far as he was concerned, the situation didn't call for words.

Honor followed him willy-nilly for a few steps. Then she dug her heels in, resisting his inexorable progress. He spun round, released her wrist and swept her up in his arms in one swift movement. Honor gave a soft cry of alarm. He could hear her quickened breathing, but she didn't struggle.

He was nearly at the door when his way was blocked by Lieutenant Gregory. The young man was pale but resolute as he faced his senior officer.

'Stand aside!' Cole growled furiously.

'No, sir!' Lieutenant Gregory lifted his chin, managing

to maintain eye contact with Cole, even though he was clearly over-matched.

Honor's wits had flown up the chimney the moment she'd set eyes on Cole. His angular face was dark with anger. The wild emotions he normally held firmly in check were boiling dangerously close to the surface. Shock and disbelief had held her paralysed as he stalked across the floor towards her. She had resisted briefly when he started to drag her out of the room, but he had easily overpowered her mild rebellion.

She was overwhelmingly aware of his fierce strength as he carried her to the door. Raven's aura of silent menace held the whole room in thrall until Lieutenant Gregory intervened.

When Honor heard Cole order the lieutenant aside she knew she had never before heard such a genuinely dangerous note in his voice. The possible consequences of a confrontation between the two men scared her into finding some of her scattered wits.

'It's all right, Lieutenant,' she said shakily. 'The Major just wishes to discuss some, some…travel arrangements…with me.'

Lieutenant Gregory ignored her. His eyes were still fixed resolutely on Cole's face. Honor knew with absolute certainty he was going to utter a further challenge.

'Lieutenant!' Real fear sharpened her voice as she tried to gain his attention. 'I'm honoured by your concern for me—but there is no need to worry.'

'Let him go, lad,' Captain Williams drawled from nearby. 'He promised her husband he'd take care of her— and we all know how straitlaced Raven is about a little harmless dancing.'

'He promised Patrick,' Honor reiterated urgently. To her

relief, after a brief hesitation, Lieutenant Gregory stepped aside.

Cole shot Captain Williams a swift, hard glance, but he didn't say a word as he carried Honor out into the night.

Honor's heart raced with apprehension. She'd always known Cole was a physically strong man, but tonight he was demonstrating his superior strength in a staggeringly direct way. He didn't set her back on her feet once they were outside; he carried her through the streets, striding easily over the uneven ground.

She looked up at his face. There was enough moonlight to see the fierce inflexibility of his expression. He jaw was clenched, his mouth pressed into a thin line. The skin was drawn tightly across his prominent cheekbones.

Honor was nervous, but she wasn't frightened. Cole had never hurt her, and even now she felt safe in his arms. She didn't struggle because she knew it wouldn't do any good—and because she needed a little time to compose her own turbulent emotions before she faced Cole's anger. One second she was furious with his brutish behaviour—the next she was exhilarated by his fierce assertion of masculine authority. Once she'd recovered from her initial shock, she even began to feel like a heroine in an Arthurian romance.

'You should have ridden Corvinus into the party,' she said, incautiously voicing her errant imaginings. 'Then you could have carried me off across the pommel of your saddle—just like a knight in shining armour.'

'I've already done that.' He sounded distinctly unamused by her suggestion.

'Oh. Yes. But the first time I was the wrong way up,' she reminded him unwarily.

He growled wordlessly and her stomach fluttered with apprehension.

'I know my experience is limited, but I'm sure this isn't how ladies are normally escorted home from parties,' she said with false brightness.

'You are not a lady,' he said tersely.

'That doesn't mean I want to be treated like a strumpet!' Her temper flared at his insult.

They'd nearly reached Honor's billet. Cole didn't reply until he'd thrust open the door and deposited her on her feet in the middle of the dark-shadowed room.

'Then you shouldn't have acted like one,' he said brutally.

'What?' Honor was first shocked, then hurt, then blindingly furious. 'How dare you! Get out!' She picked up the first thing that came to her groping hand, which happened to be a candle-holder, and hurled it at him.

In the darkness he didn't see it coming and she heard his brief curse as it struck him. He moved quickly, a looming shape in the shadows—and then she was enclosed in his unyielding embrace.

This time she did struggle, kicking and flailing until he finally managed to pin her arms to her sides. He tightened his hold inexorably, until she was locked breast-to-breast and thigh-to-thigh against him.

Honor stopped struggling and held herself rigid. In the darkness she could hear them both panting with exertion. There was no other sound in the room.

She closed her eyes, hating herself because even after Cole had rejected her and insulted her, she still loved the feel of his hard, virile body so close to hers.

Neither of them moved for several long moments. The tension between them was so potent it almost had a life of its own. Honor's heart pounded with excitement. She seemed to have heightened sensitivity for every place where Cole touched her. She knew the instant the mood of his embrace began to shift—from anger to desire—even though he remained perfectly still. She was acutely aware of his arousal, pressed hard against her stomach.

His hands slid possessively over her hips, pulling her even more tightly against him, but he was no longer holding her prisoner of anything except their mutual desire.

Honor felt his lips brush across her hair, then her temple. Two seconds later he buried his hands in her halo of curls and pulled her head back for his fierce, claim-staking kiss. She surrendered instantly to his burning, soul-shattering passion. There was no strength left in her legs. Her whole body had been transformed into a single, liquid, fiery response to Cole's lovemaking.

Then he stopped kissing her, setting her aside so suddenly that she stumbled and fell in the disorientating darkness. She sat on the hard clay floor, dizzy, shaken, and consumed by unsatisfied arousal.

She heard Cole curse and looked up to see his silhouette standing over her.

'Did I hurt you?' he asked, his voice so guttural she barely recognised it.

She shook her head. 'No,' she whispered, too bewildered to be sure what she was saying.

She heard Cole moving around the room, but she stayed where she was, her hands pressed to her cheeks. Nothing in her previous life had prepared her for the violence and confusion of her emotions at that moment.

At last Cole placed a lit candle on the table. She threw a skittering glance in his direction, then looked hastily away.

'Get up,' he said, holding out his hand towards her.

She stood without his assistance. Her legs were shaking and she sank onto a chair beside the table.

'I'm sorry. That was...unforgivable,' said Cole hoarsely.

'What was?'

'Kissing you so...'

'Oh.' Honor covered her face with her hands. 'You mean it was all right to carry me off from the dance as if you're some kind of...of border raider—but it's not all right to kiss me afterwards,' she asked, looking up at him again.

She tried to read the expression in his deep-set eyes, but the candlelight wasn't bright enough.

'It would have been better if that hadn't been necessary,' he said grittily. 'You had no business going into the officers' mess.'

'Why not?' she asked bitterly. 'I've been invited many times before. Why shouldn't I go?'

'Because you're not a camp-following strumpet,' he said harshly. 'Or you weren't until tonight. Now you've declared open season on your virtue. Half the men there wanted you in their bed tonight.'

'None of them would have had me!' she flung at him.

'Dammit, Honor! This isn't Almack's,' he ground out. 'There are no chaperons here to protect you from your own stupidity.'

Honor flinched and turned her head away. 'I don't need one when I've got a self-appointed moral guardian,' she said rebelliously. 'Hypocritical...! You want me in your bed too!'

Cole's breathing was ragged as he stared down at her.

'Oh, yes,' he said, his voice softly feral. 'I want you in my bed. I can protect you from other men. But be warned—I cannot promise I will always be able to protect you from me.'

He turned and strode out of the cottage without another word.

* * *

'Major Raven was truly magnificent last night!' Dolores exclaimed, her dark eyes glowing with excitement as she looked at Honor. 'Is he a good lover?'

Honor gasped, and flushed with embarrassment at the question. 'Major Raven is not my lover,' she stated categorically.

'But he will be,' Dolores asserted confidently. 'He is so masterful and romantic. Every girl at the party envied you. What did he do next?'

'Nothing! I mean...it was just a misunderstanding.' Honor felt far too flustered to project her normal air of calm composure.

'What was the misunderstanding about?' Dolores pressed avidly for details.

'Major Raven feels strongly that I should return to England,' Honor explained stiffly. 'He didn't think it was...appropriate for me to...to...to dance in public while I'm still in mourning.' She was so pleased with the unexceptional excuse she'd invented for Cole's dramatic behaviour she actually smiled at Dolores, although she'd rarely felt less light-hearted in her life.

'He didn't like you dancing with other men,' Dolores cheerfully reinterpreted Honor's careful explanation. 'I thought he would kill Captain Carstairs for dancing with you! He was so *magnificently* jealous and angry!'

Honor flinched. Unlike Dolores, she found the idea of men fighting over her profoundly disturbing. After Cole had left the previous night, she hadn't been able to sleep at all. She knew—beyond doubting—that Cole had strong feelings for her. But she wasn't sure how far he simply lusted after her, and how much of his behaviour towards her was motivated by warmer, deeper emotions. Sometimes she wondered if he knew himself. In the end, it didn't matter. There was only one honourable solution to the problem for both of them. She'd known that all along. It was past time for her to return to England.

'Soon he will make you his mistress,' said Dolores buoyantly. 'He will give you a donkey—and maybe even a little bird in a cage if you wish it. And we can still be friends—even though you won't be doing my hair any more.'

'That's very kind of you,' Honor said unsteadily. 'I must…fetch some water.'

She hurried out of the cottage, desperate to escape Dolores's well-meaning chatter. She knew she should have told Dolores she would be leaving in a matter of days, but she wasn't up to dealing with the Spanish girl's protests.

Unfortunately, she escaped one interrogation only to walk straight into another. Maggie Foster was striding up the street towards her.

'Well, well, well,' said Maggie, when she was close enough to speak. 'You have been making a stir.'

Honor tried to conceal her dismay. Dealing with Dolores's uncomplicated curiosity was one thing—facing Maggie's shrewd, cynical inquisition was another.

'I'm going home in the next couple of days,' she said, trying to head off Maggie's questions. 'I just wanted to tell you—'

'That's not what I heard,' Maggie interrupted, her sharp eyes scanning Honor's face. 'I heard—'

'He didn't make me his mistress—and he isn't going to,' Honor interrupted in her turn, unwilling to hear what the scandalmongers were saying about her.

'Wouldn't take much effort on your part to change that by all accounts,' Maggie said drily.

'I am a respectable woman!' Honor said fiercely. 'I was a good man's wife. I will not demean myself by becoming anyone's mistress.'

'Patrick was a good man,' Maggie agreed hardily. 'But he wasn't—and never could have been—up to Raven's weight. Wouldn't you like to know what it feels like to have a real man in your bed for a change?'

Honor flushed, furious with the insult to both Patrick and herself. Before she could speak, Maggie raised her hand in a gesture which was both an acknowledgement of Honor's right to be offended and an apology.

'I spoke out of turn,' she said roughly. 'You do what you think is best, girl. But remember—life is short and uncertain for most of us. If you get a chance to be happy— take it.' Her eyes dropped to Honor's flat belly. 'After all, it's not as if you're going to get caught out,' she added bluntly.

Honor lifted both hands to her stomach in an instinctively defensive gesture. In over three years of marriage she had not once conceived. She'd been grateful that no child had been born into the harsh conditions of life in the Peninsula, but her barren state had also caused her much sorrow. It hurt to have Maggie fling it in her face so brutally.

Maggie cleared her throat. 'Well, I've said too much,' she said gruffly. 'You'll go your own road. You always do. You're just like your mother in that respect.'

'You know my mother?' Honor said, surprised into prolonging a conversation she really wanted over.

Maggie looked uncomfortable, then grinned to disguise her uneasiness.

'*Everyone* knows your mother,' she retaliated, with a short laugh. 'I even worked for her once—before Charlie took it into his head to try soldiering.'

'I never knew that.' Honor was startled by the older woman's revelation.

'Wasn't any call for you to know,' said Maggie shortly. 'I wouldn't have left you,' she added abruptly. 'If I'd known there were no wagons coming—I wouldn't have left you. You take this chance, girl,' she concluded forcefully. 'You can have as much fun as you want—you deserve that—and when you get back to England no one will be any the wiser.'

Honor didn't know what to say to that. In the space of an hour, two women she liked had urged her to become Raven's mistress. She pulled herself together and held out her hand to Maggie. 'You've always been kind to me,' she said. 'Right from the beginning. Thank you.'

'Wasn't anything to speak of.' Maggie hunched her shoulders. 'I'll see you maybe,' she said, and stumped off through the village.

Honor stood still, watching Maggie walk away. It had been an unsettling encounter. She'd come closer to having an argument with the older woman than she'd ever done in the past, yet she believed Maggie had her best interests at heart.

She sighed, and started to turn away, knowing that several curious pairs of eyes were watching her. The melodramatic events of the previous night would be equally entertaining to the local people and to the soldiers billeted in the village. Honor thought it was ironic that, after years of taking care to be inconspicuous, she'd managed to turn herself into a prize piece of gossip just before she left army life behind forever.

She was about to go back to the cottage when a horse and rider caught her attention out of the corner of her eye. She turned and immediately recognised Cole coming towards her.

She swallowed, and resisted the urge to run and hide. It had been difficult facing him after their moonlight kisses, but this was infinitely worse. Why the devil couldn't he just stay away from her until she was safely gone? There was nothing left for either of them to say. She was acutely aware of the watching eyes and wondered if she should walk up to the barn ahead of Cole. At least that way he could speak to her in semi-privacy. She discarded the idea almost immediately. A private meeting between them would only fuel the scandalmongers' speculations. She would tell him here, in the middle of the street, that she had the funds to get herself safely home, and absolve him from any further responsibility for her.

And that would be the end of it.

She watched as he approached her. He was riding stiffly, as if he were in pain. Something was wrong. Her eyes narrowed as she scanned his face for clues. She saw the stress at the corners of his mouth, the subtle tension around his deep-set eyes. His gaze met hers, and she knew instantly that something dreadful had happened. Her heart lurched with concern. Forgetting everything else, she picked up her skirts and ran towards him.

'What's happened?' she demanded breathlessly, as soon as she was beside him. 'What's wrong?'

He swung his leg over the saddle and dropped down in front of her. His eyes were shadowed with grief. For a moment she thought he hadn't heard her.

'Cole, what's wrong?' Honor grabbed his arms and tried to shake him, anxiety thrumming through her.

'My brother's dead,' he said, his voice bleak and cold.

For another heartbeat Honor stared at him, then she wrapped her arms around him, hugging him fiercely.

He held her close, but his thoughts were elsewhere.

'His frigate was attacked by two privateers in the

Caribbean. He was shot by a sharpshooter, perhaps only wounded—but his ship was sunk,' he said unsteadily. 'Months ago. But the news was delayed reaching England, and delayed again reaching me.'

Honor looked up at him, tears shining in her eyes.

'Take me back to your billet,' she said.

'What?'

Honor took a deep breath, strengthening her resolve. 'Don't argue,' she said quietly. 'Just do it. If it'll ease your mind, I'm not planning on seducing you.'

Despite himself, a bare hint of a smile flickered in Raven's eyes. In his grief he hadn't been aware of anything except the need to seek out Honor. He hadn't thought ahead to what he'd do or say after he'd told her his terrible news. Now she'd competently taken over the task of decision-making. For once he was willing to let her do so.

He took her up before him, just as he had when he'd brought her home from Ciudad Rodrigo. He needed the comfort of having her in his arms. Gifford Raven's death meant so much more than the loss of a beloved brother, though that was pain enough to bear—Cole was now heir to a vast inheritance and all its attendant responsibilities.

Chapter Six

In Raven's quarters they at last obtained some measure of privacy, which had been Honor's purpose in suggesting it. He sat down at the table while she made up the fire, then poured him a glass of brandy.

'I remember that you were more clear-headed in this situation than I appear to be,' he said rustily. 'I should be thinking of all the arrangements I must make—instead I keep remembering when we were boys, the jaunts we used to go on. We haven't seen each other often in the past few years—but by God, we were close then. And not just Gifford, Anthony too!'

Honor knelt down in front of him.

'Anthony?' she said softly.

'Our cousin. He grew up with us,' Cole said jerkily. 'Always helping Father with his experiments. When Father died, he sailed with Giff—to see the world. God, I keep thinking of all our foolish experiments—the jokes we played...'

'Then remember those days,' Honor said huskily. 'There is nothing else you can do for them now.' She rested her hands on his thighs, just to comfort him, nothing more. 'The arrangements can wait.'

He stared at her with grief-stricken eyes, then snatched her up into his arms. He had retained his composure in front of everyone else. He was a soldier, used to the sudden loss of friends and companions, but his grief for his brother and his cousin was different. He wept against her hair, and later he lay beside her on his bed, his head on her breast.

She stroked his hair, and thought about how vulnerable he'd allowed himself to be with her. It was hard to re-member the man who had carried her out of the officers' mess in such a rage only the previous evening.

Eventually she slipped out of his arms and set about preparing a meal for them. He ate slowly, and with utter disinterest in the food she gave him.

'I must go back to England,' he said wearily, when he'd finished eating. 'Now that Giff is dead, I cannot stay in the army. I've inherited everything. There is no one else—no one to take my place if I die.'

'Sir Gifford was in the navy,' said Honor. 'Who has been taking care of things in his absence?'

'Malcolm Anderson, my mother's younger brother,' said Cole. 'I've mentioned him before. Father died a couple of years ago. Until then, he had his hands tightly on the reins. He was a younger son too.' Cole's lips twisted ironically. 'He married late when his brother died childless. He was seventy when I was twenty—but he was still a bruising rider.'

'Are you much like him?' Honor asked, eager for any-thing she could learn about Cole.

'Not to look at.' Raven raked a hand through his sun-bleached, tawny hair. 'Except the eyes. He had jet black hair, befitting his name. He was a handsome man, well into his seventies. He was fascinated by astronomy,' Cole added, as an afterthought.

'You don't think you're handsome?' Honor said, smiling a little.

'No one ever said.' He rasped a thumb down his angular jaw. 'No one who's opinion mattered to me.'

She leant over and traced the planes of his face. 'I've always thought you're handsome,' she said softly. 'Distinguished and commanding. You're a very charismatic man, Major.'

He stared at her, momentarily distracted from his worries.

She threaded her slim fingers through his spikily disordered hair.

'You were telling me about the care of the estates,' she reminded him. 'Why didn't your brother go home when your father died?'

'He did,' Cole replied. He moved his head slightly in response to her caress. He had little experience of being petted and soothed by a woman he wasn't already in bed with—but he certainly enjoyed the sensation.

'Giff was on leave at the time,' he continued huskily. 'I didn't go back. We were in the process of driving the French out of Portugal, and I didn't get the letter telling me of Father's death until two months after the funeral. Giff had just been given his first command of a frigate. He wasn't ready to give that up in exchange for running the family estates. Malcolm and Gifford decided that, as long as I was still alive, Giff could remain in the navy. If anything happened to me, Giff would have to leave…set up his nursery. Now the duty falls to me.'

Honor's hand trembled slightly, then she continued to stroke her fingers gently through his hair. It was only hours ago Maggie had flung her own inability to conceive in her face. She had never harboured much hope that she might have a future with Cole. Now she knew there was a very practical reason why she would never be a suitable wife for him.

'Will Miss Morton enjoy a large family?' she asked steadily.

'Honor…' Cole's eyes were full of silent pain when he looked at her.

'I know what you must do,' she interrupted him softly, laying her fingers against his lips. Her purpose in mentioning the matter wasn't to cause Cole further distress, but to reassure him. 'You've never misled me, or promised me things I cannot have.'

He reached for her, pulling her on to his lap, burying his face in the curve of her shoulder. She stroked and smoothed his hair.

'I'm ready to go to England now,' she said, smiling a little sadly. 'When do you wish to leave?'

Cole's hold on her tightened. A muffled, wordless exclamation escaped his throat. She was warm and soft and loving in his arms—stirring a deep painful yearning for something he couldn't have. But he also felt confused and unfamiliar with himself. He was used to being in control but, by weeping in her arms, he had displayed weakness and vulnerability to Honor. She'd finally agreed to go home, but it was hardly a victory for him. He knew she was doing exactly what she wanted to do.

He lifted his head, hunger for her—and his need to reassert his authority—destroying his few remaining scruples.

He kissed her, his mouth hard and demanding on hers. He wasn't in the mood for tender love-play. His teeth bit firmly at her lower lip, then sucked on it. She gasped and quivered. He responded by thrusting his tongue into her mouth, unequivocally claiming her as his. She opened for him, trembling and submissive beneath his passionate on-

slaught. Impatient to claim his full victory, he drew back
and started to undress her.

Honor let him, her hazel eyes large and dark in her pale
face. She was stunned by the transition in his mood, and
the unspoken bluntness with which he'd made his intentions clear. She knew he was motivated by both more—
and less—than a simple desire to make love to her. His
heart and soul were being pulled in many directions and
she was to be his brief respite from the troubles that surrounded him.

A knot of apprehension tightened her stomach and
chilled her limbs. Patrick had been her only lover. Cole
was a much larger, stronger man than her husband, with
an incomparably fiercer personality. His kisses on the
moonlit ride back from Ciudad Rodrigo had been magi-
cally seductive and last night he had fought against his
own fierce passions. Tonight he was intent on conquest.

He gave a raw sigh when he finally held her naked in
his arms. Then he laid her on the bed and unceremoniously
stripped off his own clothes.

She stared up at him, her heart racing with a confusing
combination of emotions. The candlelight threw shadows
which emphasised the strong definition of his lean, powerful body. He was a magnificent, virile man. Despite her
misgivings, excitement began to overwhelm her doubts.
She'd never before had an opportunity to look so openly
at a man—and never one so devastatingly well formed.

Her eyes explored him half-shyly, half-eagerly. His
shoulders were broad and powerful. His arms and chest
firmly muscled. His stomach flat and hard, his hips narrow...

Her eyes lingered and she swallowed, her mouth dry.
There was no doubting Cole's desire, or his intentions towards her. She looked up to meet his eyes—and caught

her breath at the raging fire which darkened the blue almost to black.

She shivered, telling herself not to be so foolish. She was no longer an inexperienced virgin, and she'd hadn't been this nervous the first time with Patrick! She'd never loved Patrick the way she loved Cole. She'd never dreamed about Patrick the way she dreamed about Cole...

So why was she suddenly so scared?

Fierce consuming need pounded through Raven. He had wanted Honor for so long—wanted her, yet denied himself. Tonight she belonged to him. His hot, possessive eyes devoured her slim, trembling body. He wanted to drive away all thoughts of the problems that beset him. He wanted to banish Patrick completely from Honor's soul. He wanted to hear her cries and moans of surrender to *him*.

Scalding heat blurred his vision and nearly destroyed his self-discipline. He dragged in an unsteady breath, dredged up a measure of self-control—and realised he was looming over Honor like an avenging warrior.

He lifted his gaze to her face, and at first he could not interpret the unfamiliar expression in her eyes. It was not an emotion he associated with Honor, and it took him a few baffled moments to recognise it as apprehension.

Remorse and frustration slammed through him. He didn't want her frightened surrender, he wanted to touch her soul, the way she'd touched his. He took several more ragged breaths and lay down beside her.

Honor wasn't quite sure what she'd been expecting, but not the surprisingly gentle kiss with which he teased her lips. She liked it, so she kissed him back. She laid her hand against the hard muscle of his arm and felt the shudder which shook his body at her lightest touch. She realised then that he was holding his passion in check for her sake, and her fear vanished. She slipped her hand up to his shoulder and pulled him closer.

He dipped his head, tracking warm kisses down the side of her neck, across her collarbone, until he found her breast. He caressed her sensitive nipple with his tongue, swirling around it with provocative circular strokes as it hardened in his mouth. He bit gently, then harder, then soothed it with his lips—except that Honor had never felt less soothed in her life.

Cole was stimulating feelings she'd never known before, creating deep aches inside her body which demanded satisfaction. She clutched at his shoulders, randomly moving her hands against his body.

Raven was in a hurry, but it was a matter of pride as well as love that Honor should be as eager for him as he was for her. He kissed and caressed her breasts until she was whimpering beneath his ministrations, her hands fluttering helplessly against him like butterfly wings. In a corner of his passion-hazed mind he was glad that she was too flustered to touch him more purposefully. Her random caresses aroused him unbearably. If she knew the power she possessed over him, she could strip him of all control. Like hot, dry tinder, he would ignite at the merest spark.

He kissed her stomach, glided his hand along the outer side of her leg, skimming across her thigh. Honor had never felt so hot, so sensitive, so sensually aroused by the lightest touch on her skin. Patrick had never made love to her like this, never propelled her to the same breathless, wonderful heights of sensation. Filled her with such an ache…

Cole's hand brushed teasingly across her blonde triangle of curls, then his fingers dipped lower—and deeper—in the most shockingly intimate caress Honor had ever experienced.

'Ohh…ohhhh…' A moan whispered from her throat.

Her muscles clenched, her legs closing instinctively against his exquisite, outrageous exploration of her most private flesh.

'Hush, sweetheart, let me.' His own voice was thickened by barely contained passion.

He took her breast in his mouth again, teasing her achingly hard nipple with his tongue, then tugging at it with his teeth. Burning currents of glorious sensation pulsed through her body, peaking where his clever fingers and mouth pleasured her. She was storm-tossed with aching ecstasy…painful yearning…

He moved over her, his big body covering hers. She opened passion-hazed eyes to stare up at him. The angular planes of his face were harsh with rigidly controlled desire. She could feel the brutal tension which gripped the whole of his muscular body. Wild emotion blazed in his eyes. He braced himself on his arms and thrust steadily into her, filling her with his fierce, hard masculinity.

'Honor!' he groaned, her name ripped from his lips.

She clutched at him, her fingers digging deep into the muscles of his arms. He held still for a moment longer, then he finally surrendered to his own overpowering need for fulfilment.

She was caught in a swirling maelstrom of overwhelming physical and emotional passion. Every urgent stroke of Cole's muscular body thrilled and stimulated her further. His earlier lovemaking had excited her so much that she matched him thrust for thrust, as demanding and wild in her need for him as he was in his need for her.

Her body clenched in an explosion of stunning rapture, closing around Cole in a deep caress. She cried out in ecstasy, and heard Cole's deep voice mingle with hers, as his own body shuddered in fierce release. He lowered his head and nuzzled her neck—then bit, open-mouthed, at her shoulder.

Her head lolled away from him. She was almost too sensitised and satiated to bear his touch. He had destroyed every preconception she'd had about what it meant to make love to the man she loved.

With a tremendous effort Cole lifted himself away from Honor and rolled to one side, pulling her into his arms. She melded bonelessly against him. He rested quietly, letting his heart rate and breathing return to normal. Gradually he became aware that Honor's skin was slick and damp beneath his idle caresses, and the room was not particularly warm. He manoeuvred them both under the covers and closed his eyes, welcoming the pleasant drowsiness which claimed him. He sensed that Honor was also drifting close to sleep and he was smugly pleased that she had been so thoroughly and satisfyingly exhausted by his lovemaking.

Cole woke an hour later to discover Honor still in his arms. His erotic dream had not been a midnight fantasy after all. His first emotion was one of overwhelming satisfaction and contentment—but then he remembered the events that had led up to this moment.

Gifford's death was a deep wound that only time could ease. It also had consequences which Cole found almost too painful to contemplate. He had spent his entire adult life in the army. He didn't want to leave it now. It was ironic, he thought bitterly, he'd been so determined to send Honor home before the next campaign season—and now he wouldn't be part of it either.

Honor.

He instinctively tightened his hold on her. She stirred and muttered in her sleep. He relaxed his grip, stroking her shoulder soothingly. She sighed, and settled against him.

He had broken the most important promise he had ever made to himself about Honor O'Donnell. He felt a twinge of self-recrimination—but not as much as he should have done under the circumstances. In the quiet shadows of night he could not regret holding her in his arms, her naked flesh warm against his.

But he wasn't being fair to her.

He stroked gentle circles on her shoulder and, for the first time, seriously considered the possibility of making her his mistress. Such arrangements were common. Captain Williams lived openly with Dolores in Spain, but he had a wife and children at home in England. Many men who'd never ventured so far afield maintained more than one household. As long as the affair was conducted discreetly, no one raised an eyebrow.

Cole contemplated a future in which he divided his time between his estates, his wife—and Honor. His gorge rose at the mental picture he'd painted. Honor deserved better than that. So did Bridget, if it came to that.

He felt the familiar anger and frustration growing within him at his predicament. But as he continued to caress Honor almost absentmindedly, he also experienced a new sense of resolve. Like it or not, he was going back to London and, for the first time in four years, would not be forced to conduct his personal business at long distance.

He drew in a deep breath, careful not to disturb Honor, and exhaled it slowly, welcoming the renewed sense of control.

His thoughts drifted to his father. For the first forty-two years of his life, Edward Raven had been a younger son, content to pursue his interests in astronomy, natural history, and scientific innovation. His dalliances with women had been limited and undemanding, far removed from the rumbustious couplings which had characterised his older brother. Then he'd been thrust into the same situation which now faced Cole.

Sir Edward had taken a young bride with the practical aim of safeguarding his inheritance—and fallen deeply in love with her. He set about exploring every aspect of his sweet Eleanor with the same enthusiastic, dedicated and somewhat innocent curiosity with which he studied the night sky. He'd been devastated when she'd died soon after Cole was born.

For the rest of his life, his cheerful personality had been sustained by his pride in his sons, his fascination with the latest scientific advances—and his absolute certainty that one day he would be reunited with his beloved Eleanor.

Sadness filled Cole as he realised neither his father nor his brother would ever meet Honor. He deliberately increased the pressure of his caresses, seeking the sweet distraction from grief she offered.

Honor woke slowly, warm and languid in her lover's arms. The muscled shoulder beneath her head was both familiar and strange to her. Memory suddenly flooded back. Her skin burned with embarrassment at her abandoned response to Cole's lovemaking. She had lost all control—allowed him to do things to her...wonderful things...

Unconsciously she rubbed herself against him, as she remembered the way he'd made her feel.

Wonderful things—but perhaps she should have retained some self-awareness, a worried voice whispered in the back of her mind. She'd let him master her completely, yet he belonged to another woman. The more she gave to him, the more fully she would be destroyed when he left her.

Cole rumbled deep in his chest and she realised he was awake. He slid his hand, butterfly light, into the indentation of her waist, over the curve of her hip, and along the outer side her thigh. She blushed again as she discovered she'd been rubbing the inner side of her leg erotically against him. He drew her leg up, and she found he was fully aroused. She tried to pull away from him, but he wouldn't let her.

'Ah, sweetheart,' he murmured, 'I thought you were never going to wake up.'

'I...' she wasn't sure what to say to him. 'Cole?' she said uncertainly.

'Mmm?' He rolled her on to her back, kissing her beneath her ear, then on her still-swollen lips. 'You can make me want you just by breathing.'

That was so demonstrably true Honor's mind immediately lost coherence. She wanted a chance to think about what had happened, possibly talk to Cole about it, but she didn't have time. She'd always known he was a man of action, she thought wildly, she just hadn't known exactly how active he could be.

Cole sent Honor back to her billet the following morning. Honor was too proud—and too unsure of herself—to protest. In the dull grey light of morning, Cole had withdrawn into himself, no longer the tender lover of the previous night. Only a few hours ago he had given her the most exquisitely passionate experience of her life—but now he was detached practicality personified.

Honor took herself and her tangled emotions back to her billet with Captain Williams and Dolores. She told them she would be leaving soon, but she didn't tell them Cole's sad news. She knew it would reach them soon enough via the camp grapevine.

Her situation was both awkward and embarrassing. If she'd stayed with Cole, at least her status as his mistress would have been clear to everyone. As it was, she knew she was the subject of an endless round of speculation. Had Raven sent her away after only one night because he found her wanting in some way? Or had Honor O'Donnell demanded too high a price for her favours?

Honor hid her own unanswered questions behind a politely expressionless face. The situation severely tried her fortitude. It was a considerable relief to her when it was finally time to leave for Lisbon.

Cole provided Honor with a riding horse for the two-hundred-mile journey. Compared to her previous experiences in the Peninsula, she considered herself to be travelling in luxury.

'You ride well,' said Cole, after watching her critically for several miles.

'Thank you.' Honor smiled tentatively at him, but he looked away without responding to her friendly overture.

She'd never known him to seem so distant. Always before she'd been able to sense the passionate emotions smouldering beneath his disciplined demeanour. Now he seemed unnaturally cool—like a polite stranger who simply happened to be travelling in the same direction for a while.

The change in him chilled Honor. Even when he'd been angry with her, she'd always felt a strong, even if intangible, connection with him. Now she sensed no warmth in him towards her at all.

They rode for miles without exchanging a word. Honor watched the changing countryside, remembering the many experiences—both good and bad—she'd had during her time in Spain and Portugal. But all the time she was acutely conscious of the silent, stiff-backed figure riding beside her.

They didn't hurry the journey, finding nightly lodgings at suitable places along the route. The first night Honor wondered briefly if Cole would come to her. But he didn't. Her fugitive hope that perhaps he'd simply been protecting her reputation over the past few days withered. They were among strangers now. No one would have known, or cared, what they did. Cole obviously regretted that moment when he'd allowed grief to overpower his declared intention not to have her.

Honor held her head high, and pretended she didn't care.

It wasn't until they'd covered over two-thirds of the journey that Joe prompted Cole to speak of his exploits early in the Peninsular campaign. Raven had carried out a variety of daring missions, including tracking the route of the French army and sending reports back to Wellington. Honor listened to the two men, fascinated by Cole's stories, but hardly daring to join in the conversation herself. She was terrified that, if she did, Cole might once more retreat into silence. But he did appear to be more relaxed and open than he had been for several days.

'I would have been scared I'd get lost,' she said at last, with total honesty.

Cole smiled slightly, his confidence in his own abilities clear. 'Not much chance of that,' he said lightly. 'Sometimes I might not know exactly where I was, but I always knew how to retrace my steps—and usually how to get from where I was to where I wanted to go.'

'You mean we aren't going to end up in Madrid by accident?' said Honor, daring to tease him. She held her breath, but Cole simply grinned and didn't bother to answer the insult.

'Do you naturally have a good sense of direction?' she queried, genuinely interested in the topic. 'Or were you given special training?'

'I had a few...educational...adventures during my boyhood,' Cole admitted. His reminiscent grin suddenly faded. For a moment his eyes were shadowed with loss, but then he roused himself to speak again. 'The 16th were stationed in Ireland for several years,' he continued. 'My commanding officer got to hear of my tendency to...roam, and decided to put me to the test. He had me sketching the countryside for him.'

'I didn't know you'd been to Ireland,' Honor said, surprised.

'I was there two years or more.'

'Strange,' Honor murmured. She'd been married to an Irishman, but she'd never visited his country. 'I'd never been further from London than Bath before we came to Portugal,' she said to Cole. 'You must have more wanderlust than I do.'

'I go where the army sends me,' Cole pointed out. 'Not the same thing at all.'

'But if you hadn't joined the army you'd have been safely toasting your toes in front of a blazing fire regardless of where the 16th or the 52nd were sent,' Honor pointed out. 'Surely that suggests you have an adventurous spirit?'

Cole didn't reply. Instead he looked away from her, scanning the vast plains of the Ribatejo with hooded eyes. Honor bit her lip, wishing she could call back her unthinking words. She was realising exactly how much Cole had lost with the death of his brother. Some men might have welcomed a respite from the gruelling campaigns, but she knew Cole wasn't one of them.

She'd been preoccupied with her own concerns and

fears for the future. Now she tried to imagine it through Cole's eyes. She knew he wasn't the kind of man to revel in the acquisition of unexpected wealth. He was too passionate and too wild to conform easily to a regulated life of fashionable domesticity. She wondered briefly if he might be tempted to find an outlet for his restlessness in the excitement of gambling—or perhaps an even more dangerous pastime. He'd come close to forcing a challenge on Lieutenant Gregory.

Honor's stomach clenched at the memory. She hastily reassured herself that that had been an unusual occasion. She'd never heard any gossip to suggest Cole was particularly prone to quarrelling with his fellow officers. Far from it—he was generally regarded as a disciplined and reasonable man, as he had been throughout their journey so far.

His temper would probably improve dramatically when she was no longer a thorn in his side. She ducked her head to hide the tears that suddenly welled up in her eyes. It was better not to think too far ahead, she decided. She'd just take each day—each hour—as it came.

Lisbon was just as Honor remembered it, surrounded by vineyards and orange groves, full of dogs and priests, and white houses with terracotta roofs. She remembered the steep, dirty streets, most of them too narrow to accommodate a carriage, the iron balconies and the decorative blue tiles on the walls of the houses.

The city was crowded with officers and men from the Allied army. Further downstream at the little town of Belem there were even more men; those who could not fight, and those who would not fight—the so-called Belem Rangers.

'It's strange to be back here,' Honor said, finding comfort in reminiscence. 'When we first arrived, I couldn't believe how many priests there were—and all the garlic and oil in the cooking! Now I think I'll miss that when I get back to England.'

'And the heat and the dust and the mud and the cold,' said Raven, but he was smiling too.

'I wouldn't have missed these four years,' said Honor sincerely. 'We'll win now, won't we?' she continued, wanting his professional opinion. 'I know we had to scuttle back to the Portuguese border last year, but we've made so many lasting advances. The French are out of Portugal now for good.'

'Yes, they are,' Cole agreed. 'I think the next push will drive the French back to their own border—out of Spain. Dammit!' His fists clenched abruptly, but then he forced his hands to relax. 'We'd better find some lodgings,' he said curtly.

They found rooms at an inn which was popular with British officers. Cole was irked to discover they'd likely have to wait several days for the packet boat. He left Honor discussing arrangements for their baggage with Joe and the inn servants and went out, intent on working off some of his restlessness striding up and down the hilly streets.

He felt as if he had an important puzzle to solve, but he didn't yet have all the pieces in his hands. He needed to get back to London, to speak to Malcolm Anderson—and to see Bridget Morton. He also needed to find an unexceptional way of providing for Honor while he dealt with all his other problems. He had no intention of showing his hand by openly setting her up as his mistress before he had a full picture of the situation.

But Honor had been unusually quiet—submissive

even—since the morning after their night together. It unsettled him. He was used to her squaring up to him and
arguing virtually every point with him. But when he'd suggested she return to her usual billet that morning, she'd
gone without a murmur.

He'd made the suggestion only in the rather vain hope
that they might have escaped the eagle-eyed attention of
the gossipmongers. Once it was obvious that had been
wishful thinking, he'd ridden over to see Honor, intending
to ask her to stay with him until they left. But she'd been
so coolly polite, and so intent on discussing only the practical details of their forthcoming journey, that he'd left his
invitation unsaid.

Perhaps she regretted her night with him, and wanted
only to forget her fall from virtue. The possibility appalled
him—but he was hardly in a position to try to change her
mind.

He was not in a good mood when he returned to the
inn. His mood didn't improve when he discovered Honor
was already on friendly terms with several other guests at
the inn. He would have preferred a more anonymous departure from Portugal.

But Honor was chatting happily to an infantry captain
and a young lady who, even to Cole's untutored eye,
seemed to be dressed in the height of London fashion. It
occurred to him for the first time that Honor was still
dressed in the same style as the local peasant girls. He'd
never been particularly interested in what Honor wore—
as long as her clothes were warm enough—but he had a
feeling this was the kind of situation most women would
find distressing.

He felt bad that he had put Honor into an awkward
situation. He should have realised she would need more
suitable clothes once they arrived in Lisbon. He knew she

would never ask for his help, she was far too proud. But when he scanned her face for signs of discomfort she looked perfectly relaxed.

'Hello, Major,' Honor greeted him with a welcoming smile. 'This is Captain Robert Bell and his wife, Lavinia. Mrs Bell and I both attended Miss Goodwin's seminary in Bath. Major Cole Raven,' she introduced him to her guests.

'How do you do?' Cole forced a smile to his lips as he shook the captain's hand. The last thing he wanted to do was make polite small talk with complete strangers, but Honor quite clearly expected him to be sociable.

'I was so thrilled when I discovered Honor—I mean, Mrs O'Donnell—was staying at the inn,' Lavinia Bell said, with a mixture of shyness and enthusiasm. 'Meeting an old friend makes Lisbon seem so much less foreign.'

'Have you only just arrived?' Cole asked, dredging up a response.

'A couple of weeks ago,' Captain Bell replied cheerfully. 'We'll be leaving to join my regiment shortly.'

'Mrs O'Donnell has promised to give me lots of advice before we go,' said Lavinia eagerly. 'I could not possibly have let Robert leave me behind, but I don't want to be a burden to him on the march.'

'You could never be a burden to me,' Robert declared, smiling at his wife fondly.

Cole observed her with a more judicious eye. He decided she looked like a cross between a sparrow and a kitten. A sweet little doll who wouldn't last five minutes on campaign.

He was just about to point out the hardships that lay ahead of her when Honor smoothly intervened.

'I'm sure you'll adapt very quickly,' she said to Lavinia. 'And Captain Bell will help you.'

'Of course I will,' said Captain Bell lovingly.

Cole frowned, uncomfortable with this public display of mawkishness. To his relief Honor directed the conversation on to other topics. Cole sat back and listened. He'd never before had an opportunity to observe her company manners under what amounted to drawing-room conditions, and he was impressed. She was poised and charming, and she knew how to maintain a light flow of conversation which was neither tedious nor controversial—a skill that Cole knew he lacked. He frowned thoughtfully, then schooled his features into an expression of polite interest before anyone questioned his momentary abstraction.

'Miss Goodwin was very proud of you,' Lavinia said suddenly to Honor.

'Proud?' Honor sounded amazed. 'Of me? Are you sure?'

Goodwin? Cole was momentarily at a loss until he remembered the name had been mentioned in connection with the seminary at Bath. He still knew very little about Honor's early life, but it was highly unusual for a serving maid's illegitimate daughter to attend a seminary for young ladies unless she had some kind of patron. He wondered again about her reluctance to return to England. Was there some particular person she was avoiding? If so, and they meant to cause Honor mischief, they would now have Cole to contend with.

'Oh, yes,' Lavinia said confidently. 'Miss Goodwin *was* proud of you. She never came right out and said so to us girls. But I know she kept copies of all your reviews. And she slipped off to London once to see you perform—I heard her telling Miss Denby about it. She said you were a fine example of what clear-thinking, perseverance, and natural talent could achieve.'

'Good heavens,' said Honor weakly. 'I had no idea.'

Cole saw her glance briefly at Captain Bell. It was the first time she had shown any sign of uneasiness during the conversation. To Cole's relief, the captain seemed unperturbed by Honor's colourful past.

'I'm sorry I never had a chance to see you perform,' Bell said to Honor. 'I wonder?' He glanced from Cole to Honor. 'Would you care to dine with us this evening?'

Cole looked at Honor, and realised she was leaving it up to him to make the decision. He accepted as graciously as he could, and was then relieved when the Captain and his wife decided to go for a stroll before eating.

Honor looked at Cole when they were alone, and for the first time in days felt a sense of connection with him. She started to laugh, she couldn't help it.

'What?' He seemed rather affronted by her amusement, although she saw a rueful gleam lurking in his blue eyes.

'You'd rather have faced a French bombardment than a hour of civilised conversation,' she teased him.

'That was hardly obvious,' he replied austerely. 'Was it?' he added with uncharacteristic doubtfulness, and she went off into a gale of laughter which only added to his discomfort.

He sighed, but he didn't look too disgruntled. In fact, she had the strangest impression that he was pleased with her.

'Did you explain how you come to be travelling with me?' he asked, a few moments later.

'Yes.' She sobered quickly. 'I told them you'd promised Patrick you would ensure I got safely home to England. And I said that, since you have to return yourself, you'd decided it would be most sensible for me to travel under your protection.' She hesitated a moment. 'I didn't tell them exactly *when* Patrick died,' she admitted.

Cole raised his eyebrows, but to her relief he didn't make a sardonic comment.

'I just didn't want our stories to conflict,' she said awkwardly.

He grinned wolfishly. 'Don't worry,' he assured her. 'You are undoubtedly the most contrary, self-willed woman I've ever met—but your secret's safe with me.'

'Where are you going?' Cole demanded the next morning.

He'd returned to the inn from an early morning walk, just in time to catch Honor on her way out, clutching a packet of documents.

'To the bank,' she replied briskly, swallowing back her nervousness. She'd been hoping to complete her errand without Cole's interference, but she held her head up and refused to be daunted by his disapproving frown.

'Why?' he demanded.

'Because I need money to pay for new clothes and my passage home,' she replied.

He stared at her through narrowed eyes. 'Who gave you the money?' he growled dangerously.

'I *earned* it!' Honor snapped, her apprehension overtaken by indignation at the implication of his question. She tried to walk around him. 'Excuse me, please,' she said coolly. 'I have business to conduct.'

'How did you earn it?' Cole barked, easily blocking her attempt to pass him.

'By performing that "preposterous nonsense" you despise so much,' she said tartly. 'You're in my way,' she pointed out.

Cole moved aside, then fell into step next to her. Honor walked quickly, although she knew she had no chance of outpacing Cole. She was frustrated by the situation which had developed. She'd known he would be difficult when he found out she had some money of her own. But she'd really hoped to complete her errand at the bank before they had this confrontation. She'd meant to work round to the subject gently, but it was too late for that now.

'You stopped acting years ago,' Cole said tautly.

'But I was always careful with my money,' she replied. 'And Patrick wouldn't let me spend it when we were married. Now it will see me safely home to England.'

When Cole didn't respond, she glanced sideways up at him. He was grim-faced, but apparently had no intention of continuing their dispute in public. She wished he would let her deal with the arrangements on her own, but she knew there was no prospect of that.

An hour later she had to admit that his formidable, uniformed presence had expedited matters. It turned out that Cole had his own business to conduct at the bank, but it aggravated Honor that the bank official handed over *her* money into Cole's safekeeping. Despite her indignation, she didn't debate the matter until they'd returned to the inn.

'Please keep back my fare for the packet boat,' she said, struggling to keep her voice pleasant and reasonable. 'I will take the rest.'

Cole smiled unpleasantly. 'This is a significant sum of money,' he said. 'What are you planning to spend it on?'

'Clothes,' said Honor briefly. She knew she ought to be more placatory, but she was annoyed by Cole's attitude. She'd respected Patrick's wishes while he was alive, but she'd worked hard for her money and she was entitled to spend it how she liked.

'All of it?'

'Of course not! I don't know why Simpson sent so much. But it doesn't matter.'

'You mean you don't intend to pay for your room here? Or the food you've eaten at my table? Or even the clothes you're currently wearing?' Cole taunted her. 'I seem to remember when I first gave them to you, you were determined to repay me for them. What happened to your all scruples about accepting charity?'

Honor stared at him, wondering how she could disentangle this situation.

'Some things are gifts, not charity,' she said quietly. 'Sometimes it's hard to tell the difference. If you wish me to pay for my room or these clothes, I will do so.'

Cole spun on his heel and took two hasty strides across the small room. He turned again and stared at her, fire flashing in his blue eyes.

'All this time you *knew* you had the funds to get safely home but you let me worry about you...think up alternative arrangements for you...' he accused her savagely.

'No! I mean, I told you I'd paid my own way since I was seventeen,' Honor replied wildly. 'I *told* you I didn't need your help. You just wouldn't believe me.'

'You do need my help,' Raven snarled. 'Having money doesn't mean you're safe—it just makes you prey to even more hazards.'

'I'm hardly an heiress!' Honor exclaimed. 'I have enough money to dress myself and get home. After that, if I'm not to starve, I'll have to find work.'

'You lied to me.' Cole's voice had sunk to a deadly purr.

'I didn't lie. You never asked.' Honor flung up her hands in dismay. 'Why are we arguing?' she demanded. 'What does it matter if I can pay my own passage home? It doesn't change anything else.'

'What else?' Cole growled menacingly.

'You're going home to be married!' Honor cried recklessly. 'You're angry with me because I'm not so poverty-stricken that I have no choice but to become your mistress.'

Dead silence followed her words.

'You presume a lot,' Cole said harshly. 'Have I asked you to be my mistress?'

Honor swallowed and looked down, trying to hide her shimmering eyes.

'Your money.' He put it down on the table. 'I'll pretend you didn't insult me with your offers of payment.'

'I was taught to pay my own way,' Honor protested helplessly.

'It's too bad you didn't remember that months ago and tell me your true situation immediately,' Cole retorted icily. 'Then it would have been a relief to know the truth—now it's an insult.' He strode out of the room, leaving Honor to brush the tears from her cheeks with trembling fingers.

Chapter Seven

Cole strode down to the edge of the Tagus, then turned to walk along the river bank towards Belem. He was furious with Honor. He'd gone back to the inn with the intention of taking Honor shopping for new clothes—and instead she'd floored him with the news that she was going to the bank.

He was outraged with her dissembling—but he was also hurt. He'd worried about her safety, but she hadn't trusted him with the truth. She'd lied to him by omission, and there was still so much he didn't know about her. Sometimes there seemed to be such harmony between them, but other times she withdrew from him as if he were her enemy. He hated it when she did that. His body lusted after hers, but his happiest memory was the night she'd confided in him on the moonlit ride back from Wellington's grand ball. He wanted her to trust him like that all the time.

He emerged from his introspection to discover he'd drawn level with the ornate little fortress of Belem, sturdily defending the Tagus. He stared out at the waves beating against the fort, a symbol of Portugal's past greatness, and felt his eyes burn with a bitter sense of loss. He was grieving for his brother, his cousin, his profession—the future he'd wanted for himself.

He also wanted Honor. And sometimes, even when she was standing right in front of him, she seemed completely out of reach.

Cole spent the rest of the day away from the inn. He wasn't in the mood to make polite conversation with Captain Bell and his wife, or any of the other guests. In the evening he went to the theatre, which he considered to be a form of self-inflicted misery in keeping with his temper.

The entertainment consisted of a play, followed by a ballet and a musical farce, all of which Cole considered badly performed, not that he regarded himself as an expert. He scrutinised his surroundings critically. The building was quite impressive, but dingy and badly lit. It reminded him of Honor's past experiences in the most negative of ways. How could she ever have put herself on public display in such a place? There was no magic here—just sordid and grimy reality.

By the time he returned to his room it was very late, and he was in a foul temper. He summoned a servant to drag off his boots, then stripped and flung himself on his bed.

In the next room, Honor listened to Raven bang around, occasionally swearing to himself, before he eventually fell silent. She knew he was in an evil mood. She felt utterly miserable herself. She hated it when they argued. She'd been trying desperately not to cry, but she couldn't contain her tears any longer. She buried her face in the lumpy pillow to muffle her sobs.

Matters hadn't much improved between Raven and Honor by the time they boarded the packet boat. Honor had, rather stiffly, tried to apologise for not telling Cole earlier about her money. She'd meant to be more conciliatory than she was, but he was so frozen and aloof that her words withered on her tongue. She had thought he was reserved on the journey to Lisbon, but now she could sense nothing from him but a chilly dislike of being in her company.

The packet boat was designed for speed. The Captain was under official orders to run rather than fight if he spotted a French ship. The quarters were cramped to say the least. Honor was assigned a cabin not much more than four feet by six feet, with no porthole. Like all the cabins, it opened on to a central dining room in which the passengers ate and, at least in theory, relaxed.

It was, thought Honor, a recipe for frayed tempers—particularly when one of the fellow passengers was the morose Cole Raven. Fortunately, he spent most of his time on deck. Joe Newton, whose presence might have helped relieve her sense of isolation, had remained in Lisbon until he could arrange to bring Corvinus back to England.

Cole stood on deck and ran his fingers through his salt-sticky hair. He welcomed the fresh breeze in his face, even though it was seasoned with a fine rain which dripped steadily from his oilskin cloak. He hated being cooped up in the cramped, stuffy conditions below decks. The packet was making good progress. Clouds obscured the stars, but the weather wasn't stormy, and the wind was in their favour.

Cole was soul-weary in a way he had never previously experienced. Honor had made no further attempts to mend the breach between them. Superficially, she seemed calm and at ease with her circumstances, but the dark circles under her eyes were more noticeable every morning. She could not avoid speaking to him completely, because that would have drawn attention to their private dispute—but she confined herself to addressing only the most commonplace remarks to him.

His fists clenched on the wooden rail. He wanted to mend the situation between them, but he didn't know how. He was no longer burningly angry with Honor's deception—but he was confused by it. He understood and even admired her fierce independence. But why hadn't she told him she was not completely impoverished? It would have been an excellent way of curtailing his interference in her life. And then he wondered why she had stayed so long in Spain. He knew from their trip to the bank that she could have left months ago. He'd gained the impression that she wasn't anxious to return home—that perhaps there were even people in England she was trying to avoid. But had she also had a compelling reason to stay in Spain? A reason that no longer existed as soon as she knew that Cole also had to return to England?

He felt a flare of hope at the possibility—followed by a sense of frustration because the cramped, public conditions of the packet boat made any kind of intimate conversation difficult to achieve. He didn't want to wait until they reached Falmouth before he made his peace with Honor.

There was a light, tentative touch on his arm. He spun round, lurching a little with the motion of the boat. Honor was standing in front of him. It was too dark to see her expression, her face was just a pale oval beneath the black shadows of her shawl.

'Cole?' she said uncertainly.

She was so transparently afraid of her welcome that his heart twisted in pain.

'I...I'm sorry,' she said unsteadily. 'Please, I don't know what...'

'Sweetheart,' he growled, unbelievably relieved that she had come to him.

He reached to pull her towards him and realised his oilskin cloak was drenched with rain. Honor had just come up from below, she was still relatively dry. He opened the cloak with shaking hands and hauled her inside, hard against his chest. He closed the cloak around her and stood with his back to the rain, bracing himself firmly so they were both secure. She trembled against him, her head tucked under his chin. He thought she was crying, but he couldn't hear above the creaking of the ship and the waves lapping against the hull.

'I'm sorry,' he whispered brokenly. 'God, I'm so sorry, Honor. I'm sorry. Forgive me, sweetheart.'

He cradled her close, one hand stroking the soft woollen shawl which covered her head, careful not to pull it back and expose her to the cold.

'No, *I'm* sorry,' she murmured against his neck. 'I should have told you...'

'Shh.' He drew her shawl away from her face just enough to kiss her forehead. 'Sweetheart...darling...' His thoughts lost all coherence. The only thing that mattered to him was that Honor was back in his arms, where she belonged. He didn't care about the rights and wrongs of their argument, only that they were reunited.

Honor lifted her head. Cole kissed her cheek, then he found her lips. His face was cold and wet from the rain. She could taste sea-salt on his lips—or was it her tears?

'Honor,' he breathed warmly against her skin.

His lips were so gentle on hers. He was apologising with his kiss, Honor thought, confused, shaken—and so relieved. Her mouth puckered and she started to cry in earnest, racked by so many tumultuous emotions.

'Oh, love…'

He tucked the shawl around her to keep her warm and held her so tenderly she cried even more.

'Raining inside and out,' he murmured eventually, wryly humorous.

She gave a hiccough of laughter. 'I'm sorry.'

'You can cry all night if it'll make you feel better,' he said, his good humour much restored.

She manoeuvred awkwardly and managed to find her handkerchief. She dried her eyes and blew her nose, all within the cramped but wonderful shelter of his arms, and relaxed against him once more.

He took the opportunity to brace his back and feet even more securely against the fittings of the packet boat. Now he was only likely to be thrown if the boat pitched very violently. Apart from the rain it was a calm night, so he didn't anticipate a problem. It wasn't a particularly comfortable position for him, but he didn't care about that. Honor was snug in his arms, and there was nowhere else for them to go. There was no privacy below deck unless they shared a cabin—which was out of the question. At least on deck the darkness and the inclement weather gave them some protection from their fellow passengers. And most of the crew seemed to take their lead from their taciturn captain, who never said a single word when none sufficed.

'I don't like this boat,' said Honor.

'I'm not overfond of it,' Cole admitted wryly.

'And I can't stand the rest of the passengers,' she added roundly.

'They don't seem too bad,' Cole said cautiously. It occurred to him he'd never heard Honor express an open dislike before. Despite her occasionally caustic comments, she was usually far more likely to make the best of a situation.

'That's because you haven't been spending any time with them,' she informed him, sounding more like her old self. 'I spent nearly all of yesterday in my cabin—in the dark—so I wouldn't have to listen to them arguing about the conduct of the war. I wouldn't mind if they knew what they're talking about, but they don't—apart from poor Lieutenant Soper, of course. Wine merchants and orange sellers!' she muttered wrathfully. 'Hah.'

Cole smiled into the darkness and hugged her close, understanding that she was talking herself back into her familiar self-confidence. God, it was good to have her in his arms again. The wind was cold against his rain-beaten back, but Honor was dry and snug against his heart. He adjusted the cloak, so that no stray draughts could destroy her comfort, and relaxed.

Honor closed her eyes. She was so tired. She thought perhaps they ought to go below, but Cole hadn't said anything and she was so cosy in his arms. He'd called her love. He'd never called her that before. She smiled contentedly.

Cole felt her body soften into sleep. He'd positioned himself so that it was possible to support her slight weight, even though they were still standing more-or-less upright. He wasn't about to let her go now.

He loved her and he thought that perhaps she... cared...about him. He wanted to ask her if she stayed in Spain to be near him, but he didn't. He couldn't quite bring himself to say the words—besides, her actions were pretty strong evidence that he was important to her. Perhaps, when they'd had a little more time together, she might even come to love him as she'd loved Patrick.

Cole decided that possession was nine-tenths of the law—and right now, as she slept in his arms, he had possession of her. He knew he couldn't do without her. The mere thought of never seeing her again after they reached England was unbearable. In his first wild grief at Gifford's death, Honor had comforted him with such loving generosity. Now he wanted her support for the gruelling task that lay ahead of him.

Cole knew he would have to learn from scratch how to manage his large inheritance, which included estates and properties in several counties as well as houses in London and Bath. He was confident he could master the practical, business skills required for his new role—but he was daunted by the endless round of obligatory socialising he would have to undertake. With Honor by his side it would all be so much easier. She would make a beautiful and gracious lady of the manor.

But first he had to deal with Bridget Morton. Cole set himself to think about the problem logically. If he withdrew from the betrothal he knew he would almost certainly be faced with an action for breach of promise. Bridget's father was not the man to leave such an insult unavenged. The scandal would rebound on both Bridget and Honor.

Cole's knowledge of polite society was limited by the years he'd spent overseas with the regiment; but he was sadly aware that, even if he married Honor without a scandal, there might be places in his world where she wouldn't be welcome; hostesses who might not be prepared to receive her into their refined and respectable drawing rooms. He wasn't sure. She'd been a respectably married woman for several years, but she had also been a well-known actress. Her success might depend not only on her own deportment, but on whether she was sponsored by one of the fashionable leaders of the *ton*. Cole had no desire to cut a dash in society, but he had no idea how Honor felt on the subject. He didn't want to spoil her social prospects by making a mess of disentangling himself from the Mortons.

He was also concerned about Bridget. He could barely remember what the woman looked like, but he'd effectively taken ten years of her life. Her family had considered her promised to him since she was eighteen. Now she would be denied the husband and family she had counted on and, at the age of twenty-eight, she would be thrust back on to the marriage mart. It was a cruel position for any woman to find herself in. Cole didn't care about the probable law suit, but he did care about his responsibility to Bridget. He listened to the creak of timber and sail and tried to think of some way he could make restitution to her.

What did women want? he wondered. He'd always assumed it was obvious—a husband and children. But his experience with Honor was teaching him not to take the obvious for granted. Perhaps Bridget didn't really want a husband. It would have been perfectly reasonable if she'd asked him to take leave of absence after her period of mourning had ended. There had been opportunities during the past three years when he could have returned to England to marry her. But she'd never asked him to do so. Perhaps she was no more eager to marry him than he was to marry her. Perhaps he could arrange for her to have what—or who—she really did want.

Unfortunately, he barely knew her. He was bad at writing letters, and hers were so dull he usually did no more than skim through them—just to make sure he didn't miss anything awkward like the fact that someone had died.

'Honor?' he murmured. She was more than half-asleep. He hoped she'd stay that way while she answered his question. 'Sweetheart?'

'Hmm?' she roused drowsily.

'If you could have anything you wanted, what would it be?' He thought if he asked Honor, it might give him a clue about Bridget. They were both female, after all.

'What?' she tensed a little. 'Why?'

'It's all right, you can say anything,' he assured her, suddenly nervous and regretting he'd spoken. Perhaps he wouldn't like her answer. He'd been thinking about Bridget, he'd forgotten he hoped for a different kind of answer from Honor.

'Really anything?' she hesitated.

'Really anything. I won't get angry,' he promised, although his apprehension was growing. 'Pretend there's a magical moon in the sky,' he suggested, remembering her comments on the night of the ball in Ciudad Rodrigo, and hoping the memory would put her in a romantic mood, 'lighting a path of silver for the packet boat to sail along to take you to your dreams.'

'Ohh,' she sighed wonderingly. 'You said you were too prosaic to believe in magic.'

'But you're not. Tell me, sweetheart,' he urged.

'Oh.' She still hesitated and he had to squash his growing anxiety. Unconsciously his arms tightened around her, silently compelling her to speak.

'If I could have anything I want,' she said tentatively. 'I'd...I'd marry you. And you'd take care of me...and—and I'd take care of you...' There was a hint of defensiveness in her voice, as if she expected him to argue the point with her. 'And we'd...love each other, of course and—if I could really have anything I wanted—we'd have babies.' She whispered the last words almost inaudibly.

Cole was tremendously, gloriously happy. He grinned into the rainy darkness like a fool. He didn't care that water was dripping down his neck, or that cramp was threatening to strike in his right leg any minute. Honor wanted to marry him and have his babies. The erotic images her words conjured up, not to mention her warm body pressed closely against his, aroused him so much he was instantly ready to try and fulfil her wish.

She stirred against him, obviously aware of the direction his thoughts had taken.

'Shush.' He held her close. 'Don't wiggle about like that, sweetheart, you'll only make things worse,' he teased her, amusement and tenderness mingling in his voice.

'Cole!'

Her face was covered by the shawl, but he suspected she was probably blushing within its protective shadows. He'd forgotten how shy she could be sometimes.

'Go back to sleep,' he soothed her.

'You can't be very comfortable,' she protested softly.

'I've never felt better in my life,' he assured her.

'You liked my answer then?' she whispered.

'Yes, love.'

'I wish there really was a moon,' she murmured.

Cole thought wishing on moonlight was unlikely to produce a satisfactory solution to their problems, but he didn't say so. Unfortunately, gratifying though Honor's answer had been for him, it hadn't got him any closer to solving the problem of Bridget Morton. In fact, if Honor was anything to go by, it seemed women really did want a husband and children. How the devil was he going to find Bridget a replacement husband—one who would take care of her properly?

Cole's father had intended Cole to receive the family estate in Oxfordshire on his marriage to Bridget. Now Cole had inherited everything, he decided to give Bridget the Oxfordshire estate as her dowry, as recompense for the years she had spent waiting for him. That was all very well and good, but he could hardly palm her off on some half-pay officer looking for a comfortable billet. Cole wanted to find Bridget someone who would love her as much as he loved Honor.

The rest of the voyage continued more happily for Cole and Honor. Cole didn't tell Honor about his plan to marry her and find a substitute husband for Bridget Morton. It didn't seem quite right to discuss marriage with one woman while he was still betrothed to another. And he also wanted to present Honor with a complete solution to their problem—like a magician pulling a rabbit out of a hat. Fortunately, she seemed reasonably content now that the rift between them was healed, and as disinclined as he was to talk about the future.

'Well, really, this is more pleasant than the voyage out,' said Honor the following afternoon, retracting her comment about not liking the packet boat.

'God, yes!' Cole winced at the thought of the misery she must have endured on the troopship.

The soldiers would have been crammed into the transport with eighteen inches of space each, wives along with their husbands, and no privacy for anyone. There was rarely adequate ventilation or even enough water to clean the decks on the ships. Cole, like many officers, was incensed by the foul conditions in which his men were forced to travel. He couldn't bear the thought that Honor had been exposed to such horrors.

'How did you manage?' he asked tightly.

'Well, it was a terrible shock. I'd never stayed in the barracks with Patrick—I couldn't bear to,' she confessed. 'They were so grim. I found lodgings nearby.' She sounded guilty. 'But when we knew Patrick was going to Portugal, of course I had to go with him.'

'You drew a ticket "to-go"?' Cole asked.

Only six wives per hundred men were officially allowed to accompany their husbands abroad.

'Yes.' Honor smiled a little at the memory. 'We were all crowded in the pay-sergeant's room. All the wives had to pull a ticket out of the hat to see if we were "to-go" or "not-to-go". It's strange, but you could tell if people liked a wife who was going—or if they didn't. There was a groan when Maggie Foster pulled her "to-go" ticket.'

'I'm not surprised!' Cole exclaimed. 'That woman's voice could saw through oak—and she drinks more than three men put together.'

'She was always kind to me,' said Honor quietly. 'When I pulled my ticket, no one knew whether to groan or be pleased,' she continued, smiling wryly. 'They didn't know me, you see.'

'If you hadn't pulled the ticket, you'd have stayed behind,' said Cole. And I'd never have known you, he thought.

'Of course not,' Honor replied briskly. 'I'd have taken a berth in a packet boat and followed Patrick. The army couldn't have turned me away if I'd made my own way to Portugal. I wasn't,' she added quietly, 'quite like the other wives who couldn't afford that option.'

She lifted her chin, almost as if she was waiting for Cole's criticism.

'The transport?' he prompted her, not wishing to pursue the subject of her financial independence. He also wasn't sure he wanted to hear about her misery on the outward journey but, at the same time, he wanted to know everything about her.

'Oh. It was horrible!' She shivered, wrapping her black shawl more tightly around her.

Cole had been ridiculously pleased that she'd gone on

wearing the shawl he'd given her, even though she had bought clothes in Lisbon more suitable for travelling in England.

'I'd never seen anything so…so *vile*,' Honor continued, her eyes clouded as she remembered the filth and stench on the crowded decks.

Cole wanted to put his arms around her and tell her she didn't need to tell him any more, but she was locked in her memories.

'Patrick was seasick, poor dear,' she said, gaze focussed on the past. 'I was beside myself. I didn't know what to do.'

'But you made it to Portugal,' said Cole tautly, torn between his irrational jealousy at Honor's undoubted affection for her late husband, and his distress at the idea she'd been so upset she hadn't known what to do—in his experience Honor *always* knew what to do. She should never have had to endure such indignities, he thought fiercely.

'Well, yes.' Honor threw Cole a cautious glance. 'I did a deal,' she confessed, as if she was admitting to a serious crime. 'Every day I gave all our rum ration to the ship's cook, and he lent me a tarpaulin we could throw over one of the ship's boats. That's how we travelled to Portugal, in relative privacy and luxury. And,' she added, determined to make a clean breast of everything, 'I did some mending and made some money on the journey.'

She looked sideways at Cole, not sure what kind of reception her confession would get. She'd always been proud of her ability to cope, but now her pride was less important than her need for harmony between them. Their time together was so limited. She didn't want it to end with an argument.

He grinned and pulled her towards him, giving her a

quick, hard kiss. Even though it was years ago, he was relieved she'd had a reasonably comfortable voyage to Portugal.

'Cole!' She pushed him away, embarrassed at being kissed when others might see them.

'I'm *glad* you managed things so well,' he declared cheerfully.

He didn't mind her taking care of Patrick, he'd spent years watching her do so. But when Honor was his wife, *he* would take care of everything. He was quite certain he would never need Honor to protect him—because he would be protecting her. Still...

'Would you carry me—if I was wounded?' he asked suddenly, and immediately wished the words unsaid. It was a stupid, weak-minded question that made him sound like a sentimental fool.

He regretted asking it even more when she didn't respond with the unequivocal 'yes' he'd expected.

She studied him carefully, little tendrils of hair blowing around her face where they'd escaped from the shawl. He tucked them back inside. Black wasn't her colour. It drained her complexion and made her look paler and more fragile than she was.

'Your legs are so long,' she said at last. 'I'd need a hatchet.'

'To cut my legs off?' He thought she had to be joking, but she looked so serious.

'No, to make a pallet,' she responded seriously. 'What do they call it? A travois. To drag you. I don't think I could carry you, Cole,' she said earnestly. 'Patrick was shorter than me, and you're so much taller—and heavier. But I'm sure I could drag you. Horses can pull much heavier weights than they can carry. I'd have to rig up some sort of harness to go around my chest, only...I haven't got a hatchet.'

Her hazel eyes were wide with anxiety that bordered on panic.

Cole couldn't believe how devastated she was by her lack of foresight. He'd done no more than ask her a hypothetical, slightly ridiculous question, yet it was as though she really was back on the muddy retreat from Salamanca, desperate to find some way of transporting him to safety. He was unbearably moved by her evident distress.

'Sweetheart.' He pulled her into his arms, heedless of witnesses. 'We're in the Bay of Biscay,' he reminded her gently. 'You don't need a hatchet.'

'No.' She pushed back a little, still in his embrace, so that she could look up at him. 'If it seems as if we're about to sink, you must instantly come and find me,' she instructed him fiercely.

She was so solemn and intense it didn't occur to him to laugh.

'Yes, love,' he agreed tenderly.

'If we're involved in a skirmish with a French ship, you will naturally want to take part in our defence,' she informed him. 'But if there's a storm in the night, you must come to my cabin. I would come to you, but you're sharing with Mr Fuller. I don't want to drown with Mr Fuller,' she concluded, frowning fiercely.

'Sweetheart!' Cole just managed to suppress an inappropriate grin. 'We're not going to drown, we're going to Falmouth. But, if the worst comes to the worst, I promise I won't let you drown with Mr Fuller,' he assured her.

'Thank you.' Honor leant against him for a moment, then she gave a horrified gasp. 'Oh, Cole, I'm so sorry!' she exclaimed. 'I forgot about Gifford.'

'That's all right.' Cole stroked reassuringly the black

shawl which covered her head. 'Luckily Giff didn't have to drown with Mr Fuller either.'

There was a pause, then Honor said uncertainly, 'That's a terrible thing to say.'

Cole didn't miss his brother on a day-to-day basis—he hadn't seen him for several years—but he missed the idea of Gifford being somewhere in the world. He wished his father and his brother could have known Honor. He was sure they would both have loved her.

He was still amazed by how earnestly she'd answered his hasty question about carrying him. And she didn't want to drown with Mr Fuller! It wasn't her preference in drowning companions which surprised him, it was the fact that she'd given so much thought to the various situations they might encounter. He'd known she sometimes had romantic ideas about magic, but could she really visualise all kinds of possibilities so clearly she could almost be living through them? Cole couldn't imagine what that might be like. He only knew Honor had said that believing in magic made life bearable.

At one time he'd been impatient with her fanciful notions, but now he knew they were an integral part of her character. And they were also part of the reason he loved her so much, even when she was driving him crazy with her wayward opinions. He decided it was understandable that she worried about the future, but he promised himself he would give her the security and happiness she needed to dream of her magic in peace.

Honor found a bittersweet pleasure in the rest of the trip to England. Cole had held her in his arms and called her 'love', and he'd asked her what she wanted most in life— but he hadn't talked about their future. She couldn't believe that she'd unwarily told him she wanted to marry him and have his babies. The memory mortified her—and thrilled her, when she recalled his very positive physical response to her wish. There was no doubt her words had pleased him. She was sure if they had been in a more comfortable, private location he would have made love to her—as tenderly and passionately as he'd made love to her the first time. Sometimes she dreamed of his lovemaking and woke hot and aroused to find she was alone. Other times she couldn't sleep at all, but simply lay wakeful, her body aching for his touch.

She thought Cole probably meant to keep her as his mistress after his marriage. It wasn't a role she'd ever intended to play for any man—but she knew it was the only way she could be part of Cole's life. He needed a woman who would give him heirs, and she couldn't do that. The knowledge hurt her bitterly. She'd regretted her childless state when she'd been with Patrick, but then it had only been a dull background sadness. Now she yearned to have Cole's baby—and the knowledge that she couldn't was a constant, grinding pain.

She didn't ask him any questions about the future because she was afraid of his answers. Instead she lived only for the moment. But she was careful what she said. She didn't want to provoke his anger again when they had so little time together.

One day Cole asked Honor if she was ill. She looked at him in surprise.

'No,' she replied immediately 'Why?'

'You haven't seemed yourself,' he said frowning.

'Oh. No, I'm fine,' she assured him.

He scowled worriedly at her. He could sense a difference in her, despite the fact that they were no longer at odds with each other. She was quieter, more subdued. Perhaps she was worried about their future. He wanted to tell her he'd sorted it all out, but he hadn't yet, so he didn't.

He stroked her hair back from her face. 'We'll reach Falmouth soon,' he said.

'I know.' She smiled at him.

He glanced round quickly, checking to see if there was anyone close by. Then he pulled her into his arms and kissed her. When he released her he was pleased to see the glow of colour in her cheeks and a new sparkle in her hazel eyes.

'Everything's going to be fine,' he assured her. 'You'll feel much better when you've got solid ground beneath your feet again. And I'll feel much better when I can…kiss you…as slowly and as often as I like.'

Honor blushed at his unmistakable meaning and lowered her eyes. Cole found her shy self-consciousness so endearing he kissed her forehead, his lips gently caressing her skin.

Later he got out Bridget's letters. If only he could stay awake long enough to re-read them, they might give him a clue as to what kind of husband she would like.

'December…we went to the Pump Room yesterday to drink the waters. Mrs Howarth introduced me to Mr Sedgeworth, a gentleman from Derbyshire who is trying to breed an improved sheep. He was most interesting on the different kinds of wool required for different purposes. I had no idea…'

Cole skimmed through a tedious description of staples and sheep breeds.

'This morning I bought a new hat. Mrs Howarth says it

is most becoming. I trust you are comfortable in your winter quarters…'

'January…this morning I bought a new pair of gloves…'

'February…I bought a length of beautiful muslin…'

Bridget needed a rich man who'd enjoy taking her shopping, Cole decided, exasperated.

'March…I visited Hookham's circulating library in Bond Street. I wished to read one of Mrs Radcliffe's romances, but Mrs Howarth says it is better to live one's adventures, rather than to read them…'

Good for Mrs Howarth, Cole thought. Who the devil was Mrs Howarth? The name sounded familiar. He decided she was probably the woman Bridget's father had hired to be her companion after her mother's death.

Cole laid the letters aside. Bridget clearly hadn't known of Gifford's death when she last wrote. Even now her next letter was probably on its way to him in his winter quarters.

He had little more sense of her after reading her letters than he'd had before. She drank the waters in Bath. She went to Almack's. She visited fashionable shops and libraries in London. She did a lot of shopping. The best he could come up with for her was a man who enjoyed Town life and had a high tolerance for boredom.

But he knew that wasn't fair. No one trying to get a sense of him from his letters would be able to deduce much more than that he could read and write and he was in the army.

For the first time it occurred to him what a difficult situation Bridget had been placed in, trapped in an endless engagement to a man she hardly knew, who had been unflatteringly slow to tie the knot. Had he inadvertently made her the object of pity or gossip? Perhaps he was fortunate that her letters were dull rather than demanding. He decided he must find her a man of wealth, influence and position to salvage her pride.

The sound of the packet's gun signalling for the pratique boat woke Honor early in the morning. She dressed hurriedly and went on deck. Cole was already there, looking towards Falmouth in the grey dawn. Several other passengers joined them, as they waited for the medical inspector to declare it was safe for them to proceed.

Honor gazed at Pendennis Castle and hugged her shawl tightly against the wind. It was the beginning of May, but the early morning air was damp and cold.

'I'll be glad to get off this damn boat,' Cole muttered, and she felt even more chilled.

Cole had made it plain he wanted to make love to her at the first opportunity. But the closer they got to London, the more worried Honor was about allowing him to do so.

The Peninsula had seemed like another world. It had been easy to believe that what she and Cole did there couldn't hurt his fiancée. But now they were back in England, and any gossip which touched Cole would also touch Miss Morton. Honor knew she would have hated it if her husband had kept a mistress. In the cold—very cold—light of dawn, she finally accepted that once they were on English soil she must say goodbye to Cole. She would find her own way back to London.

The morning was well advanced by the time they landed at Falmouth. Honor took no part in the arrangements, she simply followed Cole's lead. For the first time in her adult life, she allowed somebody else to make her decisions for her. She could imagine the scornful comments her mother would make if she knew, but Honor didn't care. She would be fending for herself soon enough.

'Thank God we're shot of that lot.' Cole breathed a sigh of relief when they'd finally seen the last of their fellow passengers. 'I didn't fancy rattling around in a mail coach all the way to London with any of them!'

Honor forced a smile. She'd been impressed by the efficiency with which Cole had separated them from their erstwhile travelling companions. She was grateful for the privacy of the private parlour he'd arranged for them in a comfortable inn.

'I think you're being a bit hard on poor Lieutenant Soper,' she said placatingly, guiltily aware that her only real grudge against her fellow passengers had been their unwitting intrusion into her limited time with Cole. 'Besides, I don't think he can afford the mail.'

'I can't imagine why anyone would want to,' said Cole frankly. 'The only time I ever travelled in one of those contraptions it made me ill!'

'And you a hardened campaigner!' Honor tried to match his bantering tone, but she found it difficult to speak at all. She was numb with awareness of what she must soon say to him. Would he accept her decision—or would their time together end with another argument? She couldn't bear it if the last words Cole said to her were angry.

Cole grinned. 'Fortunately I was never asked to go into battle under the Post Office colours. I'll hire a post chaise and we'll travel to London like civilised people. It's not as if we're in a hurry.'

'No.' Honor's throat tightened so much she couldn't swallow.

His joke about the Post Office colours heightened her sense of alienation. Cole was no longer wearing his uniform. It was strange to see him in a sober black coat and neatly tied cravat. He had already taken the first steps towards his new life. She looked away because she didn't want him to see how upset she was. This parting would be hard enough without her tears to make it worse for both of them.

'Sweetheart?' Cole crossed swiftly to her side. He took her cup and saucer away from her and dropped on one knee beside her chair.

She looked down at his strong hands holding hers in a comforting grasp and blinked quickly.

'Everything will work out,' he promised her earnestly. 'Don't worry, love. I'll take care of everything.'

He'd called her love again, Honor thought distractedly. How could she say goodbye to him when he called her love?

'I can't share you with Miss Morton,' she said jerkily. 'I don't think Miss Morton would want to share you with me. It's not right for you to take me to London, Cole. If Miss Morton finds out, it will hurt her. It would hurt me,' she whispered. 'I will make my own way to London,' she concluded, in a firmer voice. 'It's time we said goodbye.'

Chapter Eight

'No!' Cole's response was emphatic and immediate. 'Under no circumstances! You're coming to London with me.'

Honor shook her head, trying to keep her lip from trembling. She couldn't bring herself to meet his fierce eyes. 'You made a promise to Miss Morton,' she whispered doggedly. 'I've been thinking and thinking…when we were together in Spain and Portugal, that was a different place and time—perhaps what we did was excusable. But now you're home. Now you have to honour your obligations to Miss Morton and your family.'

Cole stared at her without speaking. She risked a glimpse at his austere, angular face. She knew he was in the grip of strong emotion, but she couldn't read the expression in his eyes.

'I don't mean to criticise you,' she said anxiously, suddenly afraid he thought she was condemning his behaviour, when she knew she was as much to blame as he was, 'only to make sure that you understand that I know that from now on things will have to be different.'

His stern expression relaxed into a smile. 'That was a very complicated sentence, sweetheart,' he said tenderly.

'You look tired. I think you ought to rest before we set off. We'll spend the night here, and leave in the morning.'

'Cole!' Honor was exasperated, frustrated, and perilously close to tears. 'Weren't you *listening*? We can't do this any more. *I* can't...' Her voice faltered.

In one smooth movement Cole rose, picked her up and sat down with her on his lap. She was startled into forgetting what she'd been saying. He lifted her so easily. She loved the feel of his arms around her, his muscular thighs beneath her—but she was annoyed at how easily he'd dismissed her heartfelt concerns.

He kissed her cheek. 'I won't ask you to share me with Bridget,' he murmured against her sensitive skin. His lips teasingly caressed the corner of her mouth.

Despite herself, her pulse began to race and she turned her head to meet his kiss. As she did so, she felt passion rise within him. They were alone now, just as Cole had wanted them to be on the packet boat.

His mouth was hungry as he found hers. One hand cupped the back of her head, the other rested on the curve of her hip, holding her possessively against him. She clutched his lapel like an anchor, so overwhelmed by the force of his desire she felt dizzy. But this was *not* what she'd planned, and his patronising response to her painful effort to do the right thing frustrated her.

She dragged her mouth away from his and wrenched herself out of his arms so forcefully she nearly fell on the floor. She stumbled upright and turned to face him.

'Don't!' she gasped, her cheeks blazing with indignant colour.

'What the devil...?' He thrust to his feet, shock and anger in his own angular features.

'Don't treat me as if I'm half-witted and vaporish!' she snapped at him.

'I did not!' Cole was caught up in a furious maelstrom of confusion and thwarted arousal.

'Yes, you did!' she interrupted him fiercely. 'You acted as if neither my opinions nor my morals are important to you. *"That was a very complicated sentence, sweetheart"*,' she mimicked bitterly. 'How pea-brained do you think I am?'

'Don't be so melodramatic!' Cole retaliated irritably, fighting to control his temper. His physical frustration, combined with his awareness of the problems which beset them, threatened to boil over into furious words, scalding them both in the process.

He clenched his fists, bit back the hasty words he was about to utter, and glared at Honor.

She was standing at bay on the other side of the parlour, defiance, anger and hurt in her hazel eyes. Her blunt announcement that they must part had shaken him, and the determination with which she'd wrenched herself out of his arms felt like the most bitter rejection.

'I can't be your mistress,' she said breathlessly. 'I won't! And you made a promise to Miss Morton...to your father. You have to honour that.' Her mouth twisted at what she was saying. She was, after all, named for such honour.

Cole watched her for several long minutes as he battled to clear his mind and control his emotions. He struggled to calm his ragged breathing and reminded himself that, despite her apparent rejection of him, Honor loved him and wanted to be his wife. A breach between them would drive her close to despair. He knew that, if he walked out of this room before they'd resolved their quarrel, Honor would be gone by the time he returned.

'I did not intend to belittle your worries,' he said stiffly, as he realised that was exactly what he'd done.

He hadn't wanted to admit that he still didn't know exactly how he was going to extricate himself from his engagement, so he'd brushed aside her anxieties instead.

'But you did,' she said steadily. 'And you behaved as if my integrity wasn't important to you.' She touched her slender fingers to her lips, still swollen from his kisses.

Cole opened his mouth to point out she hadn't objected to his lovemaking before, but left the words unsaid. He dimly remembered she seemed to think it made a difference that they were back in England. He thought the distinction was spurious. Morally it made no difference where they were, but on a practical level she had a point. Gossip about his conduct in England might be potentially more damaging to his cause than rumours about his activities in the Peninsula.

'I've never doubted your integrity,' he said quietly. 'Or your courage, or your determination to do the right thing.'

He saw her eyes suddenly glisten with unshed tears and a knife twisted in his gut. This whole mess was hurting Honor badly, and it was his duty—his eagerly embraced duty—to take care of her. The trick, he thought suddenly, might be to take care of her without offending the fierce independence he'd always admired in her. Like a man taming an unbroken horse, he must coax her to submit to his will without breaking her spirit.

'What are your plans?' he asked calmly.

He knew he ought to tell her his own intentions, relieve her of some of her anxieties, but he still hoped to present the solution to her on a platter, gift-wrapped and beribboned—Bridget Morton's marriage to a rich and eligible bachelor.

Honor drew in a deep breath.

'I must…Patrick wanted me…' she began.

Cole tensed. He still suffered occasional moments of jealousy when Patrick was mentioned.

'My mother,' Honor said more strongly. 'I must make peace with my mother.'

'Peace?' Cole questioned sharply.

'I have not spoken to her, or had contact with her, since Patrick was coerced into the army,' said Honor steadily. 'She condemned me for marrying him, I blamed her for...' She didn't finish.

'I see.' Cole's eyes narrowed. 'You mean to stay with her?' Honor's mother was a rather shadowy presence in his mind. 'Is she... Will you be welcome?' He'd been about to ask whether the former maidservant was respectable, but decided it would be unnecessarily provocative.

Honor smiled without amusement. 'Susannah will be pleased to see me,' she said. 'She'll be *so* pleased to see me,' she whispered, and her lips twisted.

She was very close to breaking down, Cole realised, and pressed on quickly with his questions.

'Is your estrangement from your mother the reason you didn't want to come home?' he asked gently.

Honor swallowed convulsively, and then nodded. It was clearly hard for her to speak.

'Is there anyone else?' Cole asked. 'Anyone else you could stay with who would make you welcome?'

He'd meant to ask Malcolm Anderson to find somewhere suitable for her to stay while he sorted out his affairs, but it might be better for all concerned if Honor wasn't living under the protection of his family while he dealt with the Mortons.

Honor brushed her hand across her eyes.

'Lady Durrington,' she whispered. 'She's been writing to me ever since I left England. I have an open invitation to visit her...'

Cole scoured his mind for any memories of Lady Durrington. As far as he could recall, she was a respectable woman, married to a man of unimpeachable integrity. Lady Durrington would do nicely, Cole decided.

'Very well,' he said firmly. 'We'll go to London. You'll make peace with your mother, but it would probably be best if you stay with Lady Durrington—'

'I couldn't impose upon her!' Honor protested, interrupting.

'I'm sure she won't find it an imposition,' Cole assured her, his voice softening.

'I'll have to find something to do,' Honor said distractedly, taking a few paces around the room. 'I must find work.'

'As an actress?' Cole kept his voice calm. He'd wondered if Honor's love of the theatre would be another bone of contention between them. He didn't want his wife performing on the public stage.

'No, no,' she said impatiently. 'I enjoyed acting, but the rest...'

She stopped pacing and turned to gaze at him, the energy which had briefly animated her dissolving. Strands of her sun-bleached hair fell in disarray around her slim face. She looked lost and bereft, and very fragile.

'I want you to be happy,' she said, her voice faltering. 'I know you'll be a good landlord and...husband. And I'll be fine, too. There aren't any wolves in England.' She tried to smile.

'Honor.' He closed the distance between them, careful not to provoke her into withdrawing. He put his hands gently on her upper arms. She stood frozen for a heartbeat, her eyes wide, her nostrils flaring slightly—then her self-control melted. She wrapped her arms around him, holding him tightly.

Cole closed his eyes, unutterably relieved to have her back in his arms, and praying she wouldn't push him away again. He stroked her hair, careful not to turn the comforting embrace into something more passionate.

Honor knew it was foolish to cling to Cole this way, but she couldn't help herself. When he'd calmly asked her to tell him her plans she'd felt as if her world had crumpled around her. She'd expected him to argue with her, not let her go so easily. It wasn't reasonable to expect him to love her as much as she loved him, and it was certainly better for him that he didn't—but it hurt so much.

Perhaps he'd never meant to make her his mistress, now they were back in England. She went cold at the thought. She'd made a complete fool of herself over him yet perhaps, even now, he was growing impatient with her clinging-ivy behaviour. She loosened her grip on him and tried to step away, but he wouldn't let her.

'Sweetheart…' he brushed his lips across her forehead '…I won't ask you to be my mistress, but that doesn't stop me loving you—or wanting to care for you.'

She sagged against him, so limp with relief she would have fallen if he hadn't supported her. He'd never before told her he loved her so explicitly.

'I thought…'

'What?' He cradled her tenderly.

'I don't know,' she admitted, resting her head on his shoulder. 'I've never felt so confused.'

'Trust me,' he murmured. 'I'll try not to compromise your principles, but I can't let you go, love.'

'You must.' She lifted her head to look at him.

'Shush.' He glanced around, then guided her to the chair he'd located. He made her sit down, then dropped on one knee beside her. 'You love me,' he said confidently. 'I know you do. You'd rather drown with me than Mr Fuller.'

Honor smiled waterily. 'Don't make fun of me,' she begged.

'I'm not.' He held her gaze steadily, his eyes very serious. 'Sweetheart, I know what sacrifices you are prepared to make for me. I am now a wealthy man. It is no sacrifice at all for me to provide for you. No—' he squeezed her hand as she started to protest '—I know how independent you are. But I want—I need you to realise that this is just as important to me as your independence is to you. I can't bear to hear you talk about finding work, or wondering whether your mother or Lady Durrington will make you welcome in their homes. I will give you a home of your own. And you will never have to worry about scandal, because you will never have done anything to provoke it.'

Honor stared at him, hearing the absolute sincerity in his voice. Her immediate instinct was to reject his offer, but then she hesitated.

'It would be cruel to deny me this,' he said quietly. 'You would drag me to safety on a travois if I were wounded. Even if we never make love again—even if we never see each other again after we reach London—let me provide for your future.'

Honor gazed at him, caught in the intensity of the moment. Her father had pawned his watch for her mother, she remembered suddenly, and her proud, independent mother had accepted the gift. Love meant taking, as well as giving.

'Yes,' she whispered.

'Thank God.' Cole's response was soft and heartfelt. He leant forward, briefly resting his head against her slight breasts. In his own mind, she'd just agreed to be his wife— he had no intention of providing a home for her he wouldn't share—but he wasn't yet ready to tell her that.

She looked down wonderingly at his dishevelled hair and smoothed it gently with her fingers. It was a curiously intimate moment, even though she was sure they'd just said goodbye. She wondered if this was how it had been for her parents. Feeling so unimaginably close, yet knowing they had to part.

Cole lifted his head. 'We'll go—' He broke off, suddenly perplexed. 'Does your mother live in London?' he asked, realising again how little he knew of the woman.

Honor smiled slightly. 'Yes,' she said. 'So does Lady Durrington.'

'Good,' said Cole briskly. 'We'll travel to London by easy stages. You can speak to your mother, and either stay with her or Lady Durrington, while I make arrangements.'

'I'm not sure if we should travel together,' Honor protested, although her fingers tightened around his. 'Miss Morton…'

'Patrick asked me to take care of you,' Cole reminded her, ruthlessly disposing of her objection. 'I don't think he'd want me to abandon you in Cornwall. We don't have to draw attention to ourselves, sweetheart.'

'Well…' Honor hesitated.

'Let me worry about Bridget,' said Cole firmly. 'Now, you do look tired, love. I think we should stay here tonight, and set out tomorrow morning—unless you're in a hurry to talk to your mother.' He smiled at her.

'Let's leave tomorrow,' said Honor, after a few seconds' thought.

The journey to London tried Cole's self-control to the limits. He was alone with Honor in the privacy of the chaise for hours, yet he felt honour-bound not to take advantage of the situation. Of course, if he told her he was going to marry her, that would put things in a different light—but what if it took him a while to extricate himself from his betrothal to Bridget Morton? He was looking forward to Honor bearing his child, but not before he'd got his ring safely on her finger. On the other hand, perhaps it wasn't absolutely necessary to deal with Bridget before he married Honor.

He sat watching her, opposing arguments scrambling around in his tormented mind, as they trundled on their way to London.

He was so close, Honor thought, twining her slim fingers together in her lap. She was breathlessly aware of his virile body only inches from hers. She could feel his burning gaze resting on her face. She risked a quick glance at him, flushed scarlet at the intensity in his vivid blue eyes, and turned to stare blindly out of the window. How on earth would they make it to London? Even on the packet boat she hadn't been this aware of him. But she hadn't been truly alone with him since the day he'd told her Gifford was dead, since the night she'd spent in his quarters—in his bed.

Her heartbeat quickened as she remembered the way he'd made love to her—and her own abandoned response to him. Her fingers locked painfully as she tried to control the direction of her thoughts. It was only safe to think of such things when she was alone—not when she was sitting less that three feet away from the man who made her blood burn.

She was so hot, her skin felt as if it were on fire. Her mouth was dry. She licked her lips and heard his quick intake of breath. Sensuous heat began to throb in her body. Her breasts tightened, her knees trembled. She was glad she was sitting down, if she'd been standing she would have melted in a pool of desire beside his glossy boots.

Which would have put her in an excellent position to admire his powerful thighs and—

She bit her lip, desperately trying to hold back the hysterical giggle which threatened to overcome her. She was
on her way to London, to give her beloved to another
woman—why on earth was she dangerously close to being
overcome by rampant lust?

She kept her gaze firmly on the passing countryside but,
out of the corner of her eye, she saw him move closer to
her. A flame of excited desire leapt through her. She
caught her breath, her body coiled with eager anticipation
of his touch...and the coach rolled sedately into an inn
yard.

Honor could have screamed with frustration. Cole's
muffled curse as he sat back suggested he felt the same
way.

They delayed at the inn long enough to eat a midday
meal. Honor chewed thoughtfully on a mouthful of delicious pie, and decided she'd better come up with a distraction if they were to reach London with their integrity
even minimally intact.

'I could have a small shop,' she announced, when they
were once more sitting in the chaise.

'A *what*?' The words shot out of Cole as if from a gun.

'A shop,' she repeated, glancing at him cautiously. His
expression was so stunned she decided it was safe to look
at him more fully.

'Why?' he demanded tautly. 'I said—'

'I know,' she interrupted, a conciliating note in her
voice. 'But I thought...that is...you said you'd give me a
house,' she said tentatively, stroking her dress smooth
across her lap in a nervous gesture. Then she saw Cole's
eyes following the movement of her hands and hastily

folded them demurely. 'If you gave me the means to set up a shop, I would feel less beholden,' she continued, 'and, if I made a success of it, you might even get some return on your investment. Profit, I mean,' she said brightly. 'But, of course, it would take me a while to establish a successful business,' she added warningly.

She looked up and discovered Cole was staring at her with his mouth open. After a few seconds he closed it and swallowed.

'What—what kind of shop?' he croaked.

'A dress shop.' She smiled at him, already warming to the idea. 'I'm an excellent needlewoman, and in the past I always designed my own gowns. I don't know much about business, and it would take a while to build up a fashionable clientele, but I'm sure Lady Durrington would be pleased to recommend me.'

'You want to become a modish dressmaker?' Cole said disbelievingly.

'But, Cole, I can't be your pensioner for the rest of my life,' Honor said earnestly, responding to an objection he hadn't yet made explicit.

'I don't want you to be my pensioner!' he declared passionately, then stopped abruptly, as if he'd caught himself short before he said any more.

'I know...I know you want me to live in comfort and security,' said Honor quickly. 'I understand, and I'm so grateful. But I wasn't brought up to be a well-dressed ornament, Cole. I must have rational occupation to fill my time—especially since...especially...' Her voice faltered.

Especially since she believed she would be alone, Cole realised. His rising anger abated. Sometimes he found Honor's determination to be self-sufficient frustrating, but he also respected her for it. He had no intention of letting her set up her own business, but he was quite happy to play along with her for now.

'Are you sure you want to be a dressmaker?' he asked, frowning at her. 'You would have to flatter your empty-headed customers. Not an easy task for someone of your...outspokenness.'

'I can be tactful!' She flushed indignantly. 'And not all women are empty-headed!' She rose to his bait as he'd known she would. 'And I've met many gentleman who cannot cope with anything more taxing than the set of their coat and the latest scandal.'

'So have I,' Cole agreed, aggravatingly unruffled.

She glared at him. 'You are deliberately trying to provoke me!' she said accusingly.

'Certainly not,' he denied, schooling his angular features into an expression of innocence. 'I merely wondered, since you are so at home with horses, whether you might not find blacksmithing more to your taste.'

'You think I should become a lady *blacksmith*?' Honor gasped, stunned at his suggestion. 'Getting hot and dirty in a forge? Just because I waded through the mud in Spain, doesn't mean I *like* being filthy and smelly and—'

Her eyes narrowed as she saw Cole was trying to suppress laughter.

'You beast!' she exclaimed indignantly. 'You needn't think you're going to divert me from my plans with your ridiculous suggestions. I'll be the most successful dressmaker in London. Just you wait!' She folded her arms crossly and glared out of the window.

Cole grinned. 'How will you set about it?' he asked, willing to indulge her because she'd responded so exactly as he'd known she would.

Honor looked at him suspiciously. 'I know you aren't taking this seriously,' she said.

'If it's important to you, it's important to me,' he replied soothingly.

Honor hesitated, not entirely happy with Cole's patronising manner. She was tempted not to reply to his question, but then she decided it would be more dignified if she dealt with it in a businesslike way.

'I will need to familiarise myself with the latest modes,' she said slowly, organising her thoughts. 'Then,' she began to tick points off on her fingers, 'premises in a fashionable area of London. Reliable seamstresses. The patronage of one or two influential ladies—the kind who set trends, not follow them. And the kind who pay their bills,' she added drily. She frowned. 'Men have gone out of business, waiting for the Quality to settle their debts,' she observed, tapping her fingers together consideringly. 'Perhaps I would do better to aim at a less modish and more reliable clientele. When we get to London I must look around and see what opportunities there are,' she decided.

Cole studied her, fascinated by the changing expressions that played across her face as she stared out of the window with unfocussed eyes. She was deep in contemplation, planning her future as a dressmaker. He felt a mixture of respect and discomfort at the single-mindedness with which she set about the task. He didn't like the way she could so easily exclude him from her future, yet, if he didn't tell her his true intentions, he could hardly blame her.

He comforted himself with remembering the way she'd rested in his arms on the packet boat—and the wish she'd made that night on an imaginary moon. To marry him, take care of him…and have his babies. That was what she really wanted.

Honor tried to concentrate on the practical details of her scheme, but she couldn't stop thinking how empty she'd feel when Cole was no longer part of her life. He would be married to Miss Morton. Perhaps Miss Morton—Lady Raven as she'd be then—would even come to buy a dress from Honor. Honor closed her eyes against the hurtful vision and struggled not to let her feelings show in her face.

They weren't in a hurry, and it took them three days to reach the borders of Hampshire. Three days of travelling in close proximity to Honor without touching her were enough for Cole. It was more than flesh and blood could bear to have her sitting so close and not drag her into his arms and out of her clothes. At least during the years of torment in Spain and Portugal he hadn't known exactly how rewarding it would be to make love to her. Now he knew—he remembered in excruciatingly wonderful detail at the most inopportune moments—and he wanted it again. Right now.

Unfortunately, Honor knew that, and she'd taken a moral stand not to let anything improper happen between them. Occasionally she even mentioned Miss Morton when she was particularly afraid he might be overcome with ardour.

He'd gritted his teeth and acceded to her determination to distract him. They'd talked about anything and everything—Honor knew all about Cole's childhood exploits with Gifford and Anthony, Cole knew about Honor's acting career and some amazing details about her projected dressmaking plans—but enough was enough.

'I think I'll ride beside the chaise today,' he said at breakfast on the fourth morning.

'Ride?' Honor echoed, looking at him in bewilderment. He seemed tired and on edge. 'Why?'

'Dammit, Honor!' he growled. 'I'm not used to being cooped up in a box all day. I'd rather ride.'

'*You'd* rather ride!' she exclaimed, immediately roused by his words. 'What about me? You want me to be shut up in that horrible carriage while you enjoy yourself?'

'It's a very luxurious carriage!' Cole briefly allowed himself to be sidetracked. 'Much more comfortable than the mail coach.'

'But the choice is apparently not between the chaise and the mail, but the chaise and horseback,' Honor pointed out. 'I think it's an excellent idea. Why don't you see what's available while I finish getting ready?' She stood up and whisked out of the parlour.

Cole grinned at the closing door. Until this trip with Honor, he'd had no idea how devious he could be. Before breakfast he'd already hired two fine riding horses and made arrangements for the chaise, loaded with their baggage, to meet them at an inn within easy marching distance that evening.

Honor put on the new riding habit she'd bought in Lisbon and looked at herself in the mirror. It was very plain, almost severe in its styling, but the soft moss green enhanced her hazel eyes and flattered her more than the black shawl. She smoothed her hair self-consciously, then pulled a face at herself in the mirror. It was foolish to feel so jittery and excited at the prospect of riding with Cole. They'd ridden from Ciudad Rodrigo to Lisbon without anything untoward happening, and now they were headed towards Cole's fiancée in London. It was definitely no more than an opportunity to shake off the cobwebs from the post-chaise.

She quickly packed some essential items to take with her. She was far too old a campaigner to set off, even for an innocent ride through the countryside, without at least a minimum of equipment.

*   *   *

It was a beautiful May morning. The blue sky was clear and the sun was warm and comforting. Honor smiled with pleasure at the lush green leaves all around her. Dew still sparkled on the grass and jewelled a spider's web in the hedge beside the road.

'I can hear a blackbird!' she exclaimed delightedly.

Cole smiled at her. Even though he had a foolishly sentimental attachment to her black shawl, he was pleased she was wearing something more warmly colourful. She looked poised and elegant on the grey mare he'd chosen for her.

'What a beautiful day,' she said, lifting her face to the sun. 'What a beautiful way to come home.'

'I didn't realise how much I had missed England until I came back,' Cole admitted.

'It seems odd that you're not riding Corvinus,' Honor observed. 'I hope he doesn't mind the sea passage.'

'Joe will take care of him,' Cole replied easily.

'Oh, yes,' Honor agreed. She threaded her fingers idly through the grey mare's mane. 'Perhaps I should breed horses instead,' she said thoughtfully.

'Instead of pandering to the whims of fashionable matrons?' Cole enquired, raising his eyebrows.

'I'm not completely set on that plan,' said Honor.

'I thought you were.' He was surprised.

'I was trying it out in my mind,' she said, with dignity. 'Clothes are something I know a lot about, but I also know quite a bit about horses. I could do it, I think. I have to consider all the possibilities,' she added, seeing the dubious expression in his eyes.

'So I see,' he replied drily. It suddenly occurred to him that perhaps she could contemplate such wildly different futures for herself because she didn't really want either of them. The idea cheered him enormously.

In the chaise he'd talked about his boyish pastimes with his brother, but now he started to tell her about his family estates. Eventually he admitted he knew next to nothing about land management, and he was gratified by her unhesitating confidence in him.

'I believe you'll be an excellent landlord,' she said positively. 'You know how to command men, and you know how to use each man to take the greatest advantage of his particular strengths. I often noticed it in the regiment.'

'You did?' Cole was enormously pleased, and slightly bashful at her praise.

'Yes.' She frowned thoughtfully between her horse's ears. 'I'm not sure the men felt they knew you—not the way they understood some of the officers.' She smiled mischievously and Cole suddenly realised she had an entirely different perspective on his fellow officers than he did. He was greatly intrigued but—almost—too dignified to question her further on the subject.

'They didn't know me?' he prompted her, as casually as he could.

'They did know you,' she corrected him. 'They knew the important things. They knew you were consistent and fair in your discipline and punishment. They knew you led from the front, not the rear. They knew you'd never turn sick soldiers out of their billet so you could have a comfortable night's sleep,' she added in an acid comment on one of his fellow officers. 'They knew you appreciated their efforts and their pain and suffering. That's why they gave you their loyalty and obedience.'

She turned to look at Cole, the May sunshine gilding her blonde hair.

'You don't need to know the details of tenancy agreements to be a good landlord,' she said quietly, reaching out her hand to him. 'You need to know how to deal honestly and fairly with other people. You need to be clever enough to realise when they're trying to cheat you, but you should also be compassionate when they are genuinely suffering hardship. You have all the qualities you need to be successful in your new life.'

Cole took her hand, very moved by her heartfelt testimonial.

She smiled at him. 'Another man might be contemplating what a dash he was going to cut in Town with such a grand inheritance,' she teased him gently, 'not worrying about his unexpected responsibilities.'

'Perhaps.' Cole nudged his mount closer to Honor's mare. He was enchanted by the picture she made in the spring sunshine, earnestly assuring him of his worth.

Honor felt Cole's fingers tighten around hers. The light in his eyes was warm and very intimate. She caught her breath as his gaze focussed on her mouth. He wanted to kiss her. He was going to kiss her—but it really wasn't right. They'd been talking about his inheritance. Miss Morton was part of it.

She silently urged the mare to move forward, forcing Cole to relinquish her hand. Their separation filled her with disappointment, but she was sure she'd done the right thing. Miss Morton wouldn't like it if she knew Cole was kissing another woman in the Hampshire countryside.

'What does she look like?' Honor asked abruptly.

'I can't remember,' Cole admittedly sheepishly, knowing exactly who Honor was talking about.

'You can't remember?' Honor echoed in amazement.

'It's a long time since I last saw her,' said Cole defensively. 'She's got brown hair, I think.' He hesitated. 'She's just an average female,' he said helplessly, aware his description hardly did justice to Bridget, but unable to improve upon it.

'*Average female!*' Honor exclaimed, torn between laughter and heartbreak. Cole was going to spend the rest of his life with a woman he could barely remember. 'What colour are her eyes?'

He scowled thoughtfully for a few moments. 'Damned if I know,' he admitted eventually. 'Can't picture them at all.'

'Perhaps you just aren't very observant of such things,' said Honor, looking away from him. 'What colour are my eyes?' she burst out, cursing herself for asking such a stupid question.

'Agate green and gold, with flecks of russet,' he said instantly, smiling at the back of her head.

Honor swallowed a sob at his unexpectedly poetic description of her hazel eyes. Given his prosaic description of Miss Morton she'd expected…she didn't know what she'd expected.

'What colour are my eyes?' he asked softly.

'Blue,' she whispered, still not looking at him, unable to put into words the light his vivid blue eyes illuminated in her soul whenever he looked at her. 'Schools,' she said unsteadily to change the subject.

'Schools?' Cole immediately pictured a bevy of blue-and gold-eyed children but decided that, in the present circumstances, Honor probably wasn't talking about their future offspring.

'Lady Durrington wrote to me that Lord Durrington had set up schools on his estates for the children of the farm labourers,' Honor said more coherently. 'He pays them a small allowance to attend, though of course they have to demonstrate a genuine desire to profit from the experience. He believes that everyone should have an opportunity to better themselves.'

'He's an unusual man,' said Cole slowly. 'And somewhat out of step with the rest of the world. I look forward to meeting him.'

'Meeting him?' Honor was surprised.

'Sweetheart, I'm delivering you into his wife's care,' Cole reminded her. 'It's quite likely I'm going to meet the man.'

'Oh.' She hadn't thought of that. 'I've never met him,' she said. 'I always wanted to, but somehow it was never convenient. Cole, I really don't think I should stay with Lady Durrington. I mean, I know I haven't been on good terms with Mama for a while, but I'm sure she'll offer me house-room. And if she doesn't want me, I can go to another inn. I don't want to embarrass the Durringtons or cause a scandal for you and Miss Morton.'

'Your conduct has never been scandalous,' said Cole quietly. 'Whatever scandal may arise from our situation in the future, you are not to blame, Honor. And you are not to take the weight of it upon your shoulders. Promise me.'

'I...'

He reached over and brought the mare to a standstill beside his mount. Then he looked deep into her eyes.

'Promise me,' he repeated, his voice very deep. 'Honor, I will not keep a wife and a mistress at the same time. And I will do everything I can to resolve this entanglement with as little pain and public embarrassment as possible for everyone concerned, but whatever remains is my burden—not yours or Bridget's. And I will not permit you to stay in a public inn,' he added autocratically. 'It may be best if I ask Malcolm to arrange things after all.'

Honor barely heard his last words, she was too busy struggling to divine the meaning behind his earlier declaration. Was he really implying he might end his betrothal to Miss Morton? Surely not. But...'resolve this entanglement'...? That sounded much more complicated than simply making her his pensioner and marrying Miss Morton.

She blinked and looked away. She ought to ask him to explain his meaning, but she lacked the courage. Surely he wasn't intending to marry *her*? He was already committed to Bridget. Bridget who was respectable, suitable, and could give him the heirs he needed. Even if he were free, Honor knew she couldn't marry him, because she couldn't bear him children.

'Promise me,' he insisted.

'Yes,' she whispered, not at all sure what she was promising.

Soon after midday they found a pleasant inn and ate a leisurely meal. In the afternoon they abandoned the road for less-frequented paths.

'Are you sure we won't get lost?' Honor said dubiously.

Cole raised his eyebrows at her. 'Are you doubting my sense of direction?' he asked imperiously. 'Wellington thinks quite well of it.'

'I know that,' she said, flustered. 'But I haven't got any, so if you *do* get lost, we'll probably be stuck in Hampshire for ever.'

Cole stared at her, his grin broadening as he contemplated her admission.

'You haven't got a sense of direction!' he exclaimed. 'Good God, woman! You're a seasoned campaigner. You must have some. Otherwise you'd have lost the regiment when you went out foraging for food.'

He knew that, like most of the soldiers' wives, Honor had been adept at discovering and purchasing food from the local people. There were a number of army regulations restricting the practice, but Honor had always managed to escape the sharp eye of the Provost Marshal.

She sighed. 'I did—twice,' she admitted ruefully. 'Once Maggie Foster found me, and once one of the goat boys rescued me. Why do you think I stuck to the regiment so tightly?'

'Honor!' Cole had been joking, but now he was thoroughly shaken at the possibility she might have been cast adrift in hostile surroundings. 'I didn't know…'

'Of course not!' She laughed at herself. 'I wasn't going to advertise my stupidity. After the second time I did a deal with Luis. Whenever I needed to forage, he delegated care of his goats to Pedro and came with me. He's a natural scout—and he has a wonderful sense of direction.'

Cole looked at her, remembering how often he'd seen her in the company of the ragged Portuguese goat boy. They'd made a formidable team. Until the last retreat to Ciudad Rodrigo, Honor had always managed to find food for Patrick and herself.

'Do you know how to read the stars?' he demanded abruptly.

'No,' she admitted.

'Have you got a compass?'

'No.' She bit back a smile at his frown.

'Can you read a map?'

'I don't know,' said Honor cautiously.

'Our maps of the Peninsula were very unreliable at first,' Cole observed, 'but you should have some idea of how to use one. Good God, woman!' he said forcefully. 'What is the point of rigging up a travois, if you don't know which direction to drag me in?'

'I was hoping you'd regain consciousness long enough to tell me,' Honor murmured, secretly delighted that he'd entered so fully into her imaginings.

'I'll start teaching you about the stars tonight,' said Cole decisively. 'In the meantime…' He paused, momentarily stumped at the prospect of teaching Honor a skill he instinctively possessed.

'Which way's London?' he asked.

'Um...that way,' Honor pointed hopefully along the narrow track they'd been following. 'Then why are we going that way?' she demanded, when she saw the negative response in Cole's eyes.

'Because otherwise we'd have to walk on water,' he replied, a teasing light in his eyes as he nodded to the stream that meandered on their left. 'We're taking a slightly circuitous route,' he added carelessly. 'Now, the sun's in the sky and it's about three o'clock. Which way's north?'

Honor just looked at him.

'You must have some idea!' he exclaimed. 'Within ninety degrees, say.'

'What's ninety degrees got to do with anything?' Honor asked, confused.

'It's a quarter of a full circle—or the compass,' he explained. 'I was allowing you forty-five degrees of error in either direction.'

Honor opened her mouth, then closed it again. She'd rarely felt so bewildered in her life.

'Goodness,' she said inadequately.

Cole grinned and pulled his compass out of his pocket. He flipped it open and laid it in her hand.

She looked down, fascinated by the shivering needle.

'That's north!' she said, pointing triumphantly. 'I still don't know where London is, though,' she admitted.

'No,' Cole agreed easily. 'Unless you've got some idea where we are now, you won't. And it's important to remember the compass doesn't show true north—it shows magnetic north.'

Honor stared at him in consternation and he laughed.

'I'll teach you,' he said.

Cole had inherited his father's natural curiosity, and he was a good teacher. He showed Honor how to use a compass and told her about his father's experiments, recalling some of his happiest boyhood memories as he did so.

Honor became so engrossed in her lesson that she didn't notice the passage of time until early evening—when she realised they were nowhere near any form of human habitation.

'I thought we were spending the night at the King's Head,' she said suspiciously, looking around at the place they'd fetched up in.

'We're headed in the right direction,' said Cole blandly. 'We just haven't arrived yet. What with your navigational lessons, we dawdled more than I'd anticipated.'

Honor looked around. There was an abandoned building, overgrown with weeds and brambles beside a clear flowing stream. A willow sighed into the rippling water, gilded by evening sunlight. Behind her an old, forgotten orchard of apple trees was laden with warmly flushed blossom.

'We could reach the King's Head by nightfall?' she said uncertainly.

'But these horses aren't trained for long marches,' Cole objected. 'They need rest.'

'You knew this place was here?' Honor accused him.

He smiled and refused to admit his culpability. He simply dismounted and raised his hands to lift Honor down from her saddle.

She hesitated, then slid down into his arms. He'd been so patient and relaxed while he'd been teaching her, it made her love him even more, and all afternoon she'd wondered whether he'd truly meant he intended to marry her. Of course, she knew he couldn't—and shouldn't. But even the remote possibility had given an extra glow to the beautiful day.

She looked up at him, half-expecting him to kiss her, but he set her gently aside.

'Time to set up camp,' he said briskly. 'Shouldn't take long for two such old hands.'

They selected a spot near the ruins, then took care of the horses. Honor was surprised and pleased that Cole didn't object to her looking after her mare.

She was surprised and suspicious when she discovered that, between them, they had all the essential utensils to set up a comfortable bivouac. That morning, she'd assumed it was just habit which had prompted Cole to use his Hussar saddle, complete with valise, for their ride—now she wasn't so sure...

As long as it didn't rain, they could happily sleep in the open. She contemplated the ruin, then decided to investigate it more closely. It only required a short inspection to assure her that the remaining walls and roof were quite secure, and would provide adequate shelter if the weather changed.

She tried to remember if Cole had ever described any boyhood adventures in this locality, because he'd certainly known about this place.

A pistol shot, fired nearby, jolted her out of her musings. She spun round, frantically searching her surroundings for trouble. She'd momentarily forgotten she was no longer in a war-torn country.

'Cole!' she shouted urgently.

'I'm here.' His deep voice was calm and reassuring. A moment later she saw him striding towards her through the twilight, a limp rabbit dangling from one hand.

'Supper,' he announced. 'Will you do the honours, or shall I?'

'You can prepare it,' she said tartly. 'You scared me out of my wits.'

He grinned apologetically. 'I didn't think that was possible,' he teased her.

'I'll collect some firewood,' she announced, ignoring him.

She found brittle, dead wood under the apple trees. When she returned with an armful, she discovered Cole had found dry kindling inside the ruins. She left him nursing his fire into life, and went to collect more wood.

Her emotions were in turmoil. She had no doubt that Cole had planned this night deliberately, but she didn't know how she should respond. She loved this peaceful place he'd brought her to, and she loved him, but she wasn't sure if she should surrender to the fantasy of her surroundings.

Cole was fulfilling a fantasy of his own. For years he had watched Honor make camp for Patrick. But now she belonged to him. He wanted this night with her, in peace and solitude, before he faced the hurdles he had to negotiate to claim her publicly as his wife.

When Honor returned to the fire, the rabbit was roasting and she was unsurprised to see that Cole had also provided them with bread, cheese and tea.

'No milk, I'm afraid,' he apologised, glancing up at her. He seemed relaxed and boyish as he sat by the fire, a far cry from the austere officer she'd first known in Portugal.

'I like tea better without milk,' she said vaguely, her mind on other things. 'I'm not going far,' she murmured, picking up her bag.

'Honor?' Cole twisted round, reaching up to catch her arm as he looked up at her questioningly.

'Just behind the building,' she assured him. 'You'll hear me if I call. I just…please.'

He continued to study her for several moments in the fading light, then his hand slid down her arm to briefly clasp her hand before releasing her.

'Don't go far,' he said.

'I won't.' The temptation to twine her fingers through his tousled hair was irresistible, so she gave in to it. He moved under her hand, almost like a great cat, inviting a caress. She stepped away from him, before he made it impossible to leave.

Chapter Nine

The water was clean, but cold. Honor slipped quickly out of her clothes and stood naked beside the stream in the twilight. The evening air was cool against her vulnerable skin and she shivered. She'd never before been naked beneath the open sky and she was both exhilarated and nervous at her own daring. If Cole found her like this it would be…definitely scandalous.

She sat on the grass beside the stream and dangled her legs into the water. She gasped at the cold and decided she'd better be quick. She slid into the water, feeling gingerly for the bottom. When she moved a little way into the stream, the water level came just above her knees. The current tugged gently, but not alarmingly around her legs. She lowered herself until she was submerged, focussing on the refreshing, rather than the freezing aspect of her preparations.

Then she waded out of the stream, dashed as much of the water off her slim body as she could with the flat of her hands, and dried herself on her ubiquitous black shawl. Instead of putting her riding habit on again, she pulled out a dress from her pack. It wasn't a modish dress—she'd been careful with her purchases in Lisbon—but it gave her a sense of dressing for dinner.

Finally she brushed her hair, then hesitated, unsure what to do with it next. It would be too obvious to leave it tumbling around her shoulders, but she was sick of the severe style she always wore it in.

'Honor?' Cole called.

'Coming.' She quickly stuffed her stockings and comb into her bag. Her riding habit was bulkier than the simple dress she now wore, and she had to drape it over her arm. She picked up her shoes and shawl and rejoined Cole. She draped her clothes over the branches of a sapling and sat down beside him.

The circle of firelight made the night around them seem darker than it was, and emphasised the intimacy of their situation.

'I didn't put my hair up yet,' she said breathlessly, suddenly shy in his presence. 'I didn't want you to worry I was taking too long. I'll just—'

'Leave it.' He touched her hair gently, then slipped his fingers beneath it to lift the shining weight against the back of his hand. As he did so, his fingers softly caressed the nape of her neck.

She held her breath, snared by the sensuous magic of his touch. She didn't move, or even look at him, afraid to break the spell.

'It's much prettier when it's not muddy,' he murmured provocatively, still seductively stroking her hair.

She threw a startled glance at him and a teasing smile curved his lips.

'You were not a pretty sight, when I pulled you out of the Huebra feet first,' he said reminiscently. 'A sadly bedraggled example of a fighting woman.'

Honor struggled to respond appropriately. It was hard

to feel indignant when he was touching her so distract-
ingly.

'You didn't have to haul me over your saddle bow like
a sack of corn,' she huffed unconvincingly.

'I could still feel you across my legs for hours afterwards,' he said softly. 'My hand on your waist, your
breasts against my thigh—'

'Cole!' Honor had left the top few buttons of her gown
undone, and she instinctively clutched the modest opening
together. 'You shouldn't say such things,' she scolded him.

He chuckled gently and let his hand slip around her
waist to pull her closer towards him.

'Sweetheart.' He lightly kissed her temple. 'You like it
when I touch you, why shouldn't you enjoy it when I talk
about touching you?'

'Well, because...' Honor leant against him, feeling his
breath ruffle her hair as he caressed her with his lips. They
were so close, it would be natural if she let her hand rest
on his thigh, but somehow she lacked the courage. 'It really isn't proper!'

He laughed again. 'How can you have lived such an
adventurous life, and still be such an innocent?' he enquired tenderly. 'Of course it's proper if you love me and
I love you.'

His simple, matter-of-fact comment stunned her into silence.

'But...'

'Shush. You don't really think I'd do anything to hurt
you, do you?' he murmured, kissing her temple, then her
cheek, before moving away from her to check the progress
of their supper.

Honor watched in a daze as she considered the implications of what he'd said. She should tell him not to set
his hopes in her—but perhaps he was merely intending to

make her his mistress after all. No, he'd said he wouldn't. She ought to ask him outright what he meant, but she didn't want to spoil the magical atmosphere of the evening.

'There. I have provided you with both meat and bread,' he said with considerable satisfaction as he handed her supper to her.

'Thank you. You've often provided me with food,' she said, surprised at his comment.

'Not under these circumstances,' he replied.

'You mean you hunted for me?' she asked, unable to resist teasing him a little. 'It's not real food unless you shot it and skinned it?'

'Or ploughed and sowed it,' he retorted, acknowledging her good-natured teasing with a crooked smile.

'What?' Honor asked, impulsively resting her hand on his thigh as a shadow momentarily passed over his face.

He looked into the fire for a moment, then roused himself to smile at her again. 'I always had a notion that when the war was over I might try exploring the New World. Canada, perhaps, or…'

'But…' Honor had been about to say that Miss Morton might not have liked that, but she didn't finish her observation. She didn't want to think about Bridget Morton now. Cole had far more pressing reasons why he had to abandon such dreams.

Instead of continuing the conversation, Cole laid his hand over hers where it rested on his leg. She suddenly became aware of the intimacy of her gesture and tried to draw her hand away, but he wouldn't let her. She felt the tension in the muscles of his thigh as he gently guided her hand inwards and a few inches higher.

Her breath locked in her throat. She couldn't believe how brazen he was. She was even more shocked to discover his action had filled her with pleasurable, though nervous, excitement. She had no doubt how the evening would end, but she wasn't quite ready for such bold games.

He released her hand and offered her another piece of roasted rabbit.

'No, thank you,' she said breathlessly.

She saw that he had also finished and moved with the intention of tidying up, but he forestalled her.

'Sit.' He rested his hand briefly on her shoulder. 'We've established I'm competent, and you should rest, sweetheart.'

She should have protested, but she didn't. It was very pleasant to be cared for so tenderly. She gazed into the embers of the fire, her mind a warm and comfortable haze, as Cole moved around the campsite. He made her tea, and she set it down on the grass to cool.

She sat for some time in an unthinking daydream before suddenly realising Cole wasn't nearby, and hadn't been for a while. She stood up, glancing around, not really anxious about his absence, but mildly concerned. It was colder, and she shivered in the night air. The moon had risen, silvering the stream and casting dark shadows among the apple trees. The quiet horses were silhouetted against the sky. She retrieved her shawl from the branch and threw it around her shoulders, then wandered down to the bank of the small river.

A splash from upstream attracted her attention. She approached cautiously, expecting to discover a water bird, or possibly an otter. Instead she found Cole.

He was standing in the water, his powerful body delineated by bright moonlight and dark shadows, silver ripples circling outwards from his legs. Ever since they'd made love she'd dreamed of his body; now she could see that it was as magnificent as she'd remembered. When he turned towards her she could see the strong, graceful definition of his muscular torso. Moonlight haloed his hair and high-lighted the angular planes of his face. His stomach was flat and ridged with muscle. He was unbelievably beautiful to her. It didn't occur to her that she should accord him the same privacy he'd allowed her. She couldn't take her eyes off him.

He looked up and towards her. His eyes were in shadow, but he didn't seem surprised to see her. He made no effort to cover himself and, because of his position, facing partly towards her, and partly in profile towards the moon, she knew exactly how her presence affected him. She swallowed, a little embarrassed by her own daring, but unable to retreat.

He waded towards the bank, silver ripples sparking around his legs, and stepped easily out of the water, but he didn't approach any closer to her. They were alone in the mysterious dark and pearly light. The silence between them was charged with tension. Honor took a step towards him. He waited, still and unmoving, but emanating an aura of virile power. Honor's heart thudded in her chest. This was beyond her experience. She didn't know what she was supposed to do, she only knew she was drawn inexorably towards him.

She stopped a couple of feet away from him. Still he said nothing, and made no move to touch her. Moonlight glistened on his wet shoulders. Drops of water gleamed like dewfall in the shadowy curls on his broad chest.

This close, she could see his expression a little more clearly. His lips curved in a sensuous, masculine invitation, but he didn't reach out towards her. Honor caught her lower lip between her teeth, torn between uncertainty and desire. Barely conscious of what she was doing, she pulled her shawl from around her shoulders, and began to dry him with it. She stroked the soft, slightly damp wool over his arms, his chest and his back, caressing him and glorying in his male beauty.

He didn't say anything, but she felt him tremble. She leant forward and almost timidly kissed his water-cooled back, then rested her forehead briefly against his shoulder. She was hot and quivering with her own urgent emotions, remembering the last time they'd made love—anticipating the first moment he would touch her this time.

He moved, turning to face her, and she lifted her head, her lips already parted, open and vulnerable to him.

He bent eagerly towards her, then shudderingly controlled the driving demands of his body to possess her. He brushed his mouth gently against hers, summoning a soft moan from her when he drew back without consummating the kiss. He put his hands on her hips, holding her away from him when she tried to press closer, and started to bunch her dress up in his hands, hitching it higher and higher up her legs.

Cool night air flowed around her calves, then her thighs. She felt wickedly erotic as he slowly exposed her nakedness to the moonlight. When he'd pulled her dress up to her hips, he slipped his hands beneath. His shuddering reaction when he discovered she was wearing nothing beneath it reverberated through her. He paused a moment, his hands on her waist, and lightly kissed her forehead.

'You could tempt a saint, sweetheart,' he murmured hoarsely. 'What chance have I got?'

'I like tempting you,' she whispered, completely surrendering to their mutual seduction. 'You...tempt me.'

She put her hands on his shoulders, delighting in the strong smooth feel of his muscles beneath her fingertips. The water had been cold, and his skin was still slightly cool, yet she could sense the heat radiating from his body.

He slid his palms upwards, until they grazed the sides

of her breasts. Her nipples were tight with anticipation. Her body ached and throbbed for his touch, but he made her wait.

'Cole!' she whispered, her fingers digging urgently into his shoulders.

He brushed a kiss across her cheek.

'What do you want, sweetheart?' he murmured huskily in her ear.

'Touch me!' she ordered breathlessly, twisting with frustrated need against his restraining hands.

'Like this?' His hands moved around her ribcage until he was framing her small breasts in the angle between his thumbs and index fingers.

'Ohh!' She sounded so disgruntled Cole chuckled in spite of himself.

'Like this?' he asked softly, teasing her erect nipples with the sides of his thumbs. 'Sweetheart?' He bent his head to kiss the side of her neck, his lips teasing and caressing her warm, sensitive skin.

'Mmm.' Honor's legs turned to water. Cole's touch beneath her dress was sinfully delicious. 'Oh.' Her head fell forward against his shoulder. 'You haven't even kissed me yet,' she mumbled incoherently, heedlessly voicing an errant thought. 'Not properly.'

'Sweetheart.' Cole's lips curved in a smile against her neck. 'There are a lot of things I haven't done yet. Lift your arms.'

'I might fall over,' she protested vaguely.

'I'll catch you.' He slipped her dress neatly over her head, then swept her up in his arms and carried her around the ruined building to the blanket beside the smouldering fire.

'So, you want to be kissed?' he teased her, lying on his side next to her.

'Yes.' She was amazed by her own boldness, but too aroused to be embarrassed. She rolled on to her side so that she was facing him, and brazenly rubbed her breasts against his chest.

He locked his hand in her hair and pulled her head back almost roughly to cover her mouth with his own. His kisses were fierce and possessive, completely overwhelming her. She curled her arm around his side, clinging to him as he ravaged her senses with his lips and tongue. She could feel his erection pressing against her stomach, the urgent need pulsing through his virile body. The certainty of his desire for her aroused her even further.

She rubbed her soft, inner thigh against his hard muscular leg, then tried to roll on to her back, pulling him on top of her. To her confusion, he resisted her efforts. Instead he moved on to his back, and lifted her to straddle him.

'Oh, my!' Her surprise momentarily interrupted the smooth current of their passion. 'What...?'

He guided her carefully, his hands gentle on her slim hips, though his arms trembled with the self-control he was exerting not to go too fast. His breath suddenly exploded out of him at the immense, glorious pleasure of feeling her tightly enclose him.

'Cole,' she breathed, holding herself away from him as she gazed down into his face.

'Did...I hurt you?' he asked jerkily, suddenly afraid he hadn't given her enough time.

'No.' She sounded bewildered, not hurt. 'But—'

'Shush.' He cupped her face in his hands and drew her lips down to his. 'Kiss me,' he murmured.

'Mmm.' She did, but she was distracted by other sensations, and the increasing compulsion to move. She lifted her hips experimentally and was rewarded by the tightening of Cole's embrace, and his barely stifled groan.

'Oh, you liked that!' Her voice was so breathless and thick with arousal she didn't recognise it. For the first time she realised she was not just the recipient of Cole's desire, but an active participant in their mutual arousal and ultimate satisfaction.

'Yes!' Cole's hands followed the curve of her hips and waist to find her breasts. He cupped them in his palms, caressing their hard, sensitive tips, and Honor closed her eyes with pleasure.

Then she experimented some more, concentrating on Cole's delight rather than her own. It was too dark to see his face clearly, but his body's response to her efforts, and his hoarse moans of pleasure gave her the cues she needed. In a distant part of her mind, she was surprised when he slipped his hand between them, but then he touched her intimately, and she was lost to the devastating sensations he conjured in her. Her body contracted, and she cried out as blinding ecstasy pulsed through her, overwhelming all her senses for several long, shuddering moments.

Cole's hands gripped her hips as he thrust up into her and surrendered to his own, soul-quaking release.

She lay on top of him, their hearts beating in unison, as they slowly recovered from the intense experience.

'Sweetheart.' Cole lifted his head to press a kiss against Honor's damp skin, then flopped back on to the blanket, thoroughly satisfied and spent by their lovemaking.

She barely stirred. He was still inside her, and he wanted to stay like that, but the night breeze was cool against her damp, naked flesh. He rolled them carefully to one side, ignoring Honor's mumbled protests, and wrapped them both in a cosy cocoon of blankets.

She snuggled against him, already half asleep. He held her close, enjoying the feel of her relaxed body next to his. It occurred to him that Patrick really couldn't have been much of a lover. Under any other circumstances, Honor's amazement at his reversal of what she'd expected would have been comical. They were, Cole decided, going to have so much fun discovering each other—just as soon as he'd sorted things out with Bridget. The prospect of dealing with Bridget and her father momentarily disturbed his contentment—he wasn't looking forward to his meeting with them. But then he realised his muscles were tensing in anticipation of the encounter and he deliberately pushed his concerns aside. Tomorrow would be soon enough to deal with problems. He drifted asleep, his mind full of Honor and the erotic fantasies that she'd inspired.

Honor woke up in the middle of the dawn chorus. It never failed to amaze her how much sheer noise birds could generate at the first hint of grey light. She lay close to Cole and thought about what had happened in the night. She should have been embarrassed at her uninhibited behaviour, and part of her was—but mostly she was full of happiness because she knew she had made Cole happy. She had known he liked looking at her, touching her, making love to her, but until last night she had never fully comprehended how much she could also contribute to their mutual pleasure. She wished they had more time together, but she resolutely set her mind against their future parting. She wondered if Cole had known there would be a moon last night, and decided he must have done. He knew she thought the moon was magical, and he'd given her a magical memory.

The sun was sending its first warm rays over the horizon when she heard a faint noise from the direction of the old apple orchard. She lifted her head cautiously, anxious in case they'd been discovered, and saw three deer, frozen like statues as they looked towards her. She was enchanted.

She watched as they stepped delicately through the trees, then sat up. Cole stirred in his sleep and she tucked the blankets carefully around him.

Then she got to her feet and silently followed in the path of the deer. The damp morning air was cool against her sleep-warmed skin and she shivered, but she didn't bother with her clothes. She was living in a magical adventure where the normal rules had ceased to apply.

She paused beneath an apple tree, unable to see where the deer had gone, and unwilling to go too far from the camp. She heard a sound behind her and turned to smile up at Cole. He was as naked as she was.

'You could be the nymph of the orchard,' he said softly, one hand resting on the branch above her head, 'so beautiful in the dawn.'

'Oh.' She blushed at his praise, self-conscious of her nakedness, and lifted her hands to cover herself.

He caught her wrist and shook his head.

'I like to look at you.'

'I...like to look at you too,' she said daringly.

He smiled. 'That makes me very happy,' he murmured. 'And touching me, sweetheart?' He lifted her hand and placed it against his chest.

'Yes.' She whispered. She stroked her hand across the firm muscles, softened by the mat of light brown curls. She found a flat nipple and circled it gently. Then she glanced down and discovered he was more than happy with her response to him. She looked up at him. He smiled deep into her eyes, and they shared a moment of intimate, sensual awareness.

He shook the branch above her head and apple blossom fell on her like a benediction, lying delicately on her hair, her shoulders and her breasts.

'My Honor,' he murmured, delighted with the picture

she made, and bent to kiss her, before carrying her back to their blankets.

'I must be feeding you properly,' said Cole lazily.

'Why?' Honor smiled up at him.

'Your breasts are fuller than they were in Spain,' he replied matter-of-factly.

'Oh.' She blushed.

'And your curves are generally...curvier,' he continued, inspecting them with both his eyes and appreciative fingertips.

'I thought they were a bit too,' Honor admitted, deciding there was no point in being embarrassed. 'Do you like it better?' she asked shyly.

'I like it better that you're healthy and well fed,' said Cole decidedly. 'You were too thin before. The life was too hard for you. No.' He gently laid his fingers over her lips to silence her immediate, indignant protest. 'The life was too hard for many of the men, as well, sweetheart. I know that. I know *you* never collapsed in defeated exhaustion beside the road. And I know you could do it all again if it were asked of you—but I hope to God it never is.'

'I'd do it for you,' said Honor.

'I know.' Cole kissed her, at first gently, then with increasing passion.

Honor threaded her fingers through his hair and held him close. She'd meant to talk to him about their future, but he hadn't let her, he'd been too busy loving her.

'This is such a wonderful place,' Honor said, feeling very sad as she took a last look around at the stream and apple trees before they left their camp. 'Did you know it before?'

Cole grinned. 'I'll show you,' he replied. He led the way

downstream until the little river grew broader and shallower. The horses splashed easily over to the other side and, after a few minutes riding, Honor suddenly found herself gazing at the ruined shell of a once-grand house.

'We think the fire was started by a bolt of lightning,' said Cole. 'It was about fifteen years ago. I was at school, Giff was already in the navy, and Father, Malcolm and Anthony were in London—so the stories about how it happened are a bit variable.'

'It's *your* house!' Honor exclaimed, staring in fascination at the fire-blackened remaining walls.

'Mmm.' Cole scanned his surroundings with narrowed eyes against the low rays of the early morning sun. 'Father said he'd leave it up to Giff to decide what he wanted to do about it—the house, I mean. Malcolm's still managing the land and the tenants.'

'Now it's up to you,' said Honor, urging the mare closer to the ruins. 'Will you rebuild?'

'Do you like it?' Cole asked, watching her.

'The grounds are beautiful,' she declared, smiling appreciatively at an old oak tree nearby. 'It feels so peaceful here.'

'I always liked this place,' Cole confessed. 'Not the house, particularly. My grandfather had it built and I thought it was ugly—so did Father. But the countryside, and the view of the hills—they feel like home to me. I can imagine living here.'

Honor suddenly perceived where the conversation might be heading and it made her nervous. The fire-blackened house now seemed ominous rather than merely interesting.

'We must catch up with the chaise,' she said quickly. 'Otherwise they might send out search parties for us.' She urged the mare into a brisk trot.

'The village inn is called the Raven's Arms,' Cole called

after her, grinning. 'If you keep heading in that direction you could call in for a tankard of ale—but you won't get to London.'

'So where, exactly, are we going?' asked Cole, when they were once more seated in the chaise.

'The Belle Savage, Ludgate Hill,' Honor replied, avoiding his gaze.

'The Belle Savage?' Cole echoed. Honor had just named one of the major coaching inns of London. 'Is your mother a housekeeper there?' he hazarded, frowning. He'd often wondered what had happened to the illiterate chambermaid, but Honor always seemed reluctant to talk about her mother.

Honor's smile didn't reach her eyes. 'Mama owns it,' she said tensely.

'She's the *proprietor*!' Cole exclaimed. 'How—?'

'She worked hard—and she's clever,' Honor replied tightly.

'Of course she is, she's your mother.' Cole drew in a long, deep breath, watching Honor carefully. Why was she so edgy? He decided to proceed cautiously. 'From chambermaid to proprietor of a large coaching inn is a long step up,' he observed.

'Several inns,' Honor corrected him, gripping her fingers tightly together as she recited her mother's assets. 'Mama also owns two other inns on the Bath road, and one on the Brighton road. She has stables near Epsom—it takes thousands of horses to keep Mama's coaches on the road. She owns a coach-building business—which makes coaches for the aristocracy as well as for Mama. And she is the contractor for the London ground of the London to Bath mail. Mr Hasker, he's the superintendent of the mail coaches, is a great admirer of hers. He says if all the contractors managed their affairs as efficiently as Mama, his life would be much easier. Of course...' Honor paused to catch her breath '...Mama's not the only widow woman running a successful coaching business in London—she's just the only one who never had a husband to start with.' She met Cole's eyes rather defiantly as she concluded her speech.

'Well, I'll be damned,' he said softly, watching the complicated play of emotions on Honor's face. He'd always known her feelings for her mother were far from straightforward, now he was finally beginning to see why.

'How did she achieve all that?' he asked after a moment, stunned by the magnitude of the task. Surely the woman must have had some kind of patron—even if not Honor's father?

Honor looked at him cautiously, almost as if she was anticipating his disapproval.

'I share Mr Hasker's respect,' he said hastily. He might feel hostile towards Honor's mother because of the way she'd treated her daughter—but that didn't alter his feelings for Honor.

Honor studied him in silence for a few seconds, then she started to explain.

'First she learned her trade. When I was born, my grandmother was still alive. She had Mama very late in her life—when she was forty-four years old!' Honor sounded awed by the accomplishment. 'So she was already quite old when I knew her. She died just before I married Patrick.'

'You missed her?' Cole said softly, seeing another reason why Honor might have been jolted into her hasty marriage.

'Oh, yes,' Honor agreed fervently. 'She never did learn to read, but she was the wisest person I've ever known—

and a wonderful cook! She was one of Mama's most important assets. For the first few years after I was born, Gran went on working as a cook and Mama did several jobs in various inns—learning all the time.'

'Who took care of you?' Cole demanded.

'Susannah.' Honor smiled. 'Mama's cousin. She was only eleven, but she took good care of me.'

'You were left in the care of a child?' Cole couldn't help the disapproval in his voice, though he knew far worse happened all the time.

'She took *good* care of me!' Honor fired up. 'I *liked* being with her.'

'I'm looking forward to meeting her,' said Cole.

'So'm I,' Honor whispered, wiping her eye with the back of her curled forefinger, before looking out of the carriage window.

Cole remembered then how traumatic this home-coming was going to be for her.

'Your mama learnt her trade,' he prompted, trying to divert Honor from her worries.

'When she was twenty-one she bought a rundown old inn on the Bath road. I was four years old. I can remember the roof leaking and weeds growing through the cobblestones in the yard. But Mama turned it round so fast.' Pride shone in Honor's eyes as she recalled both her own memories and the stories she'd been told by Susannah and her grandmother. 'She'd already got the best cook she could have in Gran. She'd met a lot of good people while she was still hiring herself out, and some of them were willing to take a chance on working for her. Lord Sandler's butler came to work for her when his master died—he knew everything about wine. Colin Macey kept the stables in apple-pie order. And Mama and Susannah did whatever else needed to be done. It took less than two years before their reputation was so good she was taking trade from the old-established inns nearby.'

'That must have made her popular,' Cole observed drily.

'Mama's tough.' Honor smiled slightly. 'And clever. I don't remember much about it, but Susannah told me someone tried to sabotage the stables once. Mama wasn't having any of it—nor was Colin. He can be a big, fierce man when he wants to be.' Honor chuckled.

'He's still around?'

'Oh, yes.' Honor sounded slightly surprised. 'He's not much older than Mama. He and his wife are still running that first inn Mama ever bought.'

'I see.' For a moment, Cole had wondered whether Colin Macey had had any romantic interest in Honor's formidable mama, but it seemed not.

'When Mama could afford it, she bought another inn,' Honor continued, settling into her story-telling. 'And then another. At her peak, she had several inns on the Bath road, two on the Brighton road, and a couple on the Great North Road, but what she really wanted was a centre in London. About ten years ago she sold off several of the smaller inns to buy the Belle Savage. You could say the Belle is the heart of her empire.'

'It sounds like it,' Cole agreed uneasily. Had Honor inherited her mother's fierce ambition to succeed? 'Is that the kind of thing you'd like to achieve in your own life?' he asked, his voice carefully neutral.

Honor sighed, her brief spurt of energy dying away. 'I don't want to be an innkeeper,' she said wearily. 'I never did. Dressmaking…? I think I'd rather breed horses—but not for Mama,' she added, with a hint of rebellion.

Honor wanted to marry him and have his babies, Cole reminded himself, forcing his tense muscles to relax. But he had to admit, he was quite intrigued by the story of Honor's mother.

What was it like to start with nothing and build it up into a veritable empire? He clenched his fist in a surge of excitement as he realised he didn't have to confine himself to approving tenancy agreements. He could look around and find something to do that really interested him!

'What happened?' Honor sounded bewildered. 'You look so…happy?'

'I am!' Cole exclaimed, leaning forward in the opposite seat and cupping her knees enthusiastically between his hands. 'Honor, I just realised I don't have to settle for being a landlord and gentleman of leisure, after all. If your mama can keep inns, breed horses, build coaches, and run stage coaches and the mail, I'm damn sure I can do more than one thing at a time, too!'

'Oh my God, you're just like her,' Honor breathed, half-horrified, as she stared into his blazing eyes.

'Is that bad?' he asked, momentarily disconcerted by her expression.

'Well…no.' She gave a shaken laugh. 'No, of course not. What are you going to do?'

'I don't know yet.' He sat back, unbothered by the admission. 'I'll find something. Coach-building sounds interesting. Designing a more comfortable coach—that would be worthwhile. Father was telling me about experiments with steam when I was last home. It was fascinating. I've been out of touch too long.'

Honor gazed at him, loving him, but a little bewildered by this new side of his personality. How could coach-building be interesting? And what was fascinating about steam?

Cole saw her expression and laughed, pulling her onto his lap.

'Cole!' She pushed ineffectually at his embrace. 'It's broad daylight.' She lowered her voice, even though they were alone in the chaise.

'It was broad daylight this morning, too,' he teased her.

'That was different,' she scolded him. 'We're on a busy road. People might see.'

'Pull the shades down,' he countered, grinning.

'We'll be changing horses soon.'

'You've got an answer for everything.' He cupped the back of her head with his hand and kissed her.

'So have you,' Honor gasped, when she could speak. 'Please, Cole,' she added uncertainly.

She felt confused. She didn't want him to let her go. She felt safe on his lap, but she knew that soon they would have to have a serious discussion about the future. And after that, she would be alone. She closed her eyes and rested her forehead against his cheek.

'Sweetheart.' His arms tightened comfortingly around her. 'Are you afraid of your mother?' he asked softly.

She didn't answer for a long time. Eventually she sighed.

'Not…exactly,' she said slowly. 'We've had some horrible arguments. Gran used to say it was because we're so much alike—but I don't think we are. Not really. In some ways we are—sometimes we've both got sharp tongues. But Mama always has to have the last word.' She sighed again.

Cole stroked her back reassuringly, but he didn't say anything.

'I never wanted to work in the inn,' Honor admitted. 'I don't know if that's because I don't like innkeeping—or because I just couldn't see myself working for Mama. She said I could be an idle lady of fashion, and sent me to the seminary in Bath—but how could I simper and flirt behind my fan when it was Mama's hard struggle that had made it possible for me to be idle?'

'So you ran away to become an actress,' said Cole.

'Sheridan used to visit the Belle Savage,' Honor replied. 'It's amazing the people you meet when you grow up in an inn—and the scandals you hear,' she added, smiling wryly. 'Then I had all that trouble with the Duke of Selhurst—and I couldn't bring myself to run back to Mama and have her tell me she told me so.'

'So you married Patrick instead,' said Cole.

'And Mama hasn't spoken to me since,' Honor finished. 'And I haven't spoken to her either. Not since Patrick went to see her and she upset him so much he got drunk and the recruiting party got him.'

'Sweetheart.' Cole held her close, determined that Honor's tempestuous relationship with her mother was never going to drive her into doing something foolish again.

Honor let him comfort her for a few minutes, then she pushed herself off his lap.

'I can handle her,' she said flatly. 'I will pay my respects to her, like a polite and dutiful daughter, but I will not be beholden to her. I will not go crawling back to her like the prodigal daughter. I will find somewhere else to live.'

Cole opened his mouth, then closed it again. He wanted Honor to know she wasn't the prodigal daughter, that she had a secure place in his life. But she'd just pointed out that a large inn could be a hotbed for scandal. He didn't want the scandal of his broken betrothal to reach Bridget before he'd had a chance to speak to her himself. Under normal circumstances, he didn't have any doubts about Honor's discretion, but clearly her relationship with her mother was far from normal.

* * *

They changed horses frequently and made good time. Consequently, it was mid-afternoon when they finally reached Ludgate Hill and the post-chaise swept under the arch into the outer courtyard of the Belle Savage.

Honor looked out of the window; the bustle of a busy inn was achingly familiar to her. The coffee room, the booking office, the tiered galleries that surrounded the courtyards, the horses and ostlers, private carriages and her mother's stagecoaches, the ostlers and many-caped drivers...

'Miss Honor! Miss Honor!'

Honor blinked, then smiled in delighted recognition at one of the drivers. 'Jethro!' she exclaimed holding out both hands. 'It's good to see you.'

'Miss Honor!' He seized her hands in his, holding her at arm's length as he looked her up and down. 'Miss Honor, it's so good to have you safe home,' he said, gulping, and looking as if he was too overcome to say any more. 'Ned! Sam!' he called. 'Miss Honor's come home!'

Immediately Honor found herself surrounded by a crowd of her well-wishers, all of whom worked for her mother.

Cole allowed himself to be elbowed aside by people who wanted to see for themselves that Honor was home safe and well.

'Miss Honor—' Jethro began.

'Mrs O'Donnell,' Ned hissed, nudging him in the ribs.

'But Patrick's dead, isn't he?' whispered another man.

Cole suddenly remembered that Patrick had been a coach driver. Had he once been the colleague of these men who were greeting Honor with so much excited, but respectful, affection? It was obviously more comfortable for them to ignore her widowed state and treat her as the unwed daughter of the house she'd been when they'd known her.

Cole looked around the huge courtyard, the hub of the empire Honor's mother had built, and finally realised the enormity of what Honor had done when she married Patrick. It was as if the General's daughter had upped and married a private soldier! Cole suppressed a disbelieving grin. No wonder Honor's mother had been beside herself when she'd found out.

'Honor! Honor!' A woman called from the other side of the courtyard.

Both Cole and Honor swung in the direction of the voice. Cole saw a tall, elegant woman pick up her skirts and run towards Honor.

'Susannah!' Honor met her halfway and they fell into each others arms.

Cole shouldered his way through the crowd to join them. He'd no desire to intrude upon Honor's reunions, but he did want to be close at hand if she needed him. Her mother still hadn't appeared, and he knew that would be the moment of truth for her.

'You look so well!' Honor held her mother's cousin away from her so she could gaze at her, then hugged her tightly again.

'So do you,' said Susannah warmly. 'But I've been so worried about you!' she exclaimed. 'Why'd you take so long to come home?'

'I...wasn't ready before,' Honor said unsteadily.

'Hmm.' Susannah looked straight past her into Cole's eyes.

He was momentarily surprised by how young she was. It was shocking to realise how much of a child she'd been when she'd first taken care of Honor. He wondered what she was doing now. She certainly wasn't dressed as a poor relation, and he couldn't remember the last time he'd been assessed by such a shrewd pair of eyes.

'Major Raven,' she said, obviously needing no introduction for him. He wondered what Honor had said about him in her letters. 'I'm pleased to meet you, sir,' said Susannah, holding out her hand to him.

'And I you,' he replied, shaking her hand.

'Oh, I never introduced you properly!' Honor exclaimed, looking from one to the other in mild consternation. 'This is Miss Susannah Rivers, Mama's cousin and business partner.'

'Miss Rivers,' Cole smiled.

'Let's go inside,' said Susannah, taking Honor's arm. 'Annie's out at the moment,' she added in a lower voice.

Cole saw an almost imperceptible relaxation of Honor's shoulders.

'Annie?' he said questioningly, although he'd already guessed she was Honor's elusive mama.

'Annie Howarth,' said Honor. 'My mother.'

Cole frowned as he followed Susannah and Honor inside. The name sounded familiar, but he couldn't immediately place it.

'Major Raven, I am so grateful for the way you saved Honor's life,' Susannah said sincerely, as soon as they were sitting in her private parlour.

'I think she can take most of the credit for that herself,' said Cole, uncomfortable with Susannah's gratitude.

'Honor has always been brave and determined,' Susannah agreed, 'but even she couldn't have carried Patrick all the way to Ciudad Rodrigo if you hadn't found them.'

'Did she tell you she shot a wolf?' Cole asked, turning the conversation in another direction, quite sure he wouldn't shock this self-assured woman.

'No!' Susannah exclaimed. 'Honor!' She looked at her accusingly.

'I thought it would worry you,' said Honor guiltily.

'Worry me? I'd have taken the packet to Lisbon and brought you back myself if you hadn't come home soon,' Susannah declared. 'Annie's been going crazy with worry about you.'

'Mama has?' Honor sounded as if she didn't believe it.

Cole saw a look of faint exasperation pass over Susannah's face, as if she was tired of being caught in the crossfire. Her loyalties must be uncomfortably divided by the breach between Honor and her mother.

And he suddenly realised why the name Annie Howarth was familiar to him. Before he had time to think through the implications of his realisation, he heard a commotion outside the door.

A few seconds later the parlour door flew open and a slim, flushed woman bounced inside and stopped short, staring at Honor.

'Mama,' Honor whispered, rising to her feet.

Cole automatically stood up as well. His first reaction was one of disbelief. He'd been expecting a hard-faced harridan, but the woman before him hardly looked old enough to be anyone's mother, let alone a woman of twenty-five. Then he remembered that, Annie Howarth being only sixteen when Honor was born, she was barely forty-one now.

Annie Howarth had caramel-coloured hair and blue eyes. Her face was a perfect oval. Her features were less angular than her daughter's; her figure, though slim, was more womanly. It was easy to imagine the pretty child she'd been when she'd caught the eye of Honor's father, and it made her achievements over the past twenty-five years all the more remarkable. The most likely fate for a young, poorly educated girl in Annie's situation would have been a descent into poverty and degradation. Many women in similar circumstances might have exerted their best efforts to find another, richer protector, but Annie Howarth had spurned such tactics. The fact that she had not only survived, but prospered, told Cole that she must be a truly formidable woman.

In the first few seconds after Annie first saw Honor her emotions were reflected, unguarded, in her sapphire eyes. In that instant, Cole had no doubt that Annie Howarth loved her daughter very much—and he was also sure that his half-formed deduction of only a few moments ago was correct.

Joe Newton had been writing regularly to a 'Mrs Annie Howarth' on Ludgate Hill, though Cole had only occasionally seen the letters. He wondered briefly how Annie Howarth had established contact with his servant—and then he remembered that Joe had only travelled out from England *after* Cole had transferred from the 16th Dragoons to the 52nd Foot. Cole's previous servant had been unable to stand the rigours of campaigning and he'd asked Malcolm Anderson to send him out a replacement. Somehow Annie had managed to take advantage of the situation to install her own man as Cole's servant. Annie had been kept abreast of everything that had happened to her daughter on a regular basis for the past eighteen months. Probably longer if she had other informants Cole didn't know about. And given the size of her coaching empire in England, he thought it was quite likely that she did.

Not only that, in recent months Bridget's letters had been full of references to 'Mrs Howarth'. What exactly had Honor's mother been hoping to achieve by making friends with his fiancée?

Cole started to laugh out of sheer amazement.

Chapter Ten

Honor stared at her mother. She was overwhelmed by so many cartwheeling emotions that she didn't know how she felt. Annie hadn't changed at all in the four years since they'd last seen each other. She was still perfectly beautiful, perfectly in charge of her amazing empire.

Honor couldn't speak. She could hardly breathe. Her knees were weak and trembling. She gripped her hands together tightly. She would *not* make a fool of herself in front of Annie. This was just a brief, businesslike meeting to re-establish polite contact between them.

Then Cole started to laugh. Honor was startled and disorientated by the sound. She turned her head to look at him, swaying slightly as she did so. He moved quickly to stand behind her, resting one hand reassuringly on her waist as he looked over her head at her mother.

Annie had clearly been surprised by his laughter as well. Her eyes jumped from Honor's face to Cole's.

'Was I ever in danger of being cashiered?' he asked, sounding mildly amused.

Annie raised one exquisite eyebrow in a haughty expression all too familiar to her daughter. But then, to

Honor's amazement, her mother's face softened into a smile that almost seemed to indicate approval of Cole.

'No,' she said.

'I'm glad to hear it.' Cole's deep voice vibrated reassuringly close to Honor's ear. He still kept one had firmly on her waist, but she felt him rub her gently between her shoulder blades with the knuckles of his free hand. She was grateful for the support he was offering, but she was also embarrassed that he should touch her so openly in front of her mother. She thought she ought to step away from him, but she couldn't quite bring herself to do so.

'Mama, this is Major—no, I mean...' She stumbled over the introduction as she belatedly realised Cole's title had changed.

'Sir Cole Raven,' Annie said with assurance. 'I'm delighted to meet you, Sir Cole.'

'The pleasure is all mine,' Cole reciprocated. 'I've heard a great deal about you. I understand you believe it is better to live one's own adventures—rather than read about them in someone else's novel?'

Annie raised her eyebrow. 'I may have said something of the sort,' she conceded. 'Do you disagree with my opinion, sir?'

Honor struggled to make sense of the conversation. She was sure she hadn't said anything like that about her mother to Cole—yet Annie seemed to know what he was talking about.

'No. In fact, I look forward to furthering our acquaintance very shortly, ma'am,' Cole said to Annie. 'But I have another call to make now. If you'll excuse me?'

Honor slowly registered that Cole was leaving. She twisted round to look up at him, dismayed by the prospect of his abrupt departure.

There was an odd gleam of amusement in his blue eyes

when he looked down at her, but then his expression softened into one of tenderness.

'I'm coming back,' he said gently. He pulled her shaky, unresisting body towards him and lightly kissed her forehead. She gasped and lowered her head, partly because she was embarrassed to be kissed in front of her mother, and partly because she was assailed by so many strong feelings she didn't know what to do.

Cole didn't try to make Honor look up; instead, he bent his own head and kissed her cheek.

'It's all right, sweetheart,' he murmured in her ear, too softly for anyone else to hear. 'She's pleased you're home. And I'll be back tomorrow. So don't set up in business as a dressmaker before then!'

Honor managed a slightly watery laugh as she drew away from Cole. 'You can't set up an entire business overnight,' she retorted, taking comfort from Cole's assurances. 'Not even Mama could.'

'I don't think a wise man would bet against that possibility,' Cole said, a definite—and very confusing—gleam of amusement in his eyes as he glanced from Honor to her mother. 'Good day, Mrs Howarth.'

'Goodbye, Sir Cole,' Annie replied calmly. 'We will expect to see you tomorrow.'

She stood aside so that Cole could leave the parlour. Honor distractedly noticed that Susannah left with him. She was finally alone with her mother. She couldn't quite meet Annie's eyes. She'd been dreading this confrontation for months.

'Well,' said Annie at last. 'At least this time you've chosen a man with half a brain in his head.'

'I haven't chosen him. I mean—'

'He certainly seems to have chosen you,' Annie cut briskly across Honor's denial.

'He can't. It's not how it looks at all,' Honor replied wearily. She didn't want to discuss Cole with her mother. Her heart was already aching from the pain of his loss.

'You look…thinner,' said Annie, coming closer. 'Your face is…thinner. What happened to your hair?'

The new growth was darker blonde, but the long ends were still sun-bleached from the previous summer.

Honor self-consciously brushed back a stray curl. 'It was the sun,' she whispered.

'You look older.' Annie came a few more cautious steps closer. 'You were a child when you left. Your cheeks were round like a child's. Now…' She tentatively touched one of Honor's elegantly sculptured cheekbones.

Honor gazed at her mother, shaken not only by the gentleness of her touch, but by her hesitancy. Honor had never known Annie Howarth to be uncertain about anything. Then she saw the shimmer of tears in her mother's eyes and her own self-control disintegrated. She burst into tears, and the next minute she was locked in her mother's arms.

Cole went straight to the Mortons' town house. The butler seemed a little flustered when Cole gave his name.

'This way please, sir.' The butler quickly regained his equilibrium and showed Cole into a small downstairs room. 'I will inform Mr Morton that you are here.'

Cole waited nearly ten minutes before his host finally appeared.

'Cole, dear boy!' George Morton strode across the room towards him. 'I was sorry to hear about poor Gifford.' He seized Cole's hand in a hearty grip.

'Thank you.' As ever when he thought of his brother Cole felt a pang of grief. 'You look well,' he told the other man.

'Very fit, very fit,' Morton asserted vigorously. 'You've sold out, I take it?'

'It was necessary,' Cole replied briefly. 'Sir, may I come directly to the point—?'

'Bridget,' Morton interrupted. 'You wish to discuss...sit down, boy! Sit down! Ah, Penge!' He swung round as the door opened and the butler entered carrying a silver tray. 'Brandy. I'm sure you'd welcome a glass, Raven,' he declared jerkily.

'Thank you.' Cole accepted the brandy and sat down, stretching out his long legs. Despite Morton's fulsome welcome, it was fairly clear to Cole that his arrival had unsettled the other man. He decided to leave it up to Morton to direct the conversation.

'No doubt you hoped to see Bridget,' said Morton abruptly.

'Is she not here?' Cole enquired politely.

'No. Cole, I assure you, if I'd had any idea what she planned—!' Morton burst out. He leapt to his feet and began to pace in front of the hearth.

Cole waited, trying not to look as hopeful as he felt. Despite his realisation that Annie Howarth was acquainted with Bridget, he hadn't dared to hope he might already be freed from his betrothal.

'Dammit! I've never been so embarrassed or shamed in my life!' Morton declared. 'Bridget is already married.'

'I beg your pardon!' Cole set down his glass with a sharp click. He couldn't remember the last time he'd heard such good news, but he could hardly say so. 'What the devil do you mean?'

'I mean she eloped.' Morton looked truly miserable as he met Cole's eyes.

'She fled to Gretna Green?' Cole knew it wasn't a very tactful question, but he couldn't resist asking. He'd always thought Bridget was rather dull. He found it hard to imagine her in full flight to the border.

'No, no,' Morton replied impatiently. 'She was far too old to need my consent to the marriage. She was wed by special licence in Oxford. Now she's living with her new husband in—' He broke off, glancing at Cole warily.

'I see,' said Cole drily. He wondered if Bridget's father expected him to chase vengefully after the happy couple. 'When did the marriage take place?'

Morton looked even more uncomfortable. 'A month after we heard the news from your uncle that Gifford was dead,' he said stiffly. 'I knew any letter I sent you would probably cross with you on your way home. We've kept it very quiet. There hasn't been any scandal.'

'Good,' said Cole. He didn't pretend to be heartbroken at the situation, he knew Morton wouldn't expect it of him. It had always been primarily a business arrangement.

'Bridget did not mean to insult you,' Morton said with dignity. 'You know as well as I do that this union was something your father and I hatched between us. Neither you nor Bridget ever expressed much enthusiasm for it—though you both did your duty by us. I—'

Cole held up his hand. 'There's no need to say any more,' he said quietly. 'I was away a long time. I don't feel my pride or my honour have been affronted. I hope Bridget will be very happy with her new husband.'

Morton nodded his acknowledgement of Cole's comment. 'He seems a steady enough fellow,' he replied grudgingly. 'And you'll have the pick of the Season's beauties now, hey!' he continued, striving for a more jovial note. 'A wealthy, eligible bachelor. All the pretty young girls will be throwing their handkerchiefs for you.'

Cole grimaced at the prospect. 'I'm not exactly a ladies' man,' he said.

Morton laughed and slapped Cole on the back encouragingly.

In the end the two men dined together. Their families had been neighbours for over a century and Cole preferred to stay on good terms with his father's old friend. He let Morton rib him about his new-found eligibility, but he didn't tell him about Honor. As far as possible, Cole was determined that no scandal would be attached to her name. He didn't want Bridget to experience any unnecessary discomfort as a result of her impulsive action—but he did prefer news of her marriage to be generally known before he introduced Honor to the world as his wife.

He questioned Morton discreetly about the details of Bridget's affair. To his relief, Mrs Howarth's name wasn't mentioned in connection with Bridget's elopement. Bridget had met her new husband, Mr Sedgeworth, in the Pump Room at Bath the previous December. George Morton apparently wasn't aware they'd been introduced by Annie Howarth. Bridget and Sedgeworth had continued their clandestine relationship through letters and occasional surreptitious meetings in London and Oxfordshire until the unexpected news of Gifford's death and Cole's impending return had precipitated them into taking action.

Morton began to question Cole about the progress of the war in the Peninsula, and Cole allowed the subject of Bridget's elopement to drop. He'd question Annie later. He wondered how much Honor's formidable mother would be willing to tell him.

'What kind of business are you considering?' Annie asked Honor.

Honor was momentarily disconcerted by the question, then she realised why her mother was asking.

'I mentioned to Co...Maj...*Sir* Cole,' she stumbled over

his correct form of address, and blushed at Annie's slight smile of amusement, 'that I might consider becoming a dressmaker,' she explained.

'A *dressmaker*!' Annie sounded appalled.

'I mean I thought I might have an establishment in Mayfair,' Honor explained defensively. 'I know it would require an initial investment and—'

'What does Sir Cole think of your idea?' Annie asked, arching her eyebrow quizzically.

Honor hesitated. She was having dinner with her mother and Susannah. It was a long time since they'd all eaten together. Honor was unbelievably relieved that she'd made peace with her mother, but she also felt oddly dissociated from her surroundings. So much had happened to her since she'd last stayed at the Belle Savage, and it hadn't been her childhood home. Annie had only bought the London inn shortly before Honor had gone to the seminary in Bath. Honor had visited for increasingly brief intervals between the ages of sixteen and twenty-one, but after she'd left the seminary she'd lived in the cheapest respectable lodgings she could find. She'd stopped confiding in her mother years ago because somehow Annie always seemed to criticise her plans—but now she sensed a change in their relationship. She decided to put her new-found confidence to the test.

'I did tell Cole about my dressmaking plans,' she admitted, 'but he didn't seem very convinced.'

'I'm sure you would be very successful,' Susannah said loyally. 'You were always an excellent needlewoman.'

'I thought so,' Honor agreed blandly. 'But Cole wasn't convinced. He suggested I might become a blacksmith instead—because I'm so good with horses.'

Susannah looked startled, but Annie laughed. 'A very sensible idea,' she said, without a blink. 'I employ several blacksmiths. If you wish, I could arrange for you to be apprenticed to one of them.'

Honor frowned. Her mother always managed to have the last word.

'Honor shot a wolf, Annie,' Susannah broke in hastily. 'She was so brave.'

'Of course,' Annie said matter-of-factly. 'I never doubted it.'

Honor looked down at her plate, suddenly too full of emotion to swallow, let alone eat the rest of the splendid food before her.

Her whole life was upside down. She was speaking to her mother for the first time in four years, but Cole was gone. She was so tired and emotional. She didn't want to talk about her relationship with Cole to anyone—not even Susannah, who had been her life-long confidante and ally. She just wanted to be alone, to rest and come to terms with her new circumstances.

'Come, I'll take you to your room,' said Annie briskly. 'You've travelled such a long way to get here.' Her voice cracked slightly on the last few words, but she covered her own emotions with a practised smile.

'I am a little tired,' Honor said carefully. She stood and started to follow Annie, then she turned back and hugged Susannah. The older woman held her for a long time before she released her into Annie's care.

'Ring if you need anything at all,' Annie said a few minutes later in the beautifully appointed room she'd assigned to Honor.

'Yes, Mama.' Honor caught her breath as she saw her familiar black shawl laid on the bed. She picked it up and held it against her breast. The shawl embodied so many varied memories for her. 'Mama, do you know a woman called Maggie Foster?' she asked suddenly, a snippet of conversation floating into her mind.

'Maggie?' said Annie slowly. 'I believe she worked for me once. Why do you ask?'

'I just wondered,' said Honor, feeling a growing sense of curiosity as she noticed Annie's almost imperceptible uneasiness at the question. 'She didn't mention she'd worked for you until just before I left Spain—but she must have known I was your daughter for the whole four years I knew her. I just thought it was strange.'

'Perhaps the subject never arose before,' Annie said casually.

'You didn't…discharge her?' Honor pressed, fearing the worst. 'I know she could be a bit…abrasive, but she was a very good woman. I'm sure…'

'I didn't discharge her, I asked her to look out for you,' Annie exclaimed irritably. 'I assume she did, or you wouldn't be defending her so loyally.'

'But you said you never wanted to speak to me or see my face again!' Honor exclaimed. 'Why—'

'For Heaven's sake, Honor!' Annie burst out, goaded beyond endurance. 'I didn't mean it! You can't possibly have imagined I let you go off to Portugal without taking steps to protect you!'

Honor stared at her with her mouth open. It honestly hadn't occurred to her that her mother would do such a thing. Annie had always been so insistent that her daughter should learn to be strong, independent and self-sufficient.

'And while we're on the subject, why on earth didn't you come to me when Selhurst was making such a nuisance of himself?' Annie demanded in exasperation. 'I admit I was a little distracted at the time because Brown had just set up a rival stagecoach to Liverpool—but I dealt with

the Duke as soon as I realised what was happening. And
then I found out you'd married Patrick! Good grief, girl!'

'You...dealt with...the Duke?' Honor echoed. She
didn't know whether to laugh or cry.

'Of course I did,' Annie said impatiently. 'What did you
expect me to do?'

'I don't know.' Honor flung her arm out in a wild gesture. 'Tell me to go to the devil my own way?'

There was silence for a few highly charged seconds.

'I didn't mean that either,' said Annie at last. 'I didn't
want you to go on stage. I wanted you to be a lady. I
wanted you to be happy.'

'Did you...make me such a success?' Honor whispered,
tears clogging her throat. She'd always believed her successful career as an actress was the one accomplishment
which was truly her own. Now she wondered.

'No,' said Annie quietly. 'You made yourself a success.
I couldn't have achieved that for you. I was proud of you.
I *am* proud of you.'

'Oh.' Honor didn't know which way was up any more.
She didn't know what to say, what to do or what to think.

'You must sleep,' said Annie. 'In the morning we can
talk about your plans. You're safe here.'

'I don't have any plans,' Honor said helplessly.

'But you know what you want to do,' Annie said
briskly. 'You've always known what you wanted to do
next.'

'No I haven't,' Honor cried. '*You've* always known
what you wanted to do next, Mama. I just...*do* things. I
don't know—'

Annie put her arms around Honor. She was a few inches
shorter than her daughter, although normally her forceful
personality made the discrepancy in their heights unno-
ticeable.

'But you do know what you want now,' said Annie softly.

'You can't give me this, Mama,' Honor's voice was muffled. 'No one can.'

'We'll see.' Annie cupped Honor's face in her hands and kissed her forehead. 'Wash your eyes in cold water before you sleep so they aren't puffy in the morning,' she instructed. 'Goodnight, Honor.'

Honor stumbled through her preparations for bed like an automaton. She curled up in a ball on her side as she waited for sleep to find her. It didn't matter what Cole or Annie said, she couldn't have what she wanted—because she would never be able to give Cole the heir he needed to secure the future of his inheritance.

'Good morning, Sir Cole.'

'Good morning, Mrs Howarth.' Cole had arrived at the Belle Savage a few minutes earlier and asked to see Honor. Instead he'd been brought straight to Annie, sitting in her office at the heart of her empire.

She stood up and walked around the desk, offering him her hand as she did so. He shook it and looked down at her speculatively.

'You have a question, Sir Cole?' she enquired, with a polite arch of her eyebrow.

'Possibly,' he replied. 'How is Honor?'

'She was tired after her journey,' said Annie. 'Please, sit down. Have you come to ask my permission to marry her?'

'No.' Cole sat down. 'Do you object?'

'I object if you're planning to make her your mistress,' Annie said bluntly. 'She deserves better than that.'

'Then we're in agreement,' said Cole calmly. 'Which is

rather fortunate since you've just divested me of a perfectly good fiancée.'

'Is that what Mr Morton told you?' Annie's eyebrow rose again.

'No, he didn't mention your name,' Cole replied. 'I wondered about that. Bridget's recent letters were quite full of you—how did you manage to avoid involvement in her marriage?'

'Probably because, after I introduced her to her new husband, I never mentioned him to her again,' Annie said serenely. 'I did encourage her to take a more energetic approach to her life. Of course, I've known Mr Sedgeworth for years. He always stays at the Belle when he visits London. A very steady and well-intentioned young man, with a romantic streak he has only recently learnt to explore. On a practical level, he has worked hard to improve the condition of his estates.'

'An ideal husband, in fact,' Cole observed, fascinated by Annie's revelations.

'Yes. I wish you to understand—I did not wantonly throw Miss Morton and Mr Sedgeworth together,' Annie said seriously. 'I made Miss Morton's acquaintance months before I introduced her to Sedgeworth—'

'Which you did as soon as you heard the news from Joe that Patrick was dead,' Cole interrupted.

'Patrick was dead and you held Honor in your arms while she slept,' Annie said calmly. 'Joe was most eloquent on the tenderness of the scene. Miss Morton and Mr Sedgeworth are a good match. I believe they will do very well together.'

'I suppose I must resign myself to the fact that, by the time my ring is on Honor's finger, you will have a battalion of your spies in my employ,' Cole said drily. 'In fact, you probably already have—and if I do anything to hurt her...'

'You would very much regret it,' Annie said coolly.

'Well, now.' Cole's blue eyes were as shrewd and un-flinching as Annie's as they both evaluated each other across the width of the room.

Cole didn't appreciate being spied upon, or having any-one meddle with his life as Annie had done. But he knew that she had done it for Honor, and the fact she'd taken care to select a suitable husband for Bridget was a point in her favour. He'd noticed that George Morton had made no complaints about his daughter's new husband. He'd simply been embarrassed at the way the marriage had taken place.

'For Honor's sake—and my own—I would prefer to be on good terms with you,' Cole said quietly. 'If you don't hurt her, and drive her away from you, you won't need to set spies to find out how she is.'

Annie turned her head away. 'You are direct, sir,' she said tautly.

'Sometimes it's necessary,' Cole replied, a note of steel underpinning his pleasant tone. 'I will be offended if you continue with your meddling when Honor and I are mar-ried. But if you respect our privacy, I am sure we will get along very well.'

Annie looked at him curiously. 'I think you mean that,' she said.

'I do,' said Cole. 'May I see Honor?'

'I'm afraid she went shopping with Susannah, shortly before you arrived,' Annie said apologetically.

'Shopping?' Cole was startled.

'She's very close to Susannah,' Annie explained. 'I'm sure they'll be back soon. Indeed, they may already have returned. Come this way.' She stood and led the way out of her office.

They found Susannah in the parlour, but not Honor. At Annie's sharply voiced question Susannah smiled.

'She went to call upon Lady Durrington,' she explained. 'Apparently her ladyship corresponded with Honor throughout the time she was in the Peninsula. Honor wanted to thank her for her kindness.'

'You let her go alone?' Annie's voice sounded uncharacteristically harsh.

'I've never met Lady Durrington.' Susannah frowned in surprise at Annie. 'And Honor wanted me to return home, in case Major Raven should call. So that I could—'

'Lady Durrington died two weeks ago,' Annie said grittily, jerking on the bell pull to summon a servant.

All the colour drained out of Susannah's face. 'Oh, dear, I didn't realise,' she whispered. 'Poor Honor! She was very fond of Lady Durrington.'

'I want a carriage and driver ready immediately,' Annie informed the servant who'd responded to her summons. Then she spun round to face Cole.

'Go and get her back,' she ordered tensely.

Cole didn't waste time taking offence at Annie's peremptory tone. His first consideration was Honor. He noted the address Annie gave him, and went straight there.

Honor realised there was something wrong as soon as she arrived at the Durringtons' Piccadilly town house. It was years since she'd last visited Lady Durrington but, to her surprise, the sombre butler seemed to remember her.

'This way, if you please. I'll inform Lord Durrington of your arrival,' he said solemnly.

'No, I came to see *Lady* Durrington,' Honor corrected him breathlessly.

'This way,' the butler repeated.

Honor followed him into an elegantly furnished drawing room. She'd set out to make a brief social call, but now she was filled with apprehension. The house seemed to echo with dark sorrow. The room was cold, despite the fact that it was a sunny May morning outside. She shivered, and wished she hadn't come.

She heard the door open and turned to see a tall, sombre-faced gentleman dressed in mourning come into the library.

'Forgive me for keeping you waiting,' he said. His voice was pleasant and softly spoken, but not quite steady. 'I'm Arthur Durrington.'

Even in the midst of her own discomfort, Honor thought he sounded oddly unsure of his welcome, which was strange, considering they were in his house. She suddenly realised she hadn't given her name to the butler, and he hadn't asked. She hastened to repair the omission.

'I'm...'

'Honor,' said Lord Durrington, a strange note in his voice.

'Yes.' She was surprised by his familiarity; she'd been about to introduce herself as Mrs O'Donnell. 'I suppose Lady Durrington may have mentioned me to you,' she guessed.

'Once or twice,' he agreed, his eyes still fixed on her face. The intensity of his scrutiny made her feel very unsettled.

'Lady Durrington asked—' she began.

Lord Durrington cleared his throat. 'I regret...I am sorry to tell you my wife died suddenly two weeks ago,' he said hoarsely.

'Oh! Oh, dear. I'm so sorry.' The news was a shock to Honor, even though she'd been afraid something was seriously wrong. 'I had no idea,' she said in distress. 'I only arrived in London yesterday. I shouldn't have intruded...'

'No, please, sit down,' Lord Durrington said quickly. 'My wife talked about you frequently. I have often wished to meet you. Please, sit down,' he repeated.

Honor hesitated. She didn't want to stay. She was sad for Lady Durrington, but Lord Durrington made her uncomfortable. She didn't like the way he stared at her so intently, or his eagerness to keep her with him. But it would be rude not to stay a little while when he was being so hospitable.

'Thank you.' She sat down on the edge of her chair. She would stay a few minutes, she decided. Then she would claim a prior appointment and make her escape.

When Cole arrived at the Piccadilly house he had a brief conversational tussle with the butler before he established that Honor was indeed visiting Lord Durrington.

'I'm sorry, sir,' said the butler frigidly. 'His lordship gave strict orders he didn't wish to be disturbed. If you would care to leave your card—'

Cole solved the impasse by pushing past the butler into the hallway and lifting his voice.

'Honor!' he shouted. 'Honor?'

A few moments later a door burst open and Honor ran out straight into his arms.

As Cole gathered her against him, he discovered she was trembling uncontrollably.

'Are you all right?' he demanded fiercely, filled with anger that he'd found her in such overwrought state.

'Yes,' she said, but she still clung tightly to him.

Cole looked up to find they were being observed. As soon as he saw Lord Durrington his suspicions, aroused by Annie Howarth's distress at finding where Honor had gone, were confirmed.

The man watching them had the same green, gold and russet eyes as the woman Cole loved. Not only that, but Lord Durrington and Honor also shared the same distinctive bone structure. When Honor was happy and well-fed she looked elegantly slim, but when she was hungry and anxious she looked as gaunt and hollow-cheeked as Lord Durrington now appeared. The shape of their eyebrows, their mouths—even the colour of their hair—were all very similar. If Lord Durrington had spent four years under the Iberian sun, his dark-blond hair would be as sun-bleached as Honor's. No one in the same room with the two of them could be in much doubt as to Honor's parentage. No wonder Lord Durrington had always avoided meeting her in the past.

'Honor.' Lord Durrington's voice cracked with emotion. 'I didn't mean to upset you. It just…it seemed such a miracle that you came to see me.'

'Perhaps you would be kind enough to give us a few minutes alone, Lord Durrington,' Cole said coolly.

'Of course, sir,' said Lord Durrington, stepping to one side and gesturing to the room he'd just vacated. 'I'm afraid you have the advantage of me.'

'Cole Raven,' Cole curtly introduced himself.

'Ah, yes.' Lord Durrington's mouth curved in a brief, crooked smile. 'You rescued her from drowning. I should have guessed.'

Lord Durrington's comment irritated Cole. It appeared that Annie Howarth hadn't been the only one who'd been keeping track of their activities. Had Lord Durrington relied on his wife's correspondence with Honor for his information—or had he had spies of his own in the

Peninsula? Cole decided there and then that, in future, no one was going to play devious games with Honor's life.

'He says he's my father,' Honor said a few minutes later, when her trembling had subsided and she felt safe in Cole's presence.

He nodded, apparently unsurprised, and tenderly brushed her hair back from her face.

'Did you know?' she asked in amazement.

'Not until I saw him just now,' Cole replied reassuringly. 'You look very much like him. But your mother was upset when she heard you'd come here. She sent me to fetch you. That did make me suspicious.'

'Oh. I never told Mama I was friends with Lady Durrington.' Honor twisted the material of her skirt nervously between her fingers. 'I don't understand it,' she said. 'Do you think Lord Durrington made Lady Durrington be friends with me so she would tell him about me? I don't like this. I feel so, so...*lied* to. It's horrible.'

'I'm inclined to agree,' said Cole tautly.

Honor looked up at him, distracted from her bewilderment by the censure in his tone. 'I don't know what to think about anything any more,' she admitted shakily. 'What are you doing here?' Tears suddenly started in her eyes, though she hadn't cried at her father's news. 'Miss Morton won't like it.'

'Bridget is already married to Mr Sedgeworth and no doubt living happily in Derbyshire,' Cole said, smiling at her encouragingly. 'There's nothing to worry about any more, sweetheart. I'll take you home and you can speak to Lord Durrington another time, when you've had a chance to get accustomed to his news.' He took Honor's cold hands in his, squeezing them reassuringly.

'Oh.' Honor swallowed. She was on the verge of giving

way to a tidal wave of tears, but she struggled to maintain her composure. 'I'm being stupid,' she whispered. 'I shouldn't be making such a fuss. Mama won't approve. She says you should always appraise every situation in a properly businesslike way.'

'But this isn't a business matter,' Cole pointed out gently, giving her his handkerchief.

'No.' Honor dried her eyes, but more tears welled up to replace the ones she'd wiped away. 'I'm so sad for Lady Durrington,' she whispered. 'It was such a shock...I thought everyone in London was safe—so far away from the war that nothing bad would happen to them. And then...and then he told me...' Her voice quavered and failed.

Cole had been sitting on a low stool in front of her. Now he shifted to sit beside her on the sofa. He put his arm around her comfortingly.

Honor drew in several careful breaths, exhaling slowly as she tried to assimilate all the new information she'd learned. Lady Durrington's death. The identity of her father. Bridget Morton's marriage to someone else...

She put her hand up to touch her hair. 'I must look a sight,' she said distractedly. 'Am I very dishevelled?'

'You look beautiful,' said Cole simply.

'Don't say that!' she exclaimed, feeling more tears threaten. 'I must be calm and composed. You must say practical things. Is there a mirror in here? I don't think you're a reliable witness.'

'I assure you I can be extremely practical,' Cole replied, a hint of indignation in his voice. 'Stand up, I will inspect you.'

Honor's smile was a little watery as she did as he ordered. She didn't let herself meet his eyes as he looked her over, then stroked a curl of blonde hair back from her face.

'Hmm,' he said consideringly. 'Not enough mud for a truly soldierly appearance—but you'll do. Are you ready to leave?'

'Yes.' She took the arm he offered her. 'I will tell Lord Durrington that I will speak to him another time,' she said firmly. 'But I wish…' she faltered. 'I don't want him to visit me unexpectedly,' she said in a more uncertain voice. 'Do you think that seems fair?'

'Yes.' Cole's response was immediate and unhesitating. 'You will not have to speak to him again until you are ready to do so.'

In Cole's opinion, Lord Durrington had shown an appalling lack of consideration for Honor. The man had abandoned her before she'd even been born. To claim her as his daughter only moments after he'd broken the news of Lady Durrington's death seemed both precipitant and unnecessarily cruel. Cole had no doubt Annie would protect Honor from her father while she was staying at the Belle Savage. He made a mental note to give appropriate instructions to his own servants.

'I will talk with you again,' Honor assured Lord Durrington, a few minutes later. He'd obviously been hovering nearby, because he'd appeared in the hallway as soon as Cole opened the door. 'I'm sorry Lady Durrington—' Honor broke off mid-sentence, and Cole felt her stiffen beside him.

'Did you *ask* Lady Durrington to befriend me?' she asked Lord Durrington croakily.

'No! On my honour,' Lord Durrington replied quickly. 'She saw you on stage and…forgive me, she saw the likeness between us. I did not know she'd made your acquaintance for several months. I think…she couldn't have children. You were the daughter she couldn't...' He didn't complete his explanation.

'My letters,' Honor said raspily. 'Would you return them, please?'

Cole saw the surprise and hurt in Lord Durrington's eyes at Honor's unexpected request. But he also understood why she was so shaken by the situation. She'd told him once she'd never met Lord Durrington. All the time she'd been writing to Lady Durrington, Honor would have assumed her letters were of no interest to anyone but her friend. She'd just discovered Lord Durrington had no doubt been perusing them as eagerly as his wife. Lord Durrington might be her father, but he was still a stranger to her.

'Send them to my house in Berkeley Square,' Cole told Lord Durrington.

Honor's father nodded, looking defeated.

'If you wish to be my friend, you will have to start from the beginning, the same way all new acquaintances start,' said Honor. 'I don't wish...that is, Mama always told me you were an honourable man. Lady Durrington told me only good things about you. But I must learn for myself. I'm sure I will discover that they were both right,' she added, in a softer tone.

Cole was proud of her. Her voice was steady, and contained no hint of anger or bitterness at her father's betrayal. Lord Durrington might have harboured dreams of a tearfully joyous reunion, but first he would have to gain Honor's trust.

'I will look forward to our next meeting,' said Lord Durrington huskily.

Honor nodded, and let Cole escort her out of her father's house.

'Do you think I was too unkind?' she asked, as soon as they'd gained the privacy of the carriage.

'No,' Cole replied immediately. 'He abandoned you. It's up to you if you wish to receive him.'

'Mama always told me he was an honourable man,' Honor said, chewing her lip. 'He couldn't help it. He had other responsibilities. He looked so sad…'

'I'm sure he is,' said Cole. 'But you've spent your whole life not knowing the name of your father. I think you need a little time to collect your thoughts before you speak to him again. When you do, I'm sure you'll have many things you want to say to him—and to ask him.'

'Yes.' Honor let Cole draw her against his side as the carriage trundled through the busy London streets. She rested her head on his shoulder and closed her eyes. So many, many thoughts whirled around in her head.

Her father.

Cole.

Miss Morton—who was already married to someone else…

Chapter Eleven

'Where are we?' Honor had expected Cole to take her back to the Belle Savage. Instead the carriage stopped outside a large house in Berkeley Square.

'This is my home,' Cole replied.

He helped her out of the carriage, then gave the coachman instructions to return to the Belle Savage.

'It's a very fine house,' said Honor politely, as Cole led her up the steps to the front door.

'Thank you.' Cole smiled slightly at her comment. 'Morning, Kemp. This is Mrs O'Donnell,' he introduced her to his butler. 'Please bring us some tea in the library.'

'Yes, sir.' Kemp's sharp eyes darted from Cole's face to Honor's. She knew he was curious about her, but that was the least of her concerns. Cole had brought her to his home. He'd already told her that he was no longer betrothed to Bridget Morton.

Honor gripped her hands together as she worried about what Cole might be about to say next. And what she would have to tell him…

'This was always our favourite room,' Cole said a few minutes later, as he gazed around the library.

Honor heard the sadness in Cole's voice and abruptly remembered the circumstances of his return home. She was appalled that she'd forgotten.

'I'm so sorry,' she said unsteadily. 'This must be so difficult for you.'

'Last night was the first time I'd been in this house since my father died,' Cole said distantly. He revolved slowly, his eyes roaming up and down the library shelves until his gaze came to rest on a large portrait.

There were four men in the picture. An older man, sitting in a chair, surrounded by three youths. Honor immediately recognised one of the lads as a young Cole. She saw that he shared the same vivid blue eyes as the older man. But Cole's father smiled upon the world with cheerful friendliness. He lacked the fierce intensity of his younger son which was visible even in the portrait.

Cole was standing on his father's left side. The young man standing at their father's right hand possessed the same vivid blue eyes, but jet black hair.

'Gifford?' Honor murmured.

'Yes.'

'It's easy to see you're brothers,' Honor said. 'You both have your father's eyes. And you are all very handsome.'

Cole's lips twitched in a brief smile.

Honor continued to study the portrait. She was fascinated by the picture of Cole as a younger man, but also by the images of his father and brother. At first sight she'd imagined the black man standing behind Cole's father was a favoured servant—but then she looked again. Her eyes narrowed as her gaze flicked from one man's face to another. There was a resemblance between all the men in the portrait.

'Who—?' she began.

'Anthony,' Cole replied. 'My cousin.' She sensed him stiffen beside her, but she kept her eyes on the portrait.

'He died with Gifford,' she said softly. 'You grieve for him also.'

'I do.' Cole sighed, and she felt him relax. 'Gifford is—was—five years older than me. It does not feel unusual for me to come home and he not be here. But Father and Anthony—they were always here. Working on Father's experiments...' He glanced around the library, almost as if he expected to see the familiar figures of the two men sitting in the well-worn chairs.

'How is it that Anthony is your cousin?' Honor asked.

'His father was my father's older brother,' Cole explained. 'His mother was a runaway slave Uncle James rescued. Not that I ever knew my uncle. If he hadn't died unwed years before I was born, Father wouldn't have married and I wouldn't be standing here today.'

'But Anthony grew up with you?' Honor prompted.

'He was two years older than Giff,' Cole replied. 'But his mother died in the same carriage accident that killed Uncle James. My parents took care of him, and when Giff and I were born we were all raised together.'

'Even though he was...not legitimate,' Honor whispered, seeing how Anthony gazed out of the portrait with the same self-confidence that Gifford and Cole displayed. He looked sure of his place in the world.

Honor could rarely remember feeling such certainty about her own situation. Cole had told her once she had the manners and speech of a gentlewoman. Annie had raised her daughter to be a lady, yet Annie herself had never made any attempt to enter the fashionable world for which she'd carefully prepared Honor. And Honor had spoiled all her mother's plans by running away to join the theatre.

'I don't think my father cared about that.' Cole slipped his arms around Honor from behind, drawing her back to lean against his chest as he looked up at the family portrait. 'Anthony was his nephew. He was part of our family.'

'Your father was a very fine man,' Honor said shakily. 'Some men don't recognise their own—let alone someone else's—mistakes.'

Cole didn't respond for two heartbeats, then he spun Honor round to face him.

'You are not a mistake,' he said fiercely. 'Any more than Anthony was. I was proud to have Anthony as my cousin. I am proud—'

He broke off, cupping Honor's face between his hands. He smiled at her—the sweetest smile she'd ever seen on his lips.

'I will be proud to call you my wife,' he said softly.

Tears filled her eyes and overflowed onto her cheeks. She could see him only through a distorted haze as she tasted salt on her tongue.

'I can't,' she whispered brokenly. 'I *can't*!' She dimly saw Cole's shocked expression, then she began to cry in earnest.

He pulled her into his arms, holding her with such fierce possessiveness she cried even harder. She tried to stop. She knew she had to stop. But she'd been fighting to control her turbulent emotions for too long. The calm she sought was far beyond her reach.

Cole was first shocked, then alarmed by Honor's wild tears. He'd seen her cry before, but he'd never seen her in such uncontrollable distress. He stroked her hair, trying to soothe her, but it made no difference. He resisted an urge to shake her—or even to order her to stop crying. Cold water was supposed to be good for hysterics, he thought distractedly. But he recoiled from the idea of throwing cold water over Honor. Besides, after everything she'd endured, not to mention the shocking information she'd learned from Lord Durrington, she was entitled to a few tears.

Cole sat down on the sofa and drew Honor on to his lap. He fumbled in his pocket and found his handkerchief. He pressed it into her hands, then he held her comfortingly and waited for her to stop crying.

Honor rested her head against Cole's shoulder, feeling utterly miserable. Her face was hot and swollen. She couldn't breath properly. Her head ached. Her heart ached. And now she had to tell Cole what was wrong.

She felt him stroke her hair back from her damp face, then kiss her forehead. She turned her face towards him, trying to hide in the space between his neck and shoulder.

'I'm sorry, I'm sorry,' she whispered brokenly.

'Sweetheart, what's wrong?' She heard the worry in his voice.

'I'm sorry,' she whispered again. She moved in his arms, trying to get to her feet. He tightened his hold momentarily, then he let her stand up.

She turned her back on him immediately, drying her eyes and blowing her nose. Never in her life had she had to tell anyone something this painful. Part of her had hoped she'd never have to tell Cole. Part of her had hoped for a miracle. Either way, she'd always meant to be calm and in control when they had this discussion. Now she was so overwrought she could barely speak.

She heard Cole get up, and braced herself for his touch. She was afraid she might start crying if he touched her again. Instead he went over to the door. She wondered where he was going. He went out for a few moments, then returned, closing the door carefully behind him. She threw a quick glance in his direction and saw that he was carrying a tea tray.

'Kemp can be very discreet,' he explained cheerfully. 'He left the tea tray on the hall table. Father trained him not to interrupt at crucial moments in his experiments.'

'Or w-when he had hysterical women to t-tea,' Honor said, trying to make light of her outburst.

'Bread and butter and cake as well,' Cole said approvingly. 'I meant to ask if you were hungry.' He poured two cups of tea. 'Come and sit down,' he said gently.

Honor hesitated, then sat beside him on the sofa. If she'd chosen a more distant chair she would have had to look straight into his questioning blue eyes.

She could sense the tension in Cole's large body, but he waited while she tried to compose herself. It was hard to swallow her tea. She was only just in control of her emotions. But at last her teacup was empty.

Cole took it from her and put it back on the tray. Then he took her hand in his.

'Why can't you marry me?' he asked tautly. 'On the packet boat—'

'I *wished* on the packet boat,' Honor interrupted him before he could repeat what she'd said then. It was far too painful to hear those words now.

'But I'm *free*,' Cole said with fierce impatience. 'There's nothing to stop our marriage. I don't give a damn whether your father was married to your mother—or a bigamist ten times over. It's *you* I want to marry.'

'I…' Honor swallowed and stared down at her lap. She began to pleat her skirt with nervous fingers. 'I…'

She could feel Cole's tension increasing with every second she delayed. She *had* to tell him.

'I'm barren,' she whispered, her eyes filling once more with tears.

'*What?*' The word exploded out of Cole.

'I'm barren,' she repeated more loudly, finally raising

her head to look at him. 'I can't give you children,' she added desperately as she saw he was staring at her in disbelief. 'I *can't*!'

She saw his chest expand as he drew in a deep, deep breath. He exhaled slowly, then drew in another deep breath. She could hardly bear to look at his face. She was braced for his disappointment, perhaps even his anger. He would surely feel she had betrayed him.

He drew in another deep breath and let it out slowly. His tense muscles relaxed. And he smiled at her.

'Is that all?' he asked quietly.

'All?' She couldn't believe she'd him heard correctly. 'Don't you understand what I just said?' she demanded, her voice rising with distress and frustration. 'I can't have children.'

'I know what you just said,' he replied steadily. 'I still want to marry you.'

'*No!*' Honor exclaimed. She leapt to her feet and paced about the room in her agitation. 'I admire your sense of honour—but that's just folly. You *can't* marry me. You came home to set up your nursery. You told me so yourself.'

'Yes.' Cole watched her stride around the room, flicking her skirts nervously with agitated fingers.

She came to a brief pause. 'Then it would be stupid to marry me,' she informed him curtly, and resumed her restless pacing.

'You think I'm only determined to marry you now out of some foolish sense of honour?' Cole enquired coolly, playing for time.

He hadn't been sure what to expect after her bout of frenzied weeping, but he'd seen Honor cope with too many disasters to assume her worries would be insignificant. He'd been prepared for her to tell him almost anything.

Even so, her news had come as a profound shock to him. His mind teemed with questions.

How could Honor be so sure she was barren? Why hadn't she said anything before? How was he going to protect his inheritance now?

But he didn't blame her for her condition. His father's rational yet uncomplicated teaching ran too deep in him. Cole's father had never attributed unexpected illness or other infirmity to God's punishment. He'd simply said there was a physical explanation which men had not yet discovered. Cole wanted to know why Honor believed she was barren, but he didn't judge her for her state.

It took him a few moments to absorb all the implications of her announcement. He briefly considered setting her aside as she insisted he must—and knew immediately that he couldn't do it. No matter how many difficulties might lie ahead of them, he could not imagine his life without Honor.

He stood and moved to stand in front of her. She lifted her head. Her face was pale and blotchy, her eyes puffy from crying. She watched him warily, as if anticipating his rejection. He put his hands on her shoulders, tightening his grip in an instinctive attempt to reassure her.

'I want to marry you because I cannot imagine living my life without you,' he said, his voice very deep and sure. As he spoke he felt his last remaining tension drain away. He knew beyond doubt that this was the right thing to do. 'I want to marry you because I love you. Because you are the woman my heart and soul have chosen...'

'But you must have *heirs*!' Honor cried in desperation. She shook her head at him. Her hair fell around her face in damp, untidy strands. 'I can't give them to you. You must find a woman who can!'

Cole pulled her into his arms, holding her close against

his chest despite her rather feeble efforts to escape. 'Easier said than done, love,' he said almost teasingly.

'What?' Honor abandoned her attempt to resist his embrace. It felt too good to be in his arms. She'd been so certain he would be disappointed or angry—though she'd hoped he would hide the worst of his unhappiness with her. She couldn't credit how calm he was. He probably hadn't understood the importance of what she'd told him. She braced herself to explain more fully. He had to realise that, if he married her, he would never be able to fulfil his duty to his family name.

He brushed his lips against her temple.

'The only way I could guarantee a fertile bride would be to marry a young widow who has already had a child,' he pointed out gently. 'Alternatively, I suppose I could try impregnating one of this year's debutantes. I could draw up some kind of agreement with the lucky lady's father to that effect.' A hint of amusement crept into his voice. 'She only gets my ring on her finger when I'm quite certain that she's already carrying my child.'

Honor tensed even as she allowed herself to lean against him. 'Are you taking this seriously?' she asked sharply, on the verge of losing her temper. She couldn't bear him to make fun of her at such a time.

'Oh, yes,' said Cole. His reply was simple and heartfelt. 'In this life there are no guarantees for any of us,' he said quietly. 'The only certainty I have is that I love you, and you love me, and that it would be a sin to deny that love.'

Honor tilted her head back and gazed up into his eyes. 'You really mean that,' she breathed, overwhelmed and humbled by the love and conviction she saw in his face.

'I was going to give Bridget the Oxfordshire estate as her dowry, after I had told her that I wouldn't be able to marry her,' Cole said.

Honor was momentarily confused by his change of topic, but she listened anyway.

'It turns out I didn't have to tell her anything,' Cole continued. 'Instead her father apologised to me for her elopement.'

'You were going to break off your betrothal?' Honor whispered, understanding dawning. Cole was telling her that he'd always meant to marry her—that he hadn't proposed to her just because he'd unexpectedly found himself free to do so.

'Yes.' Cole confirmed her realisation.

'Lady Durrington couldn't have children,' Honor said, her thoughts going off at another tangent. 'It was a great sadness to her. She said…that is, I understood it caused a—a coolness—in her relations with Lord Durrington.' Honor couldn't bear the idea that one day Cole's feelings towards her might change.

'I think there may have been other reasons for that coolness,' Cole said gently.

'Me?' Honor looked up at him anxiously.

'Perhaps. He didn't forget you, sweetheart. And I doubt very much whether he forgot your mother. He could have done.' Cole hesitated, she thought he was choosing his words carefully. 'A man might lie with a woman and forget her the following day,' he said slowly. 'Men do. Women too, sometimes. But I will never forget you. If you sent me to another woman, she would get the worst of me. You would always be in my heart and head.' He smiled crookedly. 'It's quite possible your mother has been in Lord Durrington's mind for the past twenty-six years,' he said. 'From all I've seen and heard of her, I don't think she'd be easy to forget.'

Honor laid her palms flat against Cole's chest as she considered what he'd said.

'Mama told me she'd never seen my father or spoken to him after he sent her away—before I was born,' she said pensively. 'But her memory might have been a powerful rival. Lady Durrington wasn't very...I mean, well, she was a bit insipid,' Honor revealed guiltily. 'Very kind, but...well...' Her voice trailed off.

Cole had his doubts about Lady Durrington's motives for befriending Honor, but he didn't mention them. He was more interested in Honor's comments about Lady Durrington's inability to have children. He guided Honor back to the sofa and sat down beside her.

'Why are you so sure you can't have children?' he asked gently.

'Well...because I was married for more than three years and I never had any,' Honor replied, surprised. 'The other women noticed. Maggie even said—' She broke off, blushing painfully.

'What?'

'That—that it wouldn't matter if I became your mistress, because I couldn't be c-caught out,' Honor stuttered uncomfortably, refusing to meet Cole's eyes.

Cole bit back a hasty retort. 'You mean your only reason for believing you're barren is because you were married for three years and didn't have a child,' he said carefully.

'Yes.' Honor looked at him warily.

'And did Lady Durrington often discuss her own problems with you?' he asked.

'She mentioned her sadness before I was married,' Honor replied, surprised by the direction of his questions. 'After I was married she discussed it more fully. She said she prayed I would be spared such sorrow.'

'Generous of her!' said Cole drily. 'Sweetheart, forgive me...you spent most of your marriage marching the length and breadth of Portugal. The conditions weren't exactly ideal. And before you went to the Peninsula—didn't you say you couldn't bring yourself to live in the barracks with Patrick?'

'Y-yes.' Honor stared at him with almost painful intensity.

'Forgive me,' he said again. 'But, Honor—were there many opportunities when you *could* have conceived a child?'

Honor's mouth formed an O as she stared at him in surprise.

'Honor…sweetheart, you do know how…?' he began tentatively, suddenly wondering exactly how sophisticated her knowledge was on this subject. She'd always been so self-sufficient it was hard to imagine she might not be well informed. On the other hand, she'd sometimes surprised him by her sweet naïvety—especially considering the conditions under which she'd lived.

'Of course I know!' She nodded her head violently. Every visible part of her face and neck flushed crimson with embarrassment and she couldn't meet his gaze. 'Susannah explained. At first I thought…I thought…' Her voice faded away.

'You thought what?' Cole prompted.

'At first I thought you could get pregnant just sitting on a sofa at the same time as a man,' Honor mumbled. 'Mama was so strict. But then Susannah explained that other…things…had to happen as well.'

'Good for Susannah!' said Cole. He was feeling almost as overheated by the conversation as Honor. His own education on this subject, as on so many others, had been matter of fact and straightforward. He realised once again how much he owed to his father.

He pulled Honor on to his lap and kissed her temple. 'I'm not trying to embarrass you,' he assured her, kissing her hair, because she still wouldn't look at him. 'But, sweetheart, you're going to be my wife, it's perfectly acceptable for us to discuss this kind of thing.'

'I didn't…I mean, Patrick didn't…' Honor mumbled.

It took a superhuman effort on Cole's part, but he managed to stop himself asking what it was Patrick hadn't done. Fortunately Honor told him before he exploded with curiosity.

'We didn't discuss this…this kind of thing,' she said. 'Patrick and me, I mean. I didn't know…'

'That's all right,' said Cole cheerfully. 'You're married to me now—or you will be, as soon as I can arrange it. And we—you and I—can discuss anything we want.'

'Oh.' Honor leant her head against his shoulder, and rubbed her finger up and down the lapel of his coat as she contemplated his proposal. 'Do you really think I might have been mistaken?' she asked hopefully. 'About children?'

'I don't know,' he said gently. 'I do know that my parents were married for a year before Gifford was conceived, and it was another five years after that before I was born. And my father knew exactly what was involved in producing an heir—and my mother was rested, well fed, well cared for, and miles from the nearest battlefield. I don't want you to worry about having my child. I don't even want you to think about it. I just want you to marry me and be happy. Will you marry me?'

Honor hesitated. She had been anxious about this for such a long time it was hard to let her worries go. She could see so many problems ahead of them. If she didn't give him a son, how would Cole feel in twenty years' time?

'I think you should have longer to think about this,' she

said at last. 'It's such an important decision, Cole. I want you to be sure.'

'I am sure,' he said firmly, a hint of impatience in his voice.

'Please.' Honor cupped the side of his face with her hand. 'This means so much to me. I want you to wait a week. If you can tell me then that you believe, with all your heart and soul, that you will be happy with just me—even if we never have children...then I'll marry you.'

'One week,' said Cole, in a voice that brooked no argument. 'Very well. But if you raise any more objections then, I swear I'll drag you to the altar!'

Honor gave him a rather watery smile. Once his autocratic manner had infuriated her—now it sounded deeply reassuring.

'You won't have to drag me,' she promised him. 'I'll be sitting on the altar steps, waiting for you.'

Cole and Honor were married exactly a week later. Cole had used the intervening period to buy the special licence and make the other necessary arrangements. The wedding was witnessed only by Annie, Susannah, Malcolm Anderson—and Lord Durrington. Cole had decided not to invite his more distant relatives. The fact that he was still in mourning for Gifford was a good reason to keep the wedding small and private. Honor had pondered for some time about her father. In the end she had chosen to invite him to her wedding, though he did not give her away and played no part in the ceremony.

Afterwards they all went back to the Belle Savage. Honor looked around the room, still a little dazed by the speed at which her fortune had changed. She had been anticipating the worst for so long—now she had almost everything she could want. Most importantly of all, she had Cole's fierce, abiding love.

Halfway through the toasts the door was flung open.

'Excuse me, sir. Excuse me.' An inn servant tugged fruitlessly, and not entirely courteously, at the intruder's arm. 'This is a private wedding party. Perhaps you might wish to hire a private parlour for yourself and your companion…'

The intruder's appearance was so disreputable that it was easy to understand the servant's evident doubts.

He was a tall, powerfully built man, who easily brushed aside the servant's efforts to detain him. His thick black hair was far too long to meet the dictates of fashion. A long scar ran down one side of his face, above and below the eyepatch which covered one eye. A streak of grey hair indicated where the scar extended across his scalp. His good eye was an intense vivid blue, and he scanned the room quickly, ignoring the servant's protests.

'Dammit, man, stop pawing at me!' he ordered. 'I'm damned if I'll miss my own brother's wedding.'

'Giff?' Cole whispered.

He was not the only one present staring at the man in the open doorway. Honor glanced around to see that all her companions were equally startled by his appearance. Malcolm Anderson looked as shaken as Cole.

But Honor was only concerned about Cole. He was staring at his brother, all colour drained from his face, his muscles tense with shock. She wasn't even sure if he'd drawn a breath since his stunned whisper.

'Cole?' She took his hand, squeezing it, trying to give him the composure and strength he needed to deal with this most amazing and wonderful apparition.

His fingers tightened convulsively around hers, although

she wasn't entirely sure he was fully aware of her. All his attention was focussed on his brother.

'Gifford?' he said, his voice unrecognisable. Suddenly he surged to his feet, knocking the table out of his way as he did so. Plates, glasses and cutlery went flying, but he didn't notice.

'I'm not so easy to kill,' said Gifford hoarsely, looking into his brother's eyes. Then they were locked in a fierce embrace.

Honor smiled, and realised she was weeping at the same time, overcome with happiness for Cole. Behind the two brothers, she saw an ebony-skinned man.

Anthony, she thought dazedly. Gifford and Anthony. They'd both come home.

It took a few minutes for Cole to recover from his shock. He turned, seeking her with his eyes, and she walked into his arms. He hugged her against his side as he introduced her to Gifford and Anthony.

'My wife, Honor,' he announced, making no attempt to disguise his pride in her. He was grinning at his brother and his cousin, drunk on happiness and relief, though his eyes were still a little blurred by tears.

'You will never know how glad I am to meet you,' said Gifford sincerely, lifting Honor's hand to his lips in a startlingly graceful gesture.

'Put on your airs for someone else,' Cole protested. 'You look more like an out-of-luck pirate than a fine courtier.'

'But that's the time when fine airs are most important,' Gifford countered, stepping back so that he could sweep Honor one of the most extravagant bows she'd ever seen. 'To fool the innkeeper you can afford the fancy dinner and private parlour you've just bespoken.' He flashed a sideways glance at Annie as he spoke, an irrepressible gleam in his blue eye.

'Have you ever thought of going on the stage?' Honor asked, unable to stop herself.

Cole groaned. 'Don't encourage him,' he protested. 'His whole life is one long performance as it is—' He broke off, his gaze locked with his brother's.

'True enough,' said Anthony, his calm voice releasing the sudden tension. 'We couldn't even get to London without having an adventure. Some fool tried to hold up the mail coach with Gifford on board—can you believe such folly? That's why we nearly missed the wedding—not that we knew you were getting married till we reached the house and Kemp told us. I swear, Gifford could not even spend a month in Bath without having some kind of adventure.' Anthony smiled at Honor as he finished speaking and she liked him immediately. In the midst of all the drama and excitement he was so calm and reassuring.

'Indeed I could.' Gifford rose to the challenge immediately. 'A month in Bath. I will be bored out of my mind—but I will not have an adventure.' He frowned. 'Perhaps we won't set off just yet,' he decided. 'I want some of the wedding feast—is there any more?' He looked around hopefully. 'And I want to hear all your adventures, brother. Mine can wait,' he forestalled Cole's response. 'It's not my wedding day. I will get to dance with the bride, won't I?' he added.

'I like your brother,' said Honor, a long time later.

'I like him too,' said Cole, grinning. 'I'd forgotten what a damn showman he can be sometimes, though. What an entrance!'

'And I like Anthony.'

'Yes.' Cole was sitting on the edge of the bed. He pulled Honor between his knees and began to unbutton her dress.

'Did you find out yet why they're still alive?' she said over her shoulder. Gifford had been resolute in not turning the evening into a recitation of his and Anthony's adventures.

'Briefly,' said Cole. 'Apparently Giff and half the crew were taken prisoner by one of the privateers that attacked him, while Anthony and the rest of the men were taken on board the other privateer. Gifford managed to escape and gain control of the privateer he was a prisoner on. Then he went off in pursuit of Anthony and the rest of his men. He didn't tell me any more than that. I do know that both he and Anthony were afraid Anthony was going to be sold into slavery. That may be why they're not talking much about it.'

'Oh my God!' said Honor, appalled at the implications of Cole's words.

'There's a shadow in Anthony's eyes that wasn't there when I last saw him,' said Cole, momentarily entirely serious. 'I didn't press for details.'

'Of course not.' Honor shivered. 'But he's safe in England now.'

'Yes.' Cole slipped the dress off her shoulders and turned her to face him.

'Wait a minute.' Honor pushed his hands away before he could finish undressing her. 'You're distracting me. I want to tell you something.'

'Sweetheart, I hope I am distracting you,' he retorted. 'This is our wedding night.'

'I know,' she said breathlessly. 'This isn't normally the kind of thing the bride tells the groom on their wedding night, but—'

She broke off, looking down at him as he sat on the

side of the bed. She slipped her fingers through his tawny hair as he gazed up at her, a half-smile on his lips, but his blue eyes narrowed questioningly.

'I was thinking,' she said, 'about what we were talking about before. And—and…I talked to Mama—because, of course, Susannah hasn't ever actually *had* any children— even though she's very well informed…'

'Honor?' Cole's hands tightened on her waist.

'And I've been thinking,' Honor continued even more breathlessly. 'About—about…well, I've been so *distracted* over the past few months, I wasn't paying proper attention. I mean, I just didn't *think* but maybe, I mean…I think it must have been the night I stayed with you in Spain—after you found out Gifford was dead—only he wasn't really, of course,' she finished in a rush.

Cole stared at her for several long, agonising seconds while he tried to disentangle what she'd just told him.

'I think I might be pregnant already!' she whispered, her eyes round with amazement and excitement. She'd held the news inside her for two days, eager to tell Cole, yet terrified that somehow she'd made a mistake.

Honor had taken Lady Durrington's sadness so deeply to heart, and made the unfortunate woman's fears so much her own, that it was hard for her to believe she might be capable of bearing a child. It was even more unbelievable to think that she might already be pregnant.

Cole took a deep breath. Much as he loved Honor, he still wasn't entirely sure she knew exactly what she was talking about. He made her explain to him in embarrassing detail why she thought she was pregnant.

By the time she'd finished she was bright pink all over and Cole was grinning with delight.

'Oh, sweetheart! I think you're right!' he exclaimed exuberantly.

He pulled her on to the bed with him and kissed her until she couldn't think straight.

'What will we do now?' she asked much later, her head resting on his shoulder as he idly stroked her back. 'Everything has changed again now Gifford has come back.'

'*Sir* Gifford,' Cole murmured lazily. 'I never did feel comfortable with that title. I was due the Oxfordshire estate if I married Bridget, but I can't say I really want to live a few miles from her father. I haven't had a chance to talk about it with Giff yet, but I thought I'd ask him for the Hampshire estate. We could rebuild the house that was burned in the fire. What do you think?'

Honor raised herself on her elbow, looking down at Cole in the dim light.

'That's where we camped on our way to London?' she said. 'Where you...' she blushed in the darkness '...covered me in apple blossom?'

'You look beautiful in apple blossom,' Cole assured her tenderly. 'We could make a good home there, Honor.'

'Yes, we could,' she agreed. 'I liked it. What are you going to do now that you won't have so many responsibilities?' she asked after a moment.

She was a little worried about Cole. Not *very* worried, just a little concerned. She didn't think managing one country estate was going to be enough for him.

'I'm not sure,' said Cole. He didn't sound perturbed. 'But if your mother can found a coaching empire out of nothing, I'm damned sure I can find something worth doing.'

'Oh, no!' Honor groaned. 'You really are just like her.'

'No, I'm not,' said Cole firmly, rolling Honor on to her back and positioning himself above her. 'In many ways I am nothing at all like your mother. But you must admit she has an admirable head for business.'

'Are we going to talk about Mama now?' Honor asked breathlessly.

'No.' Cole kissed her. 'I wasn't planning on talking at all,' he murmured against the warm skin of her cheek. 'Unless you really want to?'

'No.' Honor put her arms around him, pulling his strong body to hers. 'I don't want to talk either,' she whispered. 'Not right now. I want...' She hesitated, blushing in the darkness, and decided this was as good a time as any to overcome her shyness on certain matters. 'I want you to make love to me,' she said boldly.

Cole laughed softly. 'Yes, Mrs Raven,' he said huskily. 'Your word is my command.'

* * * * *

*Don't miss the conclusion of Claire Thornton's
Regency duet in **Volume 10** of
The Regency Lords & Ladies Collection,
available in April 2006*